JEFFERSON BASS

WITHOUT MERCY

A BODY FARM NOVEL

WM

WILLIAM MORROW

An Imprint of HarperCollins*Publishers*

This is a work of fiction. Names, characters, places, and incidents are products of the author's imagination or are used fictitiously and are not to be construed as real. Any resemblance to actual events, locales, organizations, or persons, living or dead, is entirely coincidental.

WITHOUT MERCY. Copyright © 2016 by Jefferson Bass, LLC. All rights reserved. Printed in the United States of America. No part of this book may be used or reproduced in any manner whatsoever without written permission except in the case of brief quotations embodied in critical articles and reviews. For information, address HarperCollins Publishers, 195 Broadway, New York, NY 10007.

First William Morrow premium printing: June 2017
First William Morrow hardcover printing: October 2016

Print Edition ISBN: 978-0-06-236321-3
Digital Edition ISBN: 978-0-06-236322-0

William Morrow and HarperCollins are registered trademarks of HarperCollins Publishers in the United States of America and other countries.

17 18 19 20   QGM   10 9 8 7 6 5 4 3 2 1

Books by Jefferson Bass

Fiction

Nonfiction

PART ONE

The Human Stain

> Light thinks it travels faster than
> anything but it is wrong. No matter
> how fast light travels, it finds the
> darkness has always got there first,
> and is waiting for it.
> —Terry Pratchett, *Reaper Man*

> Make a chain: for the land is full of
> bloody crimes and the city is full of
> violence.
> —Ezekiel 7:23

PROLOGUE

A WARM SPRING BREEZE stirs the stand of tulip poplars, twitching their upturned, aspiring branches, their tender new leaves and delicate flowers pale in the moonlight. A stronger wind kicks up, unleashing a blizzard of blossoms, their yellow petals splashed with orange, their feathery stamens dusted with pollen.

Soon the gust subsides, settling to a soft, steady breath soughing through the foliage, undisturbed for hour upon hour. Then, suddenly, the wind's susurration is punctuated by a series of brighter, sharper sounds: steel clinking upon steel—metallic teeth chattering, slowly at first, then faster and louder, frenzied and frantic.

A scream rends the night: a scream accompanied—or is it contradicted?—by another voice, this one deep and fearless, primitive and guttural. The scream falters, then resumes; falters, then intensifies; falters . . . and fades.

CHAPTER 1

I TURNED THE DOORKNOB of the osteology lab—or, rather, tried to—and was surprised to find it locked. Normally by eight Miranda was long since settled at her desk in the bone lab, a half-empty Starbucks cup going cold, her eyes riveted on her computer screen as her fingertips danced and her keyboard clattered, opening some new window on the virtual world she navigated with such speed and confidence.

As I unlocked the steel door and opened it, I scanned the lab's interior. The lights were off, but the front of the lab was fairly bright, thanks—or no thanks—to the venetian blinds stretching across the front wall, their metal slats kinked and broken in half a hundred places, allowing thin spokes and broad beams of the October morning sun to slant across the lab, the rays luminous and all but tan-

gible in the lab's dusty air. I still half expected to
see Miranda, if not at the desk then possibly deep
in concentration at one of the worktables, studying
some fractured fibula or shattered skull.

But the room was empty—devoid of living
humans, at any rate, though it contained gracious
plenty of dead ones: thousands of Arikara Indian
skeletons that my students and I had exhumed
during a series of summer expeditions to the Great
Plains, excavating one step ahead of rising reservoir
waters. The Arikara were neatly packed in sturdy
corrugated boxes, shelved like thousands of library
books with spines of bone. The remains should have
been returned to the Arikara tribe for reburial on
dry tribal lands—and indeed *would* have been, as required by the Native American Graves Protection
and Repatriation Act of 1990—except for a single,
insurmountable obstacle: There no longer *were* Arikara tribal lands. Decimated by multiple epidemics
of smallpox, a contagion spread by white traders
and settlers, the dwindling Arikara had been assimilated by the Mandan and Hidatsa tribes back in
the 1800s. And so it was, through an odd confluence
of river hydrology, civil engineering, field archaeology, and viral epidemiology, that the primary legacy
of the Arikara Indians—Native Americans who had
helped Lewis and Clark on the first stage of their
epic expedition to the Pacific Northwest—resided
beneath the south end zone of Neyland Stadium,
the University of Tennessee's shrine to college football.

The Arikara inhabited the back of the room, a
vast, dark complex of shelves that marched, row

upon row, toward the underside of the stadium's concrete grandstands. I generally gave them no thought, but occasionally—at moments such as this, when the university was still half asleep, the bone lab still deserted and quiet—I could almost believe I heard the whispering spirits of the vast tribe of Arikara dead. The hairs on the back of my neck prickled, and with a deep breath to refocus my attention, I turned toward the front of the lab.

This part of the room was high ceilinged and bright, its rows of worktables illuminated by the large, glass-fronted exterior wall. Atop the tables were old-style cafeteria trays, each tray laden with skulls, ribs, mandibles, vertebrae, pubic bones, arm bones, hand bones, foot bones, or some combination thereof, giving the room the look of a skeletal spare-parts shop. *"Hey, I need me a left tibia,"* I imagined a one-legged customer hopping in and saying. *"Y'all got any of them?"* *"Loads,"* my salesman-self would answer. *"What make and model you aiming for?"* The customer would look down at the stump of his leg, making sure he got the specifications right. *"A 1963 male, 'bout six foot one."* *"You're in luck,"* I'd say. *"Got one, good as new, never broken. Installation not included."*

My imaginary spare-parts sale was interrupted by a series of three dull thuds just outside the door, each thud punctuated by a curse. "Dammit. *Damn* it. *Dammit!!!*" I turned and opened the door just in time to see a two-foot stack of books teetering wildly in the overloaded left arm of my assistant, Miranda. As the leaning tower of books approached its tipping point, she reflexively swung her right hand over to stabilize it. Unfortunately, her right hand was clutching a Starbucks cup, which smacked against the books, popping off the lid, collapsing the cup, and sending liquid cascading over her hand and onto the three books that I had heard thud to the floor. I readied my ears for the litany of profanity that was sure to ensue—Miranda cussed frequently, creatively, and with considerable gusto—but she simply stared at the crushed cup, the dripping hand, and the sodden books . . . and then burst into peals of laughter. And it was the laughter that finally nudged the tower of books to its tipping point. For a moment the stack—still a single unit—seemed to hang in the air, as if both time and gravity had been suspended. Then, slowly, the structure came apart in midair, book after book tumbling into a pile at her feet.

"You do know how to make an entrance," I said. "You okay?"

She nodded, still laughing too hard to speak.

"Sorry about your coffee," I offered. "And your books."

"It's okay," she finally managed to gasp out. "I was bringing you tea." She howled afresh. "Oh, and they're your books, not mine."

Now it was my turn to stare. Sure enough, the spines and covers in the puddle were familiar ones. And, in spite of myself and my love of my books, it was my turn to laugh, too.

CHAPTER 2

THE BAD NEWS WAS, one of the books Miranda had been carrying was now thoroughly soaked, as soggy as a two-hundred-page tea bag. The good news was, the sodden mess was the osteology field guide that I myself had written years before.

"Sorry, Dr. B," Miranda said, holding the book by one corner as it drained into the trash can beside the desk.

"I have a spare copy," I said. "Actually, hundreds of spare copies. Boxes and boxes of them, crammed in the closet of my office. Peggy's been after me for years to get rid of some of them." The truth was, Peggy, my secretary, had been after me to get rid of *all* of them. "They're not the latest edition," Peggy liked to point out. "No first editions, either. Nothing worth saving. And the longer they sit in that closet, the moldier and more outdated they get."

I eyed the other books Miranda had been lugging, which ranged from osteology references to radiology texts. "Why are you bringing these back? You finally getting worried about your library fines?" It was a running joke, my pretense that she was racking up years' worth of overdue fines on the books I had loaned her.

"Why should I worry?" she cracked. "What's a few thousand bucks between indentured servant and master?"

That, too, was a running joke, one that had more than a kernel of truth in it: Graduate assistants worked long hours for low pay, and Miranda was now nearing the seven-year mark in her servitude. If she'd been a faculty member instead of a student, she'd be eligible for tenure now.

"Actually, I'm through with them," she said.

"Through?"

"Through. I sent it to the printer this morning."

"*It?*" She nodded but said nothing, waiting for me to figure out what she meant. It took me longer than it should have. "Your dissertation? You *finished*?"

"Yup. That's why I'm late—I was up all night making revisions. But it's done, by damn." She flashed me a smile—a smile that combined pride, relief, and also, I now noticed, exhaustion. And yet remarkably, she—the one who'd been up all night— had gone to the trouble to buy me a cup of tea on her way in. True, the tea was now only a puddle of good intentions, but I appreciated the gesture.

"That's great, Miranda. I'm thrilled," I said. But the word came out sounding flat and forced, and I realized that "thrilled" wasn't the whole truth. The whole truth was, now that Miranda was finishing her Ph.D. she'd be leaving, and I would miss her: her expertise, her reliability, her sassiness, and her friendship. "Thrilled" was only a small part of the large, complicated truth of what I felt as I contemplated her departure.

An awkward pause hung in the air. Finally, blessedly, it was broken by the electronic warble of the phone on the desk. Miranda lifted the receiver without looking at the display, trailing droplets of tea across the scuffed desktop. "Osteology lab, this is Miranda," she said, then, "Hi, Peggy. . . . Yeah, he's here." She handed me the phone, frowning as a few final drips spattered her forearm.

Peggy Wilhoit had been the Anthropology Department secretary and administrative assistant for most of my twenty-five years at UT. She knew where to find me, when to remind me, and how to get my goat. Much like an old married couple, we had long ago dispensed with formality, settling into a relationship that was predictable and mostly harmonious, with the exception of the occasional spat. "Morning, Peggy," I said. "Do you have a tracking device on me?"

"Darn. You've finally caught on. What I really need, though, is one of those remote-control shock collars, so I can make you mind better."

"I'd laugh," I said, "if I thought you were joking. What's up? Am I late for a meeting?"

"Sheriff O'Conner, from Cooke County, is on line two. Can you talk to him now, or should I take a message?"

"I'll take it. Thanks." I pressed the blinking light on the phone's console. "Hello, this is Dr. Brockton."

"Doc," came a familiar voice. "Jim O'Conner. Remember me?"

"Remember? Hell, how could I forget?" O'Conner, a Vietnam war hero, was a slight, soft-spoken man, yet he had a commanding presence and powerful charisma. Before becoming sheriff of Cooke County, O'Conner had built a small ginseng empire that was remarkable for being both prosperous and legal—an uncommon combination in the hills of Cooke County, which was notorious for its frontier mentality and outlaw entrepreneurs. Cooke County had long trafficked in 'sang, as the locals called ginseng root, but until O'Conner started cultivating it, the root was invariably poached from federal lands. Besides ginseng and rugged mountains, the county's other claims to fame and infamy included pot patches, cockfights, chop shops, and, more recently, meth labs.

I had first met O'Conner five or six years or so before, when I worked a murder case in Cooke County. He himself had been wrongly accused of the murder; in the end, not only was he cleared, he was elected sheriff, and he'd promised to clean up the corruption that had characterized the county for a century or more. As best I could tell from occasional news reports about undercover stings and colorful trials, he'd done a good job of keeping his promise. "My secretary told me 'Sheriff O'Conner' was calling. I reckon that means you're still wearing a badge?"

"For the moment," he said. "But it's a temporary, short-term kind of deal."

I laughed. "Isn't that what you said back when you first took the job, what, five, six years ago?"

"Well, yeah," he confessed. "My mistake was, I said I'd stick with it till I got the place cleaned up.

Turns out, cleaning up Cooke County is like getting rid of kudzu. You can cut vines all day long, but until you get at the root problem, it's just gonna keep coming back."

His analogy rang true to what I knew of Cooke County, botanically as well as criminally: it was easy to become entangled, tough to get loose. "You getting any closer? To the root problem?"

"Hard to say, Doc. Some days I think we're making progress. Other days, I think the problem is just human nature itself, stretching all the way back to Adam and Eve."

"So maybe it wasn't a snake that started the trouble," I mused, "but a kudzu vine grabbing hold of Eve's ankle?"

He gave a quick laugh. "I think you're onto something there, Doc. You ever get tired of anthropology, you should take up preaching. You make more sense than any of the hillbilly Bible-thumpers up this way."

"I'll take it under advisement," I said. "But meanwhile, I'm guessing you didn't call to ask about theology."

"You're right. We've got a death up here I'm hoping you might help us investigate."

"*Now* you're talking my language," I said. "Is the body still at the scene?"

He hesitated. "Well, no, not exactly."

My good mood evaporated, replaced by exasperation. "Dammit, Sheriff, you know better than that. I've said this to law enforcement till I'm blue in the face. It's really important not to move the body till I get there. Makes my job a *whole* lot harder if—"

"Excuse me, Doc," he interrupted. "I didn't make

myself clear. It's not that we moved the body. It's that there's not really much body *there* anymore. Just bones. And not a whole lot of 'em to speak of."

Suddenly I felt sheepish. "Well, hell, Jim, I'm sorry I snapped at you. I should've known you wouldn't compromise the evidence. My apologies."

"No worries, Doc. You think you can come help us out?"

"Sure. Miranda and I—you remember my assistant, Miranda?"

"Of course."

"We can leave in . . ." I paused and shot a questioning glance at Miranda. She'd seemed to be absorbed in checking her e-mail, but by the speed with which she met my gaze, I knew she'd been listening closely. I tapped my watch and raised my eyebrows to underscore the unspoken query. By way of an answer, she held up both hands, fingers spread wide. "Ten minutes," I told O'Conner. "We can leave in ten minutes. Where are you? How do we find you?"

"I'll have Waylon meet you at the Jonesport courthouse in an hour."

"Tell him no detours this time," I said. "The last time Waylon drove me around Cooke County, we ended up at a cockfight. Next thing I knew, my mouth was full of chewing tobacco and I was throwing up in a barrel full of dead roosters."

O'Conner chuckled. "No detours, I promise. But, hey, you got a good story out of that. People up here still talk about it."

"Great," I said. "A humiliating day that will live in infamy."

He went on, clearly relishing the tale. "If everybody who claims to've seen you barfing at that cock-fight is telling the truth, every man, woman, and child in Cooke County was at the Del Rio cock-fights that day."

"Wouldn't surprise me," I said. "Those bleachers were packed. And that concession stand was selling chicken tenders by the truckload."

"Lord help," he said. "Sometimes I wonder what people are doing with their time and money, now that we've shut down the cock pits. Then, unfortunately, I find *out* what they're doing, and I have to arrest 'em for *that*, instead. It's a shell game, Doc—you close an illegal door, folks'll crawl through a forbidden window."

"Blame it on the kudzu, Sheriff. We'll see you soon." With that, I rang off, then buzzed Peggy to tell her that Miranda and I were headed to Cooke County to work a case.

This would be our seventeenth forensic case of 2016; that meant that the victim, whoever he or she might be, would be recorded and referred to—even if we managed to identify him or her—as case 16–17, the first number referring to the year, the second to the order in which the case had arrived. *Now serving number 17*, I thought, visions of the Department of Motor Vehicles dancing in my head.

As we headed to the Anthropology Department's pickup truck, the back loaded with body bags, shovels, rakes, cameras, and anything else we might need to work a death scene, I felt a surge of energy—excitement, even—and for the moment, at least, I forgot to be morose about the prospect of Miranda's graduation and departure.

CHAPTER 3

LEAVING THE STADIUM, MIRANDA and I turned onto Neyland Drive and paralleled the emerald-green Tennessee River for a mile, then took the eastbound ramp for Interstate 40. Now that we had a forensic case I felt downright cheerful, even though the case was situated in a rough-justice jurisdiction where many an outsider had come to grief.

Cooke County was the best of counties and the worst of counties. By nature, it was a paradise: mountainsides blanketed with pines, tulip poplars, hemlocks, and rhododendron; deep valleys carved by the French Broad, Pigeon, and Nolichucky Rivers; tumbling mountain streams, brimming with trout. But by other measures—socioeconomically, ecologically, and legally—it was far from the Garden of Eden. Unemployment was high, income was low, gunshots were considered background noise, trash dumping was regarded as a constitutional right (revered only slightly less than the Second Amendment, judging by considerable roadside evidence), and crime had long been a chief source of revenue, both for Cooke County residents and for elected officials.

A COUNTY OF BAD OL' BOYS read the headline of a *Los Angeles Times* story about Cooke County a few years ago. The subhead gave more specifics: BOOTLEGGING, BROTHELS, AND CHOP SHOPS. GUILTY SHERIFFS AND FEDERAL INVESTIGATIONS.

Oddly, the article omitted mention of what was perhaps the most sensational black mark on the county's reputation: the discovery, years before, by an undercover FBI agent, that the sheriff was trafficking in cocaine, and in a big way. The sheriff turned an empty field behind the county high school into a makeshift airstrip, and as his deputies guarded the perimeter, a plane loaded with coke landed on school property. "That sure puts the 'high' in higher education," one of my FBI colleagues had remarked after the sheriff's indictment.

But that had been many years and several sheriffs ago. By all accounts—including the reckoning of the FBI, which continued to watch Cooke County closely—Sheriff Jim O'Conner had made great strides in rooting out official corruption, though Cooke County's citizenry still had a penchant for pushing the boundaries of law and order. Common lore held that anyone driving a car with an out-of-county license plate was considered fair game after dark, and a year or so ago, a friend of mine—a Knoxville writer with more curiosity than common sense—made the mistake of driving a red BMW convertible into the heart of Del Rio, a Cooke County community whose main "industry" for decades was its massive cockfighting arena. A quarter mile after he turned onto Del Rio's river road, three pickups—all equipped with loaded gun racks—pulled out of driveways and tucked in behind the BMW, following it closely until it made a U-turn and hightailed it out of there.

Miranda and I would probably be fine in Cooke County, I figured. For one thing, we'd be in the company of law enforcement officers. For another, the UT pickup truck we were driving was old and battered, and therefore not particularly tempting to thieves or kidnappers. For yet another, the truck had a feature that was sure to repel almost any ne'er-do-well: the cargo bed and camper shell reeked of death and decay, thanks to the countless bodies and bones the truck had ferried over the years. The truck was like a four-wheel version of Charon's boat, ferrying the dead across the river Styx—in this case, though, ferrying the dead across the Tennessee River to the Body Farm. Perhaps I should have felt morose about being Death's ferryman, but I didn't. Instead, I felt curious and eager as I contemplated getting to know my latest passenger—the newest resident of the Body Farm.

But my good mood didn't last long. Less than ten miles outside of Knoxville, a ghost—in the shape of a highway billboard—reared its haunting, taunting head. COMFORT INN read the faded sign, a message I always found deeply ironic on this particular billboard.

"Crap," I muttered to Miranda. "Remind me to take a different route next time."

"What? Why?" She glanced at me, then followed

my grim gaze to the billboard. "Oh. Right." She grimaced. "You'd think they'd take that down. But I guess not too many people know about it or remember it."

"It" was the series of murders Nick Satterfield had committed, two decades before, on the wooded hillside directly behind the billboard. A sadist who preyed on prostitutes, Satterfield would pick up his victims on Magnolia Avenue, Knoxville's de facto red-light district, and bring them out here to Cahaba Lane—a short cul-de-sac that was a dead end in the worst possible way. After parking directly beneath the Comfort Inn billboard, Satterfield would lead the women up a trail into the woods, where he would do brutal and lethal things to them.

"It still blows my mind," I said. "His car was parked right there, in plain sight, while he tortured and strangled those women. I still wonder if anybody driving past ever heard anything."

Miranda lowered the window and cocked her head toward it, as if listening for the echo of a long-ago scream drifting from the woods that flanked the freeway. "Lotta noise," she said doubtfully. "Even with the windows down, hard to hear anything but the wind. Though if you were stopped to change a tire . . ." She made a face. "Yuck. Yeah, next time let's take a different route."

We rode in silence for the next half hour. Then, just before the freeway began corkscrewing its way through the Great Smoky Mountains, we got off. I felt my mood lift again as we wound alongside the Pigeon River, which we followed upstream all the way into town.

Jonesport was Cooke County's seat of government and its largest town, not that the competition—from the likes of Allen Grove, Del Rio, Tom Town, Wasp, and Briar Thicket—was all that stiff. Fronting the town square was the courthouse, a brooding, fortresslike building, assembled from rough-hewn slabs of granite, its windows gridded with bars, its front doors sheathed in iron. As we approached, Miranda gave a low whistle. "Geez," she said. "That place could repel a third world army." After a moment, she added, "Although from what I know of Cooke County, a band of local outlaws is lots more likely than a foreign army."

"From what *I* know about Cooke County," I said, "the outlaws are already inside, running the place." As we passed the façade, I noticed two old men seated on a bench beside the front entrance, an enormous pile of wood shavings at their feet. I gestured in their direction to direct Miranda's attention to them. "See those two guys?" She nodded. "I think those are the same guys I saw last time I was here. Four years ago? Five? I wonder how many trees they've whittled their way through in that time."

"Well," she mused, "probably not as many as you and I have dissertated and photocopied and syllabused our way through."

"Glad to know you hold our work in such high regard," I grumbled, though without conviction.

I pulled into the gravel lot behind the stone courthouse and parked in the NO PARKING zone beside the sheriff's department, rolling down my window to take in the afternoon air. Just as I killed the engine, the sun seemed to disappear behind a cloud. Glancing out my window, I saw that it wasn't a cloud that had blocked the sun, but a mountain—a mountain of a man, his big belly and barrel chest filling my entire field of view. His shirt could scarcely contain the gargantuan form—I caught glimpses of skin through gaps between the buttons—and when he leaned on the windowsill, the truck canted to the left, causing the apple that had been sitting on the truck's bench seat to roll against my thigh.

The big man's face was out of sight above the truck's roofline, so I spoke to the immense chest—specifically, to the five-pointed star pinned to the straining shirt. "Waylon, is that you?"

"Nah, it's my baby sister," rumbled a deep growl of a voice. "How the hell you been, Doc? We ain't seen you in way too long."

A bear-paw hand clapped me on the shoulder, and the truck rocked from the force of it. "Good," I managed to grunt. "Busy, but good. Waylon, you remember Miranda?"

"Course," he said. He bent down, his bearded, bearish head occupying half the window's opening, then threaded an arm the size of an oak limb across the cab, offering her the paw, which seemed the size of a boxing glove. Miranda's hand and wrist disappeared as Waylon closed his fingers. "Mighty nice to see you again, Miss Miranda."

"Nice to see you too, Waylon," she said. "You keeping 'em honest up here?"

Her question unleashed a low, thunderous chuckle from deep in Waylon's chest. "Not so's you'd notice," he said. "I'm a deputy, not a miracle worker. Besides, if ever'body up here straightened up and toed the line, I'd be out of work, wouldn't I? Way I see it, only feller up here with more job security 'n me is the undertaker."

WE FOLLOWED WAYLON'S truck out of town on the Dixie Highway, crossing the Pigeon River and then, in a few miles, paralleling the French Broad, which had somehow, over the eons, managed to carve a channel through the high, rugged mountains between Jonesport and Asheville, North Carolina— barely thirty miles away, as the crow flew, but more than twice that far upriver as the valley twisted and turned.

We wouldn't be going all the way to Asheville— only about halfway, to the remnants of a tiny ghost town named Wasp.

As we followed the river, I didn't worry about staying particularly close to Waylon, since we could have spotted his truck from a mile away. Despite the sheriff's emblem painted on the front doors and the tailgate, the truck wasn't exactly a standard-issue law enforcement vehicle. A far cry from the Jeep Cherokees and Chevy Tahoes favored by rural sheriffs' departments, this was a hulking Dodge Ram 3500, fire-engine red, sporting a hulking diesel engine, a double cab, dual rear wheels, and twin vertical exhaust pipes, the sort normally found only on tractor-trailer rigs.

We had barely reached Jonesport's outskirts— which weren't too far from Jonesport's inskirts—

when Miranda said, "You know, if anybody else were driving that thing, I'd be tempted to diagnose a case of SPS compensation."

"Of *what* compensation?"

"SPS."

"I heard what you said," I told her. "I just don't know what it means."

"SPS? Small penis syndrome."

"Eww," I said.

"SPS compensation means driving a huge truck or a souped-up car—or shooting giant guns, or acting supermacho—to compensate for a sense of manly inadequacy. Mind you," she added, "I doubt that Waylon actually suffers from SPS."

"*Stop*," I said, my face scrunching into an involuntary grimace. "I'm sorry I asked." If I hadn't been driving, I'd have put my hands over my ears. "I can't believe we're having this conversation."

"We're anthropologists," she said matter-of-factly. "We study humans—their civilizations, their rites, their rituals, their behaviors."

"Cultural anthropologists study that stuff. We're *physical* anthropologists, remember?"

"We were also talking about physical attributes," she said, way too cheerfully.

"You were, not me," I pointed out. "*Were*. Past tense. End of discussion."

"No problem," she said. "Didn't mean to make you uncomfortable. Or . . . insecure." She snickered as soon as she said the last word.

"Ha ha. Very funny, Miss Smarty-Pants. You should do stand-up comedy, after your dissertation gets blown out of the water."

"Not gonna happen," she said. "Did I mention that harsh grading is a surefire sign of SPS?" She was grinning now, I noticed out of the corner of my eye. She *was* a smarty-pants, and she *was* funny, and she did know how to bait me, no doubt about it. Mercifully, she changed topics. "So what's that pipe sticking up above the cab of the WaylonMobile? Not the two chrome ones—even I recognize those as exhaust pipes—but that weird black one, on the right?"

I glanced at the truck's roofline. "I think that's a snorkel."

"A *snorkel*? Like, for scuba diving?"

"Basically, yeah," I said. "So the truck can ford streams—hell, probably rivers and lakes, tall as that thing is—without the engine drowning."

"So Waylon's truck is also a submarine? Does it have a periscope, too?"

I shrugged. "Knowing Waylon, I wouldn't be surprised."

She was silent for a moment—I fervently hoped she wasn't considering turning "periscope" into a bad joke—then she said, "You know how people and their dogs resemble each other?"

"Sure. My high school chemistry teacher, Miss Walpole? She had an English bulldog—short, fat, wrinkly, snuffly. Damned thing looked exactly like her, except for the strings of drool. Walked just like her, too."

"That truck is Waylon on wheels. Almost like a vehicular reincarnation."

"Don't you have to be dead to be reincarnated?"

"Correct as usual, Professor Pedant," she said.

"Okay, let me rephrase that. Waylon's truck is like a vehicular, parallel-universe avatar of him. Is that better?"

"Much," I said. I wasn't quite sure what an "avatar" was, but given our previous conversation, I was too skittish to ask.

We followed the French Broad past Del Rio, former site of the massive cockfighting arena, then continued along the river for another five miles or so. At that point, the asphalt and the water parted company, the road turning uphill away from the river. A few miles later, we turned off the highway and onto a woodsy gravel route marked Wolf Creek Road. It began promisingly enough, a lane and a half wide, but over the next few miles it gradually narrowed to a single lane, then became nothing but a pair of tracks, sometimes surfaced in gravel, sometimes in dirt, mostly in leaves. Trees crowded in from both sides and overhead, the branches slapping and clawing at Waylon's supersized truck, whose massive cab and bulging rear-wheel fenders bulked it up to a full two feet wider and at least a foot higher than the UT pickup Miranda and I were in. But if Waylon was bothered by the damage to his paint job, he didn't show it in his use of the accelerator pedal, bulling his way through the branches as if they were nothing more than clouds of gnats.

He stopped just beyond a fork in the "road"—a Y where the two faint tracks split and became four, like a backwoods version of a chromosome unzipping and replicating. Waylon had taken the right-hand arm of the Y, so I pulled a short ways up the left-hand arm before stopping. As we got out, Waylon lumbered up beside me. "Doc, snug right on up behind me, if you don't care to." His phrasing—using "don't care to" to mean "don't mind"—brought a slight smile to my lips. His next line almost made me laugh out loud: "Best not to be blockin' traffic."

"Traffic? *Here?*" I asked the question with the closest thing I could manage to a straight face.

He shrugged his massive shoulders. "Never know." He pointed in the direction my truck was facing. "This here connects up with Round Mountain Road, and Max Patch is up yonder way. Might be somebody'll be headed up thataway, or coming back down."

I nodded. I wasn't familiar with Round Mountain, but I knew Max Patch: a high, grassy bald just across the state line in North Carolina—a popular spot for Knoxville hikers and picnickers. I pointed ahead of Waylon's truck. "And that way?"

He snorted. "Ain't nothing thataway. Not now, leastwise. *Used* to be—eighty, hunnerd years ago—this here was Wasp. We'll go past what's left of the school and the post office. But ain't nobody lived here since the 1930s, when the Forest Service bought ever'body out and let the trees grow back. It'd been logged, ya see, and the land was all warshin' away, ever time it rained. 'Bout the only people goes up thisaway anymore is hunters. Them's who found it and called us."

"How far to the death scene?" I asked him.

"Hunnerd yards, give or take. Straight up thataway." He pointed past his truck. "What all you want to take up there, gear-wise? I'll help you tote it."

"If it's that close, I'll just take the camera, for now," I said. "Once we've had a look, I'll know what we need."

He nodded and headed up the track, bending and snapping branches as he squeezed past his truck and the sheriff's SUV—a much smaller Jeep that was parked twenty feet farther up the hill, in the last gasp of what had once been the road, eight decades before. As I reached the front bumper of the sheriff's Jeep, where the route narrowed to a single-track footpath, I noticed a set of crumbling, moss-covered stone steps notched into a low embankment to my left, and—on a level shelf of forest floor a stone's throw beyond—a rotting wooden building and a small cluster of gravestones. "So that must've been the church," I said, pointing at the collapsing walls.

"It was," Waylon confirmed. "And yonder's the schoolhouse." He pointed to the right, where I saw another crumbling structure, similar to the church in size, shape, and ruination, but lacking the tombstones, and standing—or, rather, leaning—rather closer to the path. "A few houses here and there, too," he added, waving a hand in a vague arc, "but they's kindly off the beaten track."

"Wait," said Miranda. "You're saying we're *on* the beaten track?"

"Yes, ma'am. Relatively speaking, that is." He stopped and cupped his hands around his mouth and called ahead, in a booming voice, "Sheriff? We're here. Hold your fire."

"I will," answered a quiet, amused voice, so close to us that I jumped. Jim O'Conner stepped out from the ruins of the schoolhouse. "I was just doing a little amateur archaeology here, while I waited. Dr. Brockton, Miranda, good to see you again. Thanks for coming."

He strode toward us, his hand extending while he was still ten feet away. He was at least a foot shorter and a hundred pounds lighter than his deputy, but there was no doubt who was in command here. I'd seen other men his size carry themselves like bantam roosters: all puffed up, preening and strutting. O'Conner carried himself easily, with quickness, grace, and wiry strength—more like a bobcat than a rooster, I decided. Ever the gentleman, he shook Miranda's hand first, then mine, with a grip that seemed somehow to be simultaneously easy and yet powerful.

"I'm always happy to help," I told O'Conner.

"He's not kidding," Miranda added. "When he's in a foul mood, I'm sometimes tempted to murder somebody, just so he'll get a case and lighten up."

O'Conner grimaced and shook his head—not to dispute what she'd said, but to express dismay, as best I could tell, about the case we'd be helping with. "Y'all might not feel the same when you see what we've got here," he said.

I held up a hand to interrupt him. "Don't tell us anything," I reminded him.

"I know, I *know*," he said. "You want to draw your own conclusions. It's a good idea; I just don't see how your conclusions can be anything but terrible when you see this." With that, he turned and led us forward, higher up the hill. The farther we went, the darker and more sinister the woods seemed to grow, though I told myself that the effect was created purely by my imagination, in response to the sheriff's ominous words.

Suddenly a man stepped from behind a tree, so unexpectedly I spooked like a horse spotting a snake in its path. He held up a hand, and I recognized Steve Morgan, a former student of mine from years back, now a special agent with the Tennessee Bureau of Investigation. Steve and his wife, Christie, had met in my osteology class, so I was always glad to see him, feeling entitled to take credit for both his professional success and his personal happiness. "Steve," I said, holding out my hand. "Good to see you. Glad to see the TBI is sending in the A-team on this one. But who'd you piss off at headquarters to get sent back to Cooke County? I thought Meffert was assigned up here."

Morgan's face fell. "I'm just temporary. Maybe. Bubba's on medical right now."

"Something serious?"

He nodded gravely. "Looks like pancreatic cancer. Not good."

"I hate to hear that." I meant it, not just because Meffert was a good agent and an old friend, but also, especially, because I had a deep and abiding hatred of cancer in all its insidious forms, ever since it had snatched my wife, Kathleen, from me years before. "Where is he? And is he up to visitors?"

"Not right now. He's out at MD Anderson. I'll let you know once he's back."

"I'd appreciate that. How about you? You glad to be back in Cooke County for a while?"

"Doc, that question is more loaded than my service weapon. Take this case here, for instance."

"Not a word," I told him, and he grinned. I turned to O'Conner. "Why didn't you tell me this guy was waiting in ambush up here, ready to give me a heart attack?"

O'Conner looked at me and shrugged, all innocence. "Hey, aren't you the one that keeps saying, 'Don't tell me anything'?"

I looked to Miranda and Waylon to chime in on my behalf, but Miranda arched a single, serves-you-right eyebrow at me, and Waylon was carefully studying his grubby fingernails.

"I see how it's gonna be with this crew," I said, feigning martyrdom. "Okay. Fine. Let's go."

The hillside steepened for ten feet or so, then plateaued into a flat, level area—possibly a natural landform, but more likely an area that had been shaped to accommodate a cabin or farmhouse a century ago. On the nearer side of the shelf, some twenty feet ahead of us, was a large tulip poplar—easily two feet in diameter, and a good eighty feet tall. All around us, other tulip poplars were just beginning to turn from green to gold—the gold that gave the Great Smoky Mountains their characteristic autumnal incandescence—but this one was completely bare: It was dead, but clearly it hadn't been dead for long, as its branches had not yet begun to rot and break.

Something near the bottom of the trunk caught my eye, and I moved closer to inspect it. It was a horizontal line, roughly the height of my waist—a line that had been etched into the trunk, an inch deep and apparently all the way around. Walking closer, I saw that what had etched the line—girdling the bark, and therefore killing the tree—was a heavy chain, its links made of steel as thick as my pinkie finger. Puzzled, I turned back and gave O'Conner a questioning look. His only response was a grim nod of his head.

Showtime, I thought, opening the case of the 35-millimeter camera that was hanging from my neck. With the zoom lens at its widest setting, I began shooting photos of the area, taking in not just the dead tulip poplar but the entire shelf. Once I was sure I had documented the overall scene, I began moving closer, ever mindful of the advice of one of my earliest law enforcement mentors, a legendary agent at the Kansas Bureau of Investigation. "Photographing a crime scene is like robbing a bank, Bill," he told me a dozen times or more. "First you shoot your way in, and then you shoot your way out." His advice had served me well throughout my career.

By the time I was arm's length from the tree, I could see the welds in each link of the chain. I could also see the smoothness of the groove worn deep into the wood: a groove worn, it would seem, by sustained movement of the chain, rotating around the trunk again and again and again, the links sliding and gouging with each revolution. How many revolutions? Hundreds, surely, to cause such wear; maybe even thousands.

When I stepped to the side, I felt a visceral shock that was like a punch in the gut. First, my peripheral vision took in the heavy padlock beside me, securing the chain around the trunk. But it took only an instant for my eyes to follow the chain outward from the tree—ten feet, twenty, twenty-five. Thirty feet out, the chain ended in another loop of padlocked links.

This loop was much smaller in diameter: perhaps five inches, no more than six—about the size of the circle I could make by touching the tips of my index fingers and my thumbs. It lay a few inches from a handful of cervical vertebrae, directly beneath the skull's location. Except that there was no skull; only a scattering of other bones, many of them splintered and incomplete.

Behind me, I heard Miranda gasp. "Sweet Jesus on the cross," she murmured. It was her strongest profanity, a phrase I'd heard her use only a handful of times in all the years we'd worked together. "Chained to a tree to die."

"Can you imagine dyin' thataway?" rumbled Waylon. It was a question no one bothered to answer; a question no one needed to answer.

I turned toward Miranda, Waylon, and the sheriff, and as I turned, I saw something I hadn't noticed before: a shallow trough in the ground, curving away from the bones in either direction; curving, in fact, in a wide circle around the tree, a uniform thirty feet from the trunk. It was a path, I realized with a new jolt: a path worn around the tree, etched in the earth, by the victim's footsteps—thousands of footsteps, maybe millions—on a long journey to nowhere. *No,* I realized, *not to nowhere. To death.*

A circuitous, ironclad journey to death.

I HAD PAUSED in my photography to absorb the horror of the gruesome death sentence imposed on the person chained to the tree, but after a moment, I got back to work. I was still standing beside the tulip poplar, some thirty feet from the bones, but I wasn't yet ready to approach them. There were more things to photograph where I stood.

I had noticed an assortment of litter strewn across the ground, though initially I hadn't focused on it. Litter is common in rural counties, where household trash isn't always collected by garbage trucks, but litter is generally confined to roadside ditches and gullies, not strewn in remote forests. I now took a closer look. Here, the litter was largely confined to the sixty-foot circle worn in the ground, and for an absurd instant, I wondered why a murderer—for unless this death was the world's strangest suicide, it was surely a murder—would choose a dump as the scene of the crime. Then the grim truth hit me, again with terrible force: The trash had accumulated *after* the victim was chained to the tree, not before; the trash—empty cans, plastic wrappers, milk jugs, shards of chicken bones—had arrived over the course of days or even weeks, during which the chained, circling victim had been fed. Had been kept terribly, terrifyingly alive. *No, Waylon*, I silently answered him, *I can't imagine dying thataway.*

I took a series of photos of the trash, once more starting with wide-angle shots, then zooming in on representative samples. Bumble Bee Tuna. Underwood Deviled Ham. Hormel Bacon. Armour Vienna Sausage. Van Camp's Beanee Weenees. The combination—a profusion of high-fat, chemical-laden processed meats, plus the terrible purpose to which they had been put—turned my stomach, and several times I had to look away and breathe deeply to keep nausea at bay. It was ironic; comical, even: In decades of forensic work, dealing with decomposing and even dismembered bodies, at every stage of decay, I had thrown up only once, on my very first case, when an exhumed coffin was opened to reveal a rotting, dripping corpse. Yet here I was, brought to the brink of vomiting by a scattering of empty cans and wrappers.

"Let's be sure to bring up a couple of rakes and trash bags," I said over my shoulder to Miranda. "I want to bag this stuff and take it back with us."

"What do you think it'll tell you?" asked the sheriff.

"Maybe nothing, maybe a lot," I said. "If we hit the jackpot, we might get fingerprints or DNA—from the victim or the suspect. Maybe from both. But even if we don't, we could still learn some things about when this happened, and how long it went on. We might not get much insight from the Vienna sausage cans—processed meat has a shelf life that's measured in years. But—"

Miranda snorted. "Decades, more like it. Maybe centuries. *Mmmm*," she said sarcastically. "Vienna sausage—every bit as tasty and nutritious in a thousand years as the day it went into the can!"

"Hey, now," Waylon protested. "Don't be talkin' bad 'bout Vienna sausage. I had me some for lunch, and like as not I'll have me some more for dinner."

"Lucky you," she said.

I ignored their culinary bickering. "The milk jugs might tell us something," I went on. "The pull dates—'sell by'—might help us pin down the time since death. Maybe even on how long he was out here." A chilling thought hit me. "Or she."

"OKAY, MIRANDA, YOU know the drill. Tell me what you see."

It was one of my favorite teaching techniques: putting my students on the spot and testing their knowledge, in the same way chief residents quiz medical students during hospital rounds. Miranda, of course, hardly counted as a student by now; she was more like a junior colleague, but this was a ritual we'd performed for years, and I suspected she had come to share my fondness for it.

After I had "shot my way in" to close-ups of the bones, we had switched gears, returning to the truck to fetch rakes, trash bags, trowels, gloves, and evidence bags. We hadn't bothered with a body bag; there *was* no body—just a skeleton, and only a partial one, at that. No point wasting an eighty-dollar vinyl bag when a few fifty-cent paper bags would do the job just fine.

Miranda bent down, then dropped to one knee and studied the bones for a long moment. Drawing a deep breath, she began. "The remains are fully skeletonized, indicating a considerable time since death—perhaps several months, though almost certainly less than a year; in fact, probably less than six months."

"Explain," I said, trying not to show that I was pleased that she had reached the same conclusion I had.

"Given the elevation here in the mountains, and the declining average temperatures in September and October, there would almost certainly be soft tissue on the bones if the death had occurred in the fall, when the weather cools off and decay slows down. But if the death occurred no later than, say, mid-August—we'll need to check the temperature records, of course—the corpse could have skeletonized fast, in just two or three weeks."

"Excuse me," said Sheriff O'Conner. "What makes you think it wasn't more than six months or so ago?"

"The remains are on top of last fall's leaf litter," she said, gesturing at the ground. "True, there are some dead leaves on the bones"—she leaned forward and picked up a brown leaf that was lying on a long-bone shaft—"but these aren't from last year." She pointed upward, toward the crown of the dead tulip poplar. "These are from the tree the victim was chained to." *Good girl, Miranda*, I thought, though of course Miranda—was she about to turn thirty?—was far from a girl now. "Also," she went on, "there's no vegetation growing up through the skeletal elements. That suggests the remains hadn't yet skeletonized by spring or early summer, when seeds germinate."

Her mention of seeds germinating reminded me of a case a few years ago—*my God*, I realized, *twenty years ago*—in the Cumberland Mountains, where I found a two-year-old black-locust seedling growing from the eye orbit of a dead girl's skull. I had so many ghosts floating around in my head by now; every new case seemed to remind me of an old case, or two or three or five old cases. *Concentrate, Brockton*, I scolded myself. *Be here now.*

"Clearly there's been a lot of carnivore activity and scatter," Miranda was saying. "Possibly dogs; more likely, coyotes. As you can see, in addition to the skull, we're missing the hands and feet, along with the ends of the long bones. In fact, we're missing a lot of the elements of the axial skeleton."

"The which of the what?" asked Waylon.

"The elements of the axial skeleton," she repeated. "The bones below the skull—the ribs, sternum, lumbar vertebrae from the lower spine—most of them are gone. So it could have been a whole pack of coyotes."

I would circle back to that shortly, but meanwhile, I wanted her to move on. "So what can you tell us about the victim?"

"Well, a lot less than I could if we had the skull," she said. "From the narrow pelvis, we can see that the victim was male. Unfortunately, that doesn't tell us anything about his geographic ancestry."

"Excuse me, Miranda," said Morgan. "Are you using 'geographic ancestry' the way we used to use 'race,' back in the age of dinosaurs, when I was in Dr. Brockton's classes?"

"I am," she said, her smile tolerant but tight. Then, looking at O'Conner and Waylon, she explained, "We used to categorize people into three 'races': Caucasoid, Negroid, and Mongoloid, which meant Asian or Native American. Now, anthropologists— most of them, anyway"—she glanced at me as she said it, knowing that I had not fully swallowed this politically correct batch of culturally sensitive Kool-Aid—"recognize 'race' to be a self-defined cultural identity. A label people choose for themselves, not an objective physical feature."

I kept silent, though inwardly I chafed a bit. *If it looks like a Caucasoid and quacks like a Caucasoid*, I thought, *it* is *a Caucasoid*. The three-race model had served forensic anthropologists extremely well, in my opinion, and it seemed a shame to discard it for the sake of what struck me as politically correct hairsplitting.

"Is 'dead redneck' a cultural identity, too?" asked Waylon. "'Cause no matter what you call it, I reckon that's most likely what we're lookin' at right here."

Miranda looked both appalled and puzzled. "Well," she hedged after an awkward pause, during which I struggled to keep a straight face, "if you're dead, it makes it hard to self-identify. But are you saying you don't think the victim is African American?" Waylon nodded but didn't elaborate, so Miranda pressed him. "Why not?"

"Not many to choose from up here," he said. "Ain't but a handful of black folks live in Cooke County. Seems like we'da heard about it if one of 'em went missing."

Seeking a second opinion, she looked at the sheriff. "Really? They're that scarce?"

O'Conner shrugged, looking slightly self-conscious. "As counties go, it's fairly monochrome," he conceded.

"How monochrome?" she persisted.

"Ninety-five percent white, as of the 2010 Census," he said. I was surprised and impressed that he knew the number off the top of his head.

"Two percent black. Two percent Hispanic, supposedly, but I'm pretty sure that number's rising,
judging by the increase in Latinos I saw at the cock-
fights, back before we shut that operation down."

"Wowzer," she said. "Double wowzer. Interesting method of demographic research, Sheriff. And
interesting Census data. I didn't know America still
had such lily-white places."

The professor in me couldn't let that stand un-
challenged. "Hey, Cooke County is a multicultural
melting pot compared to Pickett County, up on the
Kentucky border," I said. "Last time I checked, their
black population was two-tenths of a percent." She
looked dubious. "True fact," I assured her. "Zero
point two percent. One black person for every five
hundred whites."

"Must be a whole lotta fun for that one," she observed dryly. "But we digress. So: The victim might
or might not have been a white male. Let's see if we
can tell how old he was."

She picked up a clavicle—luckily, there *was* one to
pick up, though only one. "The clavicle, the collar-
bone, is a good indicator of age," she said. "The ends
of the bone, called the epiphyses, are connected to
the shaft by cartilage before adulthood, but then they
fuse, and growth stops. But luckily, the ends of the
clavicle don't fuse at the same time. The distal end,
where it joins the shoulder, fuses first, at age nineteen or twenty." She examined the bone. "And that
appears to have happened, although . . ." She peered
more closely. "Perhaps not 100 percent." She studied the other end, which had once been attached to
the sternum. "The medial epiphysis fuses later," she

went on, "usually during the twenties. Here, the fusion has just begun, so we know he's younger than thirty."

I didn't say anything—I didn't want to interrupt her—but inwardly I was cheering, *Yes! You are going to be a terrific professor someday, Miranda!*

She frowned at me, and for an absurd moment I wondered if she'd heard my thoughts and found them discomfiting, but then the reason for the frown became clear. "Too bad so many of the elements are missing," she said finally. "The skull could help us narrow down the age further. The sutures—the seams—in the roof of the mouth fuse at different ages, too. But based on the clavicle, I'd estimate the age at right around twenty. No more than twenty-five. Maybe as young as nineteen."

"What a shame," said O'Conner. "I mean, don't get me wrong, this would be awful at any age, but twenty's just a kid. Unbelievable."

"It might be unbelievable," I told him, "but I'm afraid it's all too true."

I put the sheriff, the deputy, and the TBI agent to work, helping Miranda and me inventory and bag the bones. I'd brought a diagram of the skeleton, the bones drawn as outlines. As I picked up each bone and handed it off to the lawmen to bag, I called out its name, and Miranda filled in the bone's outline on the diagram. "Cervical vertebrae," I said. "C1, C2, C3, C4, C5, C6, C7." That was the biggest collection of adjacent elements. Below the neck, the remaining bones were few, far between, and badly chewed—especially the long bones of the arms and legs. Given how many of the skeletal elements were missing, it didn't take long to collect them all. At the end, though, we got lucky: Two of the long bones—the right humerus and right femur—bore recently healed fractures. Comminuted fractures, in which the bones had been broken into several pieces. And those pieces had been fastened back together with metal plates and screws. "Look at this," I said, holding up the two shafts. "This could help a lot with identification."

Waylon gave a low whistle. "Them parts can be tracked, right, Doc? Like the serial number on a gun or a car?"

I shook my head. "I wish. But no. If we can find x-rays that match these, we'll have a positive I.D. But first we have to find a missing-person report that seems to fit, then see if we can get the medical records."

"Huh," Waylon grunted, clearly disappointed.

Once the bones were all charted and bagged, I put everyone else to work gathering up the bags, cans, and other debris. "I'll be back in a minute," I told them. They probably assumed I needed to step behind a tree and pee. Instead I ambled away, wandering the site, alternating between scanning the ground for anything that might happen to lie outside the circular path and, especially, examining the trunks of surrounding trees. After a while, I sensed that I was being watched.

"Dr. B?" I'd been so intent on my search that I hadn't heard Miranda come up behind me. "You look like you're looking for something. I mean, something specific."

"I am," I said, stepping closer to a medium-sized tulip poplar and running my fingers over the bark. "And I just found it. Y'all come take a look."

The others laid down their trash bags and approached. Waylon was the first to spot what I was looking at. "God a'mighty," he said. "I was afraid we was gonna find something like that."

"Me, too," said O'Conner, "though I didn't want to say so."

"What?" demanded Miranda, looking from their faces to mine. "Somebody want to let me in on the secret?"

I reached up and tapped the tree trunk, slightly above my head. "Claw marks," I said. "From a bear. A big one, judging by the height of the marks."

Miranda blanched. "Are you thinking what I *think* you're thinking?"

I nodded. "You mentioned coyote scavenging, but I figured it for bear," I told her.

"Why? You could tell from the tooth marks?"

I shook my head. "Hard to tell from the tooth marks themselves, though there *was* a mighty big puncture in a scapula. What tipped me off wasn't what was there, but what *wasn't*." All three of them looked puzzled. "Canids—dogs and coyotes—tend to go for the extremities. A dog'll gnaw off a hand or a foot, or even an arm or a leg, and drag it off to a safe place. Bears, though, love the torso: the ribs, the sternum, even the spine. Stuff that's too tough for dogs and coyotes. Remind me, when we get back to campus, to dig out an article for you. It was in the *Journal of Forensic Sciences* a while back. Described some cases of bear scavenging in the mountains of New Mexico. The bears ate the ribs and the sternum every single time."

"Beg pardon, Doc," said Waylon. "I don't mean to sound disrespectful, but you reckon maybe the barbecue folks are missing out on a good bet?"

I blinked and stared at him. "You mean by not putting *humans* in the smoker?"

"Lord, no!" The big man blushed and grimaced. "I mean the sternum. From pigs, not people. Smoked sternum—might taste even better'n pulled pork shoulder or baby back ribs."

"Waylon," I said, "you are one of a kind." He blushed again. "But I don't think it would work. The ribs have a fair amount of meat on them. Between them, actually. The intercostal muscles. But the sternum?" I poked around on my own chest, to underscore the point. "Lots of cartilage, to connect it to the ribs. But no real muscle to speak of. All you'd get is gristle and bone."

Waylon gave his own mammoth chest a few exploratory prods, then nodded, looking mildly disappointed. "I reckon bears ain't as picky as us."

"Maybe they don't have the luxury," I pointed out. "They're mostly eating bugs and berries and acorns, right? Not often they get a feast like this." I felt a stab of guilt when I heard myself refer to the victim that way. "I don't mean to sound callous. I just mean that if you're a big black bear in these mountains, it might be tough to find enough to eat, you know?"

"Soooo . . ." Miranda trailed off. All three of us turned to her, leaving her little choice but to finish what she'd started. "I hate to ask—I'm not sure I want to know the answer—but was the victim already dead when the bear came along, or did the bear kill him?"

I looked at Waylon and the sheriff, but they both shrugged—possibly because they didn't know, but possibly because they hated to say. "Hard to tell," I answered. "It's rare for a black bear to kill a human. Far as I know, there's only ever been one person killed by a bear in the Smokies. That was a woman back in 2000, if I remember right."

"Killed by a mama bear and a cub, lessen I disremember," offered Waylon. "The mama mighta been protectin' the cub, or thinkin' she was."

I nodded. "But this situation? A human chained in the wilderness for days or weeks, with food wrappers and maybe even scraps lying around, giving off scent? The smell would be pretty appealing to a hungry bear, and once he was here, who knows?"

"Another thing we don't know," O'Conner added, "is whether the killer kept bringing food and water, or whether he stopped at some point. The victim could've died of thirst or hunger."

"Or maybe the guy come back and shot him after a while," said Waylon. "Reckon I should bring me a metal detector up here, see if they's a bullet on the ground somewheres."

"Good idea," I agreed. "Once we're back at UT, we can x-ray the remains and see if there's a lead wipe on any of the bones."

"A which?" said Waylon.

"A lead wipe," I repeated. "A smear of lead, left by a bullet grazing the bone. A lead wipe shows up on an x-ray like a streak of white paint, much brighter than bone. I'll let you know if we find anything. How soon do you think you can get back here with the metal detector?"

"Tomorrow mornin', I reckon. I'd go get it now, 'cept it's about to get dark on us."

He was right. I hadn't noticed, but the sun was beginning to drop behind the adjoining ridge. Late-afternoon light—already golden from the low angle—was incandescent through the yellow leaves of the tulip poplars. I paused to take it in, the astounding beauty that surrounded us, even here at the scene of a terrible death. "Guess we'd better wrap this up," I said. "If we're here after dark in a vehicle with a state plate, no telling what's liable to happen to us."

Waylon chuckled. "Hellfire, Doc, I'll be behind you all the way to I-40. Ain't nobody'll mess with you, lessen they go through me first. And I don't see that happenin'."

"Neither do I," I said. "Not unless they've got a death wish. Or a huge pain wish, at the very least."

HAPPILY, NO ONE in Cooke County had a death wish, nor a Waylon-sized pain wish. Aside from the deputy's monster truck, I saw no vehicles trailing us back to Jonesport, nor on the twisting drive back to the interstate.

As we turned off River Road and onto the westbound ramp of I-40, I rolled down my window and waved. Behind us, I saw the headlights of the mammoth truck flash once, twice, three times, and the notes of the truck's aftermarket horn—tooting the opening bars of "Dixie"—came wafting through the twilight, growing fainter as we picked up speed and merged with the stream of cars meandering out of the mountains and flowing, a ceaseless river of humanity, toward the distant confluence of Knoxville.

The drive was quiet. Perhaps Miranda was preoccupied with her own thoughts—possibly thoughts of the young man whose fragmentary skeleton rode behind us in the truck's cargo bed—or perhaps she was simply giving me room to think my own thoughts. At any rate, we rode in silence.

As we neared the outskirts of the city, I overtook a slow-moving semi. Flicking my turn signal, I checked my outside mirror to be sure the left lane was clear.

It was, but in the mirror, I caught a glimpse of a lighted billboard on the other side of the median. COMFORT INN, it read. AARP. AAA. HBO. ESPN. THIS EXIT & EXIT 407.

Out of the corner of my eye, I watched as it fell farther and farther behind, shrinking and dwindling until finally it disappeared altogether, and I felt my chest loosen and lighten.

Almost as if something in the air around us had shifted, Miranda now spoke.

"At least Hugh Glass had a fighting chance," she said sadly.

"*Who* Glass?"

"No, *Hugh* Glass," she said, and I was reminded of the old "Who's on first?" joke.

"Who's Hugh, and what are you talking about?"

"Hugh Glass, the mountain man. In *The Revenant*. You're kidding, right?" Despite the darkness in the cab, I could tell she was staring at me. "Oscar-winning performance by Leonardo DiCaprio? In a movie that won two other Academy Awards this year, too?"

I shrugged, feeling sheepish. "I don't see a lot of movies," I said. "Kinda depressing to go by yourself."

"Duh," she said. "Tell me something I don't know. But you should totally see this one."

"Because?"

"Well, for one thing, the guy—this mountain man, Glass, played by DiCaprio—he's torn to pieces by a bear, a big grizzly, and gets buried alive by the guys who are supposed to be taking care of him. So there's a connection to our case, sort of. For another thing, the movie's full of Arikara Indians."

Now she had my full attention. "Arikara? But they're all gone. Died out, mostly, and assimilated with the Mandans and Hidatsu."

She made an impatient, clucking sound. "The film's historical. Set in the 1820s. Along the Missouri River."

I grinned. "Why didn't you say so? That's where all my skeletal remains come from!"

"*Duh*," she repeated. "I *know*. That's why I mentioned it. But the movie's set farther north—up in North Dakota or Montana, looks like. Serious mountains."

I turned off I-40 onto James White Parkway,

to loop along the riverfront to Neyland Stadium. Across the Tennessee, streetlights and houselights on the south shore smeared and danced in the black, rippling river. I was puzzling over the plot of the movie Miranda was describing, worrying at it, like a dog with a bone. "What are Plains Indians doing up in the Rocky Mountains?"

"Good grief, Dr. B. Don't pick it apart before you even see it. So this guy Glass is a guide for a bunch of fur trappers. The trappers get attacked by a band of Arikara Indians. The Indians are look- ing for an Arikara woman who's been abducted by a white man. Maybe that's what brought them to the mountains—the search for the woman. Anyhow, Glass spends a lot of time getting chased by them."

"I thought you said he got killed by the bear?"

She sighed. "Just see it," she said. "You'll love it. You'll laugh. You'll cry. You'll thank me." By now we had arrived back at UT. As I turned off Ney- land Drive, Miranda said, "Don't you want to take this stuff out to the facility? Put the bones in to simmer?"

I shook my head. "It's late. Just do it in the morn- ing, how 'bout?" Glancing over, I saw her shrug and nod.

I pulled in front of her pale green Prius, which was tucked beneath the stadium just outside the bone lab, and switched off the truck's engine. "So, this mountain man, Glass—is he the one who ab- ducted the Arikara woman?"

"Quit asking annoying questions. I've already told you too much." She paused, then added, "You know what? Forget I mentioned it. Don't see it. You'd probably hate it."

Now, of course, wild horses couldn't keep me from watching it.

As Miranda jolly well knew.

CHAPTER 4

OLD HABITS DIE HARD, I realized as I settled into bed. Harder, alas, than people do.

Kathleen had been dead for a decade—more than a decade, in fact—but I still slept on "my" side of the bed. Actually, for the thirty years of our marriage, "my" side had also been "our" side: no matter where she started out (usually in the middle), Kathleen had always ended up crossing the midline, and I had always ended up on the edge of the mattress, sometimes hanging partway off.

For years I had grumbled about her Territorial Imperative. Now I would have given anything—everything—to feel her crowding me, nestling me, spooning me in her sleep. "Don't it always seem to go," I serenaded myself, pulling up the covers, "that you don't know what you've got till it's gone." Truth was, though, I *had* known what I'd had with Kathleen. I'd felt lucky beyond all deserving to be with her, and bereft beyond all reckoning when I lost her.

Since Kathleen's death I had slept with only

two women—just one time apiece—and both those women were dead now, too. It wasn't as if I were responsible for their deaths, any more than I'd been responsible for Kathleen's, but all the same, I sometimes wondered if I might carry some sort of jinx, or bad karma. Could it be that immersing myself, day after day, year after year, in death, dismemberment, and decay, had somehow tainted me? That I had steadily absorbed, and now subtly emanated, mortality—and not just its faint odor of it, but its *essence* as well? That I was a carrier, like Typhoid Mary? *Mortality Bill*, I thought.

The absurdity of it almost made me smile. Almost, but not quite.

As I reached for the switch on the bedside lamp, my eye happened to light on a card that lay on the nightstand. It had arrived in the previous day's mail, sent by a California woman whose father's remains I had identified a few weeks before. His skull had recently turned up on a riverbank a few miles downstream from Knoxville, years after he'd gone missing. The man had long struggled with depression, and the general consensus, once we'd identified him, was that he had probably committed suicide by jumping from the Gay Street Bridge, Knoxville's favorite suicide spot. "Thank you for giving me closure at last," she had written. "It saddens me to know, once and for all, that he's dead, but it helps me, too. Not knowing was worse. I know I speak for others when I say how much I appreciate the work you do. Thank you, thank you, thank you."

"No, thank *you*," I whispered as I snapped off

the light, grateful for something—anything—that could counter my sense of being a jinx. "And good night."

I HAD A dream, and in my dream, I was walking, slowly and heavily, as if I were wading in waist-deep water or weighted down. After a while, I realized that indeed I *was* weighted down. A heavy chain wrapped around my neck and trailed behind me. Despite the difficulty, I kept walking, but soon I realized that I was walking in a circle, covering the same ground again and again. So I stopped.

As I rested, uncertain what to do next, I became aware of someone nearby. It was a young man—a boy, really—and like me, he was wearing a chain and walking in a circle. After he had made several turns around the tree to which he was chained, I noticed that he was being followed by an immense black bear. I opened my mouth to warn the boy, but I found myself unable to speak.

I tried to reach him, so I could turn him around, show him the bear, but my chain was too short, and he remained just out of reach. He kept walking, faster and faster, and then he began to run, as if he sensed danger even though he had not seen the bear. And then, as he ran, he began to scream, louder and louder, until his shrieking woke me.

As I lay in my bed, my heart pounding, the sheets soaked with sweat, I realized I could still hear the boy shrieking.

But the shrieking was not from the boy in my dream; the shrieking, I finally understood, was from a fire truck—a rare sound in my quiet neighborhood—and as the pounding of my heart subsided, so, too, did the wail of the siren, and I was left, awake and alone, on my side of a bed that felt as empty as a black hole in space: a void so vast and dense, not even light could escape.

CHAPTER 5

GROGGY AND OFF KILTER from my restless, night-marish night, I drove on autopilot, winding behind UT Medical Center and through the staff parking lot, then parking beside the twin gates of the Body Farm: an outer, chain-link gate, topped with razor wire, and an inner, wooden gate. The chain-link fence that surrounded our three wooded acres was there to keep out trespassers, and it worked well, although not perfectly. Occasionally fraternity boys—either as an initiation rite or as a show of bravado—tried to break in, but being drunk, they usually got snagged in the barbed wire. More seriously, we'd had one damaging robbery: someone had made off with half a dozen skulls, though the police eventually recovered three of them when the thief, who was a drug addict, tried to sell them. The inner wooden fence—eight feet high, made of pine boards butted tightly together—was there to shield the corpses from prying eyes . . . and to protect squeamish hospital employees (if there were in fact any of those) from the sight of my dead and decomposing research subjects.

I unlocked the metal gate and took a step inward to the wooden gate. The padlock's shackle clasped both ends of a loop of chain, which was threaded through a hole bored in each half of the gate. As I lifted the lock and felt the heft of the chain, I couldn't help thinking of the Cooke County victim, his neck encircled by hard, cold links, dragging that fifty-pound length of chain around and around that tree. The Tree of Death.

Just as the lock sprang open in my hand, I realized my mistake. "*Dammit*, Brockton, *think*," I scolded myself aloud. Clicking the lock shut once more, I fastened the outer gate, got back into my truck, and threaded my way down to the parking lot exit. A hundred yards beyond the exit was a small, recently paved driveway, which I turned up and followed to a new brick building, so new that its "landscaping" consisted mainly of raw, red clay. I had been here dozens of times, but now, distraught and distracted by my nightmare, I'd reverted to autopilot, following the route I'd taken thousands of times over the course of some twenty years.

The building—a combination morgue, laboratory, and classroom facility—was the culmination of years of need, hope, planning, and pleading. For more than twenty years, my decomposition research program had operated on a shoestring, my "laboratory" consisting of trees and dirt, bacteria and insects. The first version of the Body Farm had been born, so to speak, in an abandoned barn on a UT pig farm, located miles outside of town. A few years later, the facility had moved to a small fenced enclosure on what had once been a trash-burning pit for the UT hospital. But gradually the Body Farm's footprint—or was it plural: footprints?—had spread over three wooded acres. The infrastructure, though, had remained quite primitive, limited to one electrical power outlet and one water spigot.

Until now; until our new building, which was a remarkable upgrade. Inside the brick walls, beneath the green metal roof, was virtually everything I'd ever wished for: A cooler big enough to hold a dozen bodies, if need be. Two electric-jacketed kettles, each one big enough for me to curl up inside, for simmering bodies and skeletons: for separating flesh from bone. A pair of industrial-sized sinks, overhung by exhaust hoods whose whooshing fans could whisk away the last lingering odors as final bits of tissue were scrubbed and removed. Computerized workstations, complete with 3-D digitizing probes for taking skeletal measurements and plugging the data into ForDisc, our software program for determining—for "estimating," to be pedantically precise—the race or ancestry of an unknown skeleton.

In the case of our Cooke County victim, whose long bones were chewed up and whose skull was MIA, ForDisc was probably useless, our 3-D digitizing probes reduced to expensive, high-tech paperweights. Lacking more bones—especially, but not only, the skull—we had very little data for ForDisc to plug into its predictive models of race or ancestry, and that was a loss. ForDisc had shown me how well its models worked, in memorably humbling fashion, in its first forensic outing: the soggy skeleton from Polecat Creek.

Polecat Creek was a stream in Loudon County, about thirty miles southwest of Knoxville, where I'd worked a case years before. Acting on an anonymous tip, divers from the Loudon County Sheriff's Office had fished a body from the creek, directly beneath a two-lane bridge. The victim, wrapped in plastic and badly decomposed, was clearly a male, and—judging from the narrow nasal opening and the vertical structure of the mouth—a white male, of middle age. Trouble was, there were no middle-aged white males missing in Loudon County, or anywhere within a hundred miles of Loudon County.

At the time, my colleague Richard had just put the finishing touches on the first version of ForDisc. ForDisc was short for Forensic Discriminant Functions, a mouthful of a name that referred to the complicated algorithms, or equations, that Richard had written to calculate what racial group a particular skeleton best matched. To create a basis for comparison, Richard, along with helpful students and colleagues worldwide, had keyed thousands and thousands of measurements into ForDisc, from skeletons around the globe. As it happened, on that very day—long past, yet still vivid in my memory—I had grumbled about the lack of progress in identifying the John Doe from Polecat Creek. "Let's see what ForDisc says about him," Richard suggested. With an indulgent smile I handed over the bones, knowing that ForDisc would agree with me.

But ForDisc *didn't* agree with me. I had focused almost entirely on the Polecat Creek victim's skull, but ForDisc also considered measurements from the postcranial skeleton, the bones below the skull. On the basis of the postcranial elements, ForDisc judged the Polecat Creek victim to be African American, or perhaps mixed race. And sure enough, when the detective checked missing-person reports for African Americans instead of whites, he hit pay dirt immediately: A black man from Oak Ridge had gone missing a year or so before, and when we compared his dental records with the teeth from our victim, they matched perfectly. Brockton 0, ForDisc 1. Fortunately, ForDisc and I had agreed on virtually everything since Polecat Creek, but Polecat Creek had taught me the value of a second opinion, even if that opinion came from a bunch of circuit boards and arcane formulas.

Ever since Polecat Creek, I'd always been open to whatever light ForDisc could shed on an unknown skeleton. In the Cooke County case, though, ForDisc would likely be as clueless and hamstrung as I was.

Quit whining, I chided myself. *The only way forward is forward. Step by step.* The first step for case 16–17 was some quick orthopedic surgery. Normally I would do a bit of dental work instead, but here, too, I was thwarted by the lack of a skull. *My kingdom for a skull*, I silently declaimed. I had promised to send a DNA sample to the TBI lab, and teeth generally provide the best DNA samples. Tooth enamel does a good job of encapsulating and protecting the genetic material from potential damage by weather, bacteria, and other environmental or chemical factors. But there were no teeth; hence the orthopedic surgery: A bone sample would have to do.

Reaching up to a tool rack above one of the lab's counters, I took down a motorized implement that resembled a Dremel tool—a heavy, chrome-plated version, pumped up on steroids. A slender shaft projected from one end of the stainless housing, and attached to the shaft at a right angle was a flat, asymmetrical blade, one whose fanlike shape never failed to put me in mind of a ginkgo leaf, though I'd never seen tiny teeth rimming the curve of a ginkgo leaf. Hefting the tool, a Stryker autopsy saw, I felt weight, solidity, and power. I flicked the switch, and with a hum and a jolt it kicked on, the edge of the blade twitching in rapid, almost invisible oscillations.

Slowly I moved the vibrating blade toward my own forearm—closer and closer, millimeter by millimeter—and touched it to the flesh midway between my wrist and elbow. The blade buzzed and tickled, but it did not cut, my pale skin oscillating in perfect sync with the minuscule movements of the tiny teeth. This was one of the wondrous things about the Stryker saw: it could slice through bone like a hot knife through butter, but it wouldn't cut soft tissue, not unless the soft tissue was immobilized by pressure from underlying bone. If I bore down hard on my forearm, the result would be terribly different: a sudden spurt of blood, followed by the rasp of teeth chewing through my radius and ulna. But I did not bear down, my flesh and bone remained intact, and I turned, smiling, to the task at hand.

I selected one of the long bones—the left humerus, or upper arm bone—and clamped it carefully in a bench vise that was bolted to the counter beneath one of the exhaust hoods. Then I switched on the fan, switched on the Stryker saw, and bent over the bone, bringing the oscillating blade closer and closer to the bone at what had once been the middle of the shaft, before the elbow had been gnawed off by the bear. The blade sang as it began chewing into the bone, a zinging soprano pitch that always reminded me of cicadas, though more musical, somehow. As the blade bit deeper, wisps of bone dust spun and swirled upward, drawn into the fan's slipstream like tendrils of cigarette smoke. It took less than ten seconds to cut through the bone, which was roughly the diameter of my index finger. The cut I'd made had removed the bone's jagged distal end, along with an additional two inches of the shaft, creating a clean cross section through the bone, showing the dense outer, cortical bone and the inner, spongy bone.

Next I bore down with the saw again, this time cutting off only a half-inch piece: the cross section for the TBI's lab. Protected from the weather and from contaminants—bacteria, bear's saliva, and my own DNA, if the exhaust hood and my surgical mask were doing their jobs—this clean cross section would, I hoped, give the TBI's genetic technician plenty of intact, uncontaminated DNA to analyze. Sealing the disk of bone in a plastic film canister, I set it aside to send to the TBI lab later in the day.

The surgery complete, now it was time for 16–17 to have a bath. A long, hot bath.

The processing lab's equipment included two

immense electric-jacketed kettles, the sort restaurants used to cook fifty pounds of potatoes or twenty gallons of chili in a single batch. We used them to simmer skeletons—like making soup or stock, except backward: we threw away the stock and kept the bones instead. I raised the lid on one of the kettles and began filling it with hot water. As it filled, I poured a scoop of Biz Stain & Odor Eliminator into the kettle, followed by a capful of Downy Fabric Softener: the two additives I'd found most effective at helping clean and deodorize the bones. Gently I added the bones, which, being few in number and fragmented, occupied a poignantly small percentage of the kettle's capacious interior. Given how weathered and bare the bones already were, they wouldn't need to simmer overnight, as most remains did. These might be ready for a final scrubbing by the end of the day, and that was a task I would definitely delegate to Miranda.

SHE LOOKED UP from her computer screen when I walked into the bone lab. "Did you just come from the facility?" she asked. "The truck was gone when I got here, so I wondered if you might already be there."

"I was. I woke up early—"

"You *always* wake up early," she interrupted.

"I woke up even earlier than usual," I amended, "so I figured I might as well get the bones in to simmer."

"Thanks," she said. "I was planning to do it on my way to the airport, but it's taking a while to pull this stuff together, so I appreciate that."

"What stuff?" I asked, and then, "The airport? Why are you going to the airport?" Suddenly I noticed her appearance for the first time since walking into the lab. Miranda was wearing a suit, of all things—a dark gray skirt, white blouse, matching gray jacket, and—could it be?—honest-to-God *stockings*. Had I ever seen Miranda in stockings? And her hair, normally hanging in long waves of chestnut, looked oddly short and . . . springy. I stared, thunderstruck. "Did you . . . *roll your hair*?"

"What? Oh. Yeah, I did," she said, looking embarrassed. Or was it defensive?

"Okay," I demanded, "who *are* you, and what have you done with the real Miranda?" She rolled her eyes and glared. "And what's with the fancy getup? You better change into a jumpsuit. Those stockings won't last five minutes up in the woods."

"The woods? What woods? What are you talking about?"

"The Cooke County woods. I've been thinking. We need to go back. Take another look at the death scene. I can't help thinking we missed something yesterday."

Miranda stared at me, her face a study in astonishment. "Are you kidding me, or do you honestly mean you forgot?"

"Forgot what?"

"Forgot why I can't go back up to Cooke County today. Forgot why I'm in this 'getup,' as you put it. Forgot why I've been here for two hours printing out a stack of this stuff. I'm on my way to Quantico."

"Quantico? What for?" Even as I said it, I sensed a recollection beginning to bubble up from deep in the tar pit of my memory, bringing with it a bad feeling. A very, very bad feeling.

"*Jesus*, Dr. B. I have a *job* interview there. With the FBI. That didn't even register with you? It wasn't worth remembering?"

"No—I mean yes. I remembered. Of *course* I remembered. It just slipped my mind for a minute."

She concentrated on straightening her stack of printouts—her dissertation, I noticed, and reprints of several journal articles we'd written. No: several journal articles *she'd* written, but for which I got credit as a coauthor, as professors always do when their students publish.

When she looked up, her eyes were accusing and hurt. "Did that letter of recommendation slip your mind, too?" I felt myself reddening, and a bloom of sweat sprang from my brow. "*Damn* it, Dr. B," she said, before I could stammer out an explanation. Not that there *was* an explanation. Had I really failed to write the letter? Had I recently relocated—moved from the state of Tennessee to the state of Denial? What, if anything, had I been thinking? *If I ignore it, it'll go away—and she won't go away?*

Miranda was shaking her head now. "Thanks a lot," she said bitterly, scooping up her armload of credentials. "Wish me luck." And with that, she swept out of the lab.

"Good luck," I said, too lamely and too late, as the steel door slammed between us.

Standing there, abandoned by Miranda and appalled by my own thoughtlessness, I wondered if she'd ever be back.

CHAPTER 6

I HAD PLANNED TO put Miranda on trash detail, the dirty work of sifting through the debris we'd brought back from Cooke County. But in view of her trip to Quantico, and my failure to write the recommendation I'd promised, I reassigned the scut work to myself. For one thing, I didn't want to let it sit until Miranda's return. For another, the task—smelly and tedious though it was—could serve as penance, as distraction, and possibly even as a contribution to the case.

But before turning trash detective, I needed to make a phone call. I looked up the cell-phone number—I was surprised I still had it after so many years—and dialed. "Brubaker," said a crisp voice on the other end of the line.

Pete Brubaker was an FBI profiler, or had been, until his retirement a few years before. Now he worked for a forensic consulting firm, and rumor had it that he was working on a book—either a memoir or a crime novel. Either one, I figured, could be mighty interesting. "Pete, it's Dr. Bill Brockton, from the University of Tennessee," I said. "You may remember that we worked together a while back—"

"Of course," he said. "I still follow you. Anytime my colleagues visit your research facility, they always bring back gory stories. And your name pops up in my newsfeed every now and then. Glad to see you're still catching bad guys. How can I help you, Doc?"

"Two ways, I'm hoping. First, I've got a case down here," I said. "Damnedest thing I ever saw. We found . . . I can't say a body, because all that's left is some bones. A young man. Twenty, plus or minus. Race unknown. Chained to a tree in the woods to die."

"Cause of death—starvation?"

"No, bizarrely. There were empty food cans all around, so he was kept alive—until he wasn't. I think he was killed by a bear."

I heard a low whistle at the other end of the line. "Well, that's a new one even for me, Doc." There was a pause. "Could it be a kidnapping gone wrong? Chained up while they were waiting for the ransom, but the ransom never came—or it came, but they left him there anyhow?"

"Could be, I reckon, but we don't know of any kidnappings."

"Anything found at the scene that indicates some other motive?"

"Not a thing."

"Hmm. Well, it's not much to go on, but just off the top of my head? Two possibilities. One, the victim could have been mentally ill."

This hadn't occurred to me. "Interesting. Like, the hillbilly version of locking crazy cousin Vern in the attic?"

"Maybe. But I think that's less likely than the other possibility."

"Which is . . . ?"

"Revenge. The victim was being punished for some wrong—real or perceived—that he'd done to the perpetrator. That's a very personal crime. A very big power differential. Chained to a tree, totally dependent on his captor for food and water. Punishment plus degradation. It's 'I'll show you' and 'How does it feel?' and 'You messed with the wrong damn guy' all in one, right? See what I'm saying?"

"I do," I said. "I'll pass that along to the sheriff and the TBI agent."

"Have they asked for the Bureau's assistance?"

"No," I admitted. "I'll suggest it, if you think I should."

"You might wait and see if anything similar occurs," he said. "If it's a case of personal revenge, you're probably not looking for a serial killer. But if another case like it shows up, this could be the start of something bad."

"We do have a lot of trees here in Tennessee," I said. "And a lot of bears. Anything similar happens, we'll holler for help. But what you've just told me is really useful. Now I've got an angle or two we can work, and I didn't have to jump through any bureaucratic hoops to get 'em. One advantage of getting old is that you know a lot of people you can call up and ask for favors."

He laughed. "Well, ask anytime. Which reminds

me. You said you had two favors to ask. What's the second?"

I told him, and he didn't hesitate. "I might be able to help you out," he said. "No promises, but I'll do what I can."

I thanked him and hung up, then hurried to my truck. Trash detail beckoned; the crime-scene sewer awaited. And suddenly I couldn't wait to dive in.

THE BLACK GARBAGE bag glistened dully on the lab's stone counter, lumpy and ominous, stuffed with the detritus of human cruelty and depravity. I approached it warily, donning nitrile gloves and a paper surgical mask to protect myself, not just from bacteria or stinking scraps, but from subtler, more sinister contaminations—spiritual toxins and contagions, if such things existed—waiting to escape the bag we'd brought with us from the death scene.

The bag rustled, its contents shifting and clinking and rattling, when I lifted it and carried it across the room, placing it on a stainless steel counter beneath the largest of the lab's exhaust hoods. I touched the switch and the fan whirred and whooshed, smooth and powerful. The hairs on my arm moved and tickled in the rush of air, and the ruff of loose black plastic above the bag's twist tie twitched, as if something in the bag were alive and trying to get out. The hairs on my neck suddenly prickled, too— stirred not by the fan's updraft, I suspected, but by some psychic currents of superstition or premonition. *Get a grip, Brockton*, I ordered myself.

And so I did. Gripping the bag's tightly cinched neck, I untwisted the plastic-coated twist tie and laid it aside, then slowly lifted the bottom of the bag. Clattering and clanking, the contents tumbled out: Tin cans. Plastic bottles and jugs. Bags and wrappers and pouches of paper, foil, cellophane.

Where to begin? Did it even matter, my arbitrary starting point, since I'd be sifting and sorting and scrutinizing the whole mess? "Eeny . . . meeny . . . miny . . . *moe*," I said, my gloved index finger tapping a flattened milk jug at "moe." Starting with the milk jugs made good sense, I realized. For one thing, they were the largest items, so examining them first would shrink the trash heap the fastest, creating at least the illusion of rapid progress, as well as freeing up counter space for sorting the smaller items. Best of all, though, the pull dates on the cartons might tell me when the young man's captivity had begun . . . and when his feeding, and his life, had ceased.

"Okay, Moe, tell me your story," I commanded the first crumpled plastic milk jug. I picked it up by the edges, rather than the handle, on the off chance that the TBI crime lab, to which I would relay everything, might be able to coax a DNA sample or a latent print from the surface. The latter seemed doubtful; the container's textured plastic was the sort of print-defying surface I'd heard forensic technicians curse countless times. Still, it never hurt to try. "You have to try," I reminded myself, quoting from a Lyle Lovett song. "What would you be if you didn't even try?"

The jug's paper label had peeled off—it was probably curled or wadded up elsewhere in this portable trash midden—but I didn't need a label to identify the brand. A glance at the yellow polyethylene and the circular medallions embossed on the jug's sides told me that the milk had been bottled by May-field, an East Tennessee dairy that was headquartered just fifty miles south of Knoxville, in Athens. Mayfield operated a large distribution center in West Knoxville, beside Interstate 40. For decades, the industrial-looking building was elevated from eyesore to quirky landmark by the larger-than-life figure of Maggie, an immense fiberglass Jersey cow. Twelve feet high by twenty feet long, endowed with forty-gallon udders, Maggie stood serenely on a large flatbed trailer alongside I-40. Her location and her wheels made it easy for Mayfield to herd Maggie to county fairs and cornbread festivals . . . and also made it relatively simple for pranksters to borrow Maggie from time to time, during fraternity initiations or other alcohol-fueled rites of passage. Maggie had, alas, been put out to pasture in recent years, retired to Mayfield's original dairy farm, which was now open to tourists and school groups. I missed her, and I suspected the UT fraternities did, too.

The jug's pull date, printed by a dot-matrix printer around the neck, read "Sell by 10/03/16." I blinked, stunned—*He couldn't have been alive two weeks ago*, I thought—but then I looked again and saw that I had misread the year: the fading ink read 2013, not 2016. That, too, was puzzling, though, given that it seemed clear—from the lack of leaf litter atop the bones—that the death had occurred only a few months before, perhaps during summer.

Removing the jug from beneath the hood, I raised it toward my face, sniffing as I did, ready to thrust it back into the exhaust the moment I caught the stench of sour milk. But I never did, even when the open spout was practically touching my nose. *Water*, I realized: The jug had been rinsed out and used to store water. I set it on a table behind me and reached for another jug.

This one—translucent and colorless, not Mayfield yellow—didn't require the sniff test, as it had flecks of clotted milk clearly visible within the hollow handle. It also had a far more recent pull date: May 29, just five months before. The remaining half-dozen jugs followed the same pattern as the first two: three of them were clean, odorless jugs, stamped with pull dates ranging from six months to three years earlier; the other three stank of sour milk, and bore dates ranging from May 17, the earliest, to June 24, the latest. *Chained in the woods for six weeks*, I calculated. *God in heaven.*

Next I tackled the cans—a few beer cans, but mostly an assortment of pull-top tins of processed meats, including, I grimaced to see, cheap dog food. The cans, whose contents were supposedly tasty for years, were less informative than the milk jugs, so I gave each one only a quick look before setting it aside. Next came a series of crumpled wrappers and bags: Slim Jim meat sticks. Lay's Potato Chips. Armour Star Bacon. McDonald's Egg McMuffin—a delicacy consumed by the killer, I suspected, who didn't seem the sort to waste a warm, tasty breakfast sandwich on a victim he sometimes fed dog food.

Three Red Man Tobacco foil pouches, whose contents likewise had probably gone into the killer's cheek: chewing tobacco was a luxury item, an indulgence, which almost surely would not have been offered to the captive victim, except, perhaps, in the form of a stream of brown spittle, delivered to the face and followed with an insult.

I set the beer cans, the Egg McMuffin wrapper, and the Red Man pouches to one side. I would package those separately for the TBI lab, in hopes that the killer's mouth had contacted their surfaces and left behind a trace of telltale DNA. A cigarette butt might have done the job also, but apparently our perpetrator preferred saliva to smoke as his nicotine delivery system.

After I'd removed the jugs, the cans, the wrappers, and the bags, very little was left. A foil chewing-gum wrapper. A whiskey bottle. An empty Altoids tin. And, oddly, two sticks of deodorant—or, rather, two empty deodorant dispensers, their labels peeling and tightly curled. *Why on earth . . .* , I wondered. It seemed inconceivable that the victim had been provided with toiletries to keep him smelling fresh during his ordeal in the woods. But it also made no sense that our tobacco-chewing perpetrator would be attending to his own personal hygiene at the scene of the crime, either. If he *had* been, why stop with deodorant? Where were the empty toothpaste tubes, the nail clippers, the dental floss?

On a whim—curious about what brand of deodorant might appeal to the sort of person who would chain a young man in the woods for weeks—I gave the deodorant a tentative sniff. It didn't smell like my own "sport" fragrance, nor like baby powder, nor lavender, nor any other deodorant I'd ever smelled. It smelled pungent, like rancid meat. Involuntarily I made a face, then gave the curled label a tug to remove it from the dispenser. As I held the paper in my upturned palm and smoothed it flat, it gave a sudden flutter, then—caught by the exhaust hood's rising column of air—it fluttered upward and plastered against the mesh screen guarding the fan. "Crap," I muttered, switching off the fan. As the spinning blades slowed, the label detached from the screen and drifted down, landing faceup on the soiled steel counter.

I read the label—once, twice, three times—and then heard myself whispering, "Son of a bitch. You sick, sick sonofabitch."

Then I dialed Sheriff O'Conner to tell him we were looking at a case of carefully planned, meticulously executed murder.

"Bear bait," I told O'Conner when he asked how I knew. "The victim was smeared with bear bait. 'ConQuest Scent Stick. Smoked Bacon,' the label says." I had a sudden realization, and I spun around to the table where I'd piled the empty cans and wrappers to confirm that I was remembering correctly. Armour Star, the plastic wrapper still cloudy with grease. "There was actual bacon, too—raw bacon. When I saw the package, it didn't make sense—all those empty cans, all that processed food, but raw bacon? Why would he feed the kid raw bacon? But he wasn't feeding it to him."

"Lord, Doc, are you saying what I think you're saying?"

"He wasn't feeding it to him," I repeated. "He was coating him with it. The killer turned that kid into living, breathing bear bait."

CHAPTER 7

I WAS IN MY administrative office early the next morning, huddled over the mountain of paperwork that had somehow accumulated on my desk during the hours I'd spent sifting through Beanee Weenee cans and bear-bait sticks.

I was just starting to flip through the annual inventory of Anthropology Department property—a twenty-page list of stuff that, apart from the equipment in the new DNA lab and the Body Farm's processing facility, was worth about fifty bucks—when my door burst open. "You!" exclaimed Miranda, coming toward me at a brisk clip. "You are unbelievable."

"Come on, Miranda," I said. "You're still mad at me? I told you how sorry I was."

She had already made it across the room and around the end of the desk; she kept closing the distance, until she was directly beside me. "You are unbelievably wonderful." She bent over, threw her arms around my neck, and gave me a quick hug, which—given that she was standing above me—felt more than a little awkward, from where I was sitting. Mercifully, she turned me loose quickly. "How on earth did you do that?"

"Do what?" I asked. I wasn't just playing coy; I honestly didn't know what she meant.

"The director of the FBI Laboratory—the head honcho, the big cheese—he came *looking* for me. He walked in on my job interview about five minutes after it started."

"What for?"

Her eyes narrowed with suspicion. "He said he'd heard I was interviewing. Wanted to be sure he had a chance to meet me, since he'd heard 'such glowing things' about me. He grilled me for twenty minutes, then shook my hand and said he thought they'd be lucky to get me."

"Well, well," I said. "Mr. Big Cheese is clearly a smart guy. Does he have a name?"

She rattled it off, then added, "As if you didn't know."

"Actually, I didn't," I said honestly. "Never heard of him. Pretty cool, though, that he's heard of you."

"Are you telling me you didn't call him yesterday morning, after I left in a huff?"

I raised my right hand, my first three fingers nestled together and pointing upward, my pinkie and thumb folded and touching each other. "Scout's honor. How could I call him if I don't even know his name?"

"But you called *someone* at the FBI lab yesterday morning."

"No, I didn't call someone at the FBI lab," I said.

Then, realizing that Brubaker now worked for an outside consulting firm, I said, "As a matter of fact, I didn't call anyone *anywhere* in the FBI." I made a mental note to phone Brubaker again and thank him for his swift, miraculous intervention. It's possible that I wasn't entirely successful at hiding my sense of relief and self-satisfaction at how I'd managed to redeem myself, because Miranda gave me a look of knowing triumph. She appeared to be formulating her next question—if Miranda had studied law rather than anthropology, she'd have made a damned good prosecutor—so I parried, hoping to derail her cross-examination.

"Hey, did you see Chip Thornton while you were there?"

Miranda flushed. "No, I did not see Chip Thornton while I was there."

Thornton was an FBI agent specializing in weapons of mass destruction. He'd been sent down from FBI headquarters several years before to work with us on a murder committed with a powerful radiation source, and at the time, I'd noticed some serious sparks crackling between him and Miranda. "Oh well," I said, all innocence. "Too bad. He's a nice guy. Maybe if you go to work for the Bureau, you'll cross paths with him."

"The FBI's a big place," she retorted. "Besides, he's in DC, not Quantico. Not that I'm keeping track of him. But yeah, maybe I will. If I'm lucky enough to get the job."

"So you're pretty serious about it? You think you'd take it, if they offered it to you?"

"Well, duh," she said. "I'd be crazy not to, don't

you think?" She studied my face. "What?" She sighed. "I hoped you'd be excited for me."

"I am," I insisted. "It's a great opportunity. It's just . . . well, you know, we've talked about your staying on here—running the bone lab, running the body donation program. You know, as a real job, a faculty job, not an assistantship."

"Isn't that a bit like the plantation owner offering to pay his house slave actual wages, after she's been freed by the Emancipation Proclamation?" She smiled to pass it off as a joke, but her words had an edge, and I felt myself flinch as they cut into me. "I'm sorry, Dr. B. I didn't mean that. I've loved my time here—my course work, my assistantship, the forensic cases. I can't imagine a better way to learn forensic anthropology. But don't you see? If I stay here, I'll always be your assistant. And that's been great, but it's time for me to leave the nest. To be a grown-up. To be the professor or the professional that you've trained me to be." Her eyes seemed to be pleading now, and I thought I saw moisture welling up in her lower eyelids. "Besides, you can't offer me a tenure-track faculty job. UT won't allow it."

"That's true," I admitted. To make sure that the university didn't become too inbred, UT policy required that our doctoral graduates hold faculty positions at other schools for at least five years before we could hire them.

"If you create a job for me," she persisted, "I can never get tenure here—which means I can never get tenure anywhere. I'd always, only, be the hired help."

"That's not necessarily true," I protested. But it

was a weak protest, and we both knew it. Academics are notoriously snobby. If you start out in the ivory tower's minor leagues—the leagues that don't dangle the possibility of tenure after seven grueling years of teaching, research, and service—your chances of ever playing in the tenured league are slim. Skeletally slim, in fact. "I know, it's a gamble. But if anybody can do it—if anybody can make the jump from nontenured to tenured—it's you, Miranda."

"I appreciate your faith in me, boss," she said. "But it's not the way things work."

"Just don't rule out staying here," I said. "Not yet."

Our discussion was interrupted by a knock. A nanosecond after the knock, Peggy appeared in the open door looking astonished and amused.

"Excuse me, Dr. Brockton," she said, "but there's a sheriff's deputy from Cooke County here to see you. A *very large* deputy."

I grinned. "Waylon," I called through the doorway. "This is a nice surprise. Come on in."

He loomed into view, his immense bulk dwarfing Peggy. She backed out of the doorway to let him enter, but the space between her desk and the front wall wasn't designed to allow two people to pass—not, at least, if one of them was Waylon. Miranda and I watched as Peggy flattened herself against the wall and Waylon squeezed past, mumbling a red-faced "'scuse me, sorry ma'am," as his broad back rubbed across her chest, her eyes widening in . . . discomfort? dismay? delight? I shot a quick glance at Miranda, who met my gaze. Then, in unspoken agreement, we quickly looked away from each other, lest we both burst into guffaws.

I reached out and gave him a handshake. "Waylon, what brings you all the way to UT?"

"Wellsir, you asked me about going back up yonder to the scene with a metal detector," he said, "so I did. Got lucky, too." He began fishing a pair of large fingers into his shirt pocket.

I felt a rush of excitement. "A bullet? Did you find a bullet?" But even as I said it, I doubted it. I had taken the bones to the hospital's radiology department for x-rays the prior afternoon, after I finished cleaning them, and the films hadn't shown any traces of lead.

"Nah, it ain't no bullet," Waylon said. "But it's kindly interestin' all the same." He held out his hand to reveal a clear plastic sleeve that contained a silver coin, its rim ridged all the way around. In Waylon's palm, it appeared tiny—a dime, I thought at first, but then I realized it was much larger. "It's a ol' half-dollar," he said. "Almost a hunnerd years old." He handed it to me.

"I'll be," I said, examining the back. Indeed, it looked antique. Instead of the Great Seal—the stylized eagle clutching arrows in one set of talons and an olive branch in the other—this one was embossed with an eagle that looked like an Audubon engraving, wild and predatory, its wings half spread and its gaze fierce. The detail remained sharp, and the coin was virtually free of tarnish.

Miranda leaned in to look. "It's in really good shape, to've been layin' out there for all these years," she said.

Waylon looked puzzled. "Come again?"

"I said it looks great, considering how long it's been out there. Didn't you say the town shut down in the 1930s, when the government bought up all the land?"

"Yes'm, I did say that—'cause it's true—but I don't b'lieve this has been a-layin' out there all this time. Not on account of what it is. Take a closer look."

Miranda plucked the coin from my palm and held it up, angling it to catch the light. "Memorial to the Courage of the Soldier of the South," she read. She looked at Waylon. "Huh?" She flipped it over to look at the front. "And who are these guys on horseback?"

"Them's Robert E. Lee and Stonewall Jackson," he said. "The most famous generals of the Army of the Confederacy. You see that inscription right there above the year, 1925?"

She squinted. "Stone Mountain. What's that about?"

"This here's a special coin that was sold to raise money for that big monument carved in the side of Stone Mountain. Right outside Atlanta."

"Oh, right," she said. "I've actually seen it from an airplane. Huge. It's like the Mount Rushmore of the Confederacy, right?"

"Yes'm. I reckon so."

"But I thought there were *three* guys carved in that mountainside?"

"That's right." He nodded approvingly. "Somebody kicked up a fuss, so Jeff Davis, the president of the Confederacy, ended up getting hisself a piece of the rock, too."

My mind was still processing Waylon's suggestion—his guess that the coin wasn't a relic from the heyday of Wasp, the mountain hamlet that had been abandoned in the 1930s. If the coin was a collector's item, it seemed unlikely that it had belonged to the victim, since he'd been chained to the tree naked—stripped of even his clothes, much less something of value. Could it have belonged to the killer? I took it back from Miranda and studied it closely. It was in near-mint condition, that was true, so clearly it couldn't have been weathering for the past eighty years. As I shifted my grip to the coin's rim, I felt an odd sharpness, like a splinter or sliver, projecting beyond the regular ridges. Looking closer, I saw what appeared to be a bit of silver solder there, with a sharp line suggesting that a piece of it had broken off. "Hmm," I said. "Waylon, did you notice this piece of solder?"

"I sure did, Doc. That's partly what makes me think it's part of the crime scene. I'm guessing somebody used to wear that around his neck on a chain."

I nodded. "Maybe the victim pulled it off in a struggle."

"That's the way I figure it, too," he agreed.

I glanced at Miranda, whose eyes were darting to and fro, a sign that she was thinking hard. Suddenly her gaze snapped back to me. "Jesus," she said. "It's a hate crime. Has to be. Some redneck racist chained a black kid out there to die. God, I *hate* haters!"

"Hang on," I said. "We don't know the victim was black."

"But we don't know that he *wasn't*, either," she pointed out. "And aren't you always quoting Occam's razor? 'The simplest explanation that fits the facts is almost always right'?"

"I might have said that a time or two," I conceded.

"Or two hundred," she retorted.

"But we don't *have* the facts," I said. "Not enough. Not yet."

Waylon cleared his throat. "How y'all figure on tellin' was he black or white?"

"Well, it's harder without the skull," I said. "If the distal ends of the femurs weren't chewed off, we could tell by looking at the angle of Blumensaat's line."

"'Scuse me, Doc. You done lost me there."

"Blumensaat's line," I repeated. "It's a seam, basically, in the bottom of the thigh bone. Where the shaft of the bone joins the condyles, the knuckles of the knee." I touched my outer thigh, just above my knee, and traced a line angling down and backward. "Nobody knows why, but the angle of that seam—named after the doctor who first studied it—is different in blacks and whites. One of my graduate students was the first to notice and measure that difference. If we had an intact femur—or the skull—we'd have a lot more to go on."

"Still," said Miranda, "you're willing to consider the possibility that it's a racial hate crime. Right?"

"At this point," I said, sighing, "I'm willing to consider *any* possibility."

"Good," she said as she flashed a smile. Was it just my nervous imagination, or was it another look of triumph?

Waylon told us good-bye and began maneuvering his bulk toward the doorway, but then he stopped and turned back toward us. "Oh, hell, I 'bout forgot. I found something else you might want." He reached down and fished around in the thigh pocket of his cargo pants, then hauled out a large, lumpy plastic bag and laid it on my desk.

"What is it?" I asked.

"That there's some bear scat," he said. "While I was up there, I figured I might nose around a bit, see if maybe I could find the young feller's skull. Didn't have no luck finding that, but I did find some scat, with a few buttons and some pieces of bone in it."

"Great—can't wait to sink my teeth into *that*," I said, and Waylon and Miranda both laughed.

"Where did you find it?" asked Miranda.

"Three, four hunnerd yards from the tree where the boy was chained. Mr. Bear had him a den near there. He weren't none too happy to see me, I can tell you that."

"He was *there*?" Miranda said. "You *saw* him?"

"I saw him, all right. Up close and personal. He come at me just like that grizzly in that movie." Miranda shot me a meaningful, I-told-you-so glance at the reference to the film she'd been nagging me to watch. "I made out a might better than the feller in the movie, though."

"How'd you get away?" she asked.

"Get away?" The big man looked puzzled. "Well, I got away, if you want to call it that, by shootin' him. He was a big boy. Three hunnerd pounds. Like to've not dropped, but he finally did. 'Bout ten foot away from me."

"You shot the bear?" Waylon nodded, grinning.

"You *killed* the bear?" Miranda seemed to have trouble taking it in. "But . . . aren't bears endangered?"

"They are when they're chargin' at *me*," said Waylon, "that's for dang sure." He chuckled at his joke, and I smiled, but Miranda turned crimson.

"*Dammit*, Waylon," she said, her voice sounding thick and constricted. I reached out and touched her arm, hoping to calm her, but she batted my hand away. "*Shit*." Head down, she stormed out of my office, leaving in her wake a baffled deputy, an embarrassed boss, and a lumpy bag of bear excrement.

CHAPTER 8

THE BUILDING LOOMED ABOVE us like some sort of postmodern fortress: six stories of stainless steel, glass, stone, and reinforced concrete, rearing skyward from a sloping masonry base that appeared designed to deflect cannonballs or repel armored tanks. "Remind me," I said to Miranda, "why we're here?"

"Gladly." Indeed, she did look glad, not so much about the reminding as about the being here in southern Alabama. "Our Cooke County murder is a hate crime. Nobody knows more about hate crimes than the Southern Poverty Law Center."

"It *might* be a hate crime," I corrected. "But even if it is, why'd we have to drive all the way to Montgomery?"

"Duh. Because this is where the SPLC *is*." She indicated the building with a hand flourish worthy of Vanna White on *Wheel of Fortune*.

"You couldn't just set up a conference call with these folks? We couldn't just swap e-mails with them?"

She shook her head. "Not as good," she said. "Besides, you know you love a road trip. And . . . you've got no life, and it's fall break, so we're not missing anything on campus. Furthermore, there's nothing else we can do on the case until we get more leads from the sheriff's office or the TBI." She repeated the hand flourish. "Or the SPLC."

I drew a deep breath, with which I intended to deliver a devastating response, but then I realized that she was right. On all counts. "You might have a point or two," I conceded. "But what good does it do us to be in Montgomery if we can't get into the building? Where's the damn door?" We'd seen what appeared to be a sally port in the basement—a heavy, slanting steel door set deeply into the massive masonry base—but it had offered nothing that bore any resemblance to a pedestrian entrance, let alone a doorbell or welcome mat.

"Beats me." She shrugged. "Maybe they beam us up, *Star Trek* style."

As we stood, staring ineptly at the building, an armed guard—a heavyset man with thin gray hair and red cheeks—appeared, seemingly from nowhere. Perhaps the SPLC *did* possess the secret of transporter-beam technology. "Can I help you?" From his tone, I suspected that what he really meant was, *Don't y'all have someplace else you need to be?*

"We have a meeting here," I told him. "With Laurie Wood, of the Intelligence Project. But we're not quite sure how to get inside." I smiled, hoping to soften him up. "If finding the door is an intelligence test, I reckon we've flunked."

The guard's face softened; maybe he even smiled

a bit. "Right this way," he said, leading us up a narrow shelf of a walkway that angled up the building's antitank base. He swiped a key card across a magnetic reader, and a pair of glass doors, thick as bank teller's glass, whisked open. We stepped into a small, sparely furnished lobby, where another guard, a young African American woman, sat sentinel behind a counter, one end flanked by a metal detector. The older guard whisked out through the glass doors, having handed us off. "We're here to see Laurie Wood," I told our new guard. "She's expecting us."

It almost seemed as if, rather than being expected, we were *suspected*: We went through an exhaustive screening process, including a TSA-worthy metal detector, which seemed particularly dubious about me. "Third time's the charm," I muttered after I finally passed metal-detector muster.

Miranda, profiting by my example, had divested herself of her keys, two bracelets, and a wide leather belt, which sported a solid oval buckle. The buckle was made of antique silver, ornately carved and set with a cameo at the center: an elegant carving of a Victorian woman. Looking closer, I was startled to see that the "woman" in the cameo was actually a skeleton; beneath an elaborate coiffure of swirling, piled-up hair was a profile of a woman's skull and cervical spine, as well as the first three ribs. I made a mental note to ask later about the unusual fashion accessory.

Miranda made it through the metal detector on her first try, and Laurie was finally called to fetch us. As Miranda threaded her belt back on, I couldn't help noticing the contrast between her outfit and mine: Miranda was wearing jeans and a sweater, while I was in a coat and tie—fancier clothes than I normally wore on campus, but this wasn't campus. This was a nationally renowned legal organization, and in my experience, there was no such thing as being overdressed for a law office.

But when our SPLC host showed up, I suddenly felt overdressed and nerdy. Laurie Wood looked as if she might have just come from an art show, or a pottery studio. A fortysomething brunette, shorter than either Miranda or me, she wore jeans and a sweater—had the two of them conferred and co-ordinated their wardrobes?—and a large, chunky necklace of silver medallions connected by a leather cord. Her shoulder-length brown hair swayed with her relaxed, rolling gait, and her eyes had a look that struck me as curious, good-humored, and ironic. There seemed to be some sadness in it, too. My im-mediate impression was of a woman who'd seen a lot of life, and who'd learned not to take herself too seriously. "Hi, I'm Laurie," she said, offering us a warm smile, a frank gaze, and a solid, welcoming handshake.

She badged us through another security door and onto an elevator, which took us up several floors. We emerged into a large, open area, completely without walls. Everyone worked in cubicles with shoulder-high dividers, and above them, I could see across the entire floor and out two walls of thick glass that overlooked downtown Montgom-ery. The state's domed capitol was visible out the east wall; taller, newer buildings—banks and office buildings—toward the north, and, in the distance, an old railroad station perched on the bank of the Alabama River.

"Quite a view you've got here," I said admiringly. "But I'm surprised at all the glass up here. Down below, it looks designed to repel a siege."

Laurie smiled. "We've got good reason to be formidable at street level. We got firebombed back in 1983 by some of our friends in the KKK."

"Is that when y'all were suing the Klan?" asked Miranda.

Laurie nodded. "We'd won a lawsuit against a Texas Klan group a couple years before that," she said. "We'd also gotten death sentences for eleven black inmates overturned. So the Klan was pretty unhappy with us. The fire burned down our building and destroyed a lot of records. We still get targeted with death threats and bomb plots pretty regularly."

I wasn't surprised to hear this. I had friends, including more than a few law enforcement friends, who viewed the SPLC as a bunch of liberal, left-wing troublemakers, but on the six-hour drive from Knoxville, Miranda had made a convincing case for the group's importance in tracking violent extremists.

Laurie led us around a corner to the south side of the building—the side with solid walls—and ushered us into a conference room, outfitted with a large, oval table. She gestured at the high-backed leather chairs. "Please."

Laurie sat at the head of the table; Miranda sat on her right, and I sat across from Miranda, on Laurie's left. I'd brought a large manila envelope with me, and I laid it on the table in front of her. She looked at the envelope, then raised an eyebrow at me, clearly interested in whatever was in the envelope. "Miranda told me you're working on a murder case that looks like a hate crime."

I waggled my hand in a maybe, maybe-not gesture. "I'm not saying it isn't, but there's not enough evidence yet to say that it is. That's why we're here—to see if it fits the pattern."

She looked again at the envelope. "And you've got material on the case in there?"

I nodded. "Death-scene photos, mostly," I said. "I should warn you, the pictures aren't gory, but they're disturbing."

If possible, she looked even more interested than before. "Dr. Brockton, I was a crime reporter before I took this job. I saw gory and disturbing things when I was a journalist, and I've seen plenty more in this job. After twenty years of tracking violent hate groups, I don't shock easy."

"Fair enough," I said. "Sounds like you'd have made a good forensic anthropologist, too." I slid the envelope toward her. "Go for it, then. I won't say anything more until you've had a look and told us what you think."

She grinned and opened the clasp, then extricated the stack of photos and began leafing through eagerly, her eyes scanning rapidly, then freezing as she squinted and stared, with laserlike intensity, at some detail or other. Occasionally she uttered a soft "hmm" to herself.

I had included a dozen or so of the best death-scene photos, as well as shots I'd taken in the lab showing the bacon wrapper and the bear-bait stick. When she'd reviewed the entire stack from top to bottom, she reversed direction and looked at the images again, working her way back to the top. "Fascinating," she said finally, still staring at the topmost image, a wide shot showing the tree, the groove etched in its bark, the chain stretching away, and the padlocked neck loop with the postcranial bones to one side. "You want to know what I think?"

"Please."

"I think whoever did this is one sick puppy."

She glanced at me, then at Miranda, then back to me. I nodded. "I'd say that's pretty accurate. But I hope you can tell us a bit more than that."

"I don't see any clothing," she said. "Was there any?"

"None," said Miranda. "As far as we can tell, he was naked."

"You say 'he.' So the victim was male?"

"Yes," Miranda and I said in unison.

"Somewhere around twenty years old," I added.

"Black? White? Other?"

"Not sure," I said.

"Black," Miranda said.

Laurie's gaze swiveled from Miranda's face to mine, then back to Miranda's. "Okay, this is getting more interesting all the time," Laurie said. "Dr. Brockton, you first. What makes you say 'not sure'?"

I pointed at the top photo. "As you can see, the skeletal remains are far from complete. Without a skull, especially, it's hard to determine the race of the victim. Which also makes it harder to determine the nature—the motivation—of the crime. Was it a hate crime, or just a revenge killing. If it *was* a hate crime, what *sort* of hate crime? Racist? Homophobic? Vegan extremism?"

She smiled at the vegan joke, and I gathered that like Miranda and me—and most police officers I knew—she'd found gallows humor to be an essential defense against the darkness in which she was immersed day in and day out. "Miranda? What's your take?"

Miranda drew in a breath, then began. "We have a piece of evidence from the death scene that—to me, anyhow—seems to strongly indicate a racial motivation." She reached down and pulled something from the back pocket of her jeans, then laid it in front of Laurie. It was a photo of the Stone Mountain half-dollar Waylon had found with his metal detector.

"Now *that's* interesting." Laurie's eyes gleamed, and a smile—a grim one, it seemed to me—tugged at the corners of her mouth. "*Very* interesting." I could practically see the gears in her mind beginning to mesh and turn. "So. For the meantime, at least, I'm inclined to vote with Miranda. This coin's ninety years old. It's a collector's item, not a random bit of pocket change." She took another, closer look, squinting at the coin's edge. "Is that a bit of solder there on the rim?" Miranda nodded. "So this was worn as a medallion. Maybe almost like a crucifix?" I glanced at Miranda, and her face looked aglow with triumph.

Laurie shifted her gaze to me. "Tell me if I'm

reading these photographs right, Dr. Brockton. It looks to me like the victim was chained to a tree and kept alive for quite a while." I nodded. "The bacon wrapper and the bacon-scented bear bait—do those mean what I think they mean? Was he eventually killed by a bear?"

"I'm afraid so," I said.

"Murder by bear. That's a new one, at least for me." Her mental gears turned for a few more seconds before she went on. "Several top-of-the-head thoughts. The Confederate coin does suggest a white-on-black hate crime. It's simple, and it fits. Ever hear of Occam's razor?"

Miranda gave a quiet snort of laughter. "*Hear* of it? He quotes it every hour on the hour. 'The simplest explanation that fits the facts is almost always right.' I'll be surprised if it's not carved on his tombstone someday."

I felt myself blushing slightly. "It's a useful principle to teach students. And homicide detectives."

"I agree," Laurie said. "But a killer who fetishizes the Confederacy might just as readily murder a Jew or a Muslim or even a white person. Or a homosexual or transgender person of any color."

"You're a couple steps ahead of me there," I said, wondering how on earth she'd gotten all the way to transgender crime.

"Sorry. Let me back up and tell you where I'm coming from there." There was a laptop computer in front of her, connected to a projector at the center of the table. She flipped open the laptop and clicked around for a while, then leaned forward and switched on the projector. An image appeared on a projection screen that hung on the wall at the far end of the table. It was a photo of a graying, bearded man in a wheelchair; he wore a dark suit and tie and an electric-blue shirt, and his right arm was raised in a Nazi salute.

"Ever heard of Glenn Miller?" she asked.

"I'm guessing you're not talking about the 1940s big-band leader," I ventured.

"Hardly. Frazier Glenn Miller is a modern neo-Nazi. In 2014, he murdered three people outside a Jewish center in Kansas. He thought he was killing Jews, but ironically, all three victims were Christians. Two Methodists and a Catholic. Wrong place, wrong time. He shot at three other people, too, but he missed. He kept shouting, 'Heil Hitler' while he was shooting. He's on death row now."

"Swell guy," Miranda said dryly. "Thank God he's a lousy shot."

"Wish he'd been lousier. That wasn't his first run-in with the law," Laurie went on. She clicked a key on the laptop, and the image changed to a young, vigorous version of Miller, in what I guessed to be his thirties. In this photo, he wore what appeared to be a military uniform: green camo fatigues, a dark green beret adorned with a cross, and a patch on his left shoulder that I recognized as the Confederate flag. "Miller was a Green Beret who did two tours of duty in Vietnam. Shortly after Vietnam, he turned radical racist. He founded a KKK chapter in North Carolina in 1980, the Carolina Knights of the Ku Klux Klan, which morphed into the White Patriot Party. He formed a paramilitary group—he *looks* like a guerrilla leader, don't you think?—and mailed out five thousand copies of what he called his Declaration of War."

"War against whom?" I asked.

"Well, let's just see," she said, and clicked another key. Lines of typewritten words filled the screen, enlarged so that the words were six inches high. "I declare war against Niggers, Jews, Queers, assorted Mongrels, White Race traitors, and despicable informants," one sentence read. The red dot of a laser pointer squiggled across the phrase "White Race traitors." Laurie explained that the phrase could mean anyone who didn't share Miller's white-supremacist views. "One of the white race traitors he mentioned by name was Morris Dees."

"Morris Dees?" said Miranda. "Your organization's president?"

Laurie nodded. "Morris was on a hit list of liberals and civil rights leaders targeted for assassination. Miller assigned points to each target. Politicians and judges were worth fifty points apiece. 'Prominent Jews' were worth twenty-five points. Blacks were worth one point."

Appalling though the scheme was, I had to admit I found it intriguing. "And how much was your boss worth?"

She smiled slightly. "Morris was the jackpot. Killing Morris was worth 888 points to Glenn Miller."

"Wowzer," said Miranda. "Playing for keeps."

"No kidding," said Laurie. "His Declaration of War went on to say, 'Let the blood of our enemies flood the streets, rivers, and fields of the nation, in Holy vengeance and justice.' Ten days after he mailed out his manifesto, he was arrested for violating parole. The U.S. marshals who caught him found a cache of dynamite, C-4 plastic explosive, twenty pipe bombs, sawed-off shotguns, pistols, machine guns, and a thousand pounds of ammunition."

Miranda gave a low whistle of amazement. "Holy hand grenades, Batman."

"Oh, right," said Laurie. "I forgot—a bunch of grenades, too." She drew a deep breath and then blew it out, as if to clear something foul from her lungs or her soul. "I had a point in bringing all this up. What were we talking about before I went off on this Glenn Miller detour?"

It took me a moment to recall. "Oh, motivation for our murder case. Race? Religion? Sexual orientation?"

"Right, right. So Miller's an interesting case. He spews all this white-supremacy venom—calls black people 'bubble-lipped, blue-gummed niggers' and suchlike—but back in the eighties, around the time he sent out his Declaration of War on blacks and homosexuals, we hear tell Miller was picked up by the cops in Raleigh, North Carolina. Rumor is, Miller was in the backseat of his car with a prostitute—a black man in women's clothing."

"Holy hypocrisy," said Miranda.

Laurie laughed. "You think? Miller claimed he lured the prostitute into the car for a beating, but that didn't appear to be what was happening on the upholstery."

"So," I mused, "he wanted a taste of forbidden fruit?"

"*Über*forbidden," said Miranda. "Like, forbidden to the second or third power—not just an African

American, but a male African American. In drag. That's some world-class sinning, by his standards." Her brow furrowed slightly. "So all this vitriol is just overcompensation for his own dark, forbidden desires?"

Laurie shrugged. "We'll never know. Hell, maybe Miller himself doesn't even know. Guys like him don't strike me as particularly self-aware, you know?"

Miranda made a face. "So Miller's on death row for shooting Christians he mistook for Jews. Any of his fine, upstanding friends look capable of this?"

Laurie frowned. "Our Intelligence Project tracks a lot of extremists. Many of them have called, at one time or another, for the slaughter of blacks and Jews. But my guess is, it's probably not a leader—not somebody with a high profile—who did this. More likely, somebody inspired by that kind of incendiary talk. Maybe somebody who wants to impress the leadership. Somebody who wants to prove himself, get into the club, score points by committing a killing. There's multiple groups and ideologies that could fit with your case. But a lot of the groups have links to, or spun off from, one particularly influential hate group."

She fiddled with the computer again, and the projector displayed a picture of a bespectacled white man in his fifties or sixties, photographed mid-sentence, his mouth slightly open, his index finger pointing to emphasize whatever he was saying. Despite what appeared to be an angry expression on his face, the man looked slightly nerdy, even to me—a grocery-store manager or McDonald's supervisor—

but behind him was a large Nazi flag. "This cheery fellow, James Wickstrom, is a leader of what's called the Christian Identity movement," Laurie said. "Christian Identity, or Identity, hard-liners despise blacks and other people of color. They consider them subhuman, and call 'em 'mud people.' But they hate Jews even worse."

"Why?" I asked.

She rolled her eyes. "You want psychology, or theology? The Identity crazies believe the Jews were created when Eve had sex with the serpent in the Garden of Eden. Wickstrom—"

"Excuse me," Miranda interrupted, "but I misheard something there. The Jews were created when Eve *what*?"

"Had sex with the serpent. In the Garden of Eden. Cain—the 'first Jew,' according to these folks—wasn't the son of Adam and Eve, according to Identity hard-liners, but the son of Eve and the snake."

"But . . ." I paused, baffled about how to even frame a question about this bizarre twist on both biology and the creation story.

"Don't try to find any logic to it," she said. "There isn't any. Aryans are God's true Chosen People, say the Identity faithful, so they keep kosher, sort of. They don't eat pork, don't eat shellfish. They observe Jewish holidays."

"So they're trying to *be* the very people they *despise*?" I persisted. "That makes no sense."

"Like I said, don't look for logic. But they think the Jews—the evil Jews, mind you, not the good Aryan true Jews—are using the blacks to destroy whites. And they think that Armageddon will be a race war, one in which all blacks and Jews will finally be exterminated. This guy here—Wickstrom—has said he'd love to see every Jew fed through a wood chipper."

"Ewww," said Miranda.

"He's got a lot of vitriolic soul mates," Laurie went on. "You know the book called *The Turner Diaries*?" I noticed Miranda nodding, but I shook my head. "It's a racist novel about right-wing militias overthrowing the U.S. government. It's become a sort of bible for the militia types. Tim McVeigh had pages from this in his car—with his favorite passages highlighted—when he blew up the federal building in Oklahoma City. Point is, that book was written by one of the founders of the Christian Identity movement."

I held out my hands, palms up. "Where in the teachings of Christ—the guy who said 'love your enemies' and 'turn the other cheek'—do these folks find a rationale for murdering innocent people?"

"I keep telling you, it's not about logic, Dr. Brockton. Christian Identity is to mainstream Christianity as ISIS is to mainstream Islam," she said. "It's a tiny splinter group that co-opts the name and twists the message. People've been killing in the name of God—one God or another—ever since the dawn of religion."

"Reminds me of that Greek philosopher from way back," I said, "who talked about how we created God in our own image. Or images. Including our angry, hate-filled image."

Laurie nodded. "Most of these haters are just

big talkers. Unfortunately, some of them do walk the walk. They call themselves 'Phineas Priests.' A couple years ago—"

"Hang on," I said. "I hate to keep sounding so ignorant, but you've lost me again."

Miranda grinned at me from across the table. "I'm so glad you talked me out of trying to do this by phone," she teased.

I gave her a halfhearted scowl, then turned back to Laurie. "*What* kind of priests?"

"Phineas Priests. Self-proclaimed priests. Followers of an Old Testament character named Phineas."

I was almost afraid to ask. "And what did Phineas do that these people find so inspiring?"

"He ran his spear through a mixed couple—a Hebrew man and a non-Hebrew woman. In the Christian Identity movement, the title 'Phineas Priest' can be claimed by anybody who kills or beats up a mixed-race couple. Or a homosexual couple. Or someone who's considered a traitor to the white race." She moused around on her laptop for a moment, then displayed a close-up image of an embroidered shoulder patch. At first glance, it looked almost like one we'd used on our Forensic Response Team jumpsuits until recently, featuring a white skull and crossbones stitched on a shield-shaped black background. Looking closer, though, I saw that this one was captioned PHINEAS PRIEST-HOOD, and what angled down beside the skull was not a bone, but a spear shaped like a lightning bolt. Underneath the skull were the words "Yahweh's Elite."

She clicked again, and the shoulder patch was replaced by a photo of a sneering young man proudly displaying a leather jacket emblazoned with the words "Phineas Priest" across the back. "This is Daniel Lewis Lee. I took this picture of Danny at a white-power rally in Pulaski, Tennessee, in 1992. Back then, we didn't know what 'Phineas Priest' meant yet, but we could tell he was mocking us with it. In 1996, Danny Lee and two buddies robbed and killed a gun dealer—a guy named Mueller, which they thought was a Jewish name—along with his wife and eight-year-old daughter. They suffocated all three by putting plastic bags over their heads." Across the table, I saw Miranda wince. "Before they killed the girl," Laurie went on, "they tortured her with electric cattle prods, asking about hiding places for guns and money. When they finally threw the bodies in a swamp, they joked that they were putting them on a liquid diet."

She showed us another person—a handsome young man with close-cropped dark hair and a well-groomed mustache. He wore an orange jumpsuit, a bulletproof vest, and waist shackles. "Another guy strongly influenced by Christian Identity. Eric Rudolph. Remember him?"

"The guy who set off a bomb in Atlanta during the Olympics?" I ventured. "Back in, what, 1996?"

"Bingo," she said. "He also bombed two abortion clinics—one in Atlanta, the other in Birmingham—and a gay bar in Atlanta. His bombs killed three people and injured more than a hundred. He said all the bombings were motivated by his opposition to abortion and homosexuality."

"I'm having trouble connecting the dots," I said.

"What does bombing abortion clinics have to do with Christian Identity and hating Jews?"

"Remember that conversation we had about logic? My guess—and it's just a guess—is that Identity hard-liners don't give a flip about black women having abortions. But white women having abortions? They're killing God's Chosen Babies. So those white patients—and the doctors and nurses in the clinics? They're not just murderers, they're 'race traitors,' too, to folks like Rudolph."

"Rudolph's the guy who hid out in the mountains of North Carolina?" said Miranda. "For a really long time, right? Like, a year or two?"

"Like, *five* years," Laurie corrected. "Despite the best efforts of the FBI and ATF and U.S. Marshals. He probably had help—maybe from other Identity members, maybe from antigovernment militia types. The Identity movement helped spawn the militia movement of the 1980s and 1990s."

"Of course," said Miranda. "Speaking of the devil's offspring."

"Any other reason you think the Christian Identity movement could be linked to our dead guy?"

"Maybe," Laurie said again. She seemed to like the word "maybe" quite a lot. "For one thing, we've found Christian Identity groups in several parts of East Tennessee. Madisonville. Sevierville. Sweetwater. James Wickstrom—'Wood-Chipper' Wickstrom— came down for several gatherings at a farm in Sevierville. She shrugged. "Sow enough seeds of hatred—at a Christian Identity meeting or a presidential campaign rally—and sooner or later, some of those seeds will sprout, and violence will follow."

Miranda frowned. "You said, 'For one thing.' I hate to ask, but it sounds like there's another thing? Another reason?"

Laurie nodded. "These hate groups are constantly morphing. Old ones weaken or shut down, new ones spring up in their place. When SPLC got started, back in the early seventies, it was all about the Klan. Then Christian Identity and neo-Nazi and neo-Confederate groups cropped up. People looking for like-minded extremists can move from group to group, as their obsessions evolve, or as the groups rise and fall. Or people can belong to multiple groups at a time. There's a particularly scary guy named Tilden Stubbs, for instance. Stubbs started out in Christian Identity, but then he got involved in the Southern Heritage Council—another group I wouldn't entirely rule out in your murder case."

"Southern Heritage? Sounds like a bunch of history buffs," I said. "Civil War reenactors and such. Isn't that pretty tame stuff?"

She made a face. "This group doesn't stop at dress-up and playing army. This is an honest-to-God neo-Confederate group, trying to whip up enthusiasm for a secession campaign—"

"Wait," I interrupted. "Secession, as in Civil War secession?"

"Exactly. And their rhetoric's getting more and more strident. Their leaders rant about blacks taking jobs from whites, about blacks raping white women right and left. I suspect Tilden Stubbs of playing a role in the more militant tone. It started getting a lot harsher after Stubbs got involved with them, and that hasn't changed, despite the fact that he's been in prison for the past five years."

"What's he in for?" Miranda asked.

"Stealing weapons and explosives from the army. He was a Green Beret at the time."

"Holy howitzers," said Miranda. "Was he in cahoots with Heil-Hitler Glenn Miller?"

Laurie shrugged. "Not directly, far as we know. Bad apples from the same hate-family tree, though. Leaders of the neo-Nazi and Christian Identity movement encourage their followers to enlist in the military—especially the special forces, so they get specialized training in explosives and covert warfare. People like Miller and Stubbs have taken that advice and run with it. Stubbs and a buddy stole machine guns, grenades, C-4, TNT, land mines, even antiaircraft guns from Fort Campbell and Fort Bragg."

"They stole them from army bases?" squawked Miranda. "Doesn't Uncle Sam guard that stuff?"

"Not closely enough," Laurie said dryly. "Like Glenn Miller, Stubbs wrote a manifesto and printed out copies for his followers. He pledged to devote his life to defending the Aryan race against blacks and Jews. And he thanked the government for training him to fight the coming race war."

Miranda rolled her eyes. "Three cheers for God and country."

"Scary thing is, people like Stubbs and Miller really are true believers," Laurie said. "Other scary thing is, there are lots more guys out there—mostly guys—stockpiling weapons and nursing grudges—

not necessarily true believers, but if things start to get bad, they'll join the fight. Maybe they're pissed off because they're in dead-end jobs, or because they got dumped. Or maybe they're just mean so-and-sos who would love to have an excuse to start shooting people. Some people are just angry to the core, you know? And just looking for a reason to act on it. It's like road rage on steroids. Cultural, socioeconomic, racial road rage, backed by automatic weapons and explosives."

Miranda cocked her head and raised her eyebrows, studying Laurie's face with almost clinical curiosity, then asked, "*How* many years have you spent immersed in this wonderful world of hate-spewing lunatics?"

"Twenty. More than. Twenty-five, almost."

"Jesus," said Miranda. "Your job makes ours seem downright cheery by comparison."

Laurie laughed. "To each his own. I love reading about what y'all do. But to see it, and smell it, up close and in the flesh? I'd be puking in the bushes."

"Well, then," I said. "It's so nice that we all have our special gifts. So bottom line: You do think we're looking at a hate crime?"

"I do," she said. "Only question is, which variety of hate? So many to choose from. It's like Baskin-Robbins and the thirty-one flavors. Except all these flavors are toxic."

I gave Miranda a questioning, can-we-go-now look. She shrugged, which I took as assent. "Laurie, you've given us a lot to think about. Obviously we need more information, but it helps to hear that we're probably barking up the right tree. Figuratively and literally." I pushed back from the table and stood up, and Miranda followed my lead. "Thanks very much."

I held out my hand, and Laurie shook it firmly, saying, "Let me know how it goes. And call me if I can help."

I nodded. "Last question," I said. "Is it as hard to get out of here as it is to get in?"

She smiled. "Depends on how you mean that. Like I said, I've been here a whole lot of years."

THREE HOURS AFTER we'd arrived and cleared the security checkpoint, Miranda and I turned in our visitor badges, reclaimed our driver's licenses, and stepped out into the Montgomery afternoon sun. My head still spun from our whirlwind climb up the family tree of hatemongers and violence.

I still didn't know who our victim was or why he'd been killed. I also didn't have any more clarity about who the killer was. But I had a far greater understanding of the vast, entwined network of racist hate groups that might have spawned or inspired that killer. If the first step toward knowledge is indeed to recognize your own ignorance—a maxim my fellow professors and I often quoted to our students—then Miranda and I had certainly taken that step, and more, in Montgomery, I reflected as I glanced up at the SPLC headquarters once more.

"Dr. B? Before we hit the road," Miranda said, "could we look around a little? There's so much history here, and I'd love to take in some of it." I opened my mouth to protest, but she cut me off. "Please? Just the highest of the high spots?" With a shrug, I caved. "Thanks," she beamed. "Here, let's walk around the corner for a second."

On the same block as the SPLC, downhill from the law center and literally in its shadow, stood a modest brick church: Dexter Avenue Baptist Church, where Reverend Martin Luther King Jr. had served as a young pastor. Miranda led me up the stairs and into the simple sanctuary, its pale plaster walls and dark wooden pews splashed with yellow, red, and green from the stained-glass windows. "Look at that," she whispered. "That's the pulpit where he preached for four years. And downstairs, in the church basement? That's where the Montgomery bus boycott was organized, after Rosa Parks was arrested for refusing to give her seat to a white man and move to the 'colored' section at the back of the bus."

Knowing how the bus boycott had spelled the end of segregation—and knowing how King's life and death had galvanized so much of the civil rights movement—I couldn't help but feel awed by the significance of the site. I was struck, too, by the contrast between King's message of nonviolence and the bloodlust of the Christian Identity movement.

"Thank you," said Miranda. "There are three more things I'd like to see, if that's okay? We can drive to all of them in, like, five minutes."

"You're the boss," I said.

We walked back up the hill to my truck, clambered in, and left the SPLC behind. A few blocks from the church, Miranda pointed to a small white house with a full-width front porch. "That's the parsonage where King and his family lived," she said. "It was bombed early in the bus boycott. He thought he should give up, but his wife—and a prayer—convinced him not to."

A few blocks from the Kings' modest home, we passed the "first White House of the Confederacy," a grand mansion that served as the home of Jefferson Davis, the president of the Lost Cause. And two blocks from that was the Alabama state capitol, which briefly served as the Confederacy's capitol . . . and which, a century later, served as the destination for the thousands of people who marched from Selma to Montgomery to demand equal voting rights for blacks and whites.

A half mile downhill from the capitol—where the train station and the riverboat landing stood side by side—we parked briefly and got out to read a historical marker describing Montgomery's thriving slave trade in the decades before the war. Hundreds of slaves had arrived in Montgomery every day, by boat and train, for sale in the city's four slave markets. A strong field hand could fetch $1,500 at auction, I read; a skilled artisan, $3,000. By the start of the Civil War, Montgomery had a larger slave population than Natchez or New Orleans, and the state as a whole contained almost half a million slaves. Many of them, in shackles and chains, had passed through the very place where Miranda and I now stood.

"Incredible," said Miranda, reading the marker. "Montgomery is so small, but it played a huge role in the history of slavery, racism, and civil rights." She looked away from the marker, surveying the train station and the landing, where an old-fashioned riverboat—white with a big red paddle wheel at the stern—bobbed gently in its moorings, as if it had somehow churned a century and a half down the river of time to get here. Miranda raised her hands to her face, and when she pulled them away, I saw moisture gleaming on her fingertips. "So," she said quietly. "That crack I made the other day? Comparing myself to a slave? I shouldn't have said that. I'm sorry. I'm ashamed to've made light of slavery."

"Miranda," I began, but she waved me off.

"It's okay, Dr. B," she said. "You don't need to make me feel better. I do have white guilt, and I *should* have white guilt. My whole life is one big exercise in white privilege."

I didn't know how to argue with her, or whether to argue with her, so I kept quiet. She turned from the river, looking up the gentle slope of downtown Montgomery: the old business district, the white marble capitol, the sleek tower of the SPLC. "Incredible," she repeated. "Montgomery is like an American Jerusalem."

"How do you mean?"

"Sacred to two warring factions. Holy ground to die-hard racists and civil rights crusaders."

I didn't always agree with Miranda's politics—she tended to be far more liberal on virtually every issue than I was—but I had profound respect for her intelligence, idealism, and compassion. Our work together had exposed her to some of the worst of human nature, yet she still believed in the basic dignity and decency of people, whatever their color, religion, national origin, sexual orientation, or immigration status. Miranda wasn't a churchgoer—

not even a believing Christian, as far as I knew—but she embodied more of the teachings of Jesus than most Bible-thumpers I'd encountered over the years: people who made a big deal of religious faith yet seemed never to have heard or heeded Christ's teachings about charity, forgiveness, and kindness toward the poor, the sick, the hungry, the homeless.

She turned to me. "Hey," she said, "speaking of people oppressed by the white man, did you ever manage to see *The Revenant*?"

I shook my head. "I checked the movie listings, but I didn't find it. I don't think it's playing anymore."

"Oh, right," she said. "It has been almost a year since it came out. Oh well—you would've hated it. All those Arikara Indians. Not to mention the bear attack. You would've been bored out of your skull."

"Hmm," I grunted.

"Hey, boss?"

"Yeah?"

"I'm sorry I freaked out about Waylon killing the bear. I guess if the bear was charging him, he didn't really have a choice."

"I guess not," I said. "Not unless he was willing to die so the bear could live. Besides, I think the government has a policy of killing bears that have killed people. They're afraid the bears'll get a taste for humans and become habitual offenders. Seems a shame, but I can see their point."

She nodded. "Hey, boss?"

"I'm still right here."

"I'm glad we came to Montgomery. But it creeps me out, too. Let's get the hell out of here."

She didn't have to tell me twice. But all the way back to Knoxville, as the sun set and the moon rose and the auto traffic gave way to heavy trucks, it felt as if we hadn't left Montgomery entirely behind; as if we'd brought some of it with us, in the form of ghostly stowaways, polluting the air with exhalations of secondhand hate.

I still didn't know what version of hate had killed our Cooke County victim. But after Laurie's introductory course—Hate Groups 101—I now agreed with Miranda. This had to be a hate crime. But what kind of hate crime? We needed help finding out.

CHAPTER 9

IT WAS WITH DECIDEDLY mixed feelings that I dialed the local FBI field office and asked for Angela Price, and I felt more than a twinge of regret when my call went through to her, rather than to voice mail. "Special Agent Price," she said, her tone brisk and businesslike, wasting neither time nor warmth. Then she simply waited, apparently not wanting to waste words, either.

"Hello. It's Dr. Bill Brockton, from UT," I said, awkwardly adding. "Good morning." I didn't call her by name, because it felt awkward to say "Special Agent Price." I knew most of the local FBI agents, and I called the others by their first names, but Price was different. Even though I'd known her for years, and had worked with her on several cases, I didn't feel entitled—or permitted—to call her Angela.

"How are you, Dr. Brockton?" Her tone warmed. By a fraction of a degree.

"I'm good. Keeping busy, which I like, except for the fact that it means people keep killing people."

"We do depend on the dark side of human nature for our livelihoods, don't we? How can I help you, Dr. Brockton?"

"I'm wondering," I began, with less confidence than I liked, "what your criteria are for opening a hate-crime investigation?"

"First off," she said dryly, "there has to be a crime." *Duh*, I thought, parroting Miranda's standard response to patently obvious statements. "Second, there needs to be reason to believe that hate or bias—against a race, religion, disability, sexual orientation, ethnicity, gender, or gender identity—was a motivation for the crime, in whole or in part."

"How much reason?"

"Excuse me?"

"You said, 'There needs to be reason to believe' that hate was a motive. I'd just like to get a clearer picture of what you mean by that."

There was a pause. "Well," she said slowly, "for example, if you were found bludgeoned to death in your office at the university, I wouldn't be inclined to think that racial, sexual, or religious bias was the motive. Unless there's a kinky side of you that seriously rubbed somebody the wrong way." I felt myself taken aback. Was this Price's odd way of having a bit of fun with me, or was there a passive-aggressive edge to her choice of example? "But if you were an African American pastor instead of a white professor, and your house was bombed, and a big cross was burned in your front yard, I'd say there was ample reason to believe we were looking at a hate crime."

"I'd say so," I agreed.

"Although we might find out that the real motive was something else entirely."

"Such as?"

"Well, suppose the pastor were having an extra-marital affair with one of his parishioners, and the woman's husband found out he'd been cuckolded by the pastor. The husband might murder the pastor—a classic revenge killing—but make it look like a hate crime, to deflect suspicion. We'd start out investigating that murder as a hate crime, but pretty soon, I hope, we'd discover the real reason for the crime. Does that make it clearer?"

"It does," I said slowly.

"You don't sound convinced."

"I'm not unconvinced. I'm just thinking about evidence that's not as obvious as a burning cross."

"Dr. Brockton, are we talking hypotheticals here, or is there something specific on your mind? Because the Bureau doesn't generally deal in hypotheticals."

Here we go, I thought. Price was forcing me to lay my cards on the table, and I knew my hand was weak. "There's a case—actual, not hypothetical—that I'm working on. A young man was chained to a tree in the woods. He was kept alive, possibly for weeks, and then finally killed by a bear. He'd been smeared with bear bait and raw bacon, so I'm thinking the killer wanted him to suffer a while first, then be attacked by the bear. By the time he was found, he was just bones. And not that many of 'em."

"This was up in Cooke County?"

I was surprised, because I'd seen no news coverage of the murder. "You already know the case?"

"No," she said. "I already know Cooke County. Where else would you find a crime like that?"

"Ah."

"So what else can you tell me about the victim? He was young and male. Black, or white?"

She was already drilling into the nerve. "To be honest, we don't know yet. Without a skull or intact long bones, it's hard to make a determination."

A pause. "So what makes you think you're looking at a hate crime?"

"For one thing, the staging, if I'm using that term right. The victim was made powerless. Naked and chained. Fed like a dog. Smeared with bear bait and bacon grease. Seems like the killer wanted to humiliate him as much as possible. Make him less than human."

"But that doesn't prove bias or hate," she said. "Just cruelty."

"There is one piece of evidence," I began. "A coin found at the scene. A collector's item. A commemorative coin from 1925."

"Commemorative of what?"

"Of the huge Confederate monument at Stone Mountain, Georgia. Giant carvings of Stonewall Jackson, Robert E. Lee, and Jefferson Davis—the heroes of the Lost Cause."

"I know who they were," she said. "And you take an old coin as evidence of a hate crime? You can't even tell me the victim's race, but—let me guess—you have a *hunch* that the victim was a black man, and that this is a weird twist on a lynching?"

"Maybe," I said, flinching at the withering sarcasm I could hear in her voice. "This Confederate coin looks like it was worn as a pendant. Which could indicate that Confederate ideology—specifically, racism—was important to the killer." I paused, but she left me hanging, so I added, "It's the only thing we've got that might indicate motive."

There was a long silence. "Dr. Brockton, if that's the only thing you've got, you don't have much. If the sheriff's office or the TBI wants to put in a formal request for the Bureau's assistance, we'll certainly consider it. But from what you've told me, this just sounds like something out of *Deliverance*. A backwoods case of southern gothic depravity."

I mumbled a perfunctory thank-you and got off the line, stinging from Price's implicit—no, her *explicit*—rebuke. I still believed the Confederate coin to be significant, but Price was correct: Until we could pin down the victim's race, we couldn't make the case for a racially motivated hate crime. I had let myself be carried away by Miranda's certainty—Miranda's lefty-liberal *hunch*—and also, perhaps, by my hope that I'd be able to persuade her not to take a job at the FBI. And my lapse in judgment had circled back to bite me.

It added insult to injury that the fresh bite marks in my backside had been inflicted by the wickedly sharp teeth of Special Agent Angela Price. It pained me particularly that the Price was Right.

I felt on safer ground and friendlier territory with my next call. As a TBI consultant, I'd always enjoyed good working relationships with TBI field agents and supervisors, and as Steve Morgan's former teacher, I believed I had far more goodwill capital banked with Steve than I did with Price. He had certainly been friendly and helpful when I'd seen him at the death scene two days before, and I felt sure he was as eager to solve this case as I was. "Steve," I said heartily when he answered, "it's Bill Brockton."

"Morning, Dr. B," he said. I took the informality as a further good omen. "What's up? You calling to say you've I.D.'d the victim and collared the bad guy?"

"I wish," I said. "Actually, I'm calling to see if you've heard anything back from your DNA folks yet. Specifically, about the victim's race?"

"No, sir," he said, and the formality made me cringe. *Not a good omen*, I thought. Then: *Is this how Miranda will talk to me, once she's gone?* "We don't have anything quite yet. I know the lab got the evidence—I delivered it myself—but that was just the other day. Friday. And today's just Monday. They don't work on weekends, so basically this is the first workday they've even *had* the evidence."

"How soon you reckon they'll get to the DNA, Steve?" I tried to sound optimistic and encouraging, not impatient and demanding. Apparently I failed, because I heard Steve sigh.

"Thing is, Doc, they're pretty backed up in the DNA lab right now."

"*How* backed up?"

"About two months backed up, to be honest."

"Two months? You're saying they might not get around to this for two months?"

"That's pretty standard," he admitted. "Eight-week backlog is what I was told on Friday."

"Christ, Steve, that's terrible. Can you ask them to fast-track this one? I can't just spin my wheels on this for eight weeks."

"It's frustrating, I know. My wheels are spinning, too. But so are everybody else's. The DNA lab gets a hundred cases a month, and they process a hundred a month. So they're staying even, but just barely. They're treading water as fast as they can. But right now, there's nearly two hundred samples in line ahead of ours. Most of 'em murders and rapes." He hesitated, but then delivered the kicker. "Can we really say that we oughta be able to cut line, jump ahead of everybody else? I know you're in a hurry, Doc. I am, too. But so are all those homicide detectives and rape victims."

"Crap, Steve," I said. "Of course I'm not saying my case is more important than some rape victim's. I know the wheels of justice are turning. I just hate it that they turn so slow."

"You and me both, Doc. You and me both."

CHAPTER 10

IN EXPLAINING MY FASCINATION with forensic cases, and especially my ability to stomach gruesome details such as dismemberment, I often told students and police this: "I don't see a murder as a death; I see it as a puzzle. If I have the skills to solve that puzzle and bring someone to justice, I've done a good job."

But this time, my puzzle analogy was no longer just an analogy; this time, it had become completely literal. Arrayed on a table in the bone lab in front of Miranda and me were dozens of bone shards, their edges jagged and splintered, along with the shafts of the Cooke County victim's badly chewed femurs. The daunting challenge—the herculean task—was to reassemble at least one of the femurs; the payoff, if I succeeded, was the answer to a crucial question in the case: Was the victim black, and killed in a racially motivated hate crime, as the Confederate coin might suggest?

But despite decades of puzzle practice, beginning with my early fieldwork reassembling shattered Arikara Indian skulls, I wondered if I was out of my league this time. It wasn't just that this was a 3-D puzzle; every skeletal reconstruction required working in 3-D, after all. But thanks to the bear's mighty, bone-crunching jaws, many of the pieces were badly damaged, which meant that their edges would no longer match up exactly. Last but not least, this puzzle contained many extraneous pieces, from other, smaller bones, adding to the mix and the muddle.

The phone rang. Miranda rolled her chair backward and snagged the handset without even looking. "Osteology lab, this is Miranda," she said, then listened a moment. From the phone's handset, I could hear a female voice, rapid and loud. Miranda listened briefly, wincing slightly at the barrage, holding the phone slightly away from her ear. "Well, this *is* the Body Farm. It's actually called the Anthropology Research Facility—" I saw the eye roll, an early warning sign. "Yes, ma'am, I *do* know that everybody calls it the Body Farm. . . . No, ma'am, we're not *trying* to confuse people. People are just so . . . easily confused. What can I do for you, ma'am? Did you have a question?" Not surprisingly, I could hear the edge creeping into Miranda's voice; in fact, I was surprised that the edge wasn't already razor sharp. "No, I'm sorry, you *can't* come take a tour of the Body Farm. . . . Well, because it's a research facility, not a tourist attraction."

Miranda's head was shaking slowly, partly in disbelief, but mainly, I suspected, the way a bull's head shakes just before he charges. "By 'tourist,' I don't mean outsider, I just mean somebody who wants to take a tour. . . . Well, I didn't mean it to be offensive, ma'am. . . . Well, yes, there *is* another reason. We wouldn't want a tourist—or a lifelong Knoxville resident like yourself—to pick up some deadly disease from one of our corpses. . . . Well, for instance, hepatitis. Or Ebola. Or Zika." Miranda's voice was no longer edgy; during the litany of life-threatening diseases, her tone had turned chirpy. "They say there's a new airborne strain of Zika that doesn't require mosquitoes. All you have to do is breathe anywhere in the vicinity of the infection. There's even some speculation that it's transmissible by *telephone*—can you believe it?" She paused, her eyes taking on a devilish gleam. "I'm sorry we can't offer you a tour, ma'am, but we *do* have a volunteer opening right now. We just lost one of our best volunteers. A most sudden and tragic illness. If you'd like to come in for an interview . . ." She pulled the handset away from her ear and looked at it. "Huh," she said, a slight smile tugging at her mouth. "We must have gotten cut off."

"You are *so bad*," I scolded. "I can't believe you scared that poor woman like that. Zika? *Ebola?* You are going to get us in huge trouble!" But try as I might, I couldn't keep from grinning. *So much for the stern administrator,* I thought.

By the third call, my own patience was wearing thin, and when the fourth call came in, I snapped. "I'll get it," I grumbled. Snatching up the receiver, I bellowed, "Yes yes *yes*?!? What do you *want*?!?"

I heard a faint gasp on the other end, followed by a long silence. Finally, a quavery old voice—the woman must have been at least a hundred—warbled,

"Oh, dear, I must have dialed the wrong number. I was trying to reach the Anthropology Department. I . . . well, I was hoping to donate my body to science. But I seem to have made a mistake. I'm so sorry to bother you."

Stricken, I hastily reviewed my options. I could, of course, confess and grovel and try to mend the fence I'd just mowed down—unburn the bridge I'd just torched—but that seemed like an iffy bet, considering my rudeness. *Brockton, you are going to hell*, I thought, then I put on my most charming voice. "Don't you worry, ma'am. I misdial all the time. I bet if you hang up and try again, you'll get ahold of them, and they'll be so glad you called." The woman hung up, and I hung up. "I'll let you answer if she calls back," I told Miranda sheepishly. "Do be nice to her."

"Those quarterly staff trainings you like to grumble about," Miranda said. "Wasn't the last one on 'Leadership by Example'?"

"I'll take the Fifth on that," I said. "And I'll take this little project of mine down to my office. My hideaway office. Clearly I'll never get a femur put back together if I stay here."

"Clearly we'll never get another body donation if you keep scaring off the donors," she cracked. "But don't you want to work on that over at the processing facility instead?"

"Why would I want to go clear across the river?"

"Well, last time I checked, that's where the exhaust hoods are. You're hoping to glue pieces together, right?"

"Yeah. So?"

"So the fumes are nasty. Not just stinky-nasty. Toxic-nasty."

I waved a hand dismissively. "You kids today. You're so . . ."

"Intelligent?" she supplied. "Maybe that's because we haven't spent years softening our brains with solvent fumes."

"I'll be fine," I said. "I'll open a window. Besides, I've got you on speed dial. If I start to pass out, I'll call you."

"You do that," she said sweetly. "I'll come running. The last thing you'll hear, as you start climbing those stairs to the bright white light, will be the sound of my voice, saying, 'I tried to tell you, but would you listen?'"

She was kidding. Surely she was kidding.

ONE HUNDRED AND ten yards away from the bone lab—right beside Neyland's north end zone—was my sanctuary: the private, off-the-beaten-track office to which I retreated whenever I needed to hole up, bear down, or zone out. It wasn't exactly a secret hideout—my colleagues and graduate students knew where it was—but it was distant and inconvenient enough from the department's main crossroads to allow me to concentrate with minimal interruptions. My not-so-secret hideout.

I had brought with me two metal trays from the bone lab, along with the two gnawed femurs from the Cooke County victim, plus a bag filled with the bone shards I'd recovered from the bear scat Waylon had brought me. Setting the trays on my desk, I switched on my desk lamp, a gooseneck lamp featuring a large magnifying glass encircled by a doughnut-shaped fluorescent bulb. The lens magnified objects by a factor of three; if I didn't need the magnification, I could angle the light from one side, but if I wanted to see fine details—and fat fingers, kielbasa-sized beneath the lens—I could swing the lamp directly into my line of vision and peer through the glass.

I kept a small bottle of adhesive in the office, in a nozzle-tipped plastic bottle I'd gotten from a pastry chef. The chef had used it to create delicate designs with icing—swirls and inscriptions on birthday cakes and wedding cakes—but I had repurposed it to apply precise lines of a high-tech bone glue. Called Paraloid B-72, the glue was made by dissolving pellets of clear acrylic in acetone. Besides being clear, strong, and fast-setting, Paraloid had the advantage of being easy to *un*glue: all it took to break the bond was a quick brushing with acetone, and the hard plastic would soften and let go, as easily as clear nail polish dissolved with polish remover—the chemical country cousins, I supposed, of my scientific-sounding adhesive.

I had already simmered the fragments overnight to clean and deodorize them. Now, as a first step toward simplifying the two-part, 3-D puzzle of the femurs, I began by removing fragments that were clearly not femoral in origin. The easiest to exclude were the tips of fingers and toes: tiny bones that were entirely or largely intact, and therefore easily recognizable. Luckily, of the double handful of bones and fragments I'd sifted from the scat, almost half fit into this category. Once I had set those aside, my job was 50 percent simpler.

Except, of course, that it wasn't: The remaining material fragments were ten times harder to identify. It had taken only a matter of minutes to eliminate the finger and toe bones—about the same amount of time it took the bear to eliminate them, I realized—but it took the rest of the morning to sort the splintered fragments into *yes*, *no*, and *maybe* piles. The *yes* fragments tended to include the broad, convex surfaces of the condyles, the knee's knobby "knuckles." The *no* bits tended to include enough dense surface material, or cortical bone, to allow me to tell that they came from smaller bones, such as ribs or arms. The *maybes*—the pain-in-the-ass maybes—consisted largely of chunks of spongy bone—cancellous bone—from the interior of bone shafts and vertebrae. Randomly shaped, with a texture and a heft similar to volcanic pumice, these pieces struck me as capable of coming from virtually anywhere in the skeleton.

I took a break to wolf down a boring turkey sandwich I'd brought from home, washing it down with a Diet Coke from the apartment-sized fridge that Peggy restocked once a week. Then, after a pit stop and a few stretches to work the kinks out of my back and shoulders, I hunkered down and began piecing fragments together, rotating bits this way and that, seeking surfaces that would mate, and then applying a thin coating of Paraloid and holding the pieces together until the acetone evaporated and the glue set.

Luckily, a few of the pieces were fairly large, as big as the end of my thumb, and I felt a surge of optimism when I managed to cobble together most of a medial condyle and affix it to the right femur. But that was the easy part, and from there, the going got tougher and more tedious, the pieces smaller, the joints more jagged, the seams sloppier. The ragged appearance of the bone made me think of Dr. Frankenstein's monster, crudely assembled from ill-fitting parts. Reinforcing that impression was the orthopedic repair work: the compression plate—a long metal bracket—fastened to the side of the shaft by nine stainless-steel screws.

My head was pounding, possibly from neck tension and eyestrain, but also perhaps from acetone fumes. Somewhere in the back of my muddled brain, I heard an imagined Miranda saying, *I told you to work under an exhaust hood. But would you listen? Oh, no.*

I looked up, closing my eyes to rest them briefly, but even then, I couldn't escape my project: the bright light and jagged shapes left a vivid afterimage, like an x-ray or photo negative, of magnified fingers and bone fragments pulsing on my retinas. When I opened my eyes, I was surprised to see my own reflection in the grimy glass of my office window, my face looking haggard. Outside, night had fallen, transforming the window into a mirror. I had spent the past eight hours—no, nine—piecing together the femur puzzle. A line from a children's book popped into my head, from Dr. Seuss's *How the Grinch Stole Christmas*, which I'd read and watched dozens of times, first with my son, Jeff, and, years later, with Jeff's sons, Tyler and Walker: "He puzzled and puzzled, 'till his puzzler was sore."

I wasn't done yet. Still, gradually, imperfectly, the bone knitted back together, almost as if it were healing from yet another comminuted fracture—the sort that might result from falling two stories and hitting the sidewalk in a kneeling position. If I swung the magnifier to the side, held the bone at arm's length, and squinted slightly, it wasn't so bad. I'd seen far worse repair jobs done by the body's own healing processes. In fact, I realized, if this bone were inside a living leg, instead of lying on a metal tray, it would remodel and smooth out quite nicely over the course of a year or two.

Building on my initial success, I had focused entirely on the right femur, and now, although a few gaps remained in the surface of the condyles, the overall shape of the bone was restored—certainly enough for my purposes. Gently, in case the glue wasn't fully cured, I laid the femur on the desktop, positioning it so that the anterior surface of the bone—the front of the thigh—faced the ceiling and the pair of condyles was solidly planted on the desk. Then I studied the bone, scrutinized the bone, stared at it; finally I slid my hand beneath its shaft.

"I'll be damned," I murmured.

I called Richard, our resident expert—hell, the world's resident expert—on ForDisc. "So," I said, "I need a second opinion, and I'm wondering if there's any way ForDisc can give it to me. Seems a long shot, but I'm desperately trying to determine if my Cooke County John Doe is black or white." I described my painstaking reconstruction of the femur, and what I inferred from it.

"I wouldn't put much faith in a reconstruction," he said. "Let's see if ForDisc can help out. Have you got a tibia?"

"Only one," I said glumly. "And only part of it. I'm telling you, that was one hungry bear."

"Which part do you have?"

I picked up the ravaged tibia and surveyed it. "I've got ten or twelve inches of the shaft. He chewed off both ends."

"We might be in luck," Richard said. "Does your piece of shaft include the nutrient foramen?"

"Let me see," I said, rotating the bone to study the back side. Just below the ragged edge of what had once been the proximal end—the "knee" end— was a small hole angling down into the bone: an opening through which a small artery had once carried nutrients to the bone's interior. "Yes, it does. I'm looking right at it."

"Excellent. You got a caliper handy?"

"Sure. Somewhere. Hang on." I opened my desk drawer and rummaged around until I found one.

The other end of the line was silent for a moment. "Okay, I've got ForDisc booted up," Richard said.

"I didn't hear any computer keys clattering."

"It opens with a mouse click," he reminded me. "We made it easy to use."

"Right. Good work."

I heard what might have been a slightly exasperated sigh from Richard. "Measure the transverse diameter of the shaft," he said. "Right at the nutrient foramen."

"Measuring," I said. "Okay, it measures a little less than an inch. What does that tell you?"

"It tells me you need to switch to the metric system, Bill. What's the diameter in millimeters?"

"Ah." I squinted at the gauge. "Twenty-three . . . point . . . *one*."

"ForDisc doesn't take decimals," he said.

"What? How can it be accurate if it's not precise?"

This time his sigh sounded more than slightly exasperated. "You're saying your caliper reading—on a chewed-up bone—is accurate to within a tenth of a millimeter? One two-hundred-fiftieth of an inch? Besides, weren't you the one who started out by saying it was 'a little less than an inch'?"

"Okay, okay," I grumbled. "Call it twenty-three millimeters."

"And that's the transverse diameter—side to side, not front to back?"

"Yes, transverse. You asked for transverse, so I gave you transverse. I'd've given you front to back if you'd *asked* for front to back."

"No need to get snippy," Richard said. "Just making sure. You know what they say—garbage in, garbage out."

"Richard, you're killing me. Come on, what's it say?"

"Let's see." I heard a couple of clicks. "For black males in the forensic data bank, the average transverse tibial diameter, at the nutrient foramen, is twenty-seven millimeters. Average for whites is twenty-five. So statistically, ForDisc says there's a 70 percent chance your victim is white."

"Seventy? That's a pretty high percentage."

"Doesn't mean he *is* white," Richard hastened to hedge. "That's an estimate, based on averages. From one bone, which is not exactly a robust data set."

"I know, I know."

"But it does gives you some reason to question whether he's black."

"It does," I agreed. "But why in the world would a Confederate hillbilly chain a white boy in the woods to die?"

"Ah, I'm afraid ForDisc can't help you with that," he said. "That's a little beyond the capabilities of the software."

"Well, see if you can work that feature into the next upgrade," I suggested, and he chuckled. I thanked him and hung up, surprised to find that I was . . . *surprised*. Both the reconstructed femur and the tibial measurement suggested, though they certainly didn't prove, that the victim was white, not black. Individually, each was a fairly subtle, uncertain indication, but together, they seemed to carry more weight.

But what did it mean? If it wasn't a racially motivated hate crime, what was it—a simple revenge killing, as Brubaker, the retired FBI profiler, had suggested? I thought about calling him back but decided that without additional information to go on, he wasn't likely to have additional insights.

On an impulse, I rooted around in my wallet and fished out the card Laurie Wood had handed me in Montgomery, at the end of our meeting at the Southern Poverty Law Center. After we exchanged a few opening pleasantries, I cut to the chase. "This case has more twists than a kudzu vine," I told her. "Here's the latest. The victim of our Confederate hate killer—if that's what he was—was white, not black."

"Hmm," she said. "That is a twist, but it could still be a white-supremacist thing."

"How, exactly?"

"If the victim did something that made the killer consider him a 'race traitor'—someone who seriously betrayed the white race."

"For instance?"

"For instance, dating a black woman. Fathering a child by a black woman. Arresting a white man for beating up a black man. Coming to the aid of a black man who's being harassed or abused by a white man. There was a case in Mississippi in 2014, a nineteen-year-old white girl who was dating a black man. She burned to death—a car fire—and there was much rejoicing on Stormfront, a neo-Nazi website, by people who thought she got what she deserved. 'Race traitor' is in the eye of the beholder, and if your killer's looking hard for somebody to call a race traitor, it won't be hard to find." She paused, then added, "You ever had a case where your work ended up helping convict a white man for a black man's murder?"

"Well, yes—a couple of them, actually."

"There you go. You, too, might qualify as a race traitor, Dr. Brockton. Better watch your back." I sensed that she was joking. Or hoped so, at any rate.

"Takes one to know one," I countered, and she chuckled. *Whistling past the graveyard*, I thought.

Both of us. I also thought, *Takes a graveyard whistler to know a graveyard whistler.*

After I finished talking with Laurie, I dialed Sheriff O'Conner. He answered after the first ring. "Sheriff, it's Bill Brockton," I said. "I've got some interesting news. Two ways of skinning the same cat. First, I reconstructed a femur from our victim, using the pieces I fished out of the scat Waylon brought me."

"And you were able to put it back together? I'm impressed. I figured he was like Humpty Dumpty and couldn't be fixed."

"It's not perfect, but it's good enough to shed some light. The femur's shape differs slightly from one race to another. In Native Americans and Asians, the front of the bone tends to be curved. Also in whites, though not as much. But in blacks, it's almost straight. From that Confederate coin, I would've bet that this one would be straight. But I think I just lost that bet."

"So you're saying our victim wasn't black?"

"I can't be sure—there's plenty of room for individual skeletal variations, and this is just a reconstruction, so I wouldn't put a huge amount of faith in its accuracy. But there's a second thing. A measurement from another bone—a shinbone—also seems to tip the scales toward white. So just guessing, which is all I can do at this point, I'd guess we're not looking at a white-on-black hate crime."

O'Conner was silent a long while. Finally I heard him take a deep breath, then blow it out. "Well, looks like we're back to square one," he said. "I'll tell

Morgan and Waylon. And we'll go back to beating the bushes on the white side of the tracks."

"A whole lot more foliage on that side," I said. "Up in Cooke County, anyhow."

"Yeah," he said with a sigh. "Tell me about it, Doc."

I hung up, more frustrated than I could remember feeling in a long time. It was maddening, not knowing something as simple as the race of our victim—and not being likely to know for nearly eight weeks. In my mind's eye, I saw the bone sample I had sent to the TBI crime lab sitting, overlooked and forgotten and gathering dust, while other samples, and other cases, raced ahead.

Patience, Brockton, I counseled myself. *Eight weeks isn't that long. It'll go by in the blink of an eye.*

Bullshit, retorted a far less serene, far more honest version of myself.

CHAPTER 11

"DELIA ANSELMETTI," ANSWERED A warm voice.

"Good morning," I said. "It's Dr. Brockton. How's my newest assistant professor?"

"I'm good. Mostly settled in, except for some of the lab equipment, and enjoying my students."

"I'm glad to hear that. Are you in your dingy old office, or your shiny new lab?"

"I'm in the office. If you shout, I can probably hear you even without the phone."

That was true; Delia's office was only a half-dozen doors down from my administrative office, where I'd started my day. "I'd hate to shout at you, since I'm asking for a favor. Can I pop in and see you for a minute?"

"Sure. I have to teach a class in ten minutes, but come on down. Even if we don't get to finish, we can at least get started."

"I'm on my way." I hung up the phone, made a quick exit from my office, and took a right turn down the corridor.

Sometimes Stadium Hall reminded me of the interior of a space station, its curving hallway—bent by the arc of Neyland Stadium's grandstands, beneath which a wedge-shaped building had been shoehorned—calling to mind the gigantic space wheels spinning through the fantasies of sci-fi films and early NASA visionaries.

At other times, though, the building's lopsided configuration, with rooms lining only one side of the corridor, called to mind the image of a giant brain that was lacking one of its hemispheres. Since I was walking counterclockwise from my office—from south to north, along the stadium's southeastern rim—it appeared to be the brain's left hemisphere that had been removed, leaving behind only a solid wall of reinforced concrete, whose vast beige expanse was enlivened only by a few outdated bulletin boards and large, fading academic posters, dense with text, graphs, and tables.

On my way to Delia's, I passed three of these posters, which had been presented at academic conferences by job-seeking graduate students in recent years. "Morphological Variations in the Acromium Process" was the first thrilling title. "Weight Gain in Third-Instar Maggots at the Anthropology Research Facility," offered the second poster. *Or, Eating More and Enjoying It Less*, I mentally subtitled that one. "Synthetic Training Aids for Cadaver Dogs," read the third one. "What Is the Optimal Ratio of Cadaverine and Putrescine?" *Doggone if I know*, I silently responded.

Just beyond the third poster was Delia's office,

the door ajar. I knocked, heard "Come in," and did as I was told.

Delia Anselmetti had the olive complexion, dark hair, and dark eyes that her Italian name seemed to call for. Even her office seemed Mediterranean: unlike most of the drab, beige walls in Stadium Hall, Delia's were a warm reddish orange, as if by stepping through her doorway, I had suddenly been transported to a room in Venice or Florence. Delia's education and expertise were exotic, too, at least to me. A molecular anthropologist, she had focused on biochemistry, genetics, microbiology, statistics, and computer modeling—courses that only slightly overlapped my own background and interests in archaeology, anatomy, osteology, skeletal trauma, and forensics. Scarcely older than Miranda, and only just embarking on her career, Delia represented a new generation of anthropologists, a generation I admired for their scientific savvy, even as I struggled to keep up with their conversations and publications.

"Your office looks great," I said. "I didn't realize the Physical Plant folks offered any colors but hospital beige and UT Orange."

She flushed slightly. "Actually, I painted it myself—my husband and I—the weekend I moved into the office. Seemed crazy to move everything in, then have to move everything out again so they could paint it later. And duller."

"I approve," I said. "You want something done right—or done fast—you sometimes have to do it yourself." I got straight to the point, not wanting to

make her late for class. "Except when you *can't* do
it yourself. Which is why I'm hoping you can help
me. I'm wondering if you could run a DNA analysis
for me."

She frowned. "I'd be glad to, but the forensic
DNA lab isn't finished yet. They're still installing
the air-handling equipment. It's almost like we're
building a clean room for NASA. The standards for
forensic work—"

I held up a hand to interrupt her. "I'm not after
something that would be admissible in court," I
explained. "Here's my problem. I've got a murder
victim that I can't identify. I can't even tell what race
he was."

If possible, she looked even more uncomfortable.
"When you say race, do you mean geographic and
genetic ancestry, or cultural identity?"

Oh, crap, I thought, *here we go again*, remembering
Miranda's discomfort with my mention of "race" at
the death scene. The three-race model still struck
me as simple and useful—useful to me, and useful
to law enforcement. In recent years, however, "race"
had come to be hotly debated among anthropologists, and in some circles, simply saying the word
was like waving a red flag, an invitation to a shouting match or a shaming.

"Let me ask another way," I said. "I can't identify
this young man—I know his sex and his approxi-
mate age, but nothing else. I've got no skull; I don't
even have an intact femur. When I log onto the Department of Justice website and search the Missing
Persons database, DOJ tells me that *thirteen hundred* young men between the ages of eighteen and

twenty-five are missing. Two-thirds of those are described by DOJ as 'white,' one-sixth are listed as 'black' or 'African American,' a few dozen as Asian, another few dozen as Native American, and a couple hundred as 'other' or 'unsure.' My initial guess had been that my victim would be categorized as black, because the murder shows some signs of being a hate crime."

"What makes you think that?"

"We found a Confederate coin at the scene. We suspect it belonged to the killer, so we're thinking—or we *were* thinking, until just now—that he might belong to the Klan or some other white-supremacist hate group. Now, though, I'm not at all sure that the victim is African American. So it would help us a lot—me, the TBI, and the poor little Cooke County Sheriff's Office—if we didn't have to chase down all thirteen hundred of those missing-person leads." She nodded slowly. "So could you run a quick DNA test, Delia? Maybe narrow it down to one of those missing-person categories—white, black, Asian, whatever way you can match the genetics with the law enforcement descriptions? Again, it's not for court. Just to help focus the investigation."

"If that's all you need, I probably can. If the DNA's not too degraded. Can you spare a tooth? That would give me the best shot at an intact, un-contaminated sample."

I shook my head. "No skull, remember? And no scattered teeth. But I could cut a cross section from a long-bone shaft—a femur, or a humerus. That's next best, right?"

"Actually, no." She hesitated, as if she felt awkward about correcting me. "If you've got a tarsal or metatarsal or phalange—any little bone from the hands or feet—that's probably a better source." Seeing my surprise, she shrugged. "I know, I know, the conventional wisdom used to be that heavy cortical bone—the shaft of a femur or humerus—would protect the DNA better than anything except tooth enamel. But turns out it doesn't." Still dubious, I raised my eyebrows, so she went on. "That's something we learned from the team that identified victims from the World Trade Center after 9/11. They analyzed something like twenty thousand fragments for DNA—many of them not even an inch in size—and the best DNA recovery rate came from finger bones and toe bones."

"I'll be," I said. "Live and learn."

Delia's phone gave a soft chime. "Oh dear," she said, "I'm late for class."

"Sorry to keep you," I said, backing through the doorway. "Blame it on your boss."

"Aye aye, Captain." She smiled, which I took as a sign that she wouldn't be too harsh in assigning blame.

"There'll be a finger bone in your mailbox before your class lets out," I said, as she emerged and closed her door. "Special delivery. And thanks."

"Happy to help the team."

I started toward my office, and she headed the opposite direction. "Happy to have you on it," I called over my shoulder. "Even if you make me feel like a dinosaur."

CHAPTER 12

I WAS FINALLY NEARING the bottom of my in-box, having spent all afternoon sorting, signing, rerouting, delegating, and shredding, interrupting my labors periodically to grouse through the doorway at Peggy, to whom I jokingly—or half jokingly—assigned the blame for all the drudge work.

Miranda appeared in the doorway of my administrative office. "*You* look miserable," she said.

"Nonsense," I snarled. "I'm having the time of my life."

"Here," she said, sliding a large red-and-black envelope across the desktop. "Maybe this'll cheer you up."

"What is it? A new, condensed version of your dissertation? Not your resignation, I hope?"

"Neither," she laughed. "It's a Netflix DVD. *The Revenant*."

"You own this?"

She gave me a puzzled look. "What century do you live in? No, I don't own it. It's Netflix." She saw the blank look on my face. "Oh, good grief. Netflix. It's like . . . son of Blockbuster and FedEx. By way of Match.com."

"Huh?"

She shook her head. "Never mind. Forget all that. Let me start over. Netflix is an online movie service. You pay a monthly fee, you order movies off the website, and they show up in your mailbox the next day."

"How can they do it so fast?"

"The wonders of technology. You do know what a DVD is, right?" I scowled. "And you have the means to *play* a DVD?"

"Depends on the format," I said. "Is it a clay tablet, or carved in stone?"

"Point taken," she said, turning and waving good-bye on her way out. "Enjoy."

I opened the envelope and slid out the silvery disk. Unlike the DVDs I had at home—*Shakespeare in Love* and *The Princess Bride* and a handful of others Kathleen had bought years before for herself or for "us" (she claimed) or for the grandkids—this was not encased in hard plastic. Instead, it was simply tucked into a slippery Tyvek sleeve. Was that enough to protect it from the abuses of the U.S. Postal Service? It didn't appear broken or scratched, so perhaps so. Was the disk itself just like the highly packaged ones in my living room, or was this some new format that my aging DVD player wouldn't be able to handle? I had no idea.

I heard a rustle in the outer office. "Peggy? Are you still here?"

"Just leaving," she said, appearing in the door-way, one arm through the sleeve of her jacket.

"Do you know about Netflix?"

"I do," she said. "And the automobile, and the aeroplane, and Mr. Bell's telephone."

"You're as bad as Miranda," I grumbled.

"Coming from you, I'll take that as a compli-ment," she beamed.

"Do you belong, or subscribe, or whatever?"

"Doesn't everybody?" She raised her eyebrows. "I mean, everybody under ninety-five?"

"Ha ha. So this is just a regular old DVD, right? I can play it in the antique DVD player I have at home?"

"Sure. Or you can play it in your computer, if you'd rather."

"My home computer?"

"Your home computer. Your work computer. *Any* computer with a DVD drive."

I looked at the monitor sitting on my desk. "I can watch movies on *this*?"

"I wouldn't make a habit of it—you're always behind on your paperwork as it is—but yes, of course," she said. "Just pop it in the drive, and the DVD player should boot up automatically."

"Are you sure?" Instead of answering, she simply gestured at the machine, a try-it-and-see look in her eyes.

Bending beneath the desk, I touched a button on the computer's housing, and a thin tray slid open. Placing the disk in the tray's circular recess, I nudged the drawer gently and it slid shut. A moment later, I heard the disk spooling up and saw the computer monitor go black, then bright green, with white words:

**THE FOLLOWING PREVIEW HAS
BEEN APPROVED FOR APPROPRIATE
AUDIENCES BY THE MOTION PICTURE
ASSOCIATION OF AMERICA, INC.**

"Amazing," I said.

"What's the movie?"

"*The Revenant.* Fun with bears and Indians, apparently."

"So I hear," she said. "Shall I go put some popcorn in the microwave?"

I laughed. "Yeah, sure," I said, leaning down to eject the disk.

"Don't start without me," she said. "I'll be back in three minutes."

I looked up, surprised, my finger poised above the eject button. "Sorry, what?"

"I said don't start without me. The popcorn takes three minutes. I'll grab some Cokes, too."

"Oh." This was a wrinkle. I hadn't planned to watch the movie here; I'd planned to watch it at home, in my comfortable recliner. In my comfortable, empty house. Alone. *Oh, what the hell*, I thought. "Okay," I said. "I'll pause it when the FBI copyright warning comes up. Wouldn't want you to miss that."

"I've seen some movies where that was the most exciting scene," she deadpanned as she headed toward the hallway to fetch the refreshments.

"**LOOKS LIKE A** rain forest," Peggy remarked as the film's opening scene began, the camera tracking hunters sloshing through swampy woodlands, gloomy beneath towering conifers. "I thought you said the Arikara lived in the Great Plains."

"They did," I said. "At least, the ones I dug up did. South Dakota and North Dakota. This looks more like Montana. Or Oregon."

Soon, the shot widened to show us that the sloshing hunters were white men, one of them a bearded, filthy, but recognizable Leonardo DiCaprio. "Maybe the hunters are lost," Peggy offered. "Or maybe they track their prey all the way to the Plains."

"Shh," I said.

A few minutes later, the Arikara made their entrance, which they announced by shooting an arrow through the back of a running white man—a running white man who was, for some reason, buck naked. Peggy started and gasped when the arrow plowed into him and emerged halfway from his chest, just before he fell. An instant later, an Indian war party on horseback, whooping and unleashing a hail of bullets and arrows, galloped down a slope and surrounded the band of white trappers, unleashing swift, brutal death. "I thought you said the Arikara were farmers," Peggy said. "And sedentary."

"They were," I said. "At least, the ones I dug up."

"I thought you said they didn't have horses or guns."

"Artistic license," I said. "Now shh."

Miraculously, DiCaprio—or, rather, ace wilderness scout Hugh Glass, whom DiCaprio was portraying—managed to survive the slaughter, along with a dozen other men, including Glass's half-Pawnee son. Racing to their boat, hauling heavy bundles of animal pelts, they pushed off and beat a hasty retreat downriver, the Indians continuing to lob arrows at the boat until it was out of range.

But we were only ten minutes into a three-hour movie, so clearly the trappers weren't out of the woods yet. Knowing the Indians would surely race downstream to ambush them, Glass persuaded them to ditch the boat and head overland instead, angling toward the nearest fort. The battered group made camp, and Glass went hunting alone, seeking food for the group. That's when his troubles began, for Glass had the misfortune to come between a mother grizzly and her two cubs. Distracted by the cubs, Glass didn't see the mother charging until it was too late to get off a shot.

When the immense bear hit Glass, Peggy shrieked, and when it ripped him open, she grabbed my hand, squeezing so hard it hurt. After a moment, her grip eased, but she didn't let go, and I found myself only half watching the movie. Had she forgotten that she was holding my hand? Should I extricate my palm from her grip? *Probably*, I told myself. *But not yet.* It had been years since I'd held hands with anyone, but I hadn't even realized how much I'd missed it, that simple human touch. On any given day, it wasn't uncommon for me to shake hands with ten or twenty or even a hundred people, but a handshake was different—profoundly different—from holding hands.

I sat like that, silent and unmoving, though moved, for the next two hours, Peggy's grip occasionally tightening again, when yet another brutal calamity occurred on-screen. And when the end came, she gave my hand a final, gentler squeeze, as if to say "thank you" or perhaps "good night"—it was now after eight o'clock—then wiped tears from her eyes, stood up, and hurried out of the office, leaving me sitting in half darkness and utter confusion.

She also left me surrounded by ghosts. The ghost of Kathleen, my wife of thirty years, who had died a swift, unexpected death from cancer a decade before. The ghost of Jess Carter, a medical examiner from Chattanooga who had coaxed me from my cave of grief and shown me that I could love again—had shown me that I *wanted* to love again— but had been murdered by a jealous colleague. The ghost of Isabella Arakawa Morgan, a beautiful, brilliant, but deranged Japanese American librarian I'd worked with—and slept with, once—before discovering that she had murdered a scientist she blamed for the atomic blast that had killed her parents decades earlier, at the end of World War II. The only two women in my life now, apart from my son's wife, were my graduate assistant and my secretary: one of them thirty years my junior, and about to leave; the other a longtime subordinate who—despite her fearful clutching of my hand—surely knew my failings far too well to harbor romantic feelings for me.

"Every surgeon carries within himself a small cemetery," a famous French doctor wrote in his memoir. I myself carried multiple cemeteries within myself, though only one of them was small: the cemetery where the women I'd loved and lost were buried. Others—the crime victims whose bodies and bones I'd studied; the donated corpses whose decay my students and I had scrutinized and charted—numbered in the many hundreds by now.

But most numerous in my cemeteries were the Arikara Indians, some six thousand of them, carefully shelved and kept one floor beneath me, in the vast, cavernous recess beneath the stadium's south end zone. And as I locked the building—full of the dead, but emptied of the living—and headed home, it was the ghosts of the Arikara I seemed to hear whispering as I wound my way downriver alongside the dark, spooling currents of the Tennessee.

They whispered of loss: the loss of their lands, their civilization, their women and children and homes. They whispered of slaughtered bison and ferocious bears and wounded hunters. Above all they whispered of life and love, and the tenuous, fragile, crucial entwining of one with the other.

CHAPTER 13

I HAD A DREAM, and in my dream, I was standing on a grassy shore, water lapping at my work boots. It was night, and the moon was full and bright, reflecting off the rippling water. At my feet was a grave—circular, to minimize the amount of digging needed in the hard prairie soil—and within the grave, gleaming faintly in the moonlight, were bones, half covered by a buffalo robe. The skeleton was flexed into a fetal position to fit within the grave; atop and alongside and among the bones was a profusion of grave goods: heaps of beads and bangles and carved birds and bears.

Reaching down into the grave, I lifted out the skull. It was a woman's skull, an adult, and as I held it up in the moonlight, I recognized it as the skull of Kathleen, my own wife, whom I myself had buried in this spot years before. "I'm so sorry to disturb you," I said, "but I have to move you. They've dammed the river, and the water's rising. I'll go get a box and come right back to get you."

I laid the skull gently on the grass and headed to the tent camp my students and I had pitched on the flattened, grassy shelf above the water. Except for the gentle lapping of water on the shore and the soft sigh of wind through the grass, the camp was silent, the white canvas tents shining. Even the inside of my tent was faintly illuminated by the moonlight filtering through the canvas.

I knew that I had an empty bone box in the tent, but for some reason I couldn't find it. I rummaged through everything once, twice, three times, confused and growing agitated. Where was Kathleen's box? What if I'd lost it? Finally, tucked beneath my army cot, I found it. Nestling it beneath one arm, I hurried back to the shore.

But the grave was gone: vanished beneath the rising waters. "Kathleen," I called, stricken, "where are you?" The only answer was the sound of small waves lapping at my feet. Frantic now, I set the box down on the embankment and dropped to my knees, groping the submerged ground, seeking the curved edge of the circular pit. Nothing.

The water continued to rise. Soon it was up to my thighs, and then to my waist. I kept searching, now taking a deep breath and submerging myself, swimming blindly in the murky water, feeling for the grave, the buffalo robe, the bones, anything. At last my fingers closed around the straight, smooth shaft of a long bone, a bone so stout it could only have been a femur. Gripping tightly, I fought to free it. By now the water was deep, completely over my head, and I braced my feet on the muddy bottom to pull. The bone came free, and with the last bit of air in my lungs, I kicked to the surface and swam, exhausted, to the shore with the bone.

But it was not a bone. It was only a bare, brittle branch, and when I saw it, mocking in the moonlight, I knew Kathleen was lost to me forever. Dragging myself from the water, I lay in the grass and wept.

At some point in my dream I must have fallen asleep, for I felt myself awaken. It was still night; the moon still up, though low in the western sky, casting a broad, shimmering track across the rippling water: a river of moonlight. Suddenly the moon river was shattered into sparkling shards, and I saw something—someone—swimming through it, swimming down the dancing light, swimming directly toward me. Then, some distance short of the shore, the swimmer stopped and stood. It—she, an Arikara woman—was waist-deep in the water, her black hair slick and shining, water sheeting off her shoulders and dropping, like shining quicksilver, from the undercurve of her breasts and the dark tips of her nipples.

She looked at me frankly, with no trace of embarrassment or fear, and allowed me to look at her, her face mysterious and yet somehow familiar. Slowly she reached behind her neck, gathered her hair to one side, and began to twist, wringing water from it. Then, releasing the long rope of hair, she began to swing her head from side to side, back and forth, causing her hair to pendulum, faster and faster, until soon she was whipping it around and around in a great circle, an immense dark halo, surrounded by a galaxy of glowing droplets radiating outward, as if she were some dark cosmic goddess creating the very universe, spinning out stars and planets.

When she had finished, she looked at me again, then stretched a hand toward me, palm upward. Hesitant at first, I rose, then walked to the water's edge, where I stopped and stood. She waited, her hand still out, and at last I took a step, then another and another, into the water to join her. Just before I reached her, the bottom dropped from beneath me, and I sank beneath the surface. I reached out for her hand, but could not find it.

Flailing and struggling, swallowing water, I fought my way to the empty surface.

I awoke, in a fit of coughing, in my empty bed in my empty house in my sleeping Knoxville neighborhood.

CHAPTER 14

IN THE PREDAWN DARKNESS, I unlocked the door of the bone lab, the steel door grating harshly as it dragged free of the sill. Switching on the lights, I closed my eyes against the glare of the fluorescents, gradually relaxing my squint so that my eyelids glowed red, the spider work of capillaries showing through, until I opened the lids and blinked in the cold brightness.

Venturing deep into the ranks of steel shelves in the lab's inner recesses, where the stadium's grandstands sloped down from overhead, I chose three boxes at random—three from among the thousands—and carried them to an empty table at the front of the room.

The corrugated boxes, measuring three feet long by a foot square, felt as dry and brittle as the bones within them. The labels on the ends of the boxes, listing the site and grave number and date of excavation, had faded and begun to peel during the decades since they had been printed and glued to the cardboard. A thick layer of dust—some of it Tennessee dust, some of it South Dakota dust, perhaps some of it the dust of Caesar—whirled away when I puffed a breath across the top of the boxes. *Dust in the wind*, I thought. *All we are is dust in the wind.*

Opening the first box—its lid hinged along one side—I peered inside and saw a large, magnificent specimen: a tall, robust male, his bones the rich color of caramel. The skeleton was virtually complete and in remarkable condition; even the long, thinly arching ribs were unbroken. A string had been threaded through the spinal canal of each vertebra and then tied in a loop to keep them together, and for a moment I imagined them as a bizarre necklace, a trophy that a warrior might wear to strike fear into an enemy from another tribe. The bones of the man's leg—the tibia and especially the femur—were long and massive. Aligning the two and holding them alongside my own leg, I saw that the man would have towered over me.

I laid him out in anatomical position on one of the lab's long tables, and he stretched from one end all the way to the other. He was an adult, but a young one, I saw when I looked at his teeth. He had a complete set of molars—first, second, and third—so he must have been at least eighteen. But the surfaces of the molars, especially the third molars, showed little of the rapid, characteristic occlusal wear caused by the Plains Indians' gritty diet of stone-ground corn. Clearly he was in his prime, and an impressive prime it must have been. Hoping to pin down his age more closely, I checked the distal end of a femur, as well as the medial end of a clavicle. Neither end had fully fused to the shaft just yet, so the man was probably not yet twenty-five. His relative youth was also corroborated by the cranial sutures, the joints in the skull. The sutures showed up as dark, sharp lines squiggling between the bones; they were only just beginning to blur and fill and smooth, as the body began to apply its own bony spackling compound to seal and conceal the joints. By the time he was sixty, those cranial sutures would be entirely obliterated . . . except that this magnificent young man would not, could not, did not make it to sixty. At twenty years of age, his left temporal bone had been shattered by a blunt object—a war club, I suspected—wielded by a Mandan or Pawnee or Sioux warrior who had been stronger, or faster, or stealthier than this remarkable young man.

The second box contained a young woman—a girl, really, no more than fifteen, when she died. She was tall for her age, I realized when I removed the leg bones from the box, perhaps five feet eight inches already, and still growing. I could see this because the epiphyses, the ends and edges of her bones, had not yet fully fused to stop her growth. Her sacrum, the assemblage of the five lowest vertebrae, was already large, suggesting that her pelvic cavity would have had plenty of room to bear strapping babies. But her hips not yet reached their full womanly width. The iliac crest—the outer, curving edge of the hip bones—was not yet fused to the body of the ileum, so the growth plate between the two surfaces was still building. She was still growing . . . except that, because of fever or exposure or some other cause that had left no signs of trauma on her bones, she *wasn't* still growing. And she would never, of course, bear those strapping babies her body had been readying itself to bear. I laid her out in anatomical order, too, alongside the male, struck by the resemblance they bore to medieval European grave markers, the full-length stones bearing effigies of skeletons to remind the living of the inevitability of death.

The smallest, yet somehow the most powerful, was the third, a child. A meager cluster of bones—scarcely more than a handful—surrounded by crumpled newspaper and foam padding to keep it from rattling around in the vastly overscaled, adult-sized box. The teenaged girl's hipbone had been as big as my hand; this child's—there was no way to tell if it was male or female—was smaller than my ear. But what was most striking about the child—who was a month or so shy of its second birthday, judging by the presence of a full set of baby teeth—was the head: the disproportionately large cranium and eye orbits that make the skulls of babies and children look otherworldly, almost like little aliens. The child's cranial sutures—at this stage rather like jagged sawteeth or the ragged edges of splintered wood—had not yet started to interlock, as they would begin to do by adolescence. As a result, after the soft tissue had decayed, the skull had literally fallen to pieces in the grave: the frontal bone, containing the forehead and the upper halves of the immense, staring eye orbits; the parietal bones, which had formed the left and right sides of the skull; the occipital bone, whose convex outer surface and ridged inner surface reminded me of the weathered shell of a dead tortoise I had found one summer when I was a boy.

A folded piece of paper was tucked into one end of the box. I took it out, unfolded it, and read the inventory of grave goods buried with the baby:

> *This burial was associated with many artifacts:*
> *bison robe*
> *shell pendant*
> *glass marbles*
> *small glass bottle*
> *brass baby spoon*
> *blue glass pendant*
> *clay buffalo effigy*
>
> *In addition, there were many types of glass beads with this burial, including the following types and numbers: 11,067 blue glass seed beads, about 300 of which were still attached to a bison robe; 70 white glass seed beads; 9 ellipsoidal, red, transparent beads; 16 ellipsoidal, white, wire-wound beads; 10 ellipsoidal, milky white, wire-wound beads; 1 ellipsoidal green faceted transparent bead; 2 tubular blue beads; 3 compound tubular red on white beads; 22 spherical peacock blue beads; 19 yellow-and-blue spherical transparent beads; 17 spherical blue beads with white and yellow spots;*

5 spherical clear beads; 3 amber-colored spherical transparent beads; and 3 spherical green beads.

Marveling at the treasure trove of grave goods—the list took me back to the day we had unearthed the baby, and the crew and I had talked about how precious the child must have been in life, and how deeply grieved in death—I began laying out the bones, tucking them between those of the young man and the girl. Just as I finished, the bone lab's door opened.

"Good Lord," said Peggy. "What are you doing, and why are you doing it so early in the morning? It's not even seven yet."

"I woke up early," I said.

"You *always* wake up early," she said, with the same half-exasperated tone in which Miranda had said the very same words to me a few days before.

"I dreamed about Arikara Indians last night, so I came in to spend some time with them." I turned and looked at her. "What about you? What are *you* doing here at this hour?"

"I wasn't sleeping either," she said, and I thought I saw her cheeks flush slightly. "I saw the lights on and thought Miranda forgot to turn them off last night." She stepped through the doorway, came into the lab, and walked over to the table where I stood. Looking down at the three Arikara skeletons, she caught her breath. "They're beautiful," she said softly. "Were they a family?"

"What? No. At least, I don't think so."

"They look like one," she said. "Or like they could have been one, if they'd had the chance. They make me think of all those Renaissance paintings of the Holy Family, except that they're Native American." She laughed softly. "And skeletons. But still . . ."

She laid a hand on my arm for just an instant, then turned and walked out, leaving me to ponder the dead Indians, the Holy Family, and the mysterious ways of women.

CHAPTER 15

I FELT STUPID. MIRANDA was my student; I wasn't just her boss, I was her doctoral adviser and dissertation-committee chairman, so I occupied a far loftier rung of the academic and intellectual ladder. In theory, that is.

But reading her dissertation—or, rather, attempting to read it—made me feel like an impostor and ignoramus. Hell, even the title intimidated me: "An Empirical Examination of Frontal Sinus Outline Variability Using Elliptic Fourier Analysis." The good news was, I was on solid ground for the first nine words. The frontal sinus—the airspace in the bones of the forehead, just above the brow ridges— was familiar territory. Roughly fan shaped with scalloped edges, the frontal sinus sometimes reminded me of the lobes of a chanterelle mushroom. Forensically, the frontal sinus was a useful tool for confirming a dead person's identity, provided that an antemortem x-ray of the person's skull, showing the frontal sinus, could be found for comparison to the postmortem x-ray. Like fingerprints, teeth, DNA profiles, and snowflakes, frontal sinuses were unique: no two alike. So when it came to frontal sinus outline variability, and its forensic value, I was on board.

But then, after breezing through the first nine words, I slammed into those final three: "Elliptic Fourier Analysis." I knew, from looking him up, that Joseph Fourier was a French mathematician and physicist born in the 1700s. I also knew that he had found ways to use mathematical formulas to define shapes, outlines, and patterns. The main thing I knew, though, was that it took someone far more mathematically gifted than I was just to follow his thinking, let alone to harness it, to use it—as Miranda had done—to map the intricate, intracranial coastline of the frontal sinus. I didn't know what the hell regular old Fourier analysis was, let alone *elliptical* Fourier analysis.

Mercifully, Miranda's dissertation committee included members who were quite comfortable with its terminology and methodology. My colleague Richard, the developer of ForDisc, didn't bat an eye at the mention of Fourier analysis; it was quite possible that ForDisc relied on the magic of Fourier analysis—straight or elliptical or even zigzag, for all I knew—to evaluate unknown skeletons and issue its predictions about stature and race. And Dr. Gerald Grimes, who headed the Radiology Department at UT Medical Center, had seen thousands of frontal sinus x-rays in his long career, so if anybody qualified as an expert on the shape of the frontal sinus, surely he did.

I knew, having discussed the matter with them, that I could rely on Richard and Dr. Grimes to ask most of the questions at Miranda's dissertation defense. Still, I felt a responsibility to read it, even if I couldn't fully understand it. And so, with a sense of heavy foreboding—or was it rapid-onset sleepiness?—I opened the cover and began to read.

Sometime later, I felt my eyelids open, as heavily as if they had weights attached to them. Glancing down, I saw that I had made it only to page six before nodding off. Blinking and shaking off the grogginess, I realized that what had awakened me was not my subconscious sense of professorial duty, but a steady tap-tap-tapping at my door. "Come in," I called, hastily straightening up from the slumped posture in which I'd been dozing.

The door opened slowly, tentatively, and a head peered around the edge. "Dr. Brockton? Are you in there?"

"Come in, Delia," I said. "I didn't hear you knocking at first. I was . . . immersed in Miranda Lovelady's dissertation. Using elliptical Fourier analysis to compare frontal-sinus shapes. Fascinating work. Another great tool for identification."

"I'll have to take your word for that," she said. "Fourier analysis is way above my pay grade."

"Oh, it's like anything else," I told her. "Just dive in, and pretty soon you'll get the hang of it." I laid the dissertation aside before she could ask any more questions. "What brings you down here to my inner sanctum? Something important, or Peggy wouldn't have steered you here. She knows I only hide out here when I need to hunker down and think hard.

You're not having trouble with that finger bone I gave you, I hope?"

"No, not at all. I just came to give you the results from the DNA analysis."

"You got the results already? Wow, that's fast! I don't expect to hear back from the TBI crime lab for another seven and a half weeks."

She gave a slight smile. "Well, I don't get nearly as many samples as the TBI does. And I have a bit more incentive to fast-track things for you, since I'm hoping to get tenure someday."

I grinned. "Delia, if I could give you tenure right now, I would. Five years from now, if I'm still around, remind me that I owe you for this."

"Deal."

"So what can you tell me about case number 16–17, my poor bear-bait John Doe? Was ForDisc right? Is he Caucasoid, or white, or European, or whatever is today's word for folks who look like me?"

"Like you? Not exactly," she said. She handed me a printout. "According to the AIMs—the ancestry information markers—his DNA comes almost entirely from the Middle East."

"The Middle East—my God, of course!" I smacked my forehead in chagrin. "Why didn't I think of that? That explains a lot. His facial features and skin tone would be different, but his bones would look virtually the same as a white European or an American guy's."

Delia gave a slight smile. "Brothers under the skin," she observed.

"Indeed." Now that I had this piece of the puzzle, other pieces were suddenly coming together, too.

Springing up from my chair—was it possible I'd been dozing mere moments before?—I hurried to the table beneath my window and plucked a small wooden object from the tray. Placing it in my up-turned palm, I showed it to Delia. "Several of these were found in bear scat near the death scene. I thought they were just buttons, but they're not. They must be prayer beads." My mind was racing. "If that's true, then I bet this *was* a hate crime, the victim killed because he was Muslim, not because he was black." Another realization, this one horrifying, came to me. "Christ," I said, "this explains the raw bacon, too."

"Excuse me?"

"Raw bacon," I repeated. "I told you the victim was kept alive for a while, right?" Delia nodded. "So there were all these empty tin cans. Beanee Weenees, Vienna sausages, deviled ham, stuff like that. The weird thing, though, was that there with all that precooked food was an empty bacon wrap-per. Raw bacon. 'Why would they feed him raw bacon,' I kept wondering. I finally decided they smeared him with raw bacon to attract the bear. But that wasn't the only reason."

I could see Delia processing this, and when she grimaced, I knew she'd figured it out. "It's pork," she said.

I nodded. "It's pork. If you're a bad guy, and you've decided to torture and kill a young Muslim, you want to humiliate him as much as you can, right? So after you strip him of his clothes and his future and every other scrap of autonomy and dignity he's got, how else can you degrade him?"

"You cover him with something his faith says is unclean and sinful," she said.

"You do," I agreed. "So he knows death's coming—I'm sure the killer has told him he's in bear country—and he knows he's dying an unclean death."

"Wow," Delia said grimly. "Are all your killers this evil?"

"Not all," I said. Satterfield, the sadistic serial killer, popped into my mind, uninvited and unwelcome. "Some are much worse."

MIRANDA SIGHED AND pushed back from the computer screen, squinting and rubbing her eyes. "I don't get it," she said. "Why can't we find him?" She stopped rubbing her eyes and shook her head in exasperation. "It all fits. A young Muslim man is abducted, then chained to a tree by some white-supremacist sociopath. He's subjected to humiliation and abuse, then finally murdered in a god-awful way. I called Laurie Wood, at SPLC, by the way. I was wondering if she saw any inconsistency between the Confederate coin and the Muslim victim. I mean, first we think it's a white-on-black hate crime, then suddenly we decide it's white on Muslim—are they interchangeable? She said absolutely—a lot of the same people and groups who hate on blacks are now ramping up against Muslims. HGH."

"Huh?"

"HGH. Texting shorthand. Stands for 'haters gonna hate.' Laurie says it's almost certainly a hate crime."

"So does Pete Brubaker," I said. "I was on the phone with him just before I came down here."

She looked up at me. "He's the retired FBI profiler?"

"Right."

"Does he think it's somebody connected with one of the known hate groups?"

"No," I said. "He thinks it's an outlier—some wack job who's gotten all spun up by what he hears on talk radio or reads on the Internet. Those groups spew hate and violence, but when push comes to shove, Brubaker says, they're big on talk, small on action. But there are outliers even the hate-group leaders find scary. He suspects our killer is one of those fringe loonies."

"Laurie, too. She says what worries SPLC the most these days is the rise of the lone-wolf terrorist. Like Dylann Roof, the Charleston kid who killed all those people in the black church. He got obsessed with neo-Nazi and neo-Confederate groups, including the Council of Conservative Citizens."

"Who are they?"

"A white-supremacy group that denounces racial mixing and calls blacks a 'retrograde species.' After Roof shot all those people, the CCC claimed it was shocked and saddened. Yeah, right." She practically spat the words. "Hypocritical jerks." She slapped her palm on the desktop, and the sound made me jump. "So why the hell can't we find out who our victim was? I've spent hours going through these missing-person reports, and he's just not there."

I shared her frustration, though not her eyestrain. "Well," I said finally, "if there's no missing person who fits the profile, I suppose that means nobody's reported him missing."

"But why the hell not?"

I considered this. I'd worked at least a dozen murder cases in which the victims—some of them dead for weeks or months—had never been reported missing. All those victims had been women, though, and most had been prostitutes, long alienated from their families. "You think he could've been a male prostitute?" I said. "Remember what Laurie told us about Glenn Miller, the neo-Nazi caught with a black transvestite in the backseat of his car? Maybe our killer picks up the guy, has kinky sex, and then blames the victim for tempting him to go against his beliefs?"

Miranda twitched her mouth to one side, then the other, and then shook her head. "I don't buy it. For one thing, I've never heard of a Muslim male prostitute. That's not to say there aren't any, but it seems very much at odds with what I know of Muslim culture." She shrugged. "Not that I know much about Muslim law. But a young Muslim man who's carrying prayer beads? I have a hard time picturing him walking the streets and turning tricks."

The scenario struck me as a bit far-fetched, too. "Okay," I said, "let's assume he wasn't a prostitute. Why else could he go missing without being reported? Runaway?"

"Twenty's a little old to be a runaway," she said. "Besides, even if he *were* an aging runaway, seems like his family would have reported him. Could've just been a real loner, though. Or mentally ill. Or . . ."—her eyes darted back and forth as she thought—"maybe he wanted to be under the radar for some other reason."

"Because he was a terrorist?"

She shot me a sharp glance. "And some Cooke County redneck ferreted out a nefarious plot that Homeland Security and the FBI completely overlooked? Come on, Dr. B, don't tell me you've drunk the every-Muslim-is-a-terrorist Kool-Aid, too? You're smarter than that. You're better than that."

Stung by her rebuke, I didn't feel smart, and I didn't feel good. I felt small and ashamed.

CHAPTER 16

I DROVE PAST IT twice before I realized that the low, featureless building was the place I was seeking. The Muslim Community of Knoxville was housed in a drab, one-story structure made of precast concrete, the panels textured with vertical ribs and grooves—a style I'd seen mainly on the exteriors of convenience marts. The windows were protected by steel bars, and surveillance cameras stood watch over the building's doors and perimeter. The only flourishes that set the place apart from a Circle K or a liquor storage warehouse were a pair of green awnings over the doorways, plus a matching green plywood panel over the front door, featuring a cutout of a pointed dome.

Looking closer as I turned up Thirteenth Street, I noticed a small sign near the entrance identifying the building as Annoor Mosque. A sign at the entrance to the parking lot made it clear that the mosque was private property, under twenty-four-hour surveillance. *Not exactly a welcome mat*, I thought, *but not surprising.* U.S. incidents of anti-Muslim vandalism, harassment, and violence—already higher since 9/11—had tripled in 2016, I had read, egged on by the anti-Muslim rhetoric of Donald Trump and other presidential hopefuls. College students in Tucson had flung trash onto a mosque from the balconies of their luxury apartment tower. Yahoos in Georgia held a march in Atlanta at which they brandished loaded rifles and burned copies of the Quran, causing me to wonder how they'd feel if a band of armed Muslims gathered to burn copies of the Bible.

As I stepped onto the property and approached the entrance, I wondered if my progress was being tracked on a series of video monitors. The mosque had better security than the Body Farm, I realized, but that probably made sense: Although it was possible for an intruder to steal members of my flock, it wasn't possible to wound or kill them. A scrap of dialogue from *The Revenant* popped into my head, and in one of my bizarre flights of fancy, I imagined one of my corpses repeating the line to some malevolent midnight intruder: *I ain't afraid to die anymore. I done it already.*

The mosque's door, a windowless steel slab, was locked. I rapped on it, gently at first, then, when there was no answer, hard enough to sting my knuckles. *Behold, I stand at the door and knock,* I thought, with a mixture of hope and irony. Finally, my knuckles aching, I noticed the doorbell, and pressed the button. I looked up then, directly into the lens of the surveillance camera, and gave an awkward wave, plus what I meant as a friendly, trustworthy smile. My greeting must have passed muster, for a moment later, the doorknob turned and the door opened.

I stepped into the entry hall and was met by two young men. The one who had opened the door was brown skinned—Indian, perhaps—and the other was pale. Both were shoeless, and both were guarded looking. Following their footwear example, and prompted by the tall racks of cubbyholes on either side of the foyer, I removed my rubber-soled Merrell Mocs to indicate respect, then began talking, looking from one dubious face to the other. "Hello," I began. "My name is Dr. Bill Brockton. I'm the head of the Anthropology Department at the University of Tennessee." Something flickered in the face of one of the young men—the slight, brown-skinned one—so I focused more of my spiel on him, hoping he might be more receptive, although for all I knew, what I'd seen was a flicker of resentment. "I'm working on a forensic case—a murder, unfortunately— involving what we think was a young Muslim man. The victim was about twenty, and he was killed by someone who might have been a white supremacist."

The two young men—both of them around the same age as my victim, as best I could tell—looked at each other in apparent alarm, though I couldn't tell if their alarm was focused on the crime or on me, the bearer of evil tidings. "We think the victim was killed several months ago," I went on, "sometime during the summer. Trouble is, we're not having any luck identifying him. We've checked missing-person reports from all over the country"—I kept saying "we" rather than "I," in hopes of making it clear that I wasn't a solitary lunatic—"but we can't find a single report of a young Muslim man who's gone missing."

The pale one—a large young man, easily six inches taller and a hundred pounds heavier than I— said, "Excuse me. Let me make a call." He pulled out a phone, stepped away from me, and spoke softly for several minutes. Finally he returned and handed me the phone. "It's our imam," he said. "He's the one you need to speak with."

I took the phone from him to speak to the mosque's leader. During the brief pause after I told him my name and title, he said, in a formal, careful voice, "I am familiar with who you are." His voice surprised me. He didn't sound Middle Eastern; he sounded southern, and black. After my initial surprise, though, I felt stupid: Muhammad Ali and Kareem Abdul-Jabbar were far from the only African Americans to convert to Islam; for all I knew, there might be millions of other black Muslims in the United States.

In any case, taking the imam's words as a hopeful sign, I repeated what I'd told the young men, adding, "I'm here to ask for help identifying this young man. I'm hoping that you, or someone else at the mosque—or one of your colleagues at another mosque—might know of a young Muslim man who's missing."

He was silent for a moment, then he spoke slowly. "I'll need to ask around and get back to you. You must understand that an imam doesn't always know everything about every member of his mosque. I can't be the imam of just a few people. I have to be the imam of all. And that means keeping a certain distance. So I don't always know what's happening in the lives of individual members of the community."

"I understand," I said. "If you would ask around, I'd appreciate it. I'll leave my card here with these young men, so they can relay my contact information to you." With that, I thanked him and handed the phone back to the large, pale young man. Then I took two cards out of my wallet and handed one to each. "Whoever sees the imam first, please pass that along. Thank you for letting me in. I'm sorry to bring sad news."

Before leaving, I took a closer look at the interior of the mosque. I was seeing only the foyer and its intersection with the main hallway, but, except for the rack for shoes, it could have been one of a hundred small Methodist or Baptist or Presbyterian churches I had seen during my life: Beige cinderblock walls. Acoustic-tile ceilings. Bulletin boards with hand-lettered notices and printed flyers announcing upcoming events. Carpeting that was still plush and bright along the walls, but thin and worn at the center of the halls, thanks to the passage of many years and countless footsteps.

As the steel door clicked shut behind me, something in the sheen of light on its surface caught my eye, and I noticed that the paint wasn't uniform. Parts of the door had been recently repainted, I realized, and as I looked closer, I realized that the fresh paint was covering graffiti—harsh, hateful words I could still discern, faintly but unmistakably, despite the efforts to cover them, to cancel them out. *Hate always leaves a mark,* I thought sadly. *Like a break in a bone. It might heal, but you can always see where it happened.*

CHAPTER 17

I HAD INTENDED TO return to my office after my visit
to the mosque, but instead, I found myself drawn
toward I-40. I unclipped my phone and called Miranda. "I'm going back to Cooke County," I told
her. "You wanna go?"

"Why?" she asked.

"To help me," I said. "Why else?"

"No, I mean why are *you* going?"

"I still think we're missing something," I said.

"What could we be missing? We brought back
the bones, the chain, even the trash. Waylon
brought us the bear poo. We collected everything
but the tree. Unless the tree is the missing piece, we
got everything there was to get. What is it you're
imagining?"

I shrugged. "Some missing piece. I don't know
what."

"Well, duh," she said. "Funny thing about missing pieces—they're almost always . . . *missing*."

"Ha ha, Miss Smarty-Pants. But there's something else. There has to be."

"Why? Because justice always prevails? Because the good guys always win, and the bad guys never get away?"

"No," I said. "I know it doesn't always work out that way. All I know is, it feels like I've got something stuck in my teeth—stuck in my brain—and it's driving me crazy."

"And going back to the scene would be . . . mental floss?" I groaned. It was a dreadful pun, and I fervently wished I'd thought of it myself.

"Mental floss," I agreed. "Unless I go back and take another look, I'm not gonna be able to concentrate on teaching. Or grading. Or, especially, on reading your dissertation."

"A low blow," she said. "Look, I just can't go. I've *got* to get ready to defend my dissertation. But good luck chasing that wild goose."

I NEARLY MISSED the interstate exit for Jonesport. I was in the left lane, passing a Walmart truck, when I noticed the exit only a few hundred yards ahead. "Well, crap," I muttered, flooring the gas pedal. Barely clearing the front bumper of the semi, I whipped across the right lane and rocketed onto the ramp, then hit the brakes to avoid careening through the stop sign just ahead. The Walmart truck roared past, the horn blaring long and loud, the driver justifiably angry. "Sorry," I said to the truck's rear bumper as it barreled on. "Didn't mean to be a jerk."

The near miss spiked my adrenaline and also jolted me back to the present—a helpful place to be, given that it would take some concentration to find my way back up to the death scene. I'd considered calling the sheriff's office and asking if either O'Conner or Waylon could go with me, but in the end, I decided I'd rather be there alone, free to spend as much time as I wanted, unburdened by conversation or by the distraction of feeling watched as I rambled aimlessly, looking for . . . what? I had no idea.

The road up the mountain was now carpeted with leaves, mostly the bright yellow of tulip poplars. The sound of the tires was muted by the foliage, the normal crunch of gravel replaced by a rushing, swishing sound, almost like wind through treetops: almost as if the leaves contained the sound of the wind within themselves.

At the fork in the road, I bore right, then stopped at the locked gate that blocked the road to the tumbledown ruins of Wasp. Here the fresh leaf fall was so heavy that leaves swirled around my boots as I shuffled through them. When I reached the tree to which the victim had been chained, I stopped and ran my fingers through the groove in the bark, horrified all over again by the young man's cruel captivity, his ceaseless circling, and his eventual violent death.

I was probably on a fool's errand, I realized: anything we hadn't seen and collected the day we worked the scene with O'Conner and Waylon would be completely hidden now. If I'd been thinking more clearly, I'd have brought a leaf blower, and as I pictured myself wielding it, I couldn't help but smile at the absurdity of the image: an egghead professor blowing leaves in a half-million acres of forest. "For my encore, folks," I announced to the watching trees, "I'll collect every grain of sand off Miami Beach."

As if in response to my words, the wind kicked up, dislodging still more leaves from the other trees in the area. "Thank you," I said as leaves floated down. "Thank you *so much*. *Very* helpful!"

Almost as if in response, the breeze eddied and swirled, creating small cyclones of golden leaves around the base of the dead tulip poplar. I looked down, delighted, as the leaves spun upward from my feet.

And that's when I saw it—a brief flash of light, coming from a crevice in the tree's craggy roots. One brief glint of something small and shiny. Metallic and foreign. Anomalous and therefore interesting. I tried reaching in with my index finger and thumb to extricate the object, but the gap in the roots was too narrow to accommodate both my fingers. Forceps: forceps would fit, but I had driven my own truck to the mountains this time, not the Anthropology Department's truck, with its cargo bed full of tools and implements. Scanning the ground nearby, I found a promising-looking twig, about the diameter of a pencil. *Man the Toolmaker*, I thought. Angling the twig downward between the roots, I worked one end beneath the small, silvery object and gave the twig a small, deft flick. Trouble was, the flick was neither as small nor as deft as I'd intended.

The silvery object catapulted upward, tumbling end over glinting end, and then disappeared beneath the layer of leaves, as if burrowing for safety.

"Crap," I muttered. "Out of the frying pan, into the fire." I studied the spot where I thought it had gone under, doing my best to pinpoint the location before I moved. Then, still eyeing the spot, I crawled to it on all fours and stuck the twig into the ground as a reference point: a central point from which to begin searching, spiraling my way outward inch by inch, leaf by leaf. Amazing, I soon realized, how very many leaves there are on the floor of a national forest in late October. Equally amazing was how difficult it was to find a small metallic object nestled within those leaves.

Half an hour later—a mountainous pile of leaves later—I glimpsed it again, this time dropping from a handful of leaves I was sifting, as if it were making another bid for freedom. "Ha! *Gotcha*," I exclaimed, laying aside the leaves and bending down to examine my prize.

It was a cylindrical fitting of some sort, roughly the diameter of the end of my pinkie finger and less than half an inch long. The widest part was a sort of collar at one end, with flat facets on its rim that appeared designed to be gripped, by a small wrench or pliers. The collar was attached to the body of the cylinder in a way that allowed it to rotate, to spin freely without coming off. The collar's inner surface was threaded, to allow the fitting—a female coupling—to be screwed onto a male coupling. I stared at it, recognizing yet not quite recognizing the shape. It was a familiar object, a doodad I'd seen many times, but something was missing, some crucial piece of context I needed to identify it.

As I turned it over and over in my palm, gradually I ceased to look at the object and began instead to feel it, and I realized that I knew it not just by sight but by touch: My fingertips recognized the object. It was something I'd not only seen but had used; had connected and disconnected many times, twisting the collar to loosen or tighten the coupling, to connect or disconnect a video cable. The cable was the missing piece of context—the cable that must have connected to the back of a television set or a modem or a DVD player. "Or a video camera," I murmured, feeling a rising sense of horror as the implications sank in. *It's all on video*, I thought. *Somewhere out there—somewhere near here—some sick bastard has the whole thing on video.*

I hoped that we could find it.

And I prayed that we couldn't.

PART TWO

The Blood-Dimmed Tide Is Loosed

And what rough beast, its hour come
　　round at last
Slouches towards Bethlehem to be
　　born?
　　—W. B. Yeats, "The Second Coming"

CHAPTER 18

**South Central Correctional Facility
Clifton, Tennessee**

IT WAS NEARLY NOVEMBER, yet the exercise yard shimmered with unseasonal warmth, the masonry walls and concrete basketball court basking in the midday sun. Leaning against the wall of the mess hall, two guards, Testerman and Burchfield, sought the scrap of shade created by the stingy geometry of the roofline, wall, and angle of solar incidence.

Out on the cracked court, ten shirtless men—six black, two Hispanic, two white, killers all of one sort or another—shoved and elbowed and jockeyed in a tight scrum. The wet slaps of skin on sweaty skin mingled with grunts and muttered curses, the scuffing of leather soles, and the clatter of the basketball rattling the rusty rim bolted loosely to the backboard.

Suddenly inmate number 00255787—the tall,

muscled white man named Satterfield—bellowed
and dropped to his knees beneath the goal, both
hands clutching his belly. Blood oozed across his
knuckles and poured onto the pavement, and glistening loops of intestine protruded between his
splayed fingers.

The guards, both of them hefty men, heaved
themselves off from the wall and lumbered toward
the prisoners, fumbling at their belts for the only
weapons they were allowed to carry inside: small
canisters of pepper spray—absurd, sissified stand-
ins for guns. *Shit*, Testerman thought for the
thousandth time, *a man can carry a gun anywhere
in Tennessee except the one place he needs it most—in
a bunch of cold-blooded killers.* It was a favorite complaint of his. *Like sending a soldier into battle with a
damn slingshot.*

"Break it up, break it *up*," Testerman shouted,
bulling his way through the sweaty bodies. The
nine standing men had bunched up around Satterfield, either spectating or camouflaging, or—
most likely—both: watching the action, while also
making sure the guards couldn't. *Sons of bitches*, Testerman thought.

A long, bloody shank glistened on the concrete
beside Satterfield, and Testerman's first move was
to plant his left boot over the business end of the
thing. From the round shaft and hexagonal head
protruding from beneath his midsole, Testerman
saw that it had been crafted from a six-inch bolt, the
threads scraped against concrete for weeks or even
months to hone a wicked, scalpel-like blade at one
end. An opportunistic eye, a deft hand, and infinite

patience: any inmate who possessed that unholy trinity of attributes could, sooner or later, procure a piece of metal and fashion a weapon sharp enough to stab a stoolie or gut a guard.

Testerman's trigger finger twitched atop the pepper spray. "Jesus," he said, seeing the blood and entrails. Over his shoulder, without taking his eyes off the prisoners, he shouted to Burchfield: "Call for some backup. And a stretcher." Glancing around the group, he said, "Anybody wanna tell me who did this?" No one spoke. "Thought not. Too bad—I was gonna write up a commendation. Y'all go over there and line up along the fence. Go on now. *Git.*"

Once they were twenty feet away, Testerman set down the pepper spray and reached into the lower thigh pocket of his cargo pants, tugging out a pair of purple nitrile gloves. In Testerman's mind, the gloves were even more essential than the pepper spray. In here, one man in every three was HIV-positive; in here, blood and saliva and semen erupted like deadly little geysers on a daily or even hourly basis. After his hands were protected, he took another pair of gloves from his pocket, and—removing his boot from the bloody shank—he slid the weapon carefully into the purple sleeve of the index finger, using the glove as a makeshift bag, not worrying much about whether he smeared whatever fingerprints might've been on the shaft. He knotted the second glove around the blade and tucked it into his shirt pocket, careful not to pierce either the glove or himself. Only then did he turn his cursory attention to the wounded man.

Eyeing the bloody coils spilling through the

clawlike fingers, Testerman shook his head slowly. "Satterfield, Satterfield," he said, a grim smile spreading across his face. "Couldn't've happened to a nicer guy." He sat back on his heels, musing, then nodded thoughtfully. "That's a whole mess of chitlins hanging out of your belly there, stud. You might just bleed out right here in the yard." He chewed the inside of one cheek, musing. "Yep. Infirmary's probably pretty busy today. Might just take a while for them to get here with a stretcher. Might just take *quite* a while, matter of fact."

Satterfield spoke through clenched teeth. "Listen to me, you fat fuck. I've got friends. Friends in here, and friends outside. You let me die and you'll wish you hadn't. Now and for the rest of your sorry little life."

The guard snorted. "I don't think so."

"Think again," Satterfield muttered. "What's the name of that good-lookin' little wife you've got, with the blond hair and the hot body? Christie? And that boy of yours—Sammy?"

Testerman's face hardened. "You shut your mouth," he snarled. "Don't you ever talk about my family."

"Sammy," Satterfield went on, as if he hadn't heard. "Something's not right with Sammy. Autistic, or something? But making progress, I hear."

"I'm warning you, Satterfield. You keep talking, I'll finish you off myself."

"I'm thinking it might set Sammy back a bit if he was to see a few days' worth of bad things happen to his mama. Really bad things. What do you think, Testerman?"

"I think you're a dead man, Satterfield. You can't touch them."

"Can't I? They're at your place on the lake right now," he said. "Got there about an hour ago. She called to tell you they'd made it. Said it took an extra thirty minutes because there was a wreck on I-24." Testerman stared at him now, wild-eyed, trying to figure out how the hell Satterfield could possibly know that. Could the inmate really have enough connections on both the outside and the inside to keep track of her? "She didn't tell you she had company, because she didn't know it yet. But she knows it now. You better bet she knows it now." The guard's jaw clenched rhythmically, twin knots of muscle throbbing on either side. "Here's the deal, Testerman," Satterfield went on. "If I don't make it to the infirmary in five minutes, you're gonna have one hell of a mess to clean up at that cabin. And one fucked-up retard of a motherless child."

The guard's chest heaved, his nostrils flaring, electroshocks of rage pulsing down his beefy shoulders and arms and into his twitching fists. "You sick sonofabitch," he hissed at Satterfield. "If I find out you're messing with me, I'll strangle you with your own guts." Then—over his shoulder, loud and urgent: "Burchfield! We need that stretcher! And I mean *now*!"

CHAPTER 19

OVER THE COURSE OF sixteen years at the prison's infirmary, Asa Dillworth, M.D., had seen thousands of bites, hundreds of fractures, and scores of stab wounds—some minor, others fatal. A skull shattered with a baseball bat to protest an umpire's call at home plate in a softball game. A loose eyeball gouged out by a thumb in a lovers' quarrel. An ear bitten off during a dining-hall food fight that got out of hand. But never before had he seen a man clutching two handfuls of his own intestines.

Dr. Dillworth whistled appreciatively. "That's a hell of an incision," he said to Satterfield. "I'm amazed you're conscious."

"I'm tough," Satterfield said. His voice was barely above a whisper, and the doctor had to lean down to hear him.

"I need you to move your hands so I can get a better look."

"Doc?" Satterfield's voice was barely audible now. "I need to tell you something important." The doctor bent closer, not without trepidation. Was it possible this guy was about to go Hannibal Lecter on him? Lunge up and chew off his face? "Doc, you need to call your wife on her cell phone. Don't tell anyone what you're doing, or why. Stay right where I can see you and hear you. Call her right now, and keep your mouth shut and listen. Then put me in an ambulance." Dillworth stared at Satterfield, uncomprehending. "Better hurry, Doc," the inmate whispered. His eyes bored into the physician's like lasers. "There's not much time. For me or your wife."

Leaving the baffled nurse standing on the other side of the gurney, awaiting his instructions, Dillworth backpedaled a step, fumbling in a pocket for his cell phone. After a few moments he opened his mouth to speak, but whatever he heard on the other end of the line made him keep quiet. He listened, his eyes darting back and forth, as if he were watching a high-speed tennis match that he found terrifying. Sixty seconds later he closed the phone, his face ashen. "We've got to get this man to the hospital right away," he said to the nurse.

Ten minutes later, an ambulance backed up to the infirmary's loading dock, the doctor and nurse standing on either side of the gurney where Satterfield lay, the sheet over his belly glistening with blood. The two EMTs looked startled—disbelieving, even, when the doctor told them the patient had been partially eviscerated. In response, Dillworth raised the sheet to reveal the bloody coils, still clutched by Satterfield. "Holy shit," said the younger of the two, the driver.

"Take him on our gurney," said the doctor. "It'll

save time, and he shouldn't be moved. You can leave yours here for now."

"What have you done so far?" the older one asked.

"Nothing."

"Nothing? What do you mean, nothing?"

"I mean nothing."

"How much blood has he lost?" The doctor made no response. "What are his vitals?" The doctor shook his head enigmatically. "Is he in shock?"

At that, Dillworth lifted a hand, as if asking for silence or bestowing a blessing, then turned and walked away. Baffled, the EMTs looked to the nurse. She shrugged apologetically and said, "Don't ask me. Dr. Dillworth said not to touch him. Said we didn't have time, and there was nothing we could do. That's all I know."

"Christ," said the older EMT. "This guy could code any second. Let's go." Together the medics maneuvered the gurney into the ambulance and secured it, then the younger man latched the rear door and hurried to the driver's seat.

He hit the siren as soon as he cleared the prison gate and turned onto the long, straight stretch of highway headed toward town. His older colleague—riding in back with the patient—unbuckled his seat belt, leaned over the gurney, and put his stethoscope on the blood-smeared chest. His face registered surprise when he heard the heart. He'd expected it to be weak and irregular, but it thumped strongly, seventy beats a minute, steady as a metronome. He folded down the sheet far enough to expose one of the man's biceps and cinched a blood-pressure cuff around the arm. The reading—120 over 80—was better than the EMT's own blood pressure. "Damn, hoss, you're one strong son of a gun," the medic said to Satterfield. If Satterfield heard, there was no sign of it; his eyes remained closed, his face clamped in what seemed a permanent grimace of pain. "Let's just take a closer look at that belly."

The EMT folded back the sheet far enough to expose Satterfield's bloody hands, still clutching the coils of intestine. "Can you hear me?" he asked. There was no response. "I think I'd best irrigate this mess with betadine," the EMT went on, "and then wrap it. If you were to lose consciousness and let go, your insides might be all over the floor. Not good." He took hold of Satterfield's wrists and lifted them up, then laid them on the gurney beside him. Just then the ambulance hit a bump, and the gurney jounced. The pile of intestines jiggled and shifted. Then—as the EMT made a frantic but unsuccessful grab for them—they slid sideways and down, landing on his feet with a sticky plop. "Oh *shit*," he gasped. Then: "What the *hell*?" The patient's belly was covered with blood, but the gaping wound the EMT expected to see—the wound through which the intestines had emerged—was simply not there. The EMT ran an exploratory hand over the skin to make sure his eyes weren't deceiving him.

That's when his wrist was seized in a grip like a vise. "Pig," said Satterfield calmly. "Pig guts and pig blood."

The EMT stared at the prisoner's face. Satterfield stared back, holding the EMT's gaze, as he slipped a second shank—the twin of the one he'd dropped on the basketball court—out of his waistband. Driving it into the man's belly, he sliced upward until the blade hit the breastbone. The EMT grunted, his own entrails spilling out—as if in some sadistically parallel-universe echo of the sham disemboweling Satterfield had staged—and then he sank to his knees, clutching the gurney until he toppled. In a better world—a world in which rural ambulance services had ample funding—the gutting would have been captured by an interior video camera, thus alerting the driver. But this was not a better world; this was cash-strapped Wayne County, Tennessee, where one-quarter of children lived in poverty. By the time the ambulance pulled up to the hospital's emergency entrance, the dead EMT was strapped to the gurney and covered with a sheet, and by the time the unsuspecting driver switched off the engine, the blade in Satterfield's hand was already slicing the young man's carotid artery.

Thirty seconds after cutting the driver's throat, Satterfield—dressed in scrubs, his features concealed by a surgical mask—wheeled the gurney into the hospital, parked the corpse in a hallway, and followed a labyrinth of corridors to the main lobby. He walked out the front entrance, a free man, for the first time in more than twenty years.

By the time the hospital, police, and prison staff pieced together the bloody puzzle, Satterfield would be long gone: eastbound toward Knoxville, and toward Brockton, and toward the bloody reckoning Satterfield had lovingly imagined every day for two decades.

PART THREE

The Dark and Tangled Web

O, what a tangled web we weave when
    first we practice to deceive!
            —Sir Walter Scott, "Marmion"

The dark net: a place without limits,
    a place to push boundaries, a place
    to . . . sate our curiosities and
    desires, whatever they may be.
    All dangerous, magnificent, and
    uniquely human qualities.
            —Jamie Bartlett, *The Dark Net*

CHAPTER 20

I BUZZED PEGGY, AT the far end of the stadium. "Hey," I said, "would you hold my calls?"

"Napping again?" she teased.

"Not yet, but I probably will be soon," I admitted. "I'm taking another run at Miranda's dissertation. Last time I nodded off at page six."

"In that case, I'll buzz you every five minutes."

"You're *such* a help." I hung up, smiling. I still wasn't quite sure what was happening with Peggy—if, in fact, *anything* was happening: neither of us had spoken about our unexpected evening of movie-watching hand-holding—but the air around us did seem different, charged with electricity, low though the voltage might be, and full of unspoken possibilities. But was I ready for possibilities?

I had just propped my feet on the desk and opened the dissertation to page six when my intercom beeped. "Heavens, I'm not even sleepy yet," I answered.

"You have a call on line two," Peggy said.

"A call? You mean one of those things you're holding?"

"I know. But this is Captain Decker, from the Knoxville Police. He says it's urgent."

"Well, then, I reckon I'd better take it. Thanks." I pressed the blinking button. "Deck, is that you? Long time, no see. How you been?"

"Hanging in there, Doc. Keeping busy."

"Me, too. I like it that way. Keeps the ghosts at bay, you know?"

"Yessir, I do. Fact is, that's why I'm calling. One of the ghosts. Our old pal Nick Satterfield. Bad news, Doc."

"Well then, he must not be dead," I said. "That would be great news. To you and me both."

"It sure would. No, sir, it's bad. Real bad."

"He's gotten another appeal? He's getting a new trial?"

"Worse, Doc. The very worst."

I felt an icy claw clutch at my heart, and then Decker and I spoke the dreadful words in grim unison: "He's escaped."

CHAPTER 21

THE WOMAN'S FACE WAS grave, her brown eyes brimming with concern and compassion, as she looked directly at us—at me and my son, Jeff; at Jeff's wife, Jenny; at their teenaged boys, Tyler and Walker—and began to speak. "A massive manhunt is under way for an escaped serial killer," she told us, her gaze unwavering despite the dire news.

Dire, indeed, and news, literally: The woman was Beth Haynes, a coanchor of WBIR-TV's five P.M. newscast, and one of my favorite television journalists. I had watched her for years—and admired her for years, not just for her poise and charisma, but also the intellect and heart she brought to stories on complex issues such as domestic violence, homelessness, and racial tensions. When Beth talked, I listened. Always.

"Authorities say convicted killer Nick Satterfield, serving a life sentence for the murders of four prostitutes in 1992, escaped today from South Central Correctional Facility in Clifton, Tennessee," she went on, still looking directly at me, and *only* at me, or so it seemed. "Details of the escape are sketchy"—now Beth's earnest face was replaced by a full-screen shot of an ambulance parked at the emergency entrance of a hospital, the vehicle and entrance cordoned off with yellow-and-black crime-scene tape—"but early reports indicate that Satterfield overpowered and killed two emergency medical technicians, while en route to a local hospital for medical treatment."

Suddenly the screen filled with the face of Satterfield himself—a courtroom photo from his trial, an image that captured a venomous look in my direction. After more than twenty years, the malevolence of his stare still sent a spike of primal fear through me. "Satterfield was caught in 1992, during the attempted murder of University of Tennessee forensic anthropologist Bill Brockton and his family," Beth reported. "Asked today about Satterfield's escape, Dr. Brockton had this to say."

Now I had the odd sensation of looking directly into my own eyes, of being on the receiving end of a comment from myself. "He's a really bad guy," I said. "I just hope they catch him before he kills anybody else."

Jeff, standing behind me—the "me" sitting tensely in my living-room recliner—gave my shoulder a reassuring squeeze. Jenny, seated on the sofa, reached out and laid her hand on mine.

Then the camera angle widened abruptly, so that the shot included the young female reporter who had ambushed me outside my office two hours earlier. "Dr. Brockton, do you feel personally in danger?" she asked. "Nick Satterfield came after you once before. Will he come after you again?"

The me on the TV screen—looking grayer, older, and tenser than I would have liked—shook his head. "He'd have to be pretty dumb to come after me," I told the reporter—or was I telling myself? "If he comes within a mile of me, he'll be nabbed by the FBI or the TBI or the Knoxville Police Department. I'm what the fishermen call 'live bait,' and he's way too smart to take it." With that, I gave the reporter a smile—a strained, plastic smile, clearly—and walked out of the shot, hoping that what I'd said was true.

Beth Haynes's face filled the screen once more, looking even more somber than before—more somber than I'd ever seen her. "Breaking news, and a shocking update, just in. Authorities now say that family members of two prison officials from South Central Correctional Facility—the prison from which Nick Satterfield escaped—were brutally murdered today. It's not yet known whether or how these murders are connected with Satterfield's escape, but WBIR News will continue to monitor this developing story and keep you posted." In what seemed to be a return to her earlier script, she added, "Needless to say, escaped killer Nick Satterfield is considered armed and extremely dangerous. Anyone with information on his whereabouts should call the FBI or the TBI. Authorities have announced a $50,000 reward for information leading to his capture." Satterfield's photo appeared on-screen over one of Beth's shoulders, and a toll-free number materialized at the bottom of the screen, along with the caption "$50,000 Reward."

The story over, I switched off the television so we could talk.

"Fifty thousand dollars!" exclaimed Walker, who—at fifteen—still retained a boyish enthusiasm. "I wish I knew where he was! I could buy a Corvette with that!"

"Yeah, right," said Tyler, already world-weary at age seventeen. "A Corvette. Just what you need. Because you're *such* a great driver already, the way you keep one foot on the brake at all times."

"Hey, *I'm* not the one who ran over our mailbox."

"Shut up," said Tyler.

"*And* the neighbors' mailbox," Walker persisted.

In the blink of an eye, Tyler pounced, hurling his brother to the floor. "Boys! *Boys!*" Jenny yelled, to no avail, as they grappled and thrashed. "Boys!" Jeff came from behind my chair, preparing to pull them apart, but before he could enter the fray, a denim-clad leg—impossible to say whose—kicked upward, the foot careening against a ceramic lamp and sending it flying. The lamp hit the wall in a duet of destruction: the soprano notes of shattering lightbulbs accompanied by the lower, rounder clanking of fired pottery splintering into shards.

The room fell silent, except for the panting of the boys and the slow, furious breathing of their dad. "Get up," he ordered. "Get up, clean up that mess, and apologize for your stupid, *stupid* behavior." The boys lay there, looking stricken. "Dammit, I mean *now!*" he bellowed, grabbing each boy by an upper arm, and yanking with a force and a fury I had never seen in him before. Jenny stared at him, shocked, as the boys—flushed and frightened-looking— scrambled to their feet and hurried to the kitchen for the broom and the Dustbuster.

"Jeff?" She said it slowly; carefully; as if unsure whether the man in front of her was her accountant husband or a psychotic mental patient.

Jeff squeezed his eyes tightly closed, and drew a deep breath, then let it out slowly before opening his eyes. "I'm sorry," he said. "I just . . . I'm sorry."

"It's a lot to process," I said. I looked at Jenny, who still seemed shaken. "Why don't y'all go on home. I'll clean this up. To be honest, I could use the distraction. Ever since I heard the news, I've been about to jump out of my skin. I expect we're all feeling edgy. Even them." I nodded toward the kitchen, just as the boys emerged, cleaning implements in hand.

"Grandpa Bill, I'm so sorry," said Tyler. "I didn't mean to break your lamp, and I . . . I'll buy you . . ." He stopped, and I saw tears coursing down his face.

"Oh, honey, it's okay," I said, gathering him in my arms, feeling him begin to sob. "I know you didn't mean to." A moment later, I felt Walker burrowing against us, and I widened my arms to take him in, too. They were quite an armful—hardly boys anymore—yet at this moment, they seemed small and vulnerable. "Everything will be okay," I said. "Nothing's going to happen to any of us. I promise." They squeezed more tightly against me. "And you know what else, guys? For forty years, I have secretly hated that damn lamp."

THAT NIGHT I had a dream, and in my dream, I could hear Satterfield's voice inside my head, taunting me. "You should have let Decker kill me," he said. "He had the chance, and he wanted to, but you said no. You chose mercy over justice. A foolish choice. Now all your family will die. Everything you ever loved will die."

I called Decker, still in my dream, to ask him to save my family once more. Decker had reasons of his own to consider the job, for Decker hated Satterfield even more than I did. Deck's younger brother, a bomb-squad technician, had died back in 1992 in a search of Satterfield's booby-trapped house. Years later, Decker himself had nearly died, when Satterfield managed to cut his throat. It happened in a fight at the prison where Decker had gone to interview him.

Decker agreed to help, but on one condition: Only under a black flag. No arrest. No trial. Only summary execution.

"A black flag," I agreed.

In my dream. But it was only a dream. Wasn't it?

CHAPTER 22

WAS IT THE EFFECT the architect intended, or was it just my paranoid or guilty imagination? Every time I passed between the severe, three-story concrete columns flanking the entrance to the FBI building, I felt as if I'd been zapped with a shrink-ray, as if I were some Lilliputian prisoner, stepping into a mammoth, marble-floored prison cell.

The building's lobby was equally disorienting, as ornate as the exterior was austere. Floored and walled in marble and gilding, the space looked as if it had been teleported from a fancy hotel or investment bank. Did the concrete-and-brick exterior and the opulent lobby really belong to the same building? If so, the building was suffering from bipolar disorder or maybe multiple personalities.

My architectural overanalyzing was cut short by the opening of a door and the emergence of Angela Price, wearing a no-nonsense suit and no-nonsense face—exactly the face I had pictured during my uncomfortable call with her, a few days and a lifetime earlier, when all I'd had to worry about was a simple hate crime—hate that wasn't directed at me or my family.

"Dr. Brockton," she greeted me, extending a hand and shaking mine with a grip that was coolly consistent with the rest of her.

I had once made the mistake of addressing her as "Angela," and her swift, acerbic correction—"it's Special Agent Price"—ensured that I never made that particular mistake with her again.

"Special Agent Price," I replied, nodding gravely.

"Actually, it's Special Agent *in Charge* Price," she said. "I'm running the field office now." She turned and headed off, talking over her shoulder. "We're in the main conference room. Right this way." She headed briskly through the doorway and down a hall—a beige, drywalled, fluorescent-lighted corridor that seemed to have no connection to the lavish lobby—and I hurried to keep up.

She slowed but did not stop at a wide, walnut door labeled CONFI, twisting a brushed nickel handle and pushing the door inward. It opened to reveal a massive table, five feet wide by a dozen feet long, surrounded by an assortment of law enforcement officers, many of whom I'd known for years. Several were in uniform—the dark blue of the Knoxville Police Department and the Knox County Sheriff's Office—but most wore crisp dress shirts and tightly cinched ties: the unofficial but regulation uniform donned daily by detectives and agents of the FBI, TBI, and KPD.

"All right, gentlemen, let's get to it," she said, taking the chair at the head of the table. "We've got a bad guy—a really, *really* bad guy—on the loose. It's the mission of this task force to find him and put him where he belongs. In prison—or in the ground." Her bluntness surprised me, and as I glanced around the table, I saw a few other faces that appeared startled . . . and several that looked grim and gratified. "You didn't hear that from me," she added. "But no kidding, this guy's a menace, and we've got to nail him. And fast." With no further ado, she had each person around the table introduce himself—she was the only woman in the room—and talk about his agency's contribution to the manhunt. One of the group was present only acoustically: my old pal Pete Brubaker, the retired FBI profiler, linked to the meeting by speakerphone.

I knew and liked and respected all these people. For decades, after all, I had worked with the best homicide investigators that local, state, and federal law enforcement agencies had to offer, and if ever there were a case that called for pulling out all the stops, this was it: a sadistic serial killer on the loose again, a bloody trail of new bodies already in his wake.

First to talk was Wellington Meffert, a TBI agent generally known by the deceptively deprecating nickname "Bubba." I was surprised to see him here, as Steve Morgan had said Meffert was seriously ill with cancer. But I was grateful, too, for multiple reasons. Bubba and I had worked the first Satterfield case—Satterfield 1, perhaps we should call it—more than twenty years before. Now gray at the temples and gaunt to the point of looking skeletal—from the cancer, or from the chemotherapy that would kill either the cancer or himself—Meffert was one of the TBI's senior agents. "As you've probably heard," he began, "Satterfield didn't just kill the two EMTs in the ambulance. He also killed—or had accomplices kill—the families of a prison guard and the prison doctor."

Price interrupted him. "Any leads on those killings yet?"

Meffert shook his head. "Not yet. Both in isolated homes. We're interviewing neighbors, but none of 'em are close, so we might not get much. We know the doctor's wife was alive at the time of the escape, because he talked to her. And we know she was dead an hour after the escape, because that's when a sheriff's deputy found the body. Could Satterfield have gotten to her in that period, or was she killed by an accomplice right after she got off the phone? Don't know."

"And what about the prison guard's wife and son?" Price asked. "Any telephone contact with them around the time of the escape?"

"None," said Meffert. "We're also interviewing inmates, but as you know, that poses challenges of its own. The bad news is, this was a well-coordinated plan. The good news is, it was complex, which could work to our advantage." I glanced around the table, and judging by the expressions on other people's faces, I wasn't the only one puzzled by the advantage Meffert claimed we had. "This thing had lots of moving parts," Meffert explained. "Somebody got him those pig guts. Somebody fed him information about the guard's family and the doctor's family. There were lots of links in this chain of events. At least one of those links is weak, and when we pull hard enough . . ." He hooked together his thumbs and index fingers, then yanked them apart. "*Snap.*"

Price nodded. "Let's hear from Pete Brubaker next. Pete, thanks for agreeing to dust off your file and jump in on this."

"Glad to help, if I can," he said. "This guy's bad news. Sooner we get him back in prison, the better off the world is."

"Pete," said Price, "do you have an opinion on whether Satterfield himself killed the doctor's wife and the guard's family?"

"I doubt it," he said. "He killed the EMTs because he had to—they were between him and freedom. But he had no particular reason to kill the others himself. More likely, his accomplices did that. Maybe on Satterfield's orders, maybe on their own initiative, to cover their tracks. A guy like Satterfield gets off on two kinds of murders—sadistic sexual murders, like the prostitutes he murdered years ago—and revenge killings."

"Pete, this is Bill Brockton," I interrupted. "By revenge, you mean like the way he came after me all those years ago? Because he thought I'd ruined his life?"

"Exactly," said Brubaker. "The way he came after you then. The way he's almost certainly coming after you now. You and probably your family, too. The way he sees it, he's got unfinished business. With all of you."

His words hung in the air for what seemed like several minutes, and I was acutely conscious of every pair of eyes in the room focusing intently on my face. But beyond that—after that—I was conscious of very little. I vaguely heard discussion and delegation of security details, round-the-clock surveillance of my home, my office, Jeff's home, Jeff's office, the boys' school. I heard myself, my voice sounding muffled and far away, reciting phone numbers, addresses, and other information in a robotic monotone.

After the meeting, I sleepwalked out the door of the building, dwarfed once more by the massive concrete columns, feeling quite small, extremely exposed, and—despite the agent assigned to follow and protect me—very, very alone.

CHAPTER 23

"HERE," I SAID, "I'LL show you." And with that, I clambered onto the table at the front of the auditorium and knelt on all fours.

I loved teaching the intro course, giving freshmen and sophomores—plus the occasional branching-out junior and home-stretch senior—their first taste of the incredible feast that anthropology offered: Evolution. Anatomy. Archaeology. Human civilizations, from aboriginal to Zulu.

I enjoyed doing what Horace said poets should do: instruct and delight. I liked kneeling and crawling, wagging my butt to illustrate how humans—prehistoric prehuman ancestors, actually, millions of years ago—had once been quadrupeds, before eventually standing up for themselves, "or standing up for their dinner," as I liked to put it, and becoming bipeds. Students would invariably laugh, and in recent years some had taken to snapping photos with their cell phones, posting them on Facebook or Instagram or SnackChat or whatever the latest social-media network was. They laughed and they learned, and I loved it.

I *used* to love it, anyhow. But not anymore. On this occasion, as I twitched and shimmied, hamming up the prehistory of hominids, I felt silly and stupid. I resented my students for requiring entertainment, and I resented myself for stooping to it, quite literally. My heart wasn't in it, and neither were my hips, and the few token laughs I heard from the students sounded forced and embarrassed. After class, I made a beeline for the door and hurried back to the bone lab, instead of hanging around to joke with students, as I usually did.

The lab's heavy steel door banged open, hard and loud, when I entered. Miranda—sitting just inside the door, staring at her computer screen—yelped and jumped, sloshing coffee all over the desktop. "Dammit!" she said, scrambling to move papers and books out of harm's wet way, then grabbing a handful of tissues from a box to begin mopping.

"Sorry," I said. "Didn't mean to scare you." My apology came out sounding sulky, as if I felt that I was the one who had been victimized by her reaction.

"Hey, no worries," she said. "I didn't really need those ten years you just took off my life." She narrowed her eyes and examined my face. "Didn't you just come from teaching intro?"

"Yeah."

"That usually gets you superjazzed. What happened?"

I shrugged. "Nothing. It just . . . I dunno. I guess I'm just off my game."

"You've been off your game for the past week," she said. "Ever since He Who Must Not Be Named escaped from Azkaban." Under almost any other circumstances, I would have laughed at her cleverness—equating a real-life scumbag, Satter-field, to the fictional evil wizard in the Harry Potter books. But with Satterfield on the loose, and pos-sibly coming after me—or, worse, coming after my family—her attempt at humor hit me wrong.

"Glad you find this amusing," I said.

"Hey, I just . . ." She trailed off, probably afraid of antagonizing me further. "Sorry."

I saw the hurt in her eyes, and I knew my rebuke had stung her. "Yeah," I mumbled. "Me too." I held up a hand—a farewell, or a truce—and retreated to my private sanctuary. To brood.

I MUST HAVE brooded for hours, for when my in-tercom beeped, I came out of my funk enough to notice that the steel girders outside my windows were beginning to sink into shadow. I picked up the phone reluctantly, expecting Peggy. "Yes?"

For a moment I heard only ragged breathing at the other end of the line, then a hoarse whisper. "Can you come here? To the bone lab. Please."

It was not Peggy, and something was very wrong. "Miranda? Miranda, what's wrong?" I bolted up-right in my chair, then scrambled to my feet. Now I heard weeping—deep, racking sobs. "Miranda, are you hurt?" But the line had gone dead.

I considered calling the campus police—was it possible that Satterfield was here? had found his way to the bone lab, and to Miranda?—but I dared not

waste the time it would take to call and explain my
fears to them. Instead, I ran, hurtling myself down
the stairs and out the door that exited beside the
north end zone, sprinting along the one-lane service road that threaded the girders supporting the
stadium. Students stared as I passed, and I heard
one or two call my name, but I waved them off and
kept running.

When I came to a stop outside the bone lab, I
paused to look through the window, wondering if
I'd see Miranda with a gun to her head or a knife to
her neck. Instead, I saw her sitting at her desk, her
hands to her mouth, staring at her computer screen.
I burst into the door, and the expression on her
face when she looked at me was one of heartbreak
and horror. "Miranda, what's wrong?" I repeated.
"What's got you so upset?"

Instead of answering, she just shook her head,
unable to speak, and pointed at the computer. The
screen was a pale gray, as if all the color had been
bled from it, and it took me a moment to realize
what I was seeing. The instant I did, I felt a shock
wave of horror ripple through my whole body. The
monitor was showing a video, grainy and low in
contrast, but the place was clearly recognizable:
a patch of woods, shown from a high camera that
was looking down—looking down from the trunk,
I knew, of a large tulip poplar on a Cooke County
mountainside.

At first there was no movement on the screen,
but there was sound—a low whimper of fear, the
voice ragged with terror. Moments later a pale

figure—a thin, naked young man—came into the frame, lurching and staggering and clinking the chain, casting desperate glances over his shoulder. I strained to see his features but the video's quality was too poor. A few steps behind the boy lumbered a large black bear, grunting and snuffling and rumbling in a low growl.

The angle changed—to a different camera, apparently—and the chase scene continued, the boy's movements becoming jerkier, the chain's clanking more frantic. Suddenly he stumbled and fell, and the bear was upon him. The boy began screaming, in terror and agony, and the bear roared and snarled. The sound grew louder and more unbearable. Miranda covered her ears and hid her face in her elbow, and I could hear her own cries of distress mingling with the boy's screams and the bear's savagery. I didn't know how to mute the speakers, so I reached out and jerked the wires from them, then wrapped my arms around Miranda's shoulders. She turned and buried her face against my chest, shaking with sobs that quieted and then grew silent, but continued for what seemed minutes. Finally she pulled away and drew a deep, deep breath, then let it out in a shuddering sigh.

A roll of paper towels—the thick, heavy blue kind, almost like flannel, sold in Home Depots and AutoZones for use in workshops—sat on a nearby table. I tore off two and handed them to Miranda. She wiped her eyes and face with one, then blew her nose long and loudly into it. Wadding it up and dropping it into the waste can beneath the desk, she repeated the maneuver with the second one. When I offered her the roll for more, she shook her head and took two more deep breaths.

I pointed at the screen, although by now the horrific video had ended, and asked, "Where on earth did you get that?"

"The dark web," she said hoarsely.

"The what?"

"The dark web. It's like a secret, underground Internet, lurking right alongside things like Wikipedia and Facebook and YouTube and Amazon and eBay and NPR and such. The dark web is invisible and unsearchable, unless you know how to get into it and find what you're looking for. People use it to do things anonymously: Buy and sell drugs. Trade child pornography. Stream pirated movies. And share poison like this."

"But . . . how do you even know about it? How did you find this?"

She reached for the roll of paper towels and tore off one. First she blew her nose again, then she cleared her throat and spat into it. "Sorry," she said. "I'm drowning in my own effluvia here." She tossed this one, too, then took a sip of cold coffee from her Day of the Dead mug. "I called Laurie Wood at SPLC yesterday. We talked some more about the ancestry information Delia gave us, and about the prayer beads."

"But how—"

"Hang on, boss, I'm getting there. So after we talked a while, she transferred me to one of her colleagues. The SPLC's web guru. A young hipster guy, sounds like, named Sean. Sean's done some poking around in the dark web, and when I told him we thought there might be video of our victim being killed, he mentioned a site he saw once, a year or two ago, called 'Watch Niggers Die.'"

"What?"

"Yeah. Charming, right? The site showed video clips of black people in the act of dying, some of it scenes from movies, some of it real-life footage of accidents or shootings taken by security cameras and police cameras. The only requirement was that the footage show the death of a black person. The more gruesome, the better." I shook my head, in disbelief and disgust, and she went on. "So I started thinking: If there was a site called 'Watch Niggers Die'—and according to Sean, it got a huge amount of traffic before it was taken down—maybe there'd be something similar about Muslims and Jews and Middle Eastern immigrants. So I started Google searching—"

"Wait," I interrupted. "I thought you said this stuff on the deadly web—"

"The dark web," she corrected.

"I thought you said the dark web wasn't search-able."

"It's not. So I started searching on the regular web, looking for hate terms for Muslims. Guess what one of the favorites is?"

I stared at her, then shrugged. "Dunno. Maybe 'raghead'?"

"That's one, yes," she said. "So is 'towelhead.' Both relatively tame. The favorite, among the hard-core haters, is 'sand nigger.' So I did more searching on that, and I started seeing a lot of rabid, foamingat-the-mouth posts—on Facebook and Twitter and other sites—by a guy calling himself WhiteKnight. Get it?"

"Like, the white knights of the KKK?"

She nodded. "That, plus white knight as in 'savior of the white race.' All these race-baiting, race-hating posts—some about blacks, some about Jews, but more and more, in the past year, about Muslims."

I nodded. "It does seem like we've turned some kind of corner since the San Bernardino and Paris shootings."

"And since Donald Trump made racism and fascism seem patriotic," she said, her voice venomous. "Anyhow, finally I found a picture of a bloody body. The post said 'See sand nigger. See sand nigger die. Die, sand nigger, die. Die, die, die.' Somebody replied, 'Would LOVE to see that!' and so White-Knight gave him some clues for how to find it. A sort of lame, half-assed version of code. I managed to break it in a few hours. I had just found . . . *this*"— she made a face of revulsion as she nodded at the computer—"when I called you. You should watch the whole thing. The whole thing—the whole crime—is on here, edited down to ten minutes. It shows the poor kid being beaten and chained to the tree. It shows the killer—wearing a mask, so we don't see his face—throwing food at the kid and calling him all sorts of vile things. It shows the poor kid begging for his life when he's being smeared with the bear bait and the bacon grease."

"Miranda, you're amazing," I said. I felt sickened by the video, but proud of my assistant. And I felt excited about the breakthrough. "No way the FBI can say this isn't a hate crime *now*," I said. "I can't wait to see Price's face when she gets a look at this." As soon as I said it, I felt bad—turning the torture and death video into a trump card I could play, an I-told-you-so I could rub the FBI agent's nose in. "I shouldn't have said that," I told Miranda. "Not that way. I do think the FBI needs to see it, but first I want to show Jim O'Conner and Waylon."

She nodded. "That seems right. It is their case, after all. If the feds come storming in, they'll shove the locals aside and end up getting all the credit."

"*You're* the one who should get all the credit," I said.

Miranda blushed. Her glowing look was only slightly undercut by the small, sparkling droplet dangling, earringlike, from the tip of her nose.

O'CONNER AND WAYLON didn't speak during the video, but occasionally I heard what seemed to be sounds of dismay from the sheriff—sighs and clucks and *tsk*s—accompanied by low, menacing growls from Waylon. When the bear made its entrance, Waylon's growls blended with those of the animal, creating a bizarre, stereophonic duet that, because of its oddness, made it easier for me to endure the gruesome footage the second time around. Miranda, I was relieved to notice, had an easier time of it as well, emitting no sobs or wails, and requiring only one tissue at the end.

"The FBI might—*might*—be able to track down who shot and uploaded this," I said, "but it's a long shot."

"Very long," Miranda agreed. "The guy who

posted about it, 'WhiteKnight,' would be easy to find, but he's probably not the one who shot this. Just the one who blabbed about it."

"The trouble with this dark web stuff is that it's anonymous and untraceable," I added, "because it's all locked up behind something called door software."

O'Conner looked puzzled. "Door software?"

"*Tor* software," Miranda corrected, smiling slightly at my garbled explanation. "T-O-R. The letters stand for 'the onion router.' It's an encryption program—like a computerized combination lock, created by thousands of different computers, and each computer has only one digit of the combination."

"Oh, right," said O'Conner. "Waylon was telling me about this not long ago." I was surprised and mortified to be the least informed of the group. "The FBI found a way around the encryption—they busted a bunch of child pornographers by exploiting some sort of weakness—but then the Tor programmers fixed that, so now it's virtually impossible."

I shook my head. "I don't get it. Why would anybody want to shield child pornographers and drug merchants and other scum of the earth?"

"Hey, Tor's not *all* bad," Miranda said. "It was created and funded by the U.S. military—the navy and DARPA, I think—so classified intel could be sent online. It's not just used by kiddie-porn perverts; it's also used by whistleblowers and investigative journalists and groups like Human Rights Watch to protect their sources. That's the thing about free speech and privacy and other constitutional rights:

we're all for them when people like *us* want them, but not when folks we despise want them."

"Exactly," I said. "Please tell me you're not about to launch into your ACLU pitch now."

"No, I am *not*," she said, narrowing her eyes at me. "I'm saving that for the drive back to Knoxville."

"Goody," I said, then turned to O'Conner. "What do you say, Jim? Shall we take this to the FBI and push for a hate-crime investigation? They can't say no this time—not if they see this video. Maybe they could crack the encryption and track down the person who made it."

It was Waylon, not O'Conner, who responded, and his words floored me. "Hell, ain't no need to go to the FBI for that. I can tell you who done it right now."

CHAPTER 24

WAYLON'S WORDS—"I CAN TELL you that right now"—created an electric silence in the sheriff's office. Miranda, the sheriff, and I all stared at the deputy.

Finally O'Conner spoke. "Well, go ahead, Waylon. We're all ears. What do you know, and how do you know it?"

"I reco'nize the feller's voice," said the big man. "That, and the way he walks—kindly bowlegged and loose-jointed, but springy, too. Name's Jimmy Ray Shiflett. Grew up here. Always had him a big chip on his shoulder."

"That goes for all the Shifletts," said O'Conner. "Seems to be in the DNA."

Waylon nodded. "Jimmy Ray lit out when he was big enough—sixteen, maybe eighteen. Spent some time in the army, then come back a few years ago with an even bigger piece of timber on his shoulder."

"That's *right*," said O'Conner. "He left the army under some sort of cloud, if I remember right."

Waylon nodded. "Some kind of trouble in Afghanistan. Buncha villagers killed at what turned out to be a wedding. Way Shiflett tells it, the wedding was a cover for a Taliban get-together. He says the army's done gone to the dogs—not lettin' soldiers be soldiers. Lettin' in all kinda riffraff—blacks and Hispanics and A-rabs. Course, them ain't the words he used."

"Sounds like a prince," Miranda observed.

Waylon shrugged. "Shiflett says the real reason he got throwed out was for standing up for the white man. After he come back home, he took up with some of them militia folks over in North Carolina. I disremember the name of the group."

O'Conner pondered this a moment, then posed a question to the deputy. "You think he'd come in peacefully if we called and said we wanted to talk to him?"

The big man's face scrunched into an expression of disbelief. "Come in peaceful? Hell, no! He'd head for them hills like a scalded cat. He might be crazy, but he ain't stupid. Long time 'fore that boy was a soldier, he was a hunter and a tracker, good as any I ever seen. If he gets wind we're a-comin', he'll be gone just like that"—Waylon snapped his fingers—"and we won't never catch sight of him no more."

"What if he *doesn't* get wind of us?" the sheriff persisted. "What if we just show up at his door with a warrant—will he put up a fight?"

Waylon guffawed. "Will a politician lie? Will a bear shit in the woods?" He shot a quick, abashed glance at Miranda. "Sorry for the language, Miss Miranda."

"I hear worse all the time," she said. "Mostly from my own mouth."

"You could still bring in the feds," I suggested. "Sure, they'd end up taking the case away and getting credit, but they also have the resources to do it."

"Beggin' your pardon, Doc," said Waylon, shifting his enormous frame, "but if Jim and me can't bring him in, I don't reckon the FBI can. Look at how long it took 'em to nab Eric Rudolph."

It was interesting to hear Rudolph come up again so soon after our meeting in Montgomery. "And he survived up in the mountains for, what, five years?" I asked.

Waylon nodded. "Says he got by on acorns and salamanders, Dumpster scraps, that kind of thing. But word on the street is, he also got help from some Carolina militia folk. Them, and his crazy family."

"Crazy how?" asked Miranda.

Waylon snorted. "His brother cut off his own hand with a power saw—on purpose—and sent it up to the FBI. 'A message,' he called it."

I had either missed or forgotten that piece of the story. "And the message," I said, "was, 'we're *all* nuts here'?"

"I'm guessing the FBI got it," said O'Conner, "loud and clear."

I wanted to get back to the case at hand. The problem at hand. "But y'all think there's a high risk our suspect, Jimmy Ray Shiflett, could cut and run." Waylon and O'Conner both nodded. "Or put up a serious fight?"

"Hell, he's probly got enough guns up there at his

place to start a war," Waylon said. "Dynamite and such, too."

"Well," I pointed out, "that could be an argument for bringing in the FBI."

O'Conner shifted in his seat, looking uncomfortable. "Yes and no," he said. "Here's my issue with the FBI. I don't give a rat's ass who gets credit for bringing him in, if he did this. What worries me is, there's a lot of distrust of the federal government up here. Some of it goes back eighty years. Some families are still pissed off about the park." I nodded; Great Smoky Mountains National Park was America's most heavily visited park, but its creation had taken a toll on hundreds of hardscrabble mountain families, forced off their land for the sake of a park for tourists. "I'm just imagining a convoy of FBI armored vehicles rolling in here," the sheriff continued. "I hate to say it, but I'm afraid things could get ugly; spiral out of hand. You'd be surprised how many folks up here believe the stories about jackbooted soldiers and black helicopters and the New World Order. I'd hate to see this turn into some sort of Waco."

I had an idea. "Would they be less freaked out by Knoxville police? KPD has a great SWAT team. They serve a lot of high-risk warrants, and this guy Shiflett sounds about as high-risk as they come." O'Conner drummed his fingers, pondering the suggestion. "Sure, they're outsiders, too," I conceded, "but they're East Tennessee outsiders. Some of them probably have kinfolk up here."

O'Conner pondered further, then looked inquiringly at his deputy. Waylon answered the unspoken question with a fine-by-me shrug. "Sold," said the sheriff. "I'll make the call."

I took out my cell phone, searched my contacts for "KPD Decker," then slid the phone across the desk. "Captain Brian Decker. The SWAT team commander. He's a good guy."

O'Conner looked mildly surprised, then smiled, took the phone, and pressed the "call" button. After three rings, I heard Decker's familiar voice spooling from the tiny speaker in a thin thread of sound, faint but distinct. "Hey, Doc. Everything okay?"

"Captain Decker, this is Jim O'Conner, the sheriff up in Cooke County. Not to worry—everything's fine. Dr. Brockton just loaned me his phone to call you, since he's got your number in his contacts." He put the phone closer to his ear, muffling Decker's words. "Sure, I'll hand the phone back to Dr. Brockton in just a second. He suggested I call and see if your SWAT team might be able to help us serve a warrant on a fellow we think might not come quietly. . . . Murder suspect. . . . He's ex-military. Possible militia member. White supremacist. Permanently pissed off. . . . Exactly, one helluva nice guy."

They talked a while longer, then made a plan for Decker and two of his men to come to Cooke County later in the day to reconnoiter and formulate a plan.

O'Conner handed me the phone so Decker and I could finish the call. "Talk to me, Deck," I said. "What's the word on Satterfield? Any progress?"

"Well, hell," he said. "I was hoping you could tell me."

What was the line from *The Princess Bride*, that tongue-in-cheek fairy-tale movie my grandsons had made me watch a dozen times when they were younger? Oh, right: "Get used to disappointment."

MOST OF THE drive back to Knoxville was a grim, bleak blur. Miranda did not give me her ACLU lecture, although under the circumstances, a liberal rant about protecting civil liberties would have been a lot more pleasant than the dark fears and memories swirling in my mind.

Finally, as we approached the eastern outskirts of the city—about the time we passed the spot where Satterfield had killed several of his victims—Miranda spoke. She sounded as if she were far away—perhaps she'd been trying to get my attention for some time—and if I'd ever heard her voice so tentative, I couldn't remember when. "Excuse me? Dr. B?"

"Sorry," I said. "I was somewhere else. Didn't mean to ignore you."

"I didn't take it that way. And maybe I should just leave you alone."

"No, please," I said. "I'd appreciate some distraction."

"Well, if you don't want to talk about it, I understand." I waved away her concern, and she went on. "Satterfield—that all happened before my time."

I nodded. "You were probably in first grade," I said. "Twenty years ago? No, more than that—it was

1992. Bill Clinton was running for president. Clinton and Al Gore. Running against Bush the Elder." When I put it in those terms, it sounded as if several lifetimes had passed since Clinton first ran. "Wow. Elections were a lot more civilized back then, seems like. Now, campaigning's turned into a reality TV show. *Survivor* meets *Jerry Springer* or something."

"With some cage-fighting thrown in," she added. A pause. "I know Satterfield tried to kill you."

"Not just me. My whole family—Kathleen and Jeff and Jenny, who was Jeff's girlfriend at the time. They were in high school. Actually, Jeff was still in high school; Jenny had just graduated. Satterfield snuck into the house at dinnertime. He had come to UT and hidden in the back of my truck. I drove him right into our garage. Like inviting a vampire to come in, though I didn't know it, of course. We had just sat down at the kitchen table, the four of us, when he came up the stairs. The uninvited dinner guest from hell. If it hadn't been for Decker, and Tyler . . ." I trailed off, picturing the astonishing way our salvation arrived: a three-foot concrete statue of the archangel Michael, flying through the sliding glass door from the patio, his outstretched wings and raised sword pinning Satterfield to the wall.

"Tyler was your assistant?"

"He was. Tyler Wainwright, my first assistant." I looked at her. "My second-best assistant. Jeff and Jenny's son—the first one—is named for him."

"I remember you saying that once, when you introduced me to them at a cookout. One thing I never understood, though. Why did Satterfield come after you in the first place? He was a serial killer, preying on women. Prostitutes, right?" I nodded. "So why come after you—a professor—and your family?"

"Ah. For revenge. Satterfield was in the navy, and he wanted to be a SEAL. He was on the verge of getting in—*there's* a scary thought—but then he killed a woman, a stripper in San Diego. No, wait—Tijuana. Anyhow, I was called in to consult—one of the navy prosecutors was a former student of mine—and I was the one who found the evidence that the woman had been strangled."

"Her hyoid was broken?"

I nodded, smiling. "Bingo. But Satterfield was never tried. They had a circumstantial case, but no direct evidence. So all that happened was, he got kicked out of the navy."

"You're kidding. That's *it*?"

"That's it. But in his mind, I destroyed his dream. Ruined his life."

She took a moment to process this. "And then, instead of dying a painful death with your family, you lived—and helped put him behind bars." I nodded again. "So these twenty wasted years—"

"Twenty-four," I corrected.

"These twenty-four wasted years—also your fault?"

"I haven't asked him, but that'd be my guess."

"Jesus," she said. "He's coming, and he's pissed."

Never one to mince words, Miranda. "That," I agreed, "would be my guess. He's probably coming, and he's definitely pissed."

CHAPTER 25

MY CELL PHONE RANG, and I saw that the call was from Decker. "Hey, Deck," I said. "Is the cavalry all saddled up and ready to ride?"

"Cavalry? Hmm," he grunted. "Hope we make out better than Custer did at Little Bighorn. You coming?"

"Am I invited?"

"Sure you are," he said. "I mean, if you want to be."

"Absolutely. If you don't think I'll get in the way—or get shot."

"Well, dang," he said. "I was counting on you to draw fire away from my entry team, but if that's how you feel, I reckon you can hang out with me in the command post instead."

"Deal," I told him. "I wouldn't want to show up your men."

"You wanna ride with me?"

"Sure. Can't think of a safer place to be."

"Ha," he said. "Never ridden with me, have you?

But if you're feeling brave and want to come along, meet me in the south parking lot at KPD. We'll roll out in about an hour."

THE KNOXVILLE POLICE Department occupied a drab, hulking four-story building of brick and concrete atop Summit Hill, situated across a low valley from the city's downtown. Through the valley flowed the concrete ditch called First Creek and the concrete freeway called James White Parkway, both of them spanned by a series of bridges, some old and graceful, others new and boring.

By and large, Decker's SWAT team members were built like linebackers and shorn like soldiers: muscled but not fat; clean-shaven, most of them sporting crew cuts and flattops. If there was a mustache or beard anywhere, I didn't see it. Clearly they took their physical training seriously, which made sense, given the heavy thuddings and clankings of their bulletproof vests and high-powered weaponry.

If I hadn't known the target to be a lone wolf, I'd have thought the team was about to invade a third world country. Fifteen or twenty men in fatigues and vests were milling about—it was hard to count accurately, as they were coming and going between KPD's basement and a small fleet of vehicles, lugging equipment and an astonishing assortment of weaponry. I saw short-barreled shotguns, long-barreled sniper rifles, military-style automatic assault rifles, belts of machine-gun ammunition, and what appeared to be a cross between a 1920s Tommy gun and the world's biggest six-shooter, which Decker appeared to be loading with the world's largest bullets. "What the hell is *that*?" I asked. "It looks like something Arnold Schwarzenegger or Bruce Willis might use in a Hollywood shoot-'em-up."

He grinned happily. "It's a forty-millimeter grenade launcher."

"Grenades? Jesus, Deck. You guys don't mess around, do you?"

"We don't," he said, "but we're not using it to fire fragmentation grenades." Was I imagining it, or was there a trace of wistfulness in his voice? "It's the kinder, gentler grenade launcher. Tear gas or pepper powder or foam batons or distractants."

"Distractants?"

"Flashbangs. Stun grenades." He flipped open the weapon's rotary cylinder, then slid one of the cartoonishly big shells from its chamber and handed it to me. It was three inches long and nearly two inches in diameter. "It's got a one-and-a-half-second delay. Shoot it through a window, and *bam*, it goes off with enough noise and light and shock wave to disorient the bad guy for about five seconds." I nodded; I knew—from a narrow-escape personal experience several years before—what a blinding, deafening punch a stun grenade packed.

I carefully handed it back to him, and he reloaded it, flipped the cylinder back into place, and laid the weapon in the back of his truck, atop a heap of other weapons of various sizes and shapes. Amid the blocky, angular black guns, I noticed an odd outlier nestled against the wheel well. A softly lustrous silver, it appeared scuffed and old—antique, almost, yet also futuristic, like some nineteenth-century imagining of a twentieth-century weapon. I pointed at it. "What's that one? That looks almost like it should be in a museum."

"It should be." He reached in, hauled it out, and held it up, grinning. "It's an M3 submachine gun. From World War II. Better known as a grease gun."

"That's a grease gun?" He nodded. I peered at the weapon. It had a pistol grip, a stubby barrel, a long ammunition clip, and a bare-bones shoulder stock, if stock was the right word for a U-shaped length of quarter-inch steel rod. The gun's central feature, to which all these components attached, was a fat cylindrical body, the size and shape of an oversized tube of caulk. Unlike any other gun I'd ever seen, this one appeared to be made of sheet metal—a cylinder of stamped and rolled sheet metal—rather than a solid block of machined steel. Decker handed me the gun, and I raised it to my shoulder. It was surprisingly light, owing, I surmised, to its sheet-metal construction. "This is amazing," I said. "I've heard of these, but never seen one. It's called a grease gun because of the shape?"

He nodded. "Exactly. Looks like the gizmo your auto mechanic uses to squirt lube into your wheel bearings. Although this one squirts .45-caliber pistol bullets."

The gun was fascinating; also puzzling. "And . . . you actually *use* this? No offense, but it looks obsolete."

He chuckled. "It *is* obsolete, but I love it. We've got six, and yeah, we use 'em." He took it from me, slid a finger into the chamber, and pulled it back. I heard a click that I recognized as the sound of a trigger cocking. "You see how simple this is? A lot simpler than any of our other automatic weapons. We carry these if we're wearing hazmat suits and respirators and gloves—if we're going into a meth lab, for instance. The barrel's short, so the accuracy's not terrific. But for close quarters? It's a great get-off-me gun."

The loading up continued all around us—more and more weaponry packed into formidable vehicles by police who looked like commandos—and I couldn't hold back the question. "I gotta ask, Deck. Y'all really need all this firepower here in scruffy little Knoxville?"

He was returning the grease gun to the heap of weapons in the back of his truck. He paused and turned to look at me, giving a shrug that was more a gesture of politeness than an indication of doubt. "Better to have it and not need it than need it and not have it."

I RODE WITH Decker at the head of a small convoy, in his black, rubber-coated Expedition, the heavily tinted windows giving the blue-sky day a dusky aspect, as if the sun were partially eclipsed. Directly behind us was an olive-drab Humvee—"up-armored," Decker explained, with half-inch steel doors, and bulletproof windows that could keep out anything smaller than .50-caliber ammunition. Behind that came the mammoth armored vehicle the SWAT team had euphemistically dubbed the BFT—an acronym for "big fuckin' truck," Decker explained, his sheepishness mixed with obvious pride. The BFT—with room inside for twenty

SWAT team members and their weapons—was built to repel not just gunfire but chemical, biological, and radiological assaults, too. If Armageddon came calling on East Tennessee, the inside of the BFT was clearly the place with the best odds of survival.

As we barreled east on I-40, we attracted more than a few stares from passing motorists, as well as a fairly equal mixture of thumbs-up signs and worried frowns. But not even the unhappiest frowners, I noticed, dared to flip us off.

After winding along River Road into downtown Jonesport, we rendezvoused behind the courthouse with one of O'Conner's deputies. "The sheriff and Waylon's up yonder near the Shiflett place with your recon team," he told Decker. The SWAT team commander had sent a pair of two-man teams up the night before—two spotters and two snipers—to get eyes on the suspect, if possible. They'd glimpsed lights on in the house, barely visible behind heavy curtains, but they hadn't seen any movement. O'Conner and Decker had talked strategy at daybreak; they had considered simply waiting until Shiflett emerged, then surrounding his truck, the way the FBI had nabbed some of the Oregon protesters when they left the Malheur National Wildlife Refuge to drive to a nearby town. "Trouble is, he could hole up there for weeks or months," O'Conner said. "He's totally off the grid, which means we can't cut off his water or power. He's a survivalist from way back, which means he's got months' worth of food and water stockpiled. I don't have the resources to sit on him that long. Besides, if he gets wind of us, he'll just sneak out—he grew up in these mountains, and his wilderness skills are good."

"All right, then," Decker had said. "If you can't wait till he comes out, we'll go in and get him for you."

Shiflett lived in a mountain hollow just outside Del Rio, at the end of a long dirt road. Decker pulled into the turnoff and stopped at a stout metal gate, which was secured with a heavy chain and a massive padlock. The rest of the convoy eased onto the shoulder of the blacktop, although the BFT, practically scraping the trees, still occupied half the roadway.

In case the locked gate and standard red-and-black NO TRESPASSING and KEEP OUT signs weren't enough to deter visitors, a profusion of other signs wired to the gate underscored the message: One, illustrated with a skull and crossbones, read, IS THERE LIFE AFTER DEATH? TRESPASS AND FIND OUT. Another bore the image of an assault rifle; underneath was a circle containing the crosshairs of a scope, centered on a red dot labeled YOU ARE HERE. A third warned, WE DON'T DIAL 911. WE CALL THE CORONER.

In addition to the warning signs, the gate was flanked on one side by a Confederate battle flag and on the other by a yellow-and-black flag; it depicted a rattlesnake coiled around an assault rifle, captioned with the dual messages DON'T TREAD ON LIBERTY and THE RIGHT TO KEEP AND BEAR ARMS.

Decker got out, opened his truck's cargo door, and extricated an immense bolt cutter. He gave the handles a squeeze, and the padlock's shackle snapped loudly. He was about to push the gate open when I saw him freeze. After a long, tense pause, during which his body remained motionless while he scanned the woods on both sides of the driveway, he removed his hands from the gate and backed away slowly.

He clambered back into the truck. "Shit," he muttered, then reached for his radio. "Decker here. Vests on. Everybody. Now." I shot him a questioning look, and I got my answer when he keyed the radio mike again. "The gate's booby-trapped. Everybody sit tight. He's not gonna make this easy."

He exited the truck again and went to the back once more, and I heard him rummaging around. When he stepped to the gate again, he was wearing an armored vest and a helmet and was carrying a riot shield, which he held against the left side of his body. In his right hand, I glimpsed a pair of wire cutters. Threading his hand through the bars of the gate, he maneuvered the tool gingerly into position, then slowly squeezed. I felt myself brace for a bang or a boom, but neither came, and after a moment I slowly let out the breath that I'd been holding. Decker, too, seemed to unwind slightly, and after another moment, he gave the gate a tentative push, still protecting his left side with the shield. The gate swung open a couple of feet, again without triggering any sort of blast, and again I felt myself unclench.

Pocketing the wire cutters, Decker turned toward the truck but paused, midturn, facing the left side of the gate. Then, bizarrely, he lifted his right hand and gave a small wave: like a beauty queen in SWAT gear. After he'd stashed the shield in the back of the truck and climbed back in, I said, "What was *that* about?"

"He's got a surveillance camera hidden in a stump over there. Right beside the shotgun that was wired to the gate. If he's watching, he knows we're here. Might as well let him know that *we* know that *he* knows."

Once I had untangled the convoluted sentence, I nodded. "Makes sense. Show him that you're onto his tricks, and that you're not scared. Probably ups the pressure on him."

He gave a tight smile. "Doc, we have not even *begun* to apply pressure." He picked up the radio mike again and told his men the order in which he wanted the vehicles to enter: the armored Humvee first, followed by the BFT, then the two conventional, unarmored trucks. "Fan out and stop as soon as you get to the clearing," he added. "Let's keep our distance from the house."

Decker backed away from the gate and into the roadway, allowing the Humvee and the other three vehicles to enter the driveway ahead of us. Moving slowly, the Humvee pushed the gate; it opened wide and our convoy proceeded down the quarter-mile dirt lane, lurching and bucking over the ruts. The ride was relatively rough in Decker's civilized Expedition, so I imagined it to be bone-jarring in the Humvee and the BFT.

We emerged from the woods and into a large clearing, roughly the size of a football field, its center occupied by a squat, hulking log cabin, one that looked like a throwback to frontier days. The windows were few and small, and I suspected that even without curtains, the interior would have been dark as a cave. "Hmm," Decker said, then, "Christ. You see the gunports?" I took a closer look. Sure enough, several horizontal slits had been sawed through the front wall.

Decker radioed a team member named Ron. "Ron, take the BFT up close to the house and use the PA system to call him out. No point playing coy. Might as well get right up in his face."

The truck began lumbering forward, its angled windshield and hood half as high as the cabin's porch roof. "Is that safe?" I asked.

Decker gave a slight shrug. "Probably. The truck's built for threat level four—armor-piercing bullets; biological and chemical agents—so unless he's got a grenade launcher or a howitzer in there, there's not much way he can hurt it."

The vehicle stopped only a few feet from the front porch. "Jimmy Ray Shiflett, we have a warrant for your arrest," the officer's voice rang out, the drawl amplified by a factor of ten. "Come out unarmed, with your hands up and in plain sight."

We waited, but no one emerged, so we waited some more. Still no one. "Tell him again," Decker radioed Ron. Ron did as he was told, but Shiflett did not. After another long wait, Decker ordered, "See if the third time's the charm." Ron tried once more, but the third time was not the charm.

"Too bad," Decker said, "but not surprising." He got on the radio again. "Ron? Come on back to the tree line for now. Jake? Let's get some eyes in the sky." He looked at me with a grin. "Want to see our newest toy?"

"Sure, if it doesn't get me shot."

"Not to worry." He put the truck in gear and followed the BFT to the edge of the clearing, then tucked in behind it, so we were shielded. The big vehicle's rear door was already open, and one of Decker's men was leaning inside, removing tubes and motors and other parts from a large plastic case. Decker motioned me to follow him, so I got out and wandered up to the back of the truck.

"Doc, this is Jake, one of our pilots. We just got this baby last month. It's a DJI Inspire drone. This is only our third mission with it."

As I watched, Jake fitted together the drone's tubular framework—carbon-fiber tubes that snapped together to form an H, each leg about two feet long—and then began attaching rotors at each of the four corners, followed by a chunky central module that appeared to contain an electric battery and a swiveling camera. "It's powered by a twenty-four-volt lithium ion battery," Decker explained. "Like a cordless drill or circular saw. Gives us about thirty minutes of flight time. We've got a rack with spare batteries always on charge, so if we run low, we land and swap out. The camera's got high-def video and night-vision capability, so we can get HD imagery day or night. It's also got infrared—thermal—so we can look for hot spots, like people."

Decker helped Jake lift the drone out of the truck and set it on the ground. Then Jake removed a control unit from the big case and powered it up, and with a soft whir, the drone rose into the warm sky and floated toward the house, a surreal *Star Wars*-looking craft flying toward a backwoods Tennessee cabin.

A FLICKER OF movement caught my eye, a speck drifting across the sky, so subtle that at first I took it for a floater inside my eyeball. But the speck was soon joined by another, and then several more, and they drifted closer, silent and graceful, silhouetted against the brilliant blue November sky.

I nudged Decker to get his attention, then pointed at the aerial congregation that was gathering, now beginning to circle over one edge of the clearing. "Reckon your drone could slip into formation with those buzzards? Follow their noses to whatever they're smelling?"

Decker grunted, then radioed the pilot. "You see the buzzards? Just above the southeast edge of the woods?" After a pause, he added, "Sure, go on down and take a look. Let us know if you see anything."

"Too bad that drone's not carrying a smell-o-vision camera," I said, and Decker smiled.

A moment later, his head snapped up and he raised a pair of binoculars, sighting toward the distant tree line. "They've got a visual of a body on the ground," he said. "Cold. It's not showing up on infrared. I'm gonna take two teams over there. One to check it out, the other to cover them, in case there's any threat from the house. We'll move the BFT and the Humvee around there, too. Soon as we—"

Decker was interrupted by the warble of a pager. He snatched it off his hip and glanced at the display, then muttered, "Shit." He looked around for his deputy commander. "Ron," he called.

Ron jogged over. "What's up, Captain?"

"We've got a hostage situation in Knoxville," he said. "Domestic disturbance. I've got to scoot. I'll take my truck, the Humvee, and an entry team. You and the other guys follow once you've cleared the house here."

AN HOUR LATER, I found myself staring down at the bloated body and blasted face of Jimmy Ray Shiflett, if Waylon's memory and the driver's license photo could be trusted. The body lay a few feet from a massive stump. Judging by the bloating and the insect activity—swarming green blowflies, white dabs I recognized as masses of fly eggs, and swarms of small, freshly hatched maggots in the eyes, nose, and gaping crater of a mouth, he'd been dead for somewhere between twelve and twenty-four hours.

A hole freshly dug beneath one side of the stump was filled with a slurry that Waylon sniffed and then carefully tasted before pronouncing it a mixture of ammonium nitrate and nitromethane—"rocket fuel, basically," he said. "The stuff them long, skinny drag-racing cars burn." He frowned. "That right there's the same stuff Tim McVeigh used to blow up the federal building in Oklahoma City, kill all them workers and little kids."

"But what happened here?" I asked. "This stuff in the ground didn't go off, but *something* must've gone off, to do this to him." The "this" I was referring to was massive damage to the dead man's face. Much of his mandible appeared to have been blown off, along with some of his upper teeth and part of the upper jaw. His right thumb and first two fingers were destroyed as well.

Waylon gave a dismissive grunt. "What a dumb-ass," he said, peering down at the dead man. "Always thinking the fed'ral gov'mint or the U-nit-ed Na-tions was gonna come haul him off to some prison camp. But he ends up killing his own self with plain stupidity."

"Waylon, I'm not quite following you," I said. "What do you mean?"

"Hell, the stupid sumbitch, he bit down on a blasting cap. To crimp the end." He pointed at two bits of thin, insulated wire, one red and one yellow, lying on the ground nearby. "Them there's the wires. He set the fuckin' thing off in his own damn mouth."

"Ouch, man," I said. "Seems like pliers might have been a better choice."

"Pliers is for sissies, guy like him'd say," Waylon scoffed. "What's them awards for folks that do stupid stuff that kills 'em?"

"The Darwin Awards?" I asked, and he nodded. "Survival of the fittest," I agreed. "Or at least of the nonidiotic."

O'Conner, Steve Morgan of the FBI, and Deck-er's colleague Ron were off to one side conferring, and I saw the sheriff make a phone call. When he finished, the three of them joined Waylon and me beside the body. "This guy is determined to make our job harder, even after he's dead," O'Conner said to me.

"What do you mean?"

"Explosives are involved. That means we've got to call in the ATF."

"Makes sense," I said. I had worked several cases with the ATF—officially renamed the Bureau of Alcohol, Tobacco, Firearms and Explosives, but still informally called the ATF—and I respected their expertise. "Given that the gate was booby-trapped, and the guy has explosives, probably a good idea to let them check the place out, get rid of anything dangerous." I nodded at the body. "Can somebody give me and my friend a ride back to Knoxville? Not that there seems much doubt about cause of death, but the sooner we get him to the medical examiner, the less smelly he'll be."

O'Conner frowned. "Like I said, this guy's making it hard for us. *All* of us. Including you, Doc." I must have looked confused, because he added, "The ATF doesn't want us to disturb anything—not even the body—until they've made sure everything's safe."

I was about to protest—inspecting the body for explosives at this point seemed like installing a barn-door surveillance camera after the horse had been stolen—but I saw Ron and Morgan both nod, and I decided there was no point arguing about a delay designed to keep me from getting blown up. *Be a shame to win a Darwin Award of my own*, I realized. "Any idea when they'll release the body?"

"I asked the same thing. He said probably within a day."

"That's reasonable, I guess," I conceded. "The good news is, it's not hot. Tonight's low is supposed to be near forty."

"In Knoxville?" asked Waylon, and I nodded. "So

it'll get down to about freezing up here," he said. "Be just like keepin' him in the meat locker. He'll stay fresh as a daisy."

"Sure," I said, eyeing the growing number of buzzards wheeling overhead. With each spiral they edged closer, and by the time O'Conner assigned Waylon to drive me back to Knoxville, I felt as if I'd just escaped from a bad scene in the Hitchcock film *The Birds*.

CHAPTER 26

"SHALL WE BEGIN?"

Eddie Garcia's three simple words, spoken with quiet formality and a slight Spanish accent, made me smile. It had been a while since I had stood elbow to elbow with Eddie during an autopsy, and I realized I had missed the corpse-side camaraderie. In some ways Eddie—Dr. Edelberto Garcia, M.D., Knox County's medical examiner—was my polar opposite: slight and dapper, well groomed and well dressed, from an aristocratic family in Mexico City. But bring us together over a body, and those superficial differences dropped away, and we were simply colleagues and kindred spirits, equally eager to commune with the dead and hear their stories. To be sure, my anthropologist ears were attuned to older stories, while Eddie's pathologist ears tended to listen for fresher tales of tragedy. A body like Shiflett's—several days past its peak of freshness—was nearing the outer limits of Eddie's expertise and verging into my own, but the corpse's condition gave us enough overlapping interest to provide an excuse to hang out together in the autopsy suite.

Eddie folded back the sheet, exposing Shiflett's mangled face and bloating body. "I'm sorry Miranda could not join us," he said. "Her insights are always worthwhile, and sometimes quite unexpected."

"She sends regrets," I said. "*Painful* regrets. Her dissertation defense is next week, and she's frantically preparing."

He nodded. "I have read this dissertation. Twice, in fact. A remarkable piece of work, I think. Do you agree?"

"I've never read anything like it," I said truthfully; then—before he had a chance to drag me into Fourier analysis or other mathematical waters that were over my head—I changed the subject. "If you don't mind my asking, how are your hands?"

My question contained equal measures of curiosity, concern, and amazement. A few years before, Eddie's hands had been terribly burned by radiation. A physicist in Oak Ridge—"the Atomic City"—had been murdered by a radioactive pellet: a powerful imaging source hidden inside a vitamin capsule. Eddie, not realizing what he was handling, had removed the pellet from the dead man's intestine, and as he held it in his hands—for no more than sixty seconds—the radiation had inflicted irreversible damage. He had tried bionic prosthetics—a pair of i-limb hands, which looked straight out of *Star Wars*—but the lack of tactile feedback had made them only marginally useful for a physician whose work required deftness with scalpels, forceps, and microscope slides. So when he was offered the chance for a dual hand transplant at Emory University, Eddie had accepted without hesitating, despite the risk that sepsis might set in, or his body's immune system might reject the new hands completely, or the nerves might not regenerate fully. So my deceptive question carried a lot of weight, and a lot of worry.

By way of an answer, Eddie stretched out both hands, his gloved fingers extended and spread wide. Next he clenched and unclenched both hands slowly, then touched each of his fingertips to his thumbs, one by one. Finally he extended his right hand toward me—toward my own hand—offering to shake. I took his hand in mine, and when he gripped, my eyes widened, first in admiration, then in something approaching pain. "Uncle," I said, only half joking, and when he released my hand, his smile matched my own. "Eddie, that's amazing. I'm thrilled the transplants have worked so well."

"I thought my career was over," he said. "I don't often use the word 'miracle,' but I can't think of a more accurate term for this. It has given me back my work. My life. My wholeness." And with that, we hitched up our paper masks. And we began.

We started by simply looking once Eddie had cut away the clothing. Jimmy Ray Shiflett was a tall, sinewy guy, measuring six feet, two inches, weighing one hundred eighty-three pounds, clothed. He wasn't beefy, in the way of weight lifters and bodybuilders, but he was muscled in a lean, ropy way—a cowboy way—and I suspected that his military service and militia training had instilled in him a regimen of regular workouts. Hard to fight the battle of

Armageddon, I supposed—or the New Civil War, or whatever war might present itself—if you're fat and out of shape.

The most striking thing about him, of course, was his blasted face. It drew my eye irresistibly—horrifyingly—even when I tried to focus elsewhere. And there was abundant evidence of other trauma, earlier trauma, elsewhere on his body. In addition to the tattoos, Shiflett's skin bore a profusion of scars attesting to fistfights (layer upon layer of scar tissue on his knuckles), bludgeon fights (star-shaped scars on his cheek and scalp), even knife fights (long, healed gashes in an upper arm and the lower belly).

Eddie interrupted his dictated inventory of the scars long enough for a side comment to me. "Nobody would accuse him of having a soft life."

"Just a guess," I said, "but I'd hate to see the other guys. I suspect they look even worse." I caught myself looking at the face again. "Except, of course, for . . . you know."

"Indeed. By the way, do you need me to take DNA samples for identification? Dental records are perhaps not ideal in this case."

"Perhaps not," I echoed, amused by his wry understatement. "But no, we don't need DNA. The TBI took fingerprints from the hand that didn't get blasted. The prints in his service records are a match. It's Shiflett, for sure."

Eddie nodded, then, with deft strokes of a scalpel, he made a Y-shaped incision, cutting from each shoulder to the breastbone, then down the chest and abdomen to the pubic bone. He laid the scalpel aside, then tugged open the flaps he'd made, expos-

ing the rib cage and viscera. As he did, I was struck
again by his hands: if I didn't know they'd been cut
from a cadaver and stitched onto Eddie's wrists, I
wouldn't have guessed there'd ever been a thing
wrong with them.

Using a stout pair of shears, he cut the ribs and
opened the chest cavity, moving swiftly, removing
and weighing the heart and lungs, then slicing open
each and examining the interior, dictating, as he
worked, into a microphone suspended over the autopsy table. For a dead guy, Shiflett appeared remarkably healthy—except, of course, for . . . you know.

Finally I decided to stop resisting and just give
in—just *look* at the damn face. "Eddie," I said,
stretching both hands toward the head, "do you
mind?"

"Please, be my guest." And with a courtly gesture, including a slight, humorous bow, he stepped
back to give me free access.

I wasn't sure what I was looking for, never having
examined a face that had been decimated by a blasting cap, but aside from the gruesome disfigurement,
I found it fascinating. A few sluggish maggots—the
eggs laid and hatched during the day or three when
Shiflett's body had been accessible to blowflies—
were running for cover, fleeing down the throat
or up into the skull. Their numbers were far fewer
than I was accustomed to—corpses at the Body
Farm teemed with maggots by the thousands—so I
ignored them, figuring that they'd either get out of
the way or get squashed by my probing hands.

The head was already tilted back, supported by a
neck block that either Eddie or a morgue assistant

had positioned beforehand, and the mangled mandible hung down, almost as if Shiflett were wearing a grisly war trophy around his neck—the jawbone of an enemy he had killed in battle. *We have met the enemy, and he is us,* I thought, a memorable quote from my favorite childhood comic strip, "Pogo." Thanks to the neck block and the dangling mandible, I had an unobstructed view into the mouth cavity, or, rather, into what used to be the mouth cavity, once upon a time.

The blast damage was both massive and intricate: massive because the bones of the face and the floor of the skull tended to be far thinner and more delicate than, say, the cranium or the cheekbones, which were rugged enough to withstand substantial impacts; intricate because the bones were not just thin but also irregular in shape. I remembered Miranda's description of the sphenoid, the floor of the skull, as the "bat-bone" because of its winged appearance.

As I explored the abyss of carnage—my spelunking lit by the surgical light I pulled down from above, angling and swiveling it this way and that—I found myself surprised by the depth of the damage. "Look at this, Eddie," I said, stepping back so he could lean in for a better view. "If he was biting the blasting cap with his incisors, I'd expect most of the energy from the explosion to vent out of his mouth, wouldn't you?"

"That seems reasonable," he said mildly. "And yet there appears to be extensive trauma to the throat— the top of the trachea and the esophagus are macerated." He reached a finger in and moved a flap of tissue aside. "Also, two of the cervical vertebrae are partially exposed. C-3 and C-4, it appears."

"You're kidding." Eddie stepped back deferentially, and I peered in again. "I'll be damned," I murmured. "You're right." I straightened up, partly to fend off what felt like a neck cramp, partly to take a wider look, and partly to think. When I leaned down again, I focused on the teeth, and what I saw puzzled me. The incisors—which by rights ought to have been blown to kingdom come, roots and all— were simply snapped instead, folded forward in a hinge fracture.

I had seen hundreds of hinge fractures in my time. Land teeth-first on a concrete curb, or whack somebody across the mouth with a baseball bat, and the incisors will fold inward, breaking through the thin, bony walls of their sockets as they fold. Shiflett's teeth, of course, were folded outward, not inward, but it was the fact that they were folded— not shattered or pulverized—that I found puzzling. No: electrifying—a slow, building buzz of mental current.

"Eddie," I finally said, "if I didn't know better, I'd think he was swallowing that blasting cap, not biting down on the end, when it went off."

Eddie studied my own face for several seconds before turning again to Shiflett's. He leaned in again, swiveling the light, and then reached in with one hand, feeling the interior surfaces. "Jesus, Eddie, be careful. Some of that bone is really splintered. You don't want to stick yourself."

"That's true," he said. "I still have to take immunosuppressants to avoid rejection, so I need to be careful about bloodborne pathogens. But some things require touch, as you know." I held my breath until he withdrew his hand. Seeing my nervousness, he smiled and held out his fingers so we could both inspect them. "You see," he said calmly, "no damage." He looked back at the corpse's face again. "I think you are correct," he mused. "The epicenter—if I may use that word for a small explosion rather than a large earthquake?—seems to be at the back of the buccal cavity, between the base of the tongue and the posterial wall of the oropharynx. The damage seems to radiate outward in all directions from there, rather than from the front of the mouth. In fact, if you wish to feel it, you'll find a deep crater at the back of the tongue, consistent with immediate proximity to the blast."

I believed him, and I didn't particularly want to stick my hand down the guy's throat. "It might be interesting to take x-rays and a CT scan," I said, "to get a better look at the geometry of the damage—to confirm all this."

Eddie gave another of his formal, inclining nods. "An excellent suggestion."

"But unless those images contradict what we're seeing and feeling and thinking, I'd say that our man Shiflett here wasn't biting down on that blasting cap when it went off."

"No, apparently not," agreed Eddie. "It would almost appear that he was trying to swallow it."

"Or trying *not* to." I turned for one more look, and when I did, I accidentally stepped on Eddie's foot. For a moment I was off balance, and in that moment, I instinctively reached out to steady myself. My hand nudged the block that was wedged beneath the shoulders, and it shifted beneath my weight. When it did, the corpse's head turned toward me. *Flopped* toward me. I shot a startled look at Eddie, then looked back at the corpse. The head was rotated a full 90 degrees. Reaching out with both hands, I gently rotated it back to center, then continued rotating until I had turned it 180 degrees. "My God," I said, "did you know this?"

"I had no idea," Eddie said. "This case is getting very interesting."

AN HOUR LATER, after I had changed out of my surgical scrubs and returned to my office at the north end of Neyland Stadium, the Cooke County sheriff's dispatcher patched me through to Jim O'Conner, who was winding up his second day at the Shiflett place with the ATF team.

"Broken? You're sure?"

"I'm sure, Jim. His neck was snapped, and his spinal cord was severed."

"It didn't seem broken when they took the body away."

"He was still in rigor mortis then. The muscles would have stabilized the head. Now he's out of rigor, and his neck's as floppy as a limp noodle."

"Interesting," he said.

"It gets even more interesting, Jim. The severed spinal cord was the cause of death. His heart and his lungs stopped working instantly. The blasting cap was just a smokescreen, shoved down his throat and detonated after he was dead."

"What makes you think that? Couldn't the shock wave from the explosion have done the damage to his spine?"

"Could've, maybe, but didn't," I told him. "The CT scan shows torsional damage to the vertebral column and the spinal cord. His neck was broken by a hard twist, not a shock wave. Besides, there's no way he could have been biting that blasting cap when it went off. The x-ray and the CT scan both show that it was halfway down his throat when it went off."

"Damn," he said. "Are you willing to repeat all that to the ATF's point man? This definitely sounds like it could affect his investigation."

"Sure. What's his name?"

"Special Agent Tim Kidder."

"Oh, I know Kidder. I worked a case with him just a few months ago. He's good. Put him on."

I heard the phone change hands.

"Dr. Brockton? Tim Kidder here."

"Hey, Tim. Glad to hear ATF is sending in the best. You having fun up in Cooke County?"

"It's a blast," he said—a joke I felt sure he'd made countless times in his career. "Sheriff O'Conner says you've got an interesting update for me."

"I think so." I told Kidder what I'd told O'Conner. He listened without interrupting, except for a few monosyllabic grunts to register surprise or thoughtfulness.

"That *is* interesting," he said when I was finished.

"Would y'all like me to send you copies of the x-rays and CT scans? That way, you guys can tell me if I've misread anything," I said. "Besides, the images might be useful for training, too—give your folks some interesting insight into blast-related trauma."

"That'd be great, Doc," said Kidder. "I'm glad you passed this along. I think maybe it explains something we've been wondering about up here at the scene. Something that doesn't add up."

"Such as?"

"There's a shed in the woods here where our detectors are going crazy. Alerting for dynamite, nitroglycerin, ammonium nitrate, C-4, and a couple other things only demolition experts have ever heard of."

"Y'all be careful taking that stuff out," I said.

"No need to be, Doc. The shed's empty. The detectors are alerting on residues. *Only* residues. Leftover traces of stuff that isn't here anymore."

"So you're saying there was a lot of stuff in the shed at some point—"

"No. Recently. *Very* recently."

"But now it's gone?"

"Gone, baby, gone," he said. "And from what you just told me about Jimmy Ray Shiflett and his afternoon snack, I'm thinking somebody besides him cleaned out that shed."

I had a bad feeling. "So what you're saying, Tim, is that we might be looking for a killer who's got explosives and isn't afraid to use them?"

"Not 'might be' looking, Doc. *Are* looking. I just hope we find him fast."

"I'll let you get to it," I said. "And I'll get those x-rays and scans to you right away." He thanked me and hung up.

I turned, with a sigh, to page seven in Miranda's dissertation and resumed reading, my eyelids instantly feeling heavy. I'd slogged through only a paragraph when my door suddenly boomed with a frantic pounding. I whirled in my chair, muttering, "*What* the—"

"Doc? You in there? Dr. Brockton!"

My heart still hammering, I unlocked the door—I'd been careful to lock it, ever since Satterfield's escape—and opened it. "Jesus, Deck, you scared the living crap out of me. What the hell?"

"Is it true, what I heard about Shiflett?" His eyes were wild, and he looked almost unhinged.

"Come on in, Deck," I said, in what I hoped was a calming voice. "Have a seat, and tell me what you heard."

He came in, but he didn't—wouldn't—sit down. Instead, he paced back and forth, back and forth, like a caged tiger. "I heard his face was blown off. His face and part of his hand."

"Yes, that's true. And his neck was broken."

"Dammit, Doc, why didn't you tell me?"

"Hell, Deck, I just found out. I just got out of the autopsy suite an hour ago."

"But you *saw* him—you saw his face and his hand—up there at the scene. Yesterday! Why didn't you call me?"

"What difference does it make, Deck? Why are you so upset?"

He whirled on me, furious now. "Christ almighty, Doc, don't you see? It's him. Satterfield."

"The dead guy? No way."

"No, goddammit!" he shouted. "Not the dead

guy—the *killer*, dumb-ass! Don't you remember what Satterfield did to the pizza delivery guy, twenty-four years ago? He killed the guy, traded clothes with him, and put a stick of dynamite in the kid's mouth, with his hands around it. We had his house surrounded, zipped up tight, but he drove off in that shitty delivery car with the Domino's signs, right under our noses. Thirty minutes later, *bam!* We go charging in, and it looks like Satterfield has offed himself." He stared at me angrily. "How can you not even *remember* that?"

"I never saw that, Deck," I reminded him gently. "I wasn't there, remember? Y'all told me to stay away. I left my office and drove home—with Satterfield hiding in the back of my own truck. The Trojan horse, 1992-style. Thank God my assistant slowed him down, and you came charging in."

"I should've blown his head off," Decker said bitterly.

"I should've let you," I admitted. "But hindsight's always 20/20, right? So here we are."

It was easy now to understand Decker's agitation, because his brother—a bomb-squad technician—had died at Satterfield's house that day. Decker had struggled for years with PTSD, I knew—once, in my office years after his brother's death, something had triggered Deck's PTSD, and I'd had a hard time calming him. Lately, though—until this moment—he'd seemed recovered. But now, the more I grasped Decker's distress, the more agitated I felt, too. "Deck, what makes you think Satterfield had any connection to Shiflett? Do you have anything linking them?"

"The MO links them. It's exactly the same thing he did to the pizza guy. Almost exactly, anyhow. Only difference, that one was staged to look like a suicide, this one like an accident. But everything else? Explosive device detonated in the mouth, to throw us off the scent? Déjà vu all over again. It's Satterfield, Doc. *Has* to be!"

I hoped he was wrong. But that, I feared, was too much to hope for.

CHAPTER 27

MY INTERCOM BEEPED, AND I glared at it in annoyance. I was bleary and sleep deprived from another bad night: hours of restless thrashing punctuated by harrowing dreams of looming menace and terrible violence. Some of the dreams involved Satterfield, and some involved Shiflett, and one—the worst—involved both of them, teaming up to shove a blasting cap down my throat.

I resolved to ignore the call, but after half a dozen plaintive beeps, I couldn't stand it anymore. Snatching up the phone, I resisted the urge to shout. "Yes?" My voice was steady, calm, and icy.

There was a pause, then Peggy—her voice carefully casual—said, "Are you shunning me?"

"What? No, of course not." *Am I?* I wondered. *Maybe.* "I'm just preoccupied."

"Of course. Steve Morgan from the TBI is here. He's brought something he says you'll want to see. Shall I tell him you're preoccupied?"

Ouch, I thought. "No, send him down. He's been

here before. He knows how to find me." She rang off without saying good-bye. *A fine mess you've made with her,* I thought. Maybe our hand-holding was the opening of some sort of door to romance, or maybe it was simply a onetime fluke, a reflexive response to a scary scene in a movie. But I'd never know, if I kept acting as if it simply hadn't happened. What's more, I was introducing a barrier, a layer of awkwardness between Peggy and me, that hadn't existed until now.

Five minutes later I heard the stairwell door open and close, followed by a staccato tap-tap-tapping at my chamber door. I unlocked and opened the door, and Steve entered, a U-Haul book box tucked under one arm. "Looks like you've brought me a present," I said. "And it's not even my birthday." He set the box on my desk. "Can I shake it?"

"You could, but I wouldn't recommend it," he said. "You might want to glove up, though."

My pulse quickening, I snagged a pair of gloves from the box I kept at the ready—most people keep tissues on their desktops, but forensic anthropologists keep gloves—and then pulled on the gloves. Beneath the cardboard flaps was a thick wad of bubble wrap, which I grasped and lifted gingerly. "Is this what I think it is?" Steve's only answer was a one-shouldered shrug, accompanied by a we'll-see hoist of his eyebrows. I laid the bubble wrap to the side before I peered into the box's interior. "Yes," I said, reaching in with both hands, my fingers meeting at the bottom of the box. Carefully, like a priest raising the Communion host to be sanctified, I lifted the object: a human skull, surely as much in need of a blessing as any loaf of bread ever was. The skull was clean and pale, except for a vivid mark on the forehead—a reddish-brown swastika, ragged and smeared, as if traced by a finger dripped in blood.

I felt sure that the skull had come from a twenty-something male whose skeleton appeared European, both to me and to ForDisc; a male whose DNA looked Middle Eastern, to Delia's sequencing machines; and whose death, to any decent human being, had been horrific. "This was in Shiflett's house? A trophy?"

"Kinda looks that way."

The white-supremacist symbol on the forehead seemed not merely offensive but deeply ironic, for without the flesh, this skull—from a brown-skinned Middle Easterner—was indistinguishable from the skulls of the blond-haired, blue-eyed Aryans that the Nazis and the neo-Nazis considered the "master race." It had the same narrow nasal opening; the same sharp nasal sill beneath that opening; the same geometry in the cheekbones and eye orbits. *Brothers under the skin*, Delia had said when I'd given her the DNA sample a few days before. Trouble was, so many people had trouble seeing beneath the skin—beneath the surface differences—to the shared humanity at the core.

Steve nodded grimly. "That's not all. There's more in the bottom of the box."

I set the skull down gently on the bubble wrap I had already removed from the box, then peered inside again, but I saw only more bubble wrap. I took that out and saw that what I had taken for the box's bottom was actually a second box tucked inside, square but shallow. I slid my fingers down two sides of this box and lifted it out, then set it on the desk and removed a close-fitting lid. Inside, resting on a bed of odd, squiggly packing material, was a small leather-bound volume. Its dark green cover was embossed with ornate geometric designs in gold and red; the title was also stamped in gold—an exotic, swirling script I guessed to be Arabic.

The book's cover had been mutilated—the entire book had been mutilated, in fact—by what appeared to be a large-caliber gunshot. The entry wound, as I would have termed it if it were in a corpse, was a neat half-inch hole in the center of the cover. The exit, out the back, was ragged and twice that size. Bizarrely, the "wound" appeared to be bloody, and I stared in puzzlement, riffling through the volume, whose pages were all stained around the edges of the hole. I turned to Steve. "What on earth?"

"I suspect it's related to those," he said, pointing at the packing material in the shallow box. "The book and the skull were both settin' on those."

"But what are they?" He didn't answer, so I leaned down to examine the material. I had assumed they were made of cardboard, but looking closer, I saw they were furry, with longer tufts of hair at their ends. I reached in and plucked one from the box, holding it up to the light, my face a foot away. One end bore a tapered, inch-long tuft of hair; the other end was blunt—was cut—and bloody. "My God," I said. "These are pig tails?"

"Looks like it to me," he said, "but I'll ask the lab to confirm it."

I nodded in the direction of the other items. "So

I'm guessing that's pig blood on the skull and on the Quran?"

"Could be," he said, "but it might be Shiflett's—he might have wanted to mark his territory, like a dog pissing on a tree. The lab can test it with Hema-Trace, tell us if it's human or animal. Do you want to keep the skull?"

"I'd like to, yes. I want to get a facial reconstruction done. Put the likeness out there, see if anybody recognizes it. But I can scrape off some of the blood, so you can take that to the lab, too."

He nodded, and I rummaged around in my desk drawer for a scalpel. I cleaned the blade with an antibacterial wet wipe—another staple the Anthropology Department purchased in bulk and consumed at a rapid rate—and began scraping flakes of dried blood from the forehead onto a clean sheet of paper. After I'd scraped off a tiny heap of flakes—if the material were salt, I'd call the quantity a pinch—Steve said, "That's probably good." He folded the paper, marked it as evidence, and sealed it in the envelope I offered him.

"What else did y'all find?" I asked. "Hard evidence tying Shiflett to the kid chained to the tree?"

"Looks like it, though we need the computer forensics people's help."

"With what?"

"His computer's hard drive was erased."

"Crap," I said. "Although frankly, I'm kinda surprised this guy *had* a computer."

"Why, Doc? He did communications work in the military. And you know from the snuff film that he was savvy with video editing and social media."

"Good point," I conceded. "But what can the computer forensics people find, if the hard drive's been wiped clean?"

"Erased," he said, "but probably not wiped. Most people think that deleting files is enough to cover their tracks, but it's actually not."

"How's that?"

He shrugged, as if to say that he didn't fully understand it himself. "The way it was explained to me, deleting a file doesn't actually delete the file. It makes that file's space on the drive *available*, but the data doesn't really get removed. It just gets overwritten, a little at a time, as new data gets added. So a lot of the old data is still there, especially if there hasn't been a lot of new data. Sort of like deciding to paint your house a new color, but only painting for a few minutes every couple days. Gonna take a long time before that old paint's out of sight."

"Steve, you missed your calling," I said. "You should've been a computer scientist. Who dabbles in home improvements."

He laughed. "Point is, our computer nerds can probably recover a lot of the data."

"Well, I hope you're right."

He grinned and held up an index finger. "But wait, there's more. Much more. We found six video surveillance cameras, powered by a twelve-volt car battery. A video hard drive. DVDs with raw footage of the victim chained to the tree."

I felt my excitement rising. "That's great!" I winced at the way I'd said it, and he gave a shrug: absolution. He understood.

"Also a big assortment of hate literature. White

supremacy publications. Neo-Nazi stuff. A bunch of antigovernment stuff, including *The Turner Diaries*, Tim McVeigh's inspiration for Oklahoma City. Militia handbooks. DIY manuals on bomb making and sabotage."

I was afraid to ask my next question, but I was even more afraid not to ask it. "Steve, did you find anything that ties Jimmy Ray Shiflett to Nick Satterfield?"

His brow furrowed. "Satterfield? The escaped killer?" I nodded. "No, nothing. Whatever makes you ask that?"

"Forget it," I said. "Just jumpy, I guess. Hearing things go bump in the night."

MOST TABLES IN the bone lab were littered with bare bones. Joanna Hughes's table was occupied by human heads—some male, some female; some Anglo, some Latino; some smiling, some sad.

Despite the diversity, all the heads were the uniform gray of potter's clay. Joanna was a facial reconstruction artist—the first and, as far as I knew, the only student at UT to major in forensic art. She had devised the major herself, combining classes in sculpture, drawing, anatomy, and osteology: a combination that gave her detailed knowledge of how bones, muscles, and tendons meshed to create the complex structures of the human face. Reconstructing a face wasn't simply a matter of slathering clay onto a skull and mashing it around to create lips and noses and cheeks. No, reconstructing a face was a remarkably intricate process, requiring every muscle of the face to be created and applied, layered and

interwoven, just as they had been in life, before the
final covering of clay "skin," whose thickness had
to match precise scientific measurements of tissue
depth at numerous landmarks on the face and head.

In my younger days I had tried my hand at clay
facial reconstructions. The results were appalling:
my reconstructed John Does tended to look like
Neanderthals—and misshapen, stupid Neanderthals, at that. Perhaps, in hindsight, it was my failed
attempts at facial reconstruction that had taught me
to stick with things I could do well. And certainly
my own failed attempts had made it easy for me to
appreciate the remarkable blend of art and science
manifested in every one of Joanna's reconstructions.
Now, I was counting on that blend to show us what
the killer's grainy video had not: the face, in detail,
of our Cooke County murder victim.

When I walked into the bone lab with the skull
Steve Morgan had brought me, I arrived just in time
to see Joanna grab the nose of an African American
woman and twist it completely off the face. "Ouch,"
I said. "Why'd you do that?"

"I didn't like it," she said. "It didn't look right." She
frowned. "Noses are hard. There's no foundation of
bone to guide you. Nothing but a hole—the nasal
opening." She made a self-contradicting face. "Well,
actually, there is a formula for estimating breadth
and projection. But it still leaves a lot of margin—a
lot of requirement—for artistic interpretation. So
you just have to guess, from how massive or delicate
the rest of the face is, what sort of nose that particular face is asking for. And this face"—she nodded at
the one she had partially defaced—"wasn't asking

for the nose I gave her." She pushed back from the wooden table and eyed the box under my arm. "So that's him? The guy chained to the tree?" I nodded and handed her the box. She opened it and carefully removed the skull, studying it closely as she talked to me. "You said he's in his twenties?"

"Early twenties, at most. Could be as young as nineteen. But definitely not, say, twenty-seven."

"Wow, the bone structure is classic Caucasoid. But you said he's Middle Eastern?"

"According to the DNA."

"Crap," she said.

"What?"

"The nose. Narrow? Wide? Straight? Hooked? Middle Eastern noses are all over the map."

"So to speak," I said.

She laughed. "So to speak."

"You'll do fine," I assured her, as she set the skull on a cushion to one side of her table. "Just give him whatever nose the rest of his face wants to have." The last thing I saw, before I turned to go, was a scowling Joanna taking an X-acto knife to the face of the dead African American woman and, in the place where a nose had been only a few moments before, carving a two-inch question mark.

She'll do fine, I assured myself. *Really.*

CHAPTER 28

I THRASHED, AWAKE AND anxious, for most of the night—the new normal, apparently—then finally drifted off shortly before dawn. I woke up at eight, weary and bleary and astonishingly late for me, and called the bone lab. "Osteology lab, this is Miranda," answered my assistant, sounding far chirpier than I felt.

"Good morning," I said. "Sort of."

"Dr. B? Did you just wake up? I mean, *you*? Just now?"

"Ten minutes ago," I said. "I finally fell asleep at six, so I'm running behind on everything today. How would you feel about teaching today's nine o'clock forensic class?"

"Me? Sure. But . . ."

"But what? You can say if you don't want to."

"No. I mean, no, I don't want to say no. I'd love to teach it. Today is blunt-force trauma, right?"

"Right."

"But . . . you *love* teaching that class. Are you sure you can bear to let go of the reins for an hour?"

"Are you implying I have control issues?"

"No, I'm not implying it. I'm saying it, straight up. You have a teeny-tiny control issue, roughly the size of Texas, when it comes to teaching class."

"You just watch me," I said. "I'll sit in the back of the room and I won't say a word."

"Wait—I'll be up there teaching, and you'll just be *sitting* there?"

"In the back of the room," I repeated. "I won't say a word."

"Right. Sure, boss. And then hell will freeze over. And our elected leaders will all work together for the common good."

"Not a word, I tell you. Not so much as a syllable."

BY THE TIME I got to campus, I had rallied a bit, and I had mixed feelings about enlisting Miranda to teach. Unfortunately, I had painted myself into a corner, with a thick coat of paint in the unmistakable shade of Stubborn Pride. I had left myself no choice but to let her teach.

I suspected she hadn't headed to class yet, so I stopped off at the bone lab to check. At the very least, I could accompany her and offer constructive feedback. Perhaps she'd even offer the reins of class back to me.

The lab's door of the bone lab gave a particularly loud rasp as I pushed it open, setting my teeth thoroughly on edge. "How do you stand that noise?" I asked Miranda, whose desk was only three feet from the source of the sound.

"Hmm? What noise?" She looked up. "Oh, the

door? It's like anything annoying—you hear it enough times, you learn to tune it out." She smiled at me with an arch, enigmatic smile.

Across the room, I saw the familiar blond hair of Joanna Hughes, her bent head and tense shoulders a study in concentration. "You working on our Middle Eastern guy?" I called. She didn't answer, so I ambled over to take a look. Peering over her shoulder, I was stunned. Three days before, I had handed her a bare skull. Now, a pair of warm brown eyes stared back at me from a remarkably lifelike face. "Joanna, you're amazing," I said. "How on earth did you finish this so fast?"

"He's not actually finished," she said. "I haven't done anything with the hair yet, and I'm not sure about the nose. But he's getting close, I think." She took a deep breath and released it, hunching her shoulders up to her ears, then letting them drop. "You can get a lot done if you don't sleep. This guy got under my skin. Miranda told me how he died—how he was killed—and I couldn't stop thinking about him. So I figured I might as well just go flat out."

"It's remarkable," I said, studying the details: the chiseled cheekbones, the prominent eyebrows, the strong, straight nose. "This is so much better than that grainy video footage. Once the TV stations and the newspapers put this out there, somebody's sure to recognize him."

Miranda sidled up behind me. "Notice anything interesting about Joanna's reconstructions?" she asked.

"Sure," I said, eyeing the half-dozen heads on her table. "I notice they're terrific. What are you noticing?"

"They're all the same color," Miranda said. "The African American woman, the European man, the Hispanic kid from the Arizona desert, the Middle Eastern guy. All the same shade of gray." I was on the verge of pointing out that of course they were, because they were all made of clay, but I realized she was making a bigger point. "It's boring, but it's safe," she went on. "Our guy, 16–17. Maybe killed just because he was in the wrong place at the wrong time, in the wrong clothes or the wrong skin."

"Maybe so."

"Isn't it a shame," she said, "that what makes some people different—what makes them less boring— makes other people hate them?"

She looped a scarf around her neck—the morning felt more like midwinter than late fall—and said, "I need to head to class."

"I'll go with you," I said. Miranda shot me a suspicious glance. "Hey, I'm only helping carry the skulls. I won't meddle in class. Promise."

MIRANDA CLICKED TO the next slide, a close-up of a bashed-in skull, shown from behind. Thirty student faces leaned forward, captivated by the image from a forensic case we had worked a year before. "So from *this* blow," she said, using a laser pointer to highlight the crater at the back of the skull, "the fracture patterns radiate outward about the same distance in all directions." She traced several of the lines, each of them a foot long on the three-foot image of the skull. "Compare that to the other blow." She clicked to the next slide, showing the skull's shattered temporal bone. "Notice *this* fracture," she said, highlighting a crack that zigzagged from the temple toward the back of the head. "See how it starts out nice and strong, like the others? It's cracking, cracking, cracking, but then—*bam*—it stops all of a sudden, at this point where it intersects the one from the back of the head."

Looking out at the students—junior and senior undergraduates taking Introduction to Forensic Anthropology—she posed a question. "What does that tell you about the order in which the blows to the head were delivered? And therefore, what inferences can you draw about the defendant's statement to the police?"

The class was silent, possibly because they hadn't read the background materials on the case. Finally, a young woman in the front row—Mona, noteworthy for her quiet intelligence, flowing tunics, and ever-present hijab covering her hair—raised her hand. "He's lying," she said. "It wasn't self-defense."

I smiled, then—unable to stay in my seat any longer—I stood and took the reins of the class back from Miranda, along with the laser pointer. "Explain," I prompted Mona.

"The defendant said he hit the victim in the side of the head first, to avoid being stabbed, then hit him again as he fell. But the blow to the temple was the second blow, not the first one."

"Go on," I encouraged. Beside me, I heard Miranda sigh, just loudly enough to be sure I heard it, as she stepped aside. "How can you tell?"

"The way the cracks propagated."

I knew what "propagated" meant, but I suspected some of her classmates didn't. "Mona, pretend you're on the witness stand, in court," I told her. "Dr. Mona Faruz, forensic anthropologist for the prosecution. Explain your terminology and your reasoning."

"Sorry," she said, her olive skin flushing slightly. "Fractures in brittle materials propagate—they grow and spread—in a consistent way, whether the material is a ceramic cup or a steel pipeline or a human skull." Mona was an engineering major, so I suspected she knew more than anyone else in the room about fracture mechanics. "When an impact is severe enough to cause cracking, the crack, or cracks, will spread from the point of impact until their energy is dissipated, or weakened."

I didn't want her to get so detailed that she'd lose people. Using the laser pointer that I'd taken from Miranda, I traced the shortest crack. "Are you saying that something dissipated the energy of this crack? What was it? Why didn't this crack propagate any farther?"

"Cracks don't jump cracks," she said, holding up both hands to form a big T, as if calling for a time-out. "The crack from the blow to the temporal bone stopped when it intersected this crack, which was already there—from the *first* blow, which the defendant delivered to the back of the head." She held up an index finger to underscore a point she was about to make. "A blow he *couldn't* have delivered if he was face-to-face with the victim, as he claimed."

I nodded. "Class," I told the group, "you're the jury. Based on the testimony you've just heard, how many think this was murder, rather than self-defense?" All but two hands went up. "Good job,

Dr. Faruz." I checked my watch; as I suspected, we were at the end of our class period. "Okay, that's all for today. Next time, we'll talk about gunshots. Be sure to look at the cases ahead of time. I'm giving extra points for class participation next time."

The students stood and started filing out, and I began boxing up the skulls we'd brought to class. As I closed the lid to one of the boxes, I glanced up and noticed a boy in the third row nudge his neighbor. Then, to my astonishment, he stuck his foot into the aisle just as Mona was passing him. She tripped and fell, her books and papers and purse and laptop flying, and the two boys snickered. "Oops," said the boy who'd tripped her. He muttered something else; I couldn't catch all of it, but I was sure I heard the word "rag."

Before I could react, Miranda was on them like a shot. Grabbing the culprit by his shirt, she hauled him to his feet, then released him. I started toward them, half expecting her to strike him. Instead, she yanked her scarf from around her neck and wrapped it over the top of her head, like a hijab. "I'm Muslim, too, asshole," she snarled. "You want to trip me? Go on. I dare you. I fucking dare you."

As I started toward them to intervene, I heard a sharp popping sound from the back of the classroom, which made me stop and look up in alarm. Then I heard it again. One of the boys in the class, I saw, was slowly clapping his hands. A dozen other students had stopped on their way out, and now, one by one, they joined the first one in applauding. A girl hurried forward; she helped Mona to her feet and gave her a hug. Another gathered Mona's scattered possessions. A third girl, who also happened to be wearing a scarf, joined the group, and—slowly and deliberately, her eyes full of challenge—she rewound her scarf to echo Miranda's gesture of solidarity.

I admired their kindness, but I thought it best to defuse the situation. Laying a hand on Mona's shoulder, I said, "Miss Faruz, are you all right?" She nodded, not speaking, tears streaking her face. "Do you have another class now?" She nodded again. "I don't want to make you late for that. But come see me this afternoon, please. Will you do that?" I gave her shoulder a squeeze, and she managed a faint smile as she nodded a third time, then turned to go.

I touched Miranda's arm lightly; even through the sleeve of her sweater, I could feel the knotted muscles. "Miranda, can you carry these skulls back by yourself?"

She drew a long breath, then let it out slowly, and the tension in her arm eased a bit. "Yes," she said, her voice almost inaudible.

"Thank you." I squared off facing the troublemaker—Kevin McNulty was his name—and his buddy. Pointing to his buddy, I said, "You—*out*" and gestured with my head toward the doorway. Without a word, he scrambled to his feet and fled, leaving me alone in the room now with my problem student. "What do you have to say for yourself, McNulty?" I saw his jaw set and his eyes flash with defiance. He wasn't going to make this easy for me. "Start talking, son. And don't give me any crap about it being an accident. I saw the whole sorry business. Heard it, too. So if you bullshit me, I'll call the UT Police so fast it'll make your head spin, and I'll tell them how I saw you assault a woman in my classroom."

The boy blanched. Beads of sweat popped out on his forehead, and his hands began to tremble, but he remained silent. "You're running out of time, boy," I said. He still didn't speak, so I took my cell phone from my belt, scrolled through my contacts until I found "UT Police," and hit "call." I angled the phone slightly, so he could hear that the call was genuine. "UT Police," came a woman's voice through the speaker. "Hello, this is Dr. Brockton, in Anthropology," I said, looking into McNulty's eyes. "Can you send an officer to the auditorium in Mc-Clung Hall, please?"

"Yes, sir," she said. "Is this an emergency?"

McNulty finally broke. "Wait," he said. "Please. I'm sorry. Really. Please don't."

My eyes still locked on his, I told the dispatcher, "Officer, hang on. I think we've got this resolved."

"Are you sure?" she asked. "I can have somebody there in two minutes."

"Thank you, but I think we're okay here."

"All right, Dr. Brockton. You take care, and call back if you need us."

"I will," I told her. "I appreciate it." I hung up, reholstered my phone, and motioned to a chair. McNulty sat, and I did too, leaving a seat between us as a buffer. "Now you tell me, what on earth made you think that was an acceptable way to treat another student? Was it because she's a girl who's smart? Do you treat all intelligent women that way?" He shrugged and shook his head. "That's not good enough. I need you to explain. What were you thinking about her that gave you permission to demean her like that?"

He heaved a heavy sigh. "I guess . . . I guess I just snapped. I see all these Muslim immigrants everywhere, and it . . . it feels like they're taking over our country. I think they're bad for our country . . ." He trailed off and shrugged again.

"These Muslim immigrants? Like Mona?" He nodded tentatively. "Mona was born and raised here in Knoxville," I told him. "She's every bit as American as you are. Her father's a professor here. Did you know that?" He shook his head. "He's one of the best electrical engineers in the world. So you didn't know that, either, did you?"

His cheeks flushed again. "No, sir, I didn't."

"Therefore, you also don't know that her father's specialty is the U.S. electric power grid—specifically, ways to make it less vulnerable to blackouts and terrorist attacks. You think that's bad for our country?"

"No, sir, I guess not."

"I don't have to guess," I said. "I know it's not bad for our country. It's damned important for our country. But you looked at Mona, saw a head scarf, and decided she was beneath you—just another raghead immigrant, right?"

"Yes, sir, I guess I did. I'm sorry."

"I'm not the one you need to say that to, am I?"

"No, sir, probably not."

"*Probably* not?"

He sighed. "I should apologize to her."

"Well, I'll give you a chance to do so. At the beginning of class next time."

He looked pained. "In *class*? In *front* of class?"

I nodded. "If you want to stay in the class. And avoid a misconduct hearing and a police report."

Another sigh. "Yes, sir. Can I go now?"

"No, you can't," I said. "We're not quite through here. It sounds like maybe you're willing to see Mona a little differently, now that you know she's not just some pushy immigrant?" McNulty's eyes darted back and forth, and I could see him parsing my words, searching for subtext—seeking a snare—so I laid it on the table. "But what if she were? What if she were an Afghan immigrant, or a Syrian refugee? What's wrong with that?"

"Well, maybe nothing, individually. But . . . there's so *many* of them, and a lot of them are terrorists."

"Really? A lot? How many?"

"I don't know," he said. "But *any* is too many. Don't you think so? Or do you *want* terrorists coming to America?"

"McNulty, if you condescend to me one more time, you'll be out of here so fast your privileged little head will spin," I snapped. "Of course I don't want terrorists here. But I also don't want to live in a country that's got a wall around it. I still believe in the Statue of Liberty—'send me your poor'; 'I lift my lamp beside the golden door'; all that land-of-opportunity stuff. Maybe it's corny, but I still believe it's part of what made this country great."

I scrutinized the boy's face: pale skin, dark hair.

"McNulty. Is that a Native American name?" He blinked, startled. "I'm kidding. Irish, right?" He nodded warily. "You know when your ancestors came to America?"

"Not exactly. A long time ago. Early eighteen hundreds?"

"Ask your parents or grandparents. Chances are, they came in the late 1840s or early 1850s. You know why?"

He shrugged. "Looking for a better life, I suppose."

I nodded. "Sure, if by 'a better life' you mean not starving to death. They probably came during the Great Famine. Also called the Irish Potato Famine. A million people in Ireland starved to death between 1845 and 1852. A million more came to the United States. You know what they found when they got here?" He shrugged again; he was a shrugger, McNulty. "Bigotry. Prejudice. Abuse by people who thought that these scrawny, dirty Irish immigrants were second class. 'Irish need not apply,' a lot of help-wanted ads specified. People said there were too many Irish, that they were dangerous and drunkards, that they were bad for America. Sound familiar?"

"Yes, sir."

"People said similar things about immigrants from Italy and Poland and Germany and Russia. Thing is, McNulty, we're all immigrants here. Native Americans are the only ones with a legitimate beef against immigrants." I leaned toward him and squeezed his shoulder in what I hoped he'd take as a gesture of conciliation and encouragement. His deltoid was surprisingly robust. "You must work out a lot. Do you?"

"Four or five times a week."

"Don't forget to challenge your heart muscle," I said. "Most important muscle in the body. Takes a much stronger man to be kind than to be a bully and a jerk." He gave a perfunctory nod, but I could tell he'd had enough moral instruction for one day— maybe enough for a lifetime. "Now get out of here. I've got work to do."

He stood and headed for the door. "Just so you know," I called after him, "you're not out of the woods yet." He stopped in his tracks and turned, looking alarmed. "If Mona wants to file an assault charge or a conduct complaint, she's within her rights. But I'll encourage her to give you another chance. If you apologize—and I mean a sincere apology, not some half-assed, sullen sham—I hope she'll show you some compassion. Which is more than you showed her."

"Yes, sir," he said. "Thank you." And with that he was gone.

I slumped in the chair, suddenly weary—and painfully aware that I wasn't out of the woods yet either.

MIRANDA WAS IN the bone lab, as I'd thought she would be, but—contrary to my prediction—she wasn't absorbed in an e-mail or a Google search or a post for her Facebook page devoted to forensic anthropology. She was staring at half a dozen skulls, arranged in a semicircle on a lab table, their empty eye orbits all staring back at her. Surveying the lot of them, I noticed that she had three males and three females; two Caucasoids, two Negroids, and two Arikara Indians. "What are you looking for," I asked, "and what do you see?"

"I'm looking for an explanation," she said. "A reason why people choose to see differences as defects. As deficiencies."

"You're looking in the wrong place," I told her. "You won't find your answer in the dead. Only in the living. But you already know that."

She sighed. "Yeah, I guess I do. It just always surprises and saddens me when I smack up against that kind of thing."

"I know," I told her. *Quit stalling, Brockton,* I scolded myself. I drew a slow breath. "You know I admire your idealism. And your sense of justice. And your bravery." I paused. Here came the hard part. "But Miranda—"

She interrupted me with a sudden, keening cry. "I know, I know," she said, her shoulders suddenly shaking, her words so choked I could scarcely understand them. "I crossed a line. I did."

"You did," I agreed. "Never lay hands on a student in anger. Never, never, never."

"I know, I *know*," she wailed. "You've taught me better than that. You've *shown* me better than that. I'm so sorry, Dr. B. So, so sorry." She wiped a trail of tears and snot off her face with her scarf, then stared at the slimy mess. "Goddammit," she said, but there was no heat in the curse; just defeat. "Do you need to fire me? Do you want me to quit?" Her eyes, so sorrowful and vulnerable, damn near broke my heart.

"Good grief, come here," I said. I opened my

arms and enfolded her in a hug—not the first one I'd ever given her, I realized, but one of only a few, and the only one that had ever been more than a quick, awkward, surface-level gesture. "When I was a little kid," I said, "maybe five or six years old, my grandmother came to visit. Nana, we called her. She loved to take us for nature hikes, and one day, on one of these nature hikes, she was teaching me how to make a Robin Hood hat out of a great big leaf. She pulled a leaf off of this bush and made a hat for herself, to show me how, then pointed to a leaf and said, 'Now you try.' So I grabbed the leaf and pulled and pulled, but it wouldn't let go of the stem. Finally I snapped, 'How do you get these damn leaves off?!' She was shocked. Hell, *I* was shocked—I didn't even know I knew that word, let alone how to use it—and I knew I was in for it. Sure enough, when we got home, my mother said she'd have to wash out my mouth with soap."

I felt Miranda move—was it a sob, or a chuckle?—and heard her snuffle, and I went on. "But hours passed, and she didn't do it. I knew it was still coming, and the suspense was killing me. So finally, just before bedtime, I couldn't stand it any longer. I found the biggest bar of Ivory soap we had, and I crammed it into my mouth and I rubbed it all over my tongue and the roof of my mouth, and I scraped it back and forth across all my teeth. By the time I was done, I'd whittled about half of that bar into my mouth, and I was gagging from the taste."

"Good story," Miranda said, disengaging and stepping back so she could look at me. "And there's a point, too, I'm guessing?"

"Two weeks later, one of my older cousins was visiting, and said the f-word. My mother washed out his mouth on the spot, but all she did was rub the soap back and forth across his lips a couple times, like ChapStick. My point is, don't go overboard on the self-punishment. Quitting would be the worst thing you could do. Just . . . go and sin no more."

Smiling through her tears, Miranda pressed her hands together, as if in prayer, and gave the slightest, sweetest bow of her head. "No more," she said. "Never, never, never."

I believed she was telling the truth.

For both our sakes, I hoped she was.

CHAPTER 29

"SOMEONE'S ON LINE ONE for you," Peggy announced curtly when I picked up the phone. "Says it's important, but he won't give his name."

I felt a bloom of sweat on my scalp, and my mental alarms went nuts, all of them shrieking at two hundred decibels. "Does it sound like Satterfield?"

"How would I know what he sounds like? I've never talked to him. Never heard him interviewed."

"Sorry. Stupid question."

"But just guessing? I'd say he sounds young and scared, not middle-aged and murderous."

"Okay, I'll take it. And Peggy?"

"Yes?"

"I know I've been acting strange. I'm really sorry. Please try"—I almost said "not to take it personally," but that seemed like a surefire prelude to an epic case of foot-in-mouth disease—"to bear with me a little longer. Till this Satterfield storm blows over."

There was a pause. "I've borne with you for nearly

twenty-five years now," she said. "I'd say that's a pretty good testament to my patience."

"Touché," I said, feeling the unaccustomed sensation of a smile twitching at my lips.

I pressed the blinking button for line 1. "Hello, this is Dr. Bill Brockton. How can I help you?"

"Dr. Brockton?" Peggy was right, though if anything, she'd erred on the side of understatement. My caller sounded very young—the age of my grandsons, perhaps—and extremely scared. "The Dr. Brockton who's the head of the Body Farm?"

"That's me," I said. "What can I do for you?"

"My name is Hassim," he said. "I met you the other day? When you came to the mosque?"

My nervousness vanished, replaced by a sort of electric hum of hope. "Hello, Hassim. Nice to hear from you. I hope I didn't cause any trouble by showing up uninvited."

"No, sir. I mean, people *are* pretty nervous these days, with all the terrible things being said about Muslims." His voice—no discernible accent, so perhaps, like Mona, he, too, was the American-born child of immigrant parents—sounded less fearful now; more weary, perhaps, with a hint of bitterness.

"I'm not surprised," I said. "I'd be nervous, too. Not everyone feels that way. I certainly don't."

"No, sir, I didn't think you did. I remembered you when you came to the mosque. You talked at our high school last year. The STEM Academy. The new magnet school in the old L&N train depot."

"Y'all were a good group," I said, although the truth was, I didn't actually remember them. School groups tend to blur together, at least if you talk to a hundred a year. But I did remember liking the setting: a magnificent old railway station, converted into a school for science nerds. "What's on your mind, Hassim?"

"I'm not supposed to be calling you. The imam said we should keep the community's business to ourselves. But it doesn't seem right, not to help . . ." He trailed off.

"Not to help identify someone who was killed?" I said it as gently as I could. "So his family won't have to keep wondering what happened to him? Never knowing, always wondering?"

"Yes, sir. I started thinking about *my* parents, and how upset they'd be if *I* disappeared. And what it would be like for them, if they never knew . . . that I . . ."

"Who do you think it might be, Hassim? And how do I find his parents?"

"His name is Shafiq. Shafiq Mustafah. His parents are in Egypt. Cairo, I think. He was here on a student visa, studying at UT. Engineering or computer science—I'm not sure which. But he had a problem with his passport."

"What kind of problem, Hassim?"

"His parents were dissidents—they were part of the pro-democracy protests a few years ago, in the Arab Spring—and when the military took control, they got arrested, and Shafiq's passport got canceled."

I thought—or hoped—I was following him. "You're saying his passport got revoked, or canceled, by the Egyptian government? Because his parents were pro-democracy dissidents?"

"Yes, sir. At least, that's what I think happened."

"But didn't that mean he had to go back to Egypt?"

"That's the thing. He was *supposed* to go, but he didn't *want* to go. His parents were already in prison, and he was afraid he'd be arrested, too. He wanted to apply for political asylum here, but he had a hard time finding anyone to help him, and he was afraid he was about to be deported. I thought maybe he *had* been deported. And maybe he was. Maybe he's not the one who was killed."

"But maybe he went into hiding? So he wouldn't be sent back to Egypt?"

"Maybe, I don't know. I just don't know." He sounded miserable.

"Hassim, this is very helpful," I said. "I appreciate it, and I won't tell anyone you called."

"Thank you. I . . . I hope it's not him. But if it is, I appreciate what you're doing."

After I hung up, I thought—fretted—about what to do if case number 16–17 turned out to be UT student Shafiq Mustafah. How would I even go about contacting his parents, somewhere in an Egyptian prison? How would they be able to bear it, these parents who had entrusted their son to America—the nation that held itself up as the world's shining beacon of democratic enlightenment and decency—when they learned that his fate had turned out to be far worse than theirs?

Most of the time I loved my job, but as I contemplated the conversations that might lie ahead, I hated this piece of it. *Can't be helped*, I thought. *Won't be easy, but has to be done.*

Opening my desk drawer, I took out the UT Directory and flipped to the listing for the Center for International Education, the office that dealt with foreign students and the mountains of paperwork they brought and generated during their studies here. My eye was caught by a familiar name: Deborah Dwyer, the center's assistant director, had been Kathleen's secretary many years before. Kathleen had always praised the young woman's abilities, predicting that she would go on to bigger and better things than secretarial work. It pleased me to see that Kathleen had been right.

I dialed Debbie's extension, and she answered on the second ring. "International Education, Deborah Dwyer."

"Hello, Deborah Dwyer. It's Bill Brockton, in Anthropology. How in the world are you?"

"I'm doing well, Dr. Brockton. How are you? It's good to hear your voice."

"I'm hanging in," I said, then—to my own surprise—added, "I still miss her, Debbie. After all these years, I do."

There was a pause, and when she spoke again, her voice sounded thick. "I know. So do I. She was such a fine woman. Very special."

"She was. Thank you. She always spoke so highly of you. I know she'd be proud of how you're doing." I cleared my throat. "But listen, I didn't call to make you and me cry. I called to ask a favor."

"Sure. What can I do for you?"

"I'm wondering what sort of information you have on a student from Egypt—a young man named Shafiq Mustafah."

She didn't answer right away, so I went on, "He's studying engineering or computer science or some other STEM field. Or was, I think. Maybe not now."

"Is this the name of someone who's taking a class from you?" Her voice had gone guarded. *A bad sign*, I thought.

"No, it's not."

"Do you have a records release? Signed by the student?"

"No, why—do I need one?"

"I'm afraid so."

"But he's a student at a public university. I'm a faculty member. Why can't I see the file of any student I need to?"

"Same reason students can't see *your* file. It's personal information, subject to strict privacy protections. Takes a court order, a request from the Department of Homeland Security. Unless you can get a release from—what did you say his name is?"

"Shafiq. I *can't* get a release from Shafiq, Debbie, because Shafiq is *dead*." I heard a soft gasp, but I barged ahead. "That's what I'm afraid of, anyhow. I've got the skeletal remains of a twenty-year-old Middle Eastern male here, and I'm trying to identify him, but I'm having a hell of a time. I've just learned that Shafiq Mustafah went missing about six months ago. At this moment, he's my only lead. But so far all I have is a name."

"God in heaven," she said, then I heard her draw a deep breath. "Dr. Brockton, I don't think we should be talking about this on the phone. Can you come see me?"

"If you can't give me any information, I don't see

any point," I said. It came out sounding more sulky than I intended. Or maybe it came out exactly as sulky as I intended.

"The privacy protections are very clear," she said. "All the same, I wish you'd come see me. Please?"

"Well, since you put it that way. When should I come?"

"Are you free now?"

"Well . . ." I checked my calendar. "I've got a meeting with the provost in an hour, but if you think we can be done in time for me to make that?"

"Come on over," she said. "It'll be good to see you."

THE CENTER FOR International Education was housed in an aging building on Melrose Avenue, just in back of Hodges Library. The building's old bones were attractive enough; it was a typical academic building from the 1940s or 1950s, a four-story brick edifice whose doors and windows were trimmed in stone. But any scrap of elegance or dignity it had once possessed was shredded by the air-conditioning units jutting from windows on every floor. The air conditioners gave the building a sort of third world look, which was sad yet somehow appropriate, I supposed. The sign at the entrance read INTERNATIONAL EDUCATION in large letters, and, in smaller letters below, INTERNATIONAL STUDENT AND SCHOLAR SERVICES. Beside the latter label, someone had spray-painted the letters "ISIS."

Debbie Dwyer's office was on the second floor; her window—one of the few that was unobstructed by an air conditioner—looked out on a courtyard where maple trees blazed red and orange. When I knocked and entered, she stood and walked around the desk to hug me. "You're a sight for sore eyes," she said. "You haven't changed a bit."

"You have," I said. "You look a lot more . . . *important* now." She was wearing a power suit—fitted gray skirt and gray jacket, softened by a white silk blouse—but something else was different, too, although I couldn't quite tell what it was.

"It's the hair," she said. "The impression of power is inversely proportional to the length." I looked at her hair, not quite shoulder length, puzzled by the comment. "For years I wore it long," she explained, and I nodded, remembering. "Got compliments galore. But respect and responsibility? Not so much." She said it with a smile, but it was clear that she wasn't entirely joking, and I felt bad about the workplace complexities she'd had to confront and overcome. She pointed to a pair of armchairs in a corner of the office. "Please, have a seat," she said, taking one of the chairs for herself. "I am sorry about the rules," she said. "They're really quite specific."

Before I even had a chance to answer, there was a knock on her door. "Excuse me, Debbie," said an attractive young woman. Her hair was long and lovely: *compliment-worthy*, I thought ironically. "We've got a . . . situation. Could I borrow you for a few minutes?"

Debbie gave me an apologetic glance. "I'm so sorry. Can you wait right here? This shouldn't take long. I'll be back in *five minutes*." She gave me an odd look as she said it—a look that felt rather like a nudge in the ribs—and then she was gone, the door clicking shut behind her, before I had a chance to say or ask anything that might clarify whether I should wait or simply give up and go.

I glanced around the office, and then I laughed, suddenly and softly. "You *rascal*," I murmured. At my elbow was a small round table between the two armchairs, and on the table were two things: a lamp, and a manila file folder labeled MUSTAFAH, SHAFIQ.

I checked my watch. *Five minutes*, I told myself. *Better move fast, Brockton.* First I pressed the button in the door handle to lock the door—I didn't want anyone walking in and seeing me breaking a federal law—then I laid the folder on Debbie's desk and flipped it open. The first thing I saw, on the folder's inside cover, was a young man's face staring at me, wide-eyed, from a copied photograph. It was a passport photo—small and washed out and bad, embodying the special, egregious badness of every passport ever taken—and I nearly shouted with astonishment. Staring at me, from the bad photocopied photo, was a familiar face. The face Joanna Hughes had just re-created on the skull of my Cooke County victim, 16–17. But something wasn't right. This was a kid—way younger than twenty.

The entire passport had been photocopied, I realized as I continued staring. I checked the passport's date of issue and understood why the face staring back at me looked too young: the passport had been issued three years before, in 2013. Then I saw the birth date—July 1995—and a wave of sorrow washed over me. Shafiq Mustafah had turned twenty-one all alone and stark naked, chained to a tree like an abused dog, as death lumbered toward him from the dark woods of Cooke County and the dark heart of a hate-filled man.

The file was a half inch thick, and I wasn't sure how best to mine it for other useful information. For an insane moment I considered simply taking it, but taking it, I realized, could put Debbie in a very bad spot. If the file were requested while I had it, she would be held responsible for its loss. Even if the disappearance went undetected by anyone else, there would be the awkward matter of how to return it. Last but not least, if I borrowed the file, Debbie would no longer have plausible deniability, whereas if I simply scanned it here and kept my mouth shut, she could honestly say she didn't know that I had seen it.

Scan it here. The words echoed in my mind, and I checked the credenza behind Debbie's desk, desperately seeking a scanner or copier. No such luck. Suddenly I thought of my phone, with its built-in camera. I could count on one hand the number of times I had actually used my cell phone's camera, but I did know how. Or so I hoped.

The first photo I snapped made me jump—the phone made a noise like a camera shutter, but at a volume that seemed earsplitting to my paranoid ears. I flipped the toggle to silence the phone and began again, feeling a bit like a Cold War spy as I flipped pages and took photos. It wasn't as easy as I'd expected it to be; at such close range, the focus was tricky, and I ended up taking two or three shots of most pages in order to get legible images. But soon I got into a groove, snapping swiftly, keeping time to the theme music from *Mission: Impossible*, which I heard playing in my head.

I had made it halfway through the file when I heard voices approaching in the hall outside. "By the way," I heard Debbie saying, in a surprisingly loud voice, "don't forget the tailgate party we're putting together for next Saturday's game. Are you coming?" I heard a low, indistinct reply, then Debbie resumed, at bullhorn volume. "Great! Could you bring some plastic cups? And some napkins? Terrific—thank you!"

I flipped the folder closed, whirled, and placed it on the end table in its original spot, and then lunged for the door handle, just as I saw it begin to move. I gave the handle a quick twist to pop the lock button, then swung the door inward, so abruptly that Debbie, still holding the outside handle, stumbled forward with a yelp of surprise.

"Oh, I'm so sorry!" I said. "I didn't know you were there. I realized I need to get going—can't keep the provost waiting, you know."

"Never a good idea," she said. "But what a shame—we didn't even get a chance to talk!" *Methinks thou dost protest too much*, I thought, wondering if her assistant could see through our little charade; wondering, on second thought, if her assistant had actually played a supporting-actress role in our charade. "Call me and let's have lunch sometime," Debbie said, taking my elbow and steering me toward the exit, just in case I had any doubt what my next move should be. "I'd love to get caught up on your work, and the family, and . . . everything."

"I will," I said. "Soon as the dust settles. Or the smoke clears."

"Take care, Dr. Brockton."

"I'll try," I said. "Thank you. *Very* much."

"You are *most* welcome."

MY SPY MISSION at International Education had been so brief that I showed up at the provost's office thirty minutes ahead of schedule. His door was closed, which I took to mean one of two things: either he wasn't in, or he *was* in but didn't want to be disturbed. "I can come back," I told his secretary. "My office is only a football field away."

"Hang on just a minute, if you don't mind," she said. "He should be finishing up this meeting any second, and maybe you could slip in before his next one. He told me he only needs five minutes with you."

I sat down in one of those wingbacked leather armchairs that administrators high up the academic food chain seem required to own. The leather was glossy and supple, trimmed with domed brass nails along the fronts of the arms and the wings. The chair was impressive, but it wasn't actually comfortable. Then again, perhaps it wasn't meant to be comfortable.

The provost's door opened, and a young assistant professor emerged. I vaguely recognized him—English, perhaps?—but his face was ashen and drooping and his gaze downcast. As he passed, I looked up into his eyes, and I was startled to see that he'd been crying.

The provost appeared in his office, looking hale and hearty. He, clearly, had not just been crying. "Come in, come in," he boomed.

"I'm afraid to," I said, "after seeing what you did to that last guy."

He grimaced slightly. "Not everyone's cut out to be a professor," he said. He cocked his head toward another massive chair, this one in his plush inner sanctum, and settled into his own thronelike seat. "I sometimes think we should try to turn out fewer Ph.D.s, not more, so we don't flood the market with overeducated, underemployed french-fry cooks. But then I see the financials, and I tell my overworked, underpaid professors to put more butts in more seats." He gave me an ironic smile, then tented his fingers in a way that I suspected he had practiced, to make him look Solomonic. "How long have you been here at UT, Bill?"

"Twenty-five years," I said. "No—twenty-six."

"You've had a really good run."

"Uh-oh. You make it sound like it's over."

"Over? Lord, no! I'm just saying, you've done remarkable things here. Built the Anthropology Department into one of the best in the country. Created a forensic facility that's known around the world. Just when I think you've topped out, you go and prove me wrong."

He reached down and opened a manila file on his desk—a near-identical twin to the one I'd just illegally photographed—and took out a piece of stationery, thick and crisp and never folded. He made a show of reading it, then stood—at this point, he'd been sitting for all of sixty seconds—and strode toward me, the paper in his left hand, his right arm outstretched. "By golly, I just want to be the first person to shake hands with the Professor of the Year!"

I shook his hand and stood, a move made awkward and slightly perilous by the vigorous shaking he was giving my arm. "Well, thank you. I'm honored. UT has plenty of great professors, so it means a lot to be singled out by my students."

His brow furrowed. "UT? Students? What are you talking about?"

My brow furrowed. "Well, you just said I'm UT's Professor of the Year, so—"

"UT, hell!" he all but shouted. "U.S.! You've just been named National Professor of the Year! For the whole damn country!"

"Me? Are you sure?"

"Good God, man, of *course* I'm sure. Here, read it for yourself."

He handed me the letter. The stationery felt even richer than it looked—thick and stiff, with a soft texture that was closer to fabric than to paper. CASE, read the logo at the top. COUNCIL FOR THE ADVANCEMENT AND SUPPORT OF EDUCATION. The letter was actually addressed to UT's president, not the provost. "It gives me great pleasure to inform you that Dr. William Brockton has been chosen as U.S. Professor of the Year," the letter began. "This is a great honor, not just for Dr. Brockton, but for the University of Tennessee as well—a tribute to the outstanding climate the university provides for teaching, research, and academic service."

"Well, I'll be," I said. "This is a nice surprise. Like I said, I'm honored—even more, now."

"We'd like to make a big deal of this," he said. "Put you on the front page of the *News-Sentinel*. Get you on 'Alive at Five' on WBIR."

I shrugged. "Fine with me," I said. "I always have a good time with those folks."

"But I think we ought to go bigger," he said, holding a hand in the air in front of us, as if to conjure the image. "Picture this. Neyland Stadium. Halftime at the Homecoming game. A stage at the center of the field, the fifty-yard line. *One hundred thousand* people watching as I hang a medal around your neck." I nearly smiled at his phrasing and intonation—had he actually emphasized the word "I"?—but suddenly a dark cloud cast a pall on the glowing scene as I remembered: *Satterfield*. With Satterfield gunning for me, I'd be a sitting duck at a halftime ceremony. Immobilized at midfield, I'd be a human bull's-eye, smack at the center of a huge, oval target.

"That's a really nice offer," I said, "but I don't think I'd feel comfortable with that."

"But . . . of *course* you would," he said. "This is your big moment, Bill. Yours and UT's. You can't possibly pass it up."

"I'm sorry," I said, "but I can. And I do. Like I say, I'm deeply honored, and I'm very grateful to UT for providing such a supportive place for me all these years. But standing there in the middle of the stadium, in the glare of the spotlight? Can't do it."

"Oh, come on," he said, his tone somewhere between cajoling and scolding. But I was already on the way out, one hand raised in the air to wave good-bye and, in the process, to snatch away his glittering fantasy.

PEGGY FIXED ME with an odd, intense stare when I walked into the departmental office a few minutes later. "Are you okay?" she asked.

"Ish," I said. "Okay-ish. It's been a strange morning."

She raised her eyebrows, inviting me to elaborate, but I didn't want to go into it. "Tell you later," I said. "Hold my calls, would you?" And with that, I retreated—from her office, and from the interaction—leaving her looking hurt and rejected as I began the hundred-yard run the length of the football field, to my sanctuary. My hideaway. My self-imposed exile. Was it my imagination, or did she mutter *Yeah, right* as I started down the hall?

IT WAS A Dr. Jekyll and Mr. Hyde sort of day. On the sunny Dr. Jekyll side of the street, a prestigious national educational group had just decided I was the best professor in the entire United States. In the dark alley of Mr. Hyde, a sadistic serial killer wanted to destroy me, and probably my family, too, in the most painful way his twisted brain could devise. Like a Ping-Pong ball, I ricocheted back and forth, back and forth, from best to worst, from elation to despair. Finally, on the millionth bounce, I said, "Enough!" I desperately needed to reboot.

Suddenly, stunned, I remembered: *Shafiq! 16–17!* Were they indeed one and the same? Was it possible that, digitized within the phone clipped to my belt, was another nugget of information that could answer the question once and for all?

I opened the phone's camera application and began scrolling through the images I had taken. There were more than a hundred of them—some crisp, some blurred, all maddeningly, illegibly tiny. I would die of eyestrain, I realized, before I made it halfway through the documents I had photographed.

Miranda picked up the intercom on the second beep. "Hey," I said, not bothering with a greeting. "You're pretty savvy with a cell phone, right?"

"Compared to the average twelve-year-old, I'm a dolt. Compared to you, I'm Stephen Hawking."

"Then come be brilliant," I said. "I took a bunch of pictures with my phone, but they're tiny. Is there a way to see them on a computer screen, lots bigger?"

"There is," she said, "but it would take a genius. I'll be right there."

MIRANDA LOADED THE pictures—all 127 of them—onto her laptop, which she'd brought from the bone lab. "I've got Photoshop and iPhoto on this machine," she said. "You're probably still running Hieroglyph 1.0. Here, give me your phone." She connected a short cable and pressed a few keys. As if by magic, photos began flashing across her laptop screen. "First thing, let's get rid of the ones that aren't in focus. That'll cut out the number in half, at least." She began scrolling through the photos at a blistering pace, hitting the delete key with a staccato speed that put me in mind of an old-time telegrapher.

"How do you even know the ones you're deleting aren't good?" I said. "They're only on the screen for a nanosecond before you get rid of them."

"Trust me, they're bad," she said. "If they look like a Weather Channel satellite photo, we're not going to be able to read the words, no matter how long we stare at them. Here, I'll show you." She went into the trash file and pulled out one of the deleted pictures. Everything was a swirling blur.

"Looks like Hurricane Miranda," I acknowledged grudgingly. "Okay, carry on. Sorry I doubted you."

"Never do it again," she said, quoting one of her favorite lines from *The Princess Bride*. Once she had separated the fuzzy chaff from the crisp wheat, she went back to the beginning, starting with the passport images. The first one showed the document's two-page spread, but the next one was a close-up, zoomed in on the young man's face. "Wow," said Miranda. "Joanna really nailed it, didn't she? I mean, the only thing she missed is that mole on his left cheek." She shook her head. "Poor kid."

Filling the screen, the image was more poignant than it had been as a thumbnail. The boy's face was slender, his brown eyes large and frightened. Was he afraid of traveling to an unknown land, or afraid because he lived in a country ruled by military tyrants his parents despised? Or was he afraid—was it possible?—because he possessed, somehow, some uncanny, sixth-sense premonition about the terrible darkness that lay in wait for him in the not-too-distant future?

After the passport came contact information: the address of the apartment where he was living; the name and number of his landlord and roommates; the address and telephone number, back in Egypt, of his parents—before they were arrested, I assumed, not in the hellhole where they were probably now being beaten and "interrogated."

Miranda had been overly generous when she estimated that half my images might be usable; as it turned out, only 31 of the original 127 had survived her merciless culling, and it was number 31 that made me jump to my feet. "Look," I said, tapping the screen with one hand and grabbing Miranda's arm with the other. "Look!"

"*Oww*," she said. "Use your words, not your painful viselike grip. What?"

"Sorry. It's a letter from a doctor. He says Shafiq needs a reduced course load because he's been injured in a car accident."

"So it does. 'Orthopedic surgery on the right humerus and right femur.' Golly." Miranda read more, her tone becoming as excited as mine. "'Bones repaired with plates and screws'—my God, it really *is* him!"

"It really is," I echoed. "We'll need to see if we can rustle up some x-rays or some DNA—maybe he left some personal effects at the apartment where he lived, like a hairbrush or a cap that would have some hair and follicles. But it's him. It's got to be him."

"This is *awesome*," said Miranda.

"It is," I agreed. "Awful, too."

"Awful, too," she echoed.

CHAPTER 30

THE NUMBER THREE HAS long been considered a magic number—a mystically powerful number—in many cultures around the world. And so it is, judging by three events that occurred in swift succession in my forensic-anthropology classroom, two days after Kevin McNulty had tripped Mona Faruz.

Event number one: I arrived early for class, as I generally do, but for once, I wasn't the first one in the auditorium. Two students—girls who tended to sit in the back and disappear behind their computer screens, e-mailing or posting on Facebook, judging by their grades—stood just inside the doorway. "Well, *you're* certainly here early," I observed cheerily. They blushed and looked from me to each other, as if they had some sort of secret about which they felt both self-conscious and pleased. They didn't seem inclined to confide it to me, though, so I gave them a generic smile and headed up to the table at the front, to unpack today's teaching specimens. It wasn't long before their secret came to light, though: As soon as another female student entered, the two girls at the door offered her an assortment of brightly colored scarves. The new arrival selected one, then arranged it over her hair like a hijab, and the two scarf-bearers did likewise. As more students arrived, the ritual was repeated: the scarves were offered to every female student, and every one chose and donned a scarf. The male students—initially puzzled, then swiftly grasping the message—reacted, for the most part, by giving thumbs-up signs and smiles of approval. One, though, reacted rather differently: Kevin McNulty arrived only moments before class was due to start; seeing the display of hijab solidarity, he blanched, then turned crimson. I half expected him to turn and flee, but surprisingly—bravely—he walked slowly to the front row and took a seat, all eyes riveted to him. I, too, looked at him, raising my eyebrows, and he responded with a barely perceptible nod.

Event number two: I checked my watch, then cleared my throat. "All right, let's get started," I said. "We're talking about postcranial skeletal trauma today, and we've got a lot to cover. But first, I believe, Mr. McNulty has something to say?"

With a slowness that seemed painful, McNulty stood, took two steps toward me, and then turned to face the class. His eyes swept the room until they found Mona, who was seated, for once, in the very back row. "I behaved badly at the end of the last class," he began. "Rudely, meanly, and stupidly. I should have known better. My great-grandfather's grandfather—or maybe it was his great-grandfather, I lose track of the 'greats'—came to America in

1838. He was about my age, and about my size, but he weighed half as much as I do. That's because he was starving, like a lot of people in Ireland were. I found this out by talking to my grandmother for a long time last night. 'Big Paddy,' that's what they called him—even his nickname was a joke. He barely survived the voyage from Ireland, and then he nearly starved once he got to New York, because he couldn't find work. He got beaten up, more than once, and got called a lot of names, and got treated like dirt." He paused, and looked down, collecting himself, then looked at Mona again and went on. "The point is, my family got treated the same way I treated Mona the other day. Mona, I apologize. You didn't deserve to be treated that way. I'm sorry, and I'm ashamed." He extended his arms to either side, palms up. "I hope you can forgive me."

The room was silent—silent, but electric—and everyone turned toward Mona, following his gaze. After what seemed a long time, Mona stood, as slowly as McNulty had. "Yes," she said finally. "I can. I do." Then she pressed her hands together as if in prayer and bowed slightly. Another charged silence followed, and then—almost like a replay of the prior class ending—one student began to clap, and soon the entire auditorium was filled with applause, the students on their feet clapping and cheering, some of them smiling, some of them crying.

Event number three: As the students quieted and settled into their seats, Miranda—whom I hadn't even realized was present—came from one side of the auditorium and said to me, "Dr. B? May I have a moment?" I nodded, and she turned to face the class, her coppery hair, like that of the other female students, covered with a scarf. "I behaved badly last time, too. I let my anger run away with me. I said things and I did things that I'm embarrassed about and sorry for. I apologize to all of you for my outburst. Kevin, I particularly apologize to you. I was wrong to grab you, and I was wrong to speak to you the way I did. And I hope that *you* can forgive *me*." McNulty stood up again. He looked at her for a long moment, then gave a slow, sheepish smile and stretched out his hand, and they shook.

Class—even to me; even though I was showing my favorite examples of skeletal trauma—was more than a bit anticlimactic.

"DOC," GROWLED THE voice on my phone shortly after I had returned to my office, still processing the remarkable events of class. "Bubba Meffert. Listen, I'm just leaving the prison. Been talking to inmates about ol' Satterfield. Found out some mighty interesting stuff. Got a minute?"

"Sure, Bubba, go ahead. Whatcha got?"

"Well, first off, Steve Morgan was tellin' me—"

I couldn't resist interrupting. "Steve's an inmate now? About time. I knew he couldn't keep scamming the TBI forever."

Bubba chuckled, though the laugh sounded forced and feeble. I hoped he wasn't pushing himself too hard so soon after chemo. "Nah, Steve's still got his badge—he's still half a step ahead of Internal Affairs. Anywho, I was swapping notes with Steve yesterday evening, and he said you'd asked him if there was anything up at Shiflett's place that tied him to Satterfield."

"I did ask him that."

"At the time," he went on, "Steve thought it was a weird question. Thought it came outta left field, or outta a certain lower part of your anatomy. Actually, though, it was a brilliant question."

My Spidey Sense was starting to tingle. "Go on."

"Turns out Satterfield and Shiflett were thick as thieves. They developed quite the bromance, apparently."

I drew back and gave the phone a puzzled, questioning look. "They had a sexual relationship?"

"God, no," said Meffert. "Not as far as I know, anyhow. Buddies. Brotherly love. Well, brotherly hate, more like it. They were both mixed up with skinhead groups, neo-Nazis, neo-Klan. It all kinda runs together, you know? Anything that helps the whites and hurt the blacks and the browns—the 'mud people,' they called 'em."

"But how did Shiflett and Satterfield even meet? Satterfield was in prison for more than twenty years. Did Shiflett do time there, too?"

"No, but that's where they met. They met through Satterfield's cellmate. Guy name of Stubbs. Shiflett was in the army with Stubbs—they served in Afghanistan together, ten or twelve years ago."

Now my Spidey Sense was shrieking. I sat bolt upright in my chair, then leaned forward, closer to the phone, as if by getting right next to it, I could hear better and therefore hear a different name.

"Stubbs? Did you say Satterfield's cellmate was named Stubbs?"

"Yeah. Stubbs."

"Tell me you're not talking about *Tilden* Stubbs. Militant racist? Doing time for stealing weapons from the army?"

"I am. He was," said Meffert.

"Come again?"

"*Was* doing time. Did the time. Served five years. Got out a month ago."

"Wait. He's out? Crap. I hate to hear that, Bubba."

"Sorry to be the bearer of bad tidings." Meffert's tone seemed to suggest that he had something else to say, but he was silent.

"Bubba? You got more bad news?"

"Yeah." He drew out the word—easing into it on the front end, dragging out the vowels, trailing off reluctantly at the end. "This is where it gets creepy, Doc."

"You're saying that neo-Nazis, militias, and army heists aren't creepy?"

"Not compared to this."

"Hell, Bubba. You do know how to sugarcoat the pill, don't you? Just spill it. What is it you're so worried about telling me?"

"The Cooke County case—the murder by bear?"

"Yeah? What about it? Creepy, for sure, but I already know all about it."

"No, you don't. That was supposed to be you. Chained to the tree."

"*What?*" My skin prickled, my hackles rose, and sweat popped out on my forehead.

"I heard it from two different inmates."

"But that's crazy," I said. "I never heard of Jimmy Ray Shiflett. Why in hell would some Cooke County redneck want to chain me to a tree and feed me to a bear?"

"It wasn't Shiflett."

"What do you mean?"

"Shiflett wasn't the one planning to do it to you. Wasn't Stubbs, either."

A wave of nausea crashed over me as his meaning sank in. "Satterfield," I breathed.

"Satterfield. Satterfield must've told Stubbs about it. Maybe Satterfield told Shiflett, too. Or maybe Shiflett heard it from Stubbs on a prison visit. Doesn't matter. It was completely Satterfield's plan. For you."

WHEN I CALLED Angela Price to relay Meffert's update, she agreed that the Satterfield task force needed to discuss it. An hour later, I dialed a special phone number, to join a conference call that Price's assistant had set up. Rattled as I was, I kept misdialing the second set of numbers, the sequence needed to connect me with Price's group, rather than some other group of, say, investment bankers or Las Vegas bookies or whoever else was huddled around phones at this particular moment.

After my third botched attempt to make the connection—and my third string of profanities—Peggy came through the doorway from the outer office. "Let me help," she said. She came behind the desk and stood beside me, leaning forward to read the numbers I had scrawled on a notepad. She put the phone on speaker to free up her hands. Her left hand deftly dialed the numbers; her right hand came to rest on my shoulder, a calming weight that seemed to add some ballast and balance to my unsteady keel. Reaching up with my right hand, I laid it on hers and gave a grateful squeeze. Funny thing: I still didn't know how to talk to her, except as my secretary, but somehow her hand and my hand were better at bridging the awkward gap.

A computerized voice in my phone announced, "You have joined the conference. There are five other people in the conference." Peggy slid her hand off my shoulder, tiptoed from the room, and closed the door. "Hello, it's Bill Brockton," I said. "Am I the last one to the party?"

"I think so," said Price. "A couple of folks couldn't make it, but I think we've got most of the key players. From the TBI, we've got Special Agents Meffert and Morgan. From ATF, Special Agent Kidder. From KPD, Captain Decker. And our retired behavioral consultant, Pete Brubaker."

"Can't think of anybody I'd rather have on the case," I said. "Where do we start?"

"Agent Meffert," she said, "would you start us off? Tell us what you learned at the prison."

"Sure," he said and led the group through the connections between Satterfield, Stubbs, and Shiflett.

"Sounds like a real shitstorm's brewing," said someone. "This is Kidder, by the way."

"Say some more, Agent Kidder," said Price.

"Three guys, all of them racist Rambo wannabes. Two are in prison, one's holed up in a fortified hollow in the mountains. One of the jailbirds is released, and two weeks later, the other one busts out. And a few days after that, the mountain man's murdered, and his shed full of weapons and bomb-making ingredients gets cleaned out."

I heard a ruminative grunt. "Meffert here. Let me see if I follow you, Agent Kidder. You thinking Satterfield busted out of prison to team up with Stubbs? Start some kind of race war?"

"Could be," Kidder said. "But these Far Right nuts are always talking big about race war. Never quite happens, but they keep hoping. They could be starting a new militia group. Lotta those folks are pissed off by the way that latest Bundy thing turned out—the takeover of that wildlife refuge out in Oregon. I don't know what these guys are up to, but I do think the timing is important. Satterfield never made an escape attempt in more than twenty years—is that right, Agent Meffert?"

"That's right," said Bubba.

"But then, two weeks after his buddy gets out, *bam*! Satterfield busts a move."

"Could be. Oh, sorry—Steve Morgan, TBI. But then what about Shiflett? You think Satterfield and Stubbs turned on him? Why would they kill their buddy?"

"Decker, KPD SWAT team. Maybe they wanted some of his stash, and he didn't want to share. Maybe they wanted to blow up a black church, and he got cold feet. Wouldn't be the first time bad guys turned on one another."

"This is Dr. Brockton," I chimed in. "Shiflett had his driveway monitored, and he'd booby-trapped the gate, with a shotgun rigged to a trip wire. And he died of a broken neck."

"Go on, Dr. Brockton," Price nudged. "Connect those dots."

"Shiflett was killed by somebody standing right behind him. Somebody he knew and trusted. Somebody he let in. The killer was strong, and he'd been trained to kill. Could've been either Satterfield or Stubbs. Or both."

"No, it couldn't. This is Brubaker, by the way."

"Couldn't what, Pete?" asked Price. "Couldn't be both? Couldn't be either—as in somebody else altogether?"

"I'm saying it was Satterfield. Only Satterfield."

"Why?" Price persisted.

"Because Shiflett stole Satterfield's prize possession."

"This is one very confused Meffert here. Stole *what*?"

"You told us yourself, Agent Meffert," said Brubaker. "Satterfield comes up with the perfect way to get revenge on Dr. Brockton. Chain him to a tree, torture him, feed him to a bear. But then Satterfield makes a mistake. He brags about his bright idea to his buddies, and then one of the buddies—Shiflett, the dumb shit—has the nerve to use the idea himself. Squanders the brilliant, magnificent plan on some pissant little foreign kid. Steals the precious gem that Satterfield spent twenty long years honing and polishing. To someone like Satterfield, that's unforgivable. A killing offense."

"Meffert here. Brubaker, you'd've made one hell of a preacher," Bubba said.

"How's that?"

"'Cause right now, you're makin' a believer out of me." I heard Meffert breathe deeply. "Well, shit, folks," he said. "I guess I got to pay a call on the charming Mr. Stubbs now. And I guess I'd best take a bit of backup with me, in case he's keepin' bad company."

CHAPTER 31

STILL RATTLED BY THE conference call—especially by Brubaker's reminder of how implacably Satterfield hated me—I decided to stretch my legs and get some air. Peggy gave me a searching look as I passed her desk, but I waved her off. "I'll be right back," I said. "I just need some air." Ducking into the stairwell, I headed down to the bone lab. Just as I reached the door, I heard what could have been a war cry from one of my Arikara Indians, if my Arikara had not all been dead. The whoop was followed by a "Yes! *Hell*, yes!" in what seemed to be Miranda's voice. On drugs. Specifically, the drug called ecstasy.

Peering through the small window in the door, I saw my assistant jumping and waving her arms, in the exuberant, awkward combination of movements she called her Happy Dance. She capped the dance with a series of exaggerated pelvic thrusts, which I devoutly wished I had not witnessed. When I opened the door, the metallic rasp caught her attention and she looked in my direction, frozen, her hips still thrust forward. "Keep it down," I said. "Some of us are trying to nap." I waved a hand vaguely in the direction of her contorted torso. "By the way, a chiropractor might be able to help you with that."

Straightening up and rushing to me, she flung her arms around my neck. "I got it, Dr. B! I *got* it!"

"Can you get rid of it? A double dose of antibiotics, perhaps?"

"I *got* it," she repeated, unwinding herself and stepping back. "The FBI job!"

"Miranda, that's . . . great," I said, wishing I felt as happy as I was supposed to. "Congratulations!"

"It was your phone call, or e-mail—or whatever it was you did or said or sent that you keep pretending you didn't. I'm sure that's what tipped the scales. So thank you. Thank you, thank you, thank you."

"You're welcome," I said. *Me and my big mouth*, I thought. "When do they want you to start?"

"January second—two months! Can you believe it?"

"Of course I can believe it. They're lucky to get you."

She gave a slight frown. "There's one condition attached to the offer. It's contingent on my finishing my Ph.D."

"Hmm," I said. "*Inter*-esting. And *how* much did you say you'll be depositing in my Cayman Islands account, the day you defend your dissertation?"

She raised not one but both middle fingers at me. And both corners of her mouth, in the biggest smile I'd ever seen.

"ONE MOMENT, DR. BROCKTON," said the provost's secretary. "He just walked in. I'll transfer your call now."

I heard a double beep, followed by the electronic ring tone and then by the provost's voice. "Hello, Dr. Brockton," he said coolly. It had been years since he'd addressed me so formally. "Looks like you've been trying to reach me for quite a while—I see half a dozen notes on my desk saying you called." He paused briefly. "All of them within the last thirty minutes. Is there a crisis in Anthropology?"

"In a manner of speaking, yes. My graduate assistant has a job offer from the FBI Laboratory."

"Well, I can understand how that might throw you for a loop," he said with exaggerated cheerfulness, "job offers in anthropology being virtually nonexistent."

"Not funny," I snapped. "This is the best Ph.D. candidate we've ever had. She's a huge asset to our forensic program. She runs the osteology lab and the Body Farm donor program. I don't want to lose her."

"Then don't. Put her on staff. A lab tech or instructor or something."

"Won't work," I said. "I've got to be able to offer her a tenure-track job."

"You can't. UT policy is very clear on that. We don't hire our own Ph.D.s—not until they've held a tenure-track position at another university first."

"I need an exception to the policy," I said. The phone went dead. "Hello?"

"I'm still here," he said. "I'm just thinking about

this. Let me see if I have this right. You're asking us to trample on a policy that's crucial to our academic strength and integrity . . ."

"Well, I wouldn't necessarily call it 'trample'—" I began.

"*I* would," he snapped. "And yet *you* don't want to do this institution the simple courtesy of showing up to accept an award, at a ceremony that would be a big boost to our reputation?"

"Oh, come on," I protested. "You've got to help me out."

"No," he said. "Actually, I don't."

And then the phone went dead for real. The university provost—my dean's boss; my boss's boss—had just hung up, ending the call, and ending my hopes.

CHAPTER 32

IT MUST BE STRANGE *to be my neighbors*, I thought. At the end of my driveway, where I'd ambled to pick up the morning paper, I waved at the FBI agent in the black sedan that was parked across the street. He raised an index finger an inch off the steering wheel—an extravagant gesture, in my experience with these guys—and I considered pushing my luck and striking up a chat.

To give the agents their due, most mornings—weekdays—I was in my truck when I picked up the latest edition of the *News-Sentinel*. Pausing at the end of the driveway, I would open the door, lean out—hanging practically upside down to snag the paper, like some modern-day cowboy leaning from his saddle—and snag the plastic bag, giving it a vigorous shake to remove most of the morning's dew before straightening up, tossing the paper on the passenger seat, and closing the door. Then I would turn onto my street, make my way to Cherokee Boulevard, and wind along the foggy Tennessee

River, an FBI car behind me, as the street curved uphill, away from the water, and toward the main artery of Kingston Pike. A mile east on Kingston Pike, I'd take a right onto Neyland Drive, following the river once more, wondering if the agent behind me was able to take in the beauty of the wispy fog spooling downstream, the herons wading and flying along the shore, the occasional tree trunk gliding along like some ghost ship or botanical submarine, its periscopic branches peering out from the secret emerald depths.

But today was Saturday, so I did not need to head to campus at daybreak. Today, I could relax at home—not that relaxing was something that came easily these days. And not that being at home was any great treat, either. Home was merely where I slept—or where I mostly failed to sleep, these days.

Today's newspaper was half buried in the leaves—maples, mainly, though with a fair number of tulip poplar and a smattering of Bradford pear—that had accumulated over the past several weeks. The leaves had gotten so deep that it was difficult to tell where my driveway left off and my lawn began. *It must be annoying to be my neighbors*, I amended. I glanced skyward, saw abundant blue through the scattering of stubborn leaves still clinging to branches. The day was bright and crisp; cool, but not cold. A perfect day to rake.

I ventured across the street, approaching the unmarked car that screamed "law enforcement," and the tinted window slid down. "Good morning," I said.

"Morning," replied the agent, a clean-cut, close-cropped, strapping young man I didn't recognize.

"I'm Bill Brockton," I said, offering my hand.

"Travis Joyner," he said, reaching across his chest to give me the requisite manly vise grip.

"Thank you for watching my back," I said. "My front and sides, too. I suspect this isn't the most interesting assignment, but I appreciate you."

"All part of the job," he said, a study in politeness and impenetrability, as if his personality was wearing reflective sunglasses.

"Can I bring you anything? Coffee? Tea? A bowl of oatmeal?"

"No, sir, I'm fine. Thanks just the same."

"Well, if you need anything—water, a restroom, whatever—just knock."

"Thank you. I'll be fine."

So y'all are trained to hold your pee? I considered asking, but he didn't strike me as a guy who'd see the humor in the question. "All right, then. Oh, I'm thinking about raking up some of these leaves, so the city doesn't decide my property's abandoned. That's okay, right? It's not a big risk for me to rake leaves, is it?"

"Rake away," he said. "You just pretend I'm not here."

"Right. Of course. I didn't even know it was you till you rolled down the window. Have a good one."

I turned back toward the leaf-covered driveway—I knew it lay just to the left of the mailbox—and I noticed that the mailbox was open, and a large manila envelope was curled inside. Strange: I had collected

Friday's mail when I arrived home that evening, and it was far too early for the Saturday mail delivery. I pulled the envelope from the mailbox and looked it over. No return address; no address of *any* kind, in fact, not even mine. I felt a surge of fear—I'd once received a sinister missive from Satterfield in this way—but I fought back, scolding myself for being paranoid.

I strolled back to the FBI agent's sedan, and the window slid down again. "Agent Joyner, did you see who dropped this off?"

He nodded. "A kid on a skateboard—nine or ten, maybe. Friendly. Waved at me, but didn't talk. Turned at that next corner."

I felt relieved. Something from a neighbor, then—an American Cancer Society fund-raising packet? A sheaf of petitions protesting my lackadaisical lawn care? It wasn't even sealed; simply held closed by the two thin tabs of the metal clasp, like the delicate wings of a damsel fly. I folded them upward, side by side—wing to wing—and raised the envelope's flap.

Inside was a quarter-inch sheaf of papers. Photographs. I smiled as soon as I saw the first one: Tyler on the soccer field, his right leg extended in a powerful kick, the ball—distorted by the kick and blurred by speed—streaking out of one corner of the frame. The second one, of Walker, was fun but not remarkable; it showed him behind the wheel of their minivan, leaning out the open window, checking the half inch of clearance between the vehicle and the mailbox. The third one showed Jenny, kneeling in the yard, her face intent as she planted pansies along their front sidewalk.

I took out my cell phone and called Jeff. "Hey, thanks for the pictures," I said when he answered. "But who was the delivery boy?"

"What pictures?"

"This packet of pictures in my mailbox," I said. "The boys and Jenny. They're from you, right?" His silence spoke volumes, and every page of every volume terrified me. "They're not from you," I said, needlessly. Cradling the phone with my shoulder, I began leafing through the pictures, and with each picture—each increasingly intimate, invasive, voyeuristic image—I felt my revulsion and panic rising. As I neared the bottom of the sheaf, I came to a series that showed each member of my family in close-up, and on each face was superimposed the crosshairs of a rifle scope. The final four images were identical, with one addition: each face was smeared with what appeared to be blood.

"Dad? Dad!" Faintly, from far away, I heard Jeff shouting, his voice tinny and distorted by the cell phone's minuscule speaker.

"Y'all keep together, Jeff," I told him. "Stay close to home. Tell your security detail that Satterfield's circling. I'll call Price, tell her we need reinforcements."

"Shit," he said. "Shit shit shit."

My sentiments exactly.

CHAPTER 33

WHEN IT RAINS, SOMETIMES it only pours. Sometimes, though, you need an ark.

"Doc, it's Bubba," Meffert's voice drawled in my ear. "How's it going?"

"Been better, Bubba. I just found out that Satterfield's stalking my family."

A pause. "Damn, Doc. I'm sorry to hear that. Really, really sorry. You got security?"

"Some. Not enough. I just got off the phone with Agent Price, at the FBI. I've asked her to assign more agents to us, but I'm not sure she can. Meanwhile, it feels like we're swimming around in a fishbowl while a hungry tiger circles, planning his menu." I desperately wanted to change the subject. "How're you doing? Better news on your end, I hope?"

"It's been an interesting twenty-four hours," he said. "But 'better'? I wouldn't necessarily put it that way."

"Crap," I said. "Spill it, Bubba. What's happening?"

"Tilden Stubbs is dead. Single gunshot to the head. Could be suicide, could be homicide."

"Christ. Time of death?"

"Judging by the stink and the bugs, it's been a while. The M.E. called in an entomologist to look at the maggots, figure out how long ago they hatched."

"What'd he say?"

"She, actually. She took some samples back to her lab—some alive and wiggling, some that she put in a kill jar—"

"Sounds like she knows what she's doing," I said. "She'll study the dead ones under a microscope to get a better idea how developed they are, and she'll let the live ones complete their life cycle and pupate into adult flies. That helps pin down how long ago they hatched from eggs. Generally, it takes about fourteen days to go from egg to fly."

"Yeah, that's just about how she explained it, too," he said. "Based on her first look, she thinks he was killed five to seven days ago."

I did some quick math. "Right about the time Shiflett was killed. That doesn't shed much light."

"Try this," said Meffert. "Satterfield kills Shiflett for stealing his idea about the bear—I think Brubaker's right about that—and then Stubbs finds out about the murder. Stubbs feels guilty—after all, he's the one who introduced Shiflett to his cellmate Satterfield, right? So Stubbs starts drinking, and the more he drinks, the worse he feels. Finally he decides he's a sorry sumbitch who doesn't deserve to live. Puts a gun to his head and offs himself. You buy it?"

"I don't," I said. "*Stubbs?* Killing himself out of *remorse*? Guys like that don't feel remorse, Bubba. Guys like that don't shoot themselves. Guys like that shoot other people. Guys like that blame anybody but themselves when things go wrong." I felt a surprising head of steam building inside me. "Guys like that think they shouldn't have to pay taxes, even though they want good roads and a strong military and a well-trained fire department and plenty of Border Patrol agents. Guys like that think it's your fault if they break their hand by punching you in the face. Guys like that—" I stopped, because I could hear that I was getting spun up, loud and angry. "Sorry, Bubba," I said. "I tried it, and I guess I don't buy it."

He gave a brief laugh. "Yeah, I was starting to get the picture. Okay, so if it's not suicide, it's homicide. Shiflett, or Satterfield?"

"Satterfield, of course."

"Why not Shiflett? Maybe Shiflett shot Stubbs over some kinda disagreement, and then Satterfield went after Shiflett 'cause Shiflett had killed his buddy."

"I don't buy that, either, Bubba. Redneck racists like Stubbs and Shiflett—they're mean, hateful bullies and jerks. But they're not bad-to-the-bone monsters. Satterfield is."

"I don't dispute that," he said. "And I get why Satterfield would go after Shiflett, for stealing his plan. But Stubbs—why would Satterfield kill Stubbs, too?"

I said it before I even thought it. "To cover his tracks. Satterfield needed two accomplices on the outside to help him escape, right? Stubbs and Shiflett. They killed the prison doctor's wife and the guard's family. They were useful to him. But once they'd done that—once they'd helped him get out of prison—he didn't need them anymore, and they became liabilities. By killing Stubbs and Shiflett, he made himself harder to trace, and—at least at Shiflett's place—he was able to stock up on weapons."

Bubba heaved a sigh. "At Stubbs's, too," he said glumly. "Stubbs was renting a storage unit a few miles down the road. Looks like it was cleaned out within the past week or so. ATF's coming over to check it out, but my guess? They'll find residues of explosives and ammunition in there, just like they did in Shiflett's shed."

The news was bad, but it wasn't surprising. In fact, it seemed almost inevitable. "So Satterfield's got himself one hell of an arsenal now," I said. "Sure would be good to know where he's keeping it."

"And what he's aiming to do with it," said Meffert. "Race war?"

"Hell, no," I said without hesitation. "Shiflett and Stubbs might believe that crap, but Satterfield doesn't give a damn about a race war. He was just telling them what they wanted to hear. He played those guys like fish, reeling 'em in till they were flopping on the dock. And them he stomped 'em."

After I hung up, and feeling like I did—like a walking, talking target—I wished Meffert had chosen a different word for Satterfield's next move.

Aiming.

CHAPTER 34

"I'M SORRY, DR. BROCKTON." ANGELA Price—Special Agent Price—sounded as if she was, in truth, sorry. But not as sorry as I was.

"Can't you request additional agents from another field office? Just until he's caught?"

"I told you, I've already asked. Twice. And been turned down twice. We don't know how long it might be until he's caught. Maybe days, but possibly years."

"God spare us," I said.

"I agree. But we can't do an open-ended expansion of your family's security detail. For one thing, we don't have the budget. Even if we had the money, we don't have the personnel—here *or* elsewhere. We're dealing with multiple terrorism threats these days—credible threats of coordinated attacks—and we are stretched to the breaking point. My agents are averaging sixty hours a week, Dr. Brockton. *Averaging*."

I mumbled my understanding and my thanks—they were, after all, still posting agents outside my house, and at Jeff's house and office, and even the boys' school. Then I hung up and repeated my request to higher-ups at the TBI and at KPD. They, too, turned me down; they, too, expressed genuine regret.

"If you'd be interested in hiring some off-duty officers, I can ask around," Decker said, sounding slightly embarrassed at the prospect of bringing money into the equation. "I hadn't thought of that," I said, "but it might make sense. See what you find out, and give me a buzz back."

But in the end, it wasn't one of Decker's guys, or anyone from KPD, who came to our aid. It was Waylon—big-hearted, big-bodied, big-trucked Waylon—who phoned back to say he'd help, after I'd talked to O'Conner. "Jim figgers he can spare me for a while," Waylon said, "seein's how we're all done with that Shiflett mess."

"Y'all aren't worried about Satterfield killing off more of the fine citizens of Cooke County?"

"Fine citizens?" Waylon guffawed. "Well, that narrows it down to one—and I reckon Jim can look after his own self. Where do you live and when you want me to show up?"

"Actually, I want you looking after my son and his family," I told him. "If Satterfield really wants to hurt me, it's them he'll go after, not me." I told him about the pictures I'd found in my mailbox, and by the time I described the final, blood-smeared images, I could hear a low, rumbling growl coming from Waylon's end of the line. I gave him Jeff's address—in a neighborhood in the western suburb of Farragut—and arranged to meet him there, so I could introduce him to Jeff and the family, as well as to the FBI agent posted outside the house. I hung up feeling relieved and grateful to have the big man as backup.

WE WERE GATHERED—JEFF, Jenny, their boys, Waylon, and I—in their living room, making small talk after introductions. Visually, Waylon stood out like a sore thumb in the suburban living room: the hulking, homespun man perched on a fancy sofa three sizes too small for him. Yet there was a gracious ease about Waylon—an openness and genuine warmth—that I hadn't fully appreciated before, and it quickly put everyone else at ease, too. Waylon, talking to Tyler about soccer: "I never even seen a soccer ball till I was twenty-five, maybe thirty. But we started gettin' some of them Hispanics in Cooke County, we got us a couple Mexican restaurants, and they got a channel that's always showing soccer. So I got kindly interested. Still got a lot to learn, though—lost a couple hunnerd bucks on that last World Cup." Waylon, talking to Walker about his learner's permit: "I learnt to drive on my daddy's tractor when I was twelve. He took me out to the south field one morning, showed me how to work the gas and the clutch and the gearshift, and said, 'Don't come home till you kin *drive* home.' 'Bout sundown, I finally made it back to the barn. Trouble was, Daddy didn't really show me about the brake, and I drove plumb through the back wall and into the pigsty."

The chime of the doorbell made me jump. "It's just the pizza delivery, Dad," said Jeff.

"I'll get it," said Waylon, getting to his feet with surprising swiftness for a man of his bulk. As he passed, he shot me a glance, and I remembered telling him how Satterfield had escaped capture years before by trading places with a Domino's driver. The deputy took a quick peek through the peephole before opening the door, where a scrawny, pimply-faced teenager strained beneath the weight of three huge pizzas. Waylon took the boxes and followed Jenny's motion beckoning him into the kitchen, while Jeff smoothly rotated in to pay for the food and tip the driver.

"Waylon," I heard Jenny say, "you'll have some pizza with us, won't you, before you disappear into the darkness?" Given the FBI agent's prominent presence in front of the house, Waylon had suggested that he watch the back, and he'd brought night-vision gear and camouflage—including a leaf-laden ghillie suit—so he could stand guard unseen. It was as if Waylon had studied the FBI's agent's example and done exactly the opposite. I decided to join them in the kitchen. "We ordered way too much," Jenny was saying when I walked in. "I hate to send you out there hungry. Say you'll have some."

"If you're sure you've got plenty," Waylon said, "I don't care to have a slice."

I could see Jenny's puzzlement—was he accepting or declining?—so I chimed in with, "I could go for a couple pieces myself," giving Jenny a nod that I hoped made it clear that Waylon and I were both on the meal plan.

"Great," she said. "Do y'all mind paper plates? We like to give the dishwasher the night off when we order pizza."

Waylon shook his big, shaggy head. "Paper plates is fancy china for me," he said. "Unless my girlfriend's cooking, I eat straight outta the can."

Jenny laughed. "Tell me about your girlfriend."

"Miss Jenny, you get me started on her and I won't never shut up. She's my favorite subject." He grinned. "She's a teacher. Junior high math. Name's Gracie. She's got two boys, seven and nine. Sweet little guys." Waylon suddenly looked self-conscious, even shy. "You know what? I never thought I'd be a dad. And I'm not, exactly. Maybe more like a uncle. But them two boys get to me like nothin' else in this world, you know what I mean?"

Jenny beamed. "I think I do, Waylon. They're lucky to have you in their lives."

I was surprised by this tender side of Waylon—surprised and ashamed, I realized: ashamed that I had assumed Waylon would be with a woman of low class or intelligence, and ashamed that in all my years of acquaintance with him, I had never delved into Waylon's personal life as deeply as Jenny managed to do in sixty seconds.

"And how did you and Gracie meet?" asked Jenny.

"Ha. Now that's a good story. I stopped her for speeding. She was doin' about sixty on River Road, which is kinkier than a hunnerd-dollar—" Waylon stopped himself, blushing. "Kinkier than a worm on a hook. And there was something about her . . ." He paused, seemingly caught up in the memory, but then his gaze snapped toward the back door.

I followed his gaze. "Waylon?"

He held up a big hand, listening. Then, very softly, he said, "Would y'all 'scuse me just a minute?

I think I'll just step outside." He walked—casually, it seemed—but not to the kitchen door. Instead, he returned to the living room, and I heard the front door open and then close quietly.

Jenny stared at me; I shrugged, as if Waylon's sudden departure meant nothing, then said, "Maybe we should go back into the living room for now." Her eyes widened, and she nodded wordlessly.

Jeff glanced from my face to Jenny's, and what he saw there made him go pale. "What's going on?"

"I don't know," said Jenny. "Waylon got a funny look on his face and said he needed to go outside for a minute."

Walker smirked. "Did he need to have a chew?"

His brother groaned. "Walker, you are *such* a dumb-ass."

"Tyler!" snapped Jenny.

"Sorry, Mom," he said, and I saw something in the boys' faces shift—saw alarm setting in—as they took the measure of Jenny's agitation.

Jeff's gaze drilled into me. "Dad?"

"I'm sure everything's fine," I said. "Waylon's just being careful. That's what he's here for."

I was about to add, "He'll be back any second," when I was interrupted by scuffling sounds coming from the backyard. We turned toward the kitchen, all of us, and stared, frozen, as if by looking hard enough, we might be able to see through the walls and out into the night, where grunts and thuds and snarls hinted at a desperate struggle in the dark.

"Y'all stay together," I said. "Jenny, call 911. Jeff, do you have a gun?" He nodded. "Get it, right now. Everybody go together. Stay together. In a room without windows. The laundry room, or a walk-in closet. You hear anybody at the door, you start shooting."

"You're coming with us," said Jenny.

"No, I'm not. Now go. Hurry!" Turning from them, I ran to the front door, and outside, hurtling down the steps and running to the street, where the FBI sedan idled at the curb, dark and imposing. And empty.

Except that it *wasn't*. When I leaned against the driver's window, cupping my hands around my face to block the streetlight's glare, I saw a man slumped across the front seat, his starched white shirt slowly going crimson as blood oozed over the collar and seeped downward.

Yanking open the door, I held a palm in front of the agent's face and waited, but I felt no breath. Grabbing his left wrist, I sought a pulse, but felt none. Reaching under his arm, I clutched the pocket of his shoulder holster, but felt no gun.

What to do, what to do? Standing in the glare of a suburban streetlight, beside the dead FBI agent in his idling car, I heard the wail of a siren—no, of multiple sirens—in the distance, headed my direction. *Hurry. Hurry.* Help was coming—but help would be too late.

I turned toward the house, its front windows brimming with cozy amber light. Behind it, the dark tops of pines and oaks. "Waylon!" I ran, sprinting up the driveway and around the end of the house. "Waylon! He's here! Watch out!"

But I knew that my warning, like the police, was too late. Suddenly, somewhere in the darkness

behind the house, I heard a loud grunt and a sharp
gasp, followed by a groan of great pain. I froze,
and in the stillness that followed, a shot rang out,
and then another. Another cry of pain—this one
sharper, higher in pitch—and the sound of footsteps, staggering and uneven, across the back of the
yard and around the far end of the house, toward
the front yard and the street. For an instant I hesitated, then I set off in pursuit.

I rounded the corner just in time to see the FBI
sedan rocket down the street, tires squealing and
rear end fishtailing. *Too late*, I cursed myself. *Too late*.

Filled with dread, I turned back toward the darkness. "Waylon? It's Bill. Are you there? Waylon?
Can you hear me?"

Just beyond the tree line, I heard it: a deep guttural noise, somewhere between a grunt, a groan,
and a growl—the sort of sound a bear or buffalo
might make if it were gravely wounded. I froze,
gripped by a reflexive rush of alertness and primal
fear. The sound seemed to be coming from my
left—from deep in the trees, near the distant corner
of the lot. *Get the hell out of here*, I thought. *Wait
for the police*. But something in the sound was familiar: a bass note whose frequency resonated in my
memory. *Oh, shit*, I thought, my feet moving now,
taking me toward the darkness. "Waylon? Hey,
Waylon, where are you?" Halfway across the yard, I
stopped again to listen. A wet, rasping sound emanated from somewhere just beyond me. I hurried
toward it, but could not find the source. "Waylon?"
I heard a fainter groan, a softer rasp.

Easing into the woods, holding my own breath to

listen, I caught the sound of labored breathing. I un-holstered my phone and touched the menu button to wake it up and illuminate the screen, which I used as a makeshift flashlight. "*Waylon!* Oh Jesus." The big man was lying faceup on the ground, blood bubbling and burbling from a hole in his chest. "*God.* Waylon, hang on, man. I'm calling 911." Fingers shaking, I punched the numbers, and when a woman answered in a flat, bored voice—"911, what's the nature of your emergency?"—I found it hard to force out audible words. "I . . . need . . . an ambulance," I finally managed.

"Speak up, sir. I can barely hear you."

"I need an ambulance," I said again, louder this time. "A man has been shot. Or stabbed. He's bleeding—a lot—from his chest."

"What's the location, sir?"

"My son's house. In Farragut."

"I need a street address, sir."

Address? My mind was blank. *What's Jeff's address? What the bloody hell is Jeff's address?* "Uh . . . Fox Den Drive. . . . 9125 Fox Den Drive."

A pause. "Sir, is that East Fox Den Drive, West Fox Den Drive, or North Fox Den Drive?"

"Jesus, I don't know. I don't know! *I don't know!*"

"Sir, I can't send an ambulance if I don't know which street."

"Christ. It's . . . West. West! The same place police cars are heading right now. Send the fucking ambulance!"

"Sir—"

I hung up, then dropped the phone to the ground and leaned closer.

Waylon's rasping sounded different now—urgent, with an undertone of grim determination. As if he was trying to summon up strength for a last stand, or last words. I knelt beside the gasping, burbling being. "Waylon? Waylon, it's Bill Brockton. I'm right here with you, Waylon." Groping in the darkness, I found one of his huge hands, slick with blood and God-knows-what, and took it in one of mine. With my other hand, I tried to cover and seal the gurgling hole in Waylon's chest. "Help's coming, Waylon," I said. "You hear the sirens? They're almost here. Hang on, big man." Waylon gave another bestial groan—from the pain of his shredded insides, or the pain of my pressing palm? *God, what do I do?* I thought, then—in an absurd echo from my college fantasies of medical school—I thought, *First, do no harm.* I felt a wave of grim despair. *What does that even mean, 'Do no harm'? We do harm just by breathing. I did harm—terrible harm—by asking Waylon to guard my family.*

I felt a hand encircling and clutching my arm—a painful, powerful grip, coming as it did from a man sliding through death's door. I saw, or sensed, Waylon's lips moving, so I leaned closer. "You trying to tell me something, Waylon?"

"Gracie." It was scarcely a whisper, more like a feather of air fluttering against my eardrum. Almost the way he might have whispered her name in her ear, as her boys slept in the next room.

Out in the street, I heard sirens. Screeching tires. Slamming doors. Thundering feet. "They're here. Hang on, Waylon." I turned my head toward the house, toward help. "Here!" I shouted. "In the backyard. Hurry!" Then, to Waylon, "They're coming. Hang on, buddy."

The big man shook his head slightly, then grunted, as if he'd just taken a punch to the gut, a knife to the ribs. "Can't. Tell . . . Gracie."

"Tell Gracie what, Waylon?"

"I wanted . . . marry her. . . . Adopt . . . boys."

"You tell her, Waylon. Hang on, so you can tell her yourself. Please."

Waylon made a sound that started as a growl, then became a primal, guttural groan. "*Uhhhnnn.*"

"Help! Hurry!" I called.

I heard voices shouting, and gradually I realized they were shouting my name. "Dr. Brockton? Are you here? Are you hurt? Dr. Brockton?"

Do no harm, a voice was shrieking in my head, louder than any siren. *No harm! No harm! No harm!*

Another voice, soft and sinister, responded with a hiss: *Too late. Too late. Too late.*

CHAPTER 35

THE TSA SUPERVISOR AT the Knoxville airport nodded, then motioned me through the checkpoint, allowing me to walk to the gate with Jeff and his family. The plane was almost finished boarding; the phalanx of FBI agents had held us back until the last minute.

"Please change your mind," Jenny pleaded. "Get on the plane; we'll pay for the ticket when we land. Come to Toronto with us. We'll buy you some more clothes there." She tried a smile, but her tears gave her away.

"I'll see you soon," I said. "This'll be over soon."

She hugged me tight. "I'm so afraid," she whispered fiercely. "What if we never see you again?"

"You'll see me again," I said. "I promise."

Jeff hugged me next. He tried to speak, but could not, so I spoke for both of us. "I know," I said. "I love you, too. You're a good man—a good son, a good husband, a good father—and I'm so proud to be your dad."

Tyler and Walker came up, one on each side of us, and wrapped their arms around us. "I love you, Grandpa Bill," said Walker.

"I love you, too," I told him.

"Be careful," said Tyler. "Remember, you promised you'd speak at my high school graduation."

"I'll be there," I said. "Now go."

And they went, through the gate and down the Jetway and up into an empty, ice-blue November sky.

"GET YOUR FAMILY to safety," Brubaker had said, when the task force had conferred the day after Waylon's death. "Send them away. Someplace that requires a passport; someplace he can't get to. Make him come after you."

It was a brilliantly simple idea. And a terrifying one.

"You're saying I should turn myself into bait on a hook?"

"You already *are* bait on a hook," Brubaker clarified. "Trouble is, there's other bait, on other hooks. What you need to do is get the other bait out of the water. Make yourself the only bait. *Irresistible* bait."

"How do I do that? Mock him?" I seemed to remember that sometimes investigators would make disparaging comments at news conferences, insulting the intelligence of serial killers, hoping to goad them into acting rashly. "Go on television and talk about what a tiny penis he's compensating for?"

"That only works for presidential candidates," he said, and several of the people at the conference table smiled grimly. "Satterfield's too smart to fall for it."

"Then what?"

"Well, let's think about this. Bait on a hook. What kind of bait do fish go for?"

"Worms," I said. "I should make myself wriggly and slimy?"

"Think 'lures.' Artificial lures. Shiny. Sparkly. The shinier you look, the more he'll notice you. The more he'll *hate* you. The more satisfaction he'll get out of reeling you in and gutting you on the dock."

"Wait, wait," I said. "I thought he was the fish, not the fisherman. You're saying the *fisherman* is gonna take the bait?"

"Don't be so literal, Doc. What I mean is, the shinier you look, the more he'll want to chew you up and shit you out. How's that?"

"More consistent but still gross," I said. "But let me see if I'm following you. If I were put under a big, bright spotlight—if I were hailed as the greatest thing ever to happen to UT and Knoxville and the state of Tennessee—that might make Satterfield come after me sooner?"

"Well, yeah, it might. But that's a big if, Doc. It's not always easy to arrange a coronation on a week's notice."

"Watch me," I said.

"I'M SORRY, DR. BROCKTON, he's still tied up," said the provost's secretary, for what must have been the hundredth time. I had been back from the task force meeting for more than an hour, and for more than an hour, she'd been telling me that the provost was tied up.

"Well, go untie him," I snapped.

"I've given him your messages," she said. "All seventeen of them. I'm sure he'll return your call— your many, *many* calls—at his first opportunity."

I sighed. Clearly I was being punished. Banished to the doghouse. As far as I could tell, there was no telephone service in the doghouse, so I doubted that the provost would call me at his first opportunity, or at *any* opportunity. Clearly it was time to up the ante. "Tell him I'll do it," I said.

"Excuse me?"

"Tell him I'll do it. Accept the award in Neyland Stadium. At Homecoming. At halftime."

"I'll relay that message," she said, and then, suddenly, "Oh, excuse me, Dr. Brockton, my other line is ringing. Can I put you on hold for just a moment?" Before I had a chance to ask if I had a choice, she had already done it. I remained in limbo for several minutes, and when she came back on the line, she said, nice as pie, "Dr. Brockton? The provost has just gotten out of his meeting. He can speak with you now, if you like."

I considered saying, *No, I've changed my mind—it really wasn't important*, but I decided she probably wouldn't see the humor in it, so I played it straight. "Excellent. Thank you."

"Bill," the provost said in his warmest voice. "Sorry to be so slow getting back to you. You wouldn't believe the day I've been having."

"Probably not," I replied, matching his tone as best I could. "Listen, I've given a lot of thought to what you said, and I certainly don't want to deny UT a chance to shine. I wouldn't have won this award without all the support I've gotten from the university over the years, so I'd really like to be part of a big Homecoming celebration after all." Suddenly I had another idea. A simple, brilliant idea. I tacked on three more words: "If I can."

"Of course you can!" He paused. "What do you mean, 'If I can'?"

"I might be away," I said slowly, as if reluctantly deciding to reveal a secret. "On a job interview."

He made a brief barking sound, which might have been either laughing or choking. "You can't be serious."

"Sounds crazy," I said, "but the thing is, I really like working with my assistant, Miranda. So if I can't convince her to stay here, the only thing to do is go with her. To the FBI lab. They have a supervisory position—senior scientist—that just came open, and the interview schedule is . . . challenging. It might conflict with Homecoming."

"Have you lost your mind? You would actually consider leaving UT to follow your *assistant*? Christ, Bill, don't tell me you're sleeping with her?"

"No! *God* no. It's just that she's one of a kind. Truly . . . exceptional."

I heard a grunt. "So that's what you're after— you're still angling for an exception to the damn hiring policy. Blackmailing me so you can offer her a tenure-track job."

"Blackmail? I would never stoop to blackmail," I said cheerfully. "This is extortion. A far kinder, gentler tactic."

I could practically see him glaring as he said, "And this really means that much to you."

"It does," I said.

After a pause and a sigh, he said, "All right. The Faculty Senate will have my hide, but I'll do it. Oh, and Bill?" His voice lost all its prior warmth. "Don't ask me for anything else. *Ever.*"

"I won't," I said. In my mind, I added, *Especially if I'm dead.* Aloud, I added, "Thank you. I can't wait for Homecoming." And before he could change his mind or question me more closely about my FBI job interview—an interview that existed only in my imagination—I hung up.

I PRACTICALLY LEAPED down the two flights of steps to the bone lab, and when I opened the door, I gave it such a push, it rebounded off the wall and nearly hit me in the face. "Impressive," said Miranda, looking up from a notepad. "You must've eaten your spinach this morning."

"I have good news," I told her.

"We could all use some good news." Miranda had taken Waylon's death hard—I knew she had been fond of the deputy, but the depth of her grief had surprised me. "And this good news is? You've decided that my dissertation is so brilliant, I don't have to defend it?"

"Better than that."

"You don't mean—you *can't* mean—that you've sworn off terrible puns forever?"

"Even better."

"What could possibly be better than that?"

"I talked some sense into the provost," I said. "He's agreed to make an exception to the hiring policy. Tenure track—yours for the taking!"

"How the hell did you manage that? You've got

pictures of him boffing a freshman on the president's desk?"

"Ewww. No, I do not. I just explained what a devastating blow it would be if UT lost you. The point—the good news—is that now you can stay here after all." I beamed, waiting for her response—a hug, a Happy Dance, a face-splitting smile.

Instead, she furrowed her brow. Then, remarkably, she frowned. "But . . . Dr. B . . . I've already accepted the FBI job."

"I know, I know, but that was because I couldn't offer you a tenure-track job here. Or thought I couldn't. But turns out I can!" She continued to frown. "Miranda, it's okay—the FBI'll understand. Sure, they'll be disappointed, but they'll get over it. Hell, there must be a dozen other people who could do that job—not as well as you, of course, but very capably. I can call the Bureau for you, if you want."

"No!" The speed and the force of it surprised me, and it seemed to have surprised her, too. "I mean, thank you, but . . . please don't." Now she looked on the verge of tears. "Here's the thing, Dr. B. I appreciate your faith in me. And I appreciate how you went to bat for me, because I know it couldn't have been easy to get an exception to the hiring policy. But you're not just my mentor. You're my hero. My role model. I want to be like you. And I can't be like you if I stay here. Don't you see? I've got to leave the nest and spread my wings—branch out on my own—if I want to do it right. If I want to do it the way *you* did it."

When I had first broached the idea of her staying on here—it seemed a lifetime ago, but in reality it had been only a few weeks—Miranda had compared me to a plantation owner at the end of the Civil War, offering to pay a former slave for labor that had previously been free. That comment, half joking, had wounded me, but only superficially: a paper cut, nothing more. But this—this talk of heroes and role models: this was a blade slicing straight into my heart—slicing all the more keenly because of the kindness and generosity behind the pointed words.

And couch it however she might, the bottom-line fact remained unchanged: I still could not bear the idea of her not being here. "I'm late for a meeting," I lied, my voice suddenly thick and unfamiliar. "I think you're doing the right thing," I lied again. "The FBI is so lucky to get you." I ended, at least, by speaking a truth.

I gave her shoulder a quick squeeze, then turned and hurried out of the bone lab. "Dr. B? Hey, Dr. B," she called after me.

I held up a hand—my fist closed, my thumb raised in a gesture of false jauntiness—and turned the corner into the safe, obscuring shadow of the stairwell, the steel door closing between us as I trudged up the steps.

CHAPTER 36

EIGHT DAYS HAD PASSED since Waylon had died; six days since Jeff's family had flown off to exile in Canada and since I had agreed to accept my Professor of the Year award during halftime of the Homecoming game. The ceremony had been announced with full-page ads in the *News-Sentinel* and on billboards flanking every highway into town. I'd spent a half hour on camera at WBIR, waxing rhapsodic to Beth Haynes about how the ceremony would be the high point of my life.

And now it was time.

Overhead and all around us, Neyland Stadium rumbled and shook with the stamping of multitudinous feet. "Sounds like the Vols just put some more points on the board," Decker said. We were in my administrative office, awaiting the buzzer that signaled halftime.

"I'm glad the Vols are moving the ball well," I grumbled. "Me, I can barely move at all." Two of Decker's SWAT guys hoisted my academic robes over my head, then clumsily threaded my arms through the sleeves. The gown was a strangely snug fit, and I felt like the Michelin man, or a kid in a snowsuit.

Except it wasn't a snowsuit I was wearing under the gown; it was a bomb suit. I wasn't wearing the high collar or the helmet, but I was wearing a bulletproof vest under the bomb suit, just in case. "You're trading mobility for survivability," Decker said. "Not a bad trade-off, I'd say. In this rig, only thing you need to worry about is a rocket-propelled grenade. That, or a tactical nuke."

"I worry about a head shot," I said. "What if he shoots me in the head?"

"Oh, that." He gave a philosophical-looking shrug. "He shoots you in the head, we shoot *him*. Then we clean up the mess and feel really bad." He frowned. "Seriously, Doc, you don't have to do this. I know you want to draw him out, but you really don't have to take this risk."

"Deck, there are ninety thousand people out there expecting to see me get a medal draped around my neck. I can't back out."

He smiled. "No offense, Doc, but eighty-nine point nine thousand of 'em came to see the game, not you. As long as the Vols come back out and play the second half, nobody's gonna be heartbroken. We make a PA announcement that you've been called out on a forensic case, and everybody'll say, 'Good ol' Dr. Brockton—there he goes again!' No shame in choosing to be safe."

I shook my head. "If I chicken out now, it just means I have to keep looking over my shoulder, jumping every time a car backfires or a kid lights a firecracker. I'm sick of that, Deck. Let's get this over with."

He frowned. "He might not try anything today, Doc. He's gotta know we're on high alert."

"He might know, but he won't care. Look at it from his point of view: If he shoots me out there on that field, not only does he win, he wins in front of ninety thousand people. Plus a TV audience of millions. How could he resist?"

Decker shrugged. "I know, he's bound to find it tempting. Still, there's no guarantee he'll take the risk."

"No guarantee," I agreed. "But there's a chance. And if he's out there waiting, and I don't show up? I'll have pissed away a golden opportunity. When will I ever have this much protection again? You've got, what, fifty, sixty guys out there?"

"More like two hundred," he said, "once you count the FBI and TBI agents and UT police. Hell, you've got better security today than Obama had when he came to town."

"Deck, that's not your politics showing, is it?"

"I better take the Fifth on that." He grinned slyly. "But you? It would be a real shame if we lost *you*." From overhead came another roar, and I saw Decker's eyes flicker as he put a hand to his ear to catch a transmission on his radio. "Okay, Doc, it's halftime. Showtime."

"But Daddy, I have to pee."

"LADIES AND GENTLEMEN," the PA system boomed, "you've seen him featured on *60 Minutes* and *Cold Case Files*. You've read about him in *USA Today* and the *New York Times.* Please welcome America's top forensic scientist . . . the creator of the world-famous Body Farm . . . and now, the man who's just been chosen as *National* Professor of the Year . . . the one, the only . . . *Dr. Bill Brockton!*"

Perhaps Decker was right—perhaps everyone in the stadium had come only for the game—but even so, the crowd did a commendable job of feigning enthusiasm, for as I stepped out of the dark access tunnel and lumbered, blinking and waddling, out to the sunlit center of the field, I could have sworn that all ninety thousand people rose to their feet, clapping and cheering. *A good day to die*, I told myself. *Far worse ways to go.*

I struggled up the steps of the platform that had been rolled to midfield, my bomb-suited legs as stiff as those of the Tin Man in need of his oil can. The provost welcomed me with a handshake and a huge, fake smile, then turned to the microphone and talked. And talked. And talked. Was he actually so fond of the sound of his own voice, or was he making sure Satterfield had plenty of time to line up a clean shot to the head? He talked so long, I found myself doing mental calculations: If Satterfield fired from one hundred yards away—say, from the top of the Jumbotron scoreboard, or the top of the press box, or the interior of a skybox, or the roof of the geology building—how long would it take the bullet to reach me, assuming it was traveling three thousand feet per second, which Deck had told me was the muzzle velocity of a high-powered rifle? *Easy*, I thought. *A tenth of a second.* And how much time beween the arrival of the bullet and the arrival of the *rack* of the gunshot, which would travel at the con- iderably slower speed of sound, eleven hundred feet per second? *Not quite two-tenths of a second.* So if I vere still alive and conscious for half a second after he bullet left the muzzle, I might—might—hear he sound of the shot that nailed me. *But not if my rains are spattered all over the provost*, I concluded.

Eventually, miraculously, the provost finished saying all he had to say, apparently, for he stepped forward, hoisted a loop of satin ribbon over my head, and hung a heavy medal on me.

But why was I still alive? And why was there no commotion—no shrieking from the spectators, no shouting on the platform, no fusillade of bullets from the SWAT officers—exploding around me? I surveyed the stadium, turning in a complete circle, seeking some sign of Satterfield. I stretched out my arms, raising them shoulder-high—the highest I could manage, within the confines of the bomb suit and vest. *Here I am*, I yelled wordlessly. *Do it. Come on, damn you—do it.*

The crowd—understandably misunderstanding my gesture, misreading it as a sign of exuberance, not frustration—went wild, woke from their provost- induced slumbers and erupted, cheering and stomp- ing and bellowing their approval. I heard air horns and cowbells and whistles.

But still I did not hear a gunshot, and by the time I had rotated in two complete circles, seeing police galore, but no assassin, I knew that the plan had failed, that Satterfield had been too smart to take the bait. Bowing my head—not in modesty, but in defeat—I waved a feeble farewell, waddled down the platform steps, and lumbered off the field.

Decker met me just inside the access tunnel. Even in the semidarkness, I could read the mixture of disappointment and relief on his face.

"Deck, there's good news and bad news," I said. "The good news is, Satterfield didn't kill me. The bad news is, he didn't try."

"Maybe we came on too strong, Doc, scared him off. Maybe we should've played it a little lower key. Blended into the crowd more, you know?"

"Maybe I'd be dead now if you'd gone low-key," I countered. "Or maybe he's dead—for all we know, Satterfield bled to death after Waylon winged him, or choked to death on a chimichanga last night—or he's in lockup somewhere, busted for DUI. Who knows. Who the *hell* knows."

"Sorry, Doc. It was worth a try, and you were brave to do it."

"Thanks. Now get me out of this getup, because by now I really do need to pee."

THE BATHROOM WAS down one flight of stairs from my office, positioned halfway down the staircase that descended to the bone lab. As I was about to enter the restroom, I thought I heard footsteps, followed by the rasp of the lab's steel door scraping across its sill. "Miranda?" I called, "are you here?" There was no answer, and the noise filtering down from the crowd in the stadium made it difficult to know what, if anything, I'd heard at the base of the tairs. I hurried into the restroom, grateful for the chance to pee at last.

Leaving the restroom, I heard another sound from below, definitely—a forceful thud, and then another. *What the hell?* I trotted down the stairs, delighted by how easy it was to move, and move quickly, now that I was no longer encased in the bomb suit. I tried the doorknob and was surprised to find it unlocked—surprised because the UT Police required the entire building to be secured and empty during football games. The sole exception, of course, was professors who were being trussed up in body armor and trotted out on stage as live targets for psychopaths to shoot at. Or not.

Just as I was about to open the lab's door, I looked outside—out the glass exit door at the base of the stairwell—and paused. Something had caught my eye . . . but what? I looked down at the floor, at my feet, to reset my vision, then quickly looked up again, hoping that whatever had caught my attention subliminally would do it again, but overtly this time. The Homecoming bunting was unusual, of course, as was the "Congratulations Dr. Bill Brockton—U.S. Professor of the Year" banner. But neither of those was the thing that had flipped a switch in my subconscious. The thing that had flipped a switch in my subconscious was smaller and subtler than either of those gaudy decorations. The thing that had flipped a switch in my subconscious was barely noticeable, up there amid the spiderwork of steel I-beams supporting the stadium. The thing that had flipped a switch in my subconscious was . . .

a slender, horizontal aluminum angle bracket, attached to a vertical I-beam with what appeared to be a cable tie. Looking left and right, I saw identical brackets, their silvery luster contrasting with the reddish brown of the steel, fastened to the neighboring I-beams as well. Fingers shaking, I grabbed my phone, found Decker's number, and hit the "call" button. *Answer, Deck,* I prayed. *For God's sake, answer the damn phone.*

"Doc? What's taking you so long? Did you get lost, or did you need to download a file, as my kids would say?"

"Deck, listen. Are you still in my office?"

"Yeah. I thought you were—"

"Shut up. Listen. Go to the window and look out."

"What?"

"Go look out my window. At the vertical I-beams. What do you see?"

"Doc? Are you okay? I don't quite—"

"Do it *now,* Deck—*look!*"

"Okay, *okay.* Don't get your panties in a twist. I'm at the window. I'm looking out. I see two big ol' grimy I-beams . . ." The phone went silent.

"You see them?" I said in an urgent whisper. "Those brackets? Aren't those demolition charges? Cutting charges?" What was the term I'd learned at the ATF lab a few months before? "LSCs? Linear shaped charges?"

In my ear, I heard Decker begin to whisper, "Holy Mary, Mother of God, pray for us sinners, now and at the hour of our death."

"Deck, what do we do?"

"Holy Mary, Holy Mary, Mother of God, pray for us sinners, now and at the hour of our death."

Christ, I realized, *it's his PTSD again*. "Decker, come on, man—get a grip. I need you. *We* need you. Stop praying and start being a cop."

Behind me, I heard the bone lab door rasp open. I turned and saw Miranda's face leaning around the door frame, her hair rumpled, her eyes wide and wild. "Hey," I said. "What are you doing here? You know the campus police don't want us using the building on game days, don't you?"

Instead of answering, she took a step forward, and I saw a huge handgun pressed to her head. Then, prodded by the barrel of the gun, she took another step, and I saw one of Decker's SWAT guys behind her, in olive-drab fatigues and a vest. Only it wasn't one of Decker's men; it was Nick Satterfield close behind Miranda, his left hand gripping her upper arm. "Do come in," Satterfield said. "We didn't want to start the party without you."

Stunned, I walked slowly toward them, my hands up, my fingers spread wide. He was leaning against the door to hold it wide, and as I passed them in the doorway, entering the lab, he shifted the barrel, pressing it hard beneath her ear, causing her to grunt in pain. "We were just about to call you, weren't we, Miranda? But you saved us the trouble. Very thoughtful of you."

"This place is crawling with cops," I said. I turned to face him, my knees weak, halfway sitting on the table at the center of the lab for support. "If I'm not back in my office in five minutes, they'll start looking for me."

"And I'll be part of the search party," he said, a cold, smug smile on his serpent's face. "In fact, I'm going to be the one who finds you." On the desk just inside the door sat a matching helmet, and I realized with horror that once he put the helmet on, Satterfield would look exactly like all the other SWAT team officers. "And then I'm going to lead you and your teacher's pet back onto the field—we'll have to call a time-out—and we'll get a microphone. And then you'll tell all those people that you're a fraud. That you pose as a good man, but you're not."

There was the sting of truth in his words. I'd gotten Waylon killed, and now I'd led Miranda into deadly peril. And as the implications of what I'd seen through the window continued to sink in, I realized that perhaps I had led thousands of people—no, tens of thousands—to their deaths. If Satterfield had rigged the stadium's supports with demolition charges, the entire upper deck could come crashing down. "You'll tell them you're an evil man, and you're about to prove it."

I snuck a glance at Miranda. She was motionless and silent, but tears coursed down her face, and the sight ripped my heart open. *Stall, Brockton,* I thought. *Keep calm and stall. Get him talking—isn't that what they do on TV?* "And how am I going to prove it?"

"By pressing this button," he said, holding up a gizmo that resembled a cell phone or a garage-door opener.

"And how will pressing that button prove I'm an evil man?"

"By killing everyone in this stadium, while you

watch from center field, untouched by the carnage happening all around you."

Do something, Decker, I prayed. "You're insane," I said. "You can't possibly kill everyone in the stadium."

"I won't," he said. "*You* will."

"Bullshit. I don't believe you." I saw Miranda's eyes flicking back and forth, from me to Satterfield and back again, and my sense of helplessness was maddening.

"Oh, but you will soon," he told me. "Seeing is believing. You will see, and you'll believe, and you'll wish you were never born."

"Can't be done," I said. "You can't kill all those people unless you've managed to hide a nuclear weapon in the stadium. And you don't have the ability to do that."

"I don't need a nuclear weapon. The stadium is my weapon."

"You're bluffing. You aren't capable of it," I said, hoping my face didn't betray the fact that I knew he was.

"Oh, but I am," he said. "It doesn't really matter if you believe me. But I'll explain it, so you can start dreading it in detail. There are demolition charges—cutting charges—all around the stadium. When you press that button, they'll slice through every support, every girder, and the entire stadium will collapse. And there you'll stand, untouched, like Joshua at the battle of Jericho, as the walls come tumbling down . . . and everybody around you dies."

"Why would you do that? You want to kill me—I

know that. I even understand it. But why try to kill all those innocent people instead of me?"

"To make you suffer." Satterfield practically spat the words. "Killing you isn't enough. You have to suffer. I can't make you suffer for thirty years, like I did—not unless I let you live. Maybe I should kill your family—slowly and painfully—but let you live. Cut off your hands and feet, put out your eyes, slice off your dick and make you eat it. That would be perfect. But what is it the business gurus say? 'The perfect is the enemy of the good'? Perfect revenge isn't an option. But I think this'll do. You know why?"

I didn't want to hear it; everything that came out of his mouth was like poison spewing into the air, seeping into my soul, but I knew the only hope—for me, and Miranda, and the unsuspecting crowd above us—was to keep him talking. "I've thought about you a lot over the years," Satterfield said. "Who do you love, and what do you care about? Your family, sure. It goes without saying that they'll be dying very soon, and very painfully. But who else do you love—and *what* else—as much as your family? *More* than your family?" He looked around the bone lab, his expression somewhere between a smile and a sneer. "That's your dirty little secret, isn't it, Brockton? You love this place—your precious job, your precious university, your precious reputation—even more than you love your family. And so your legacy—the thing you'll go down in history for—will be wholesale destruction and mass fatalities. Twenty times the death toll of the World Trade Center. And your finger will be the one pushing the button, Dr. Brockton. Doctor of Death. The man who singlehandedly destroyed the University of Tennessee."

"I won't do it," I said. "So just go ahead and kill me and be done with it."

"Oh, I will kill you. But only after you push the button. Only after you commit the massacre. On national television."

I shook my head. "I won't do it," I repeated. "You can't make me."

"I think I can," he said. He looked at Miranda, the gun still pressed against her head. Slowly he slid the barrel down her neck, her chest, her belly, her crotch. "I think I can find ways to motivate you. A knife, I think, might be a better motivational tool. Or a scalpel. There must be scalpels in here somewhere." Miranda was trembling. I could see it, and I knew he could feel it, and the knowledge was bitter beyond all reckoning.

"You sick bastard," I said. But I was the one who was on the verge of vomiting and fainting. Dizzy and breathing hard, I put more of my weight on the table behind me, steadying myself with both hands.

And that's when I felt it: the shaft of a femur. The femur of a robust male Arikara Indian. The bone was twenty inches long, topped with a hard round knob—the femoral head—measuring a good two inches in diameter. *The Holy Family*, I thought, in a bizarre flashback to Peggy's characterization of the Arikara man, woman, and child. Then—another bizarre flashback—I thought of Decker's whispered, panicked prayer: *Holy Mary, Mother of God, pray for us sinners, now and at the hour of our death.* My fingers curled reflexively around the bone, midshaft.

The femur felt smooth and strong, solid in my grip, and it was the comforting familiarity of it—a shape I had clasped thousands of times over the decades—that slowly eased my distress and cleared my mind. I remembered my order, my plea, to Decker—"Stop praying and *do* something"—and I eased my fingers down the shaft toward the distal end, to a point just above the flare of the condyles, before tightening my grip. The bone felt awkwardly thick in my hand—I would rather have gripped it near the proximal end, where it was thinner—but as Satterfield himself had just said, "The perfect is the enemy of the good." The femur felt ergonomically imperfect but savagely good. Taking care not to scrape the bone on the table, or rattle it against other bones, I began to lift it with one hand, with agonizing slowness, holding the rest of my body motionless, using my torso as a screen, a shield, to conceal what I was doing.

"Showtime, kids," said Satterfield, motioning toward the door with the hand that held the detonator. "Let's go." Any moment, he would don the helmet and become—to all outward appearances, at least—one of the good guys.

It's now or never, Brockton, I thought, my arm tensing. But the gun was pressed against Miranda's head once more, his right index finger curled around the trigger, his left index finger hovering above the button of the remote control. A flex of either finger would be catastrophic.

"Don't make me tell you again," Satterfield said. "Let's *go*." He gave the gun a push, jabbing it hard against Miranda's skull.

"*Fuck* you, asshole," she snarled, and then—so fast, my conscious mind didn't even realize what was happening—he raked the end of the barrel across Miranda's face, the gun sight tearing a ragged furrow up her cheek, over the zygomatic bone, and across her forehead.

I saw her yank away and spin toward him, her "fight" reflex fully engaged. "Miranda, *no*," I shouted as Satterfield swung the gun toward her forehead. My arm, seemingly of its own will, with no conscious thought on my part, arced from behind me in a sidearm swing, impelled by terror or rage or some lizard-brain hatred deep in my DNA. I felt the femur slam into Satterfield's temporal bone with crushing force, the shaft snapping from the stress of the impact. Satterfield's head seemed to burst, the entire back of his skull erupting in a geyser of blood and brain matter and bone. He began toppling backward, and I heard myself shout "no!" as I lunged—dove—for his hand, in a desperate effort to grab the detonator. But I was too late, and too far away, and as he hit the floor, my hand a maddening eighteen inches from his, I saw his knuckles slam down onto the concrete, saw the fingers clench, even saw the movement of the button and a blinding flash of light.

Then the world itself seemed to explode, with a deafening roar and a force that shook my entire body. I tried reaching out for Miranda. If I could at least hold her hand as I died—and as she died, and as throngs of people above us died, burying us deep beneath the rubble, with the bones of the

Arikara—my death would not be utterly devoid of grace or comfort. *Pray for us now, and at the hour of our death.* The room faded to black.

And then it faded to gray, and green—olive drab—and swirling figures amid the dust. "Doc? *Doc.* Can you hear me?" I squeezed my eyes shut, then opened them, struggling to focus on the figure kneeling beside me. "Talk to me, Doc."

"Deck? Is that you? Are we alive?"

"It is. We are."

"But . . . *how?* The detonator—I saw his fingers push the button when he fell."

"Didn't matter," Decker said. "The detonator was dead. After you called, one of our bomb techs crawled out your window, shinnied across a beam, and broke the circuit—cut the wires connecting the charges. I got the word literally five seconds before things went crazy in here."

Suddenly I felt a rush of panic. "Miranda—my God, what about Miranda?"

"I'm over here." Her voice was weak, but it was *hers.* Unmistakably, miraculously hers. "I'm okay."

"Oh, thank God." I pushed myself into a sitting position. Miranda was by the desk, half leaning, half sitting on it, dabbing her face with a bloody paper towel. The gash from the gun sight would require stitches—possibly dozens of stitches—and would probably leave a scar, but at the moment, I had never seen a more beautiful sight than that torn and bleeding face. "Thank God."

"Actually, I give the credit to mere mortals. Mainly you." She smiled broadly but briefly, then the smile morphed into a flinch. "*Oww*," she said. "It only hurts when I blaspheme."

I looked down, for the first time, at the motionless form of Satterfield, his shattered skull lying in a puddle of its former contents, the head of the Arikara femur embedded deep in Satterfield's temporal bone. "Jesus," I said. "So much for mercy. I guess I went for justice instead. Big time. I don't even know how I did all that damage."

"You had a little help," said Decker. "I was watching y'all through the blinds—good thing the slats are so crooked and busted. When it looked like he was about to shoot Miranda, I said a prayer and squeezed off a round. The Hail Mary pass of gunshots."

I looked closer, and this time I saw the entry wound, centered in Satterfield's forehead. The exit wound must have blown off the back of his head. "That was an amazing shot."

"Mostly lucky," Decker said. "Really, really lucky. But just in case you were gonna feel bad about killing him, you can take that off your worry list. I killed him. And I won't lose one second of sleep over it."

"I appreciate your trying to ease my mind," I told him. "But the whack I gave him—this temporal fracture? Fatal, for sure." The bullet and the bone, I realized, must have hit Satterfield at exactly the same instant. "Truth is, we both killed him, Deck. And maybe that's how it should be." He stared at me, then nodded slowly.

I looked around the bone lab now—the locus of so much of my life and work; this crossroads of the dusty dead and the miraculously alive; this little world we had created out of bones and study and the quest for justice—and I saw that it was good.

Through the broken blinds—the lifesavingly broken blinds—I saw men in uniform erecting barricades and stretching crime-scene tape to create a wide perimeter around the bone lab. From somewhere above us, a roar of excitement drifted down, and the stadium vibrated, like some vast musical instrument, tuned to the key of gladness, resonating with life.

And again I saw—and I felt—that it was good. Very, very good.

CHAPTER 37

IT WAS ONLY WHEN I glanced out and saw a towboat passing—we were at a big round table flanked by windows overlooking the water—that I realized: This was the very same table where some of us had sat almost twenty-five years before, when Satterfield had entered a guilty plea and been sentenced to life in prison. Jeff and Jenny, seated to my left now along with Tyler and Walker, had been at that lunch, although their teenaged boys—not yet a gleam in their parents' eyes, way back then—had not, of course. Nor had Miranda, who had been busy coloring, doubtless outside the lines, in elementary school at the time.

Brian Decker, halfway through his slab of ribs, had been there on that prior occasion, eating exactly the same meal, I seemed to recall, of ribs, fries, and coleslaw. Beside him, Meffert picked at a chicken salad; he was still gaunt and haggard from his chemo, but he looked a hell of a lot stronger than he had at the FBI task force meeting a few weeks earlier. Meffert also, for that matter, looked more robust than the man seated on his left, Sheriff Jim O'Conner, who was clearly devastated by the death of Waylon.

The gathering felt momentous, but not celebratory. We had survived Satterfield's onslaught—those of us gathered around the table had—and we'd narrowly averted a mass-casualty act of domestic terrorism. But the events of the past few weeks had been harrowing, and all of us, I felt sure, would carry scars—figurative or literal—for the rest of our lives. But we would heal, too, in part or in full, because the human body and the human heart are remarkably resilient. Case in point: In the space of a week, the gash Satterfield had raked down Miranda's cheek had already shed its scab, leaving only a thin pink line, one that would steadily fade. My hunch—my hope—was that her scar would be gone by the time winter gave way to spring: roughly the same time, I suspected, that it would take for Satterfield's unclaimed mortal remains—laid out at the Body Farm—to be reduced to bare bone. Satterfield would be an interesting addition to our forensic teaching collection: a robust male specimen, the postcranial skeleton unblemished, the skull marked by three holes: a small, circular entry wound in the frontal bone, a large, irregular exit wound in the occipital, and a two-inch hole in the left temporal bone—a signature fracture, I would explain to students, as I demonstrated how neatly and perfectly the hole meshed with the spherical head of the Arikara Indian femur that had punched through the thinnest part of the skull.

I tapped my knife on the side of my glass of iced tea. The subdued voices around the table fell silent, the faces turned toward me. I hesitated, knowing that my words would surely fall short of the momentous things that ought to be said. I cleared my throat, which was already constricting. "To all of you," I began, "who showed such courage and perseverance in the midst of darkness and danger. To friends present, and friends absent." I thought first, and mainly, of Waylon, but I also thought of Shafiq, the murdered young Egyptian, whose DNA the TBI had managed to match with the bones, and whose parents had been notified, perhaps sneeringly, by the authorities in Egypt. "To Waylon," I said, "gentle giant, guardian angel, and fallen comrade. 'Greater love hath no man than this, that he lay down his life for his friends.' My family and I will always, always . . ." I stopped, unable to speak. Across the table, Jim O'Conner wept openly, unashamedly, and Miranda—seated on his left—stood up, moved behind him, and bent forward, enfolding him in a fierce hug.

I felt a hand take hold of mine and squeeze. I glanced to my right—at Peggy, smiling through tears—then took a deep breath to steady myself. "To Waylon," I resumed, "who died, that we might live." Around the table, glasses were raised and clinked in a toast, the name murmured softly all around, sounding rather like a collective "a-men."

I took another breath, blew it out as a way of shifting gears. "Today marks a painful end, but also a new beginning. And so I have another toast to make, a happier toast. To Miranda, who defended her dissertation this morning—with such clarity and brilliance that for one brief shining moment, even *I* seemed to grasp the wonders and forensic capabilities of elliptic Fourier analysis." The group laughed, no one harder than Miranda. I raised my glass high. "To my irreplaceable assistant, amazing colleague, and dear friend, off to a stellar career at the FBI. To *Dr.* Miranda Lovelady!" Miranda blushed and beamed, to the accompaniment of whoops, whistles, and clinking glasses.

To new beginnings, I silently toasted once more—thinking not just of Miranda's job, but also of the sabbatical I had requested, and the leave of absence Peggy had been granted.

As if reading my thoughts, Peggy gave my hand another squeeze, and I gave her slender, capable fingers a hopeful answering squeeze.

—The End—

WRITER'S NOTE: ON FACT AND FICTION

THE OPENING CRIME IN this novel—the horrifying fate of a young man chained to a tree, fed and kept alive for weeks or months as he paced in a circle, gradually wearing a path in the ground and a groove in the bark—is, we're told, one that actually occurred. Not recently, and not as a hate crime, but as a revenge killing: a rural Southern father's version of rough justice, the vengeance he took on a privileged young man who had raped his daughter. We haven't yet confirmed the accuracy of the story, but we hope to.

What we can, alas, confirm, is a shrill polarization in American public discourse, along with a rise in hate speech, hate groups, and hate crime. After three years of declines, in 2015 the number of hate groups rose by 14 percent, according to the Southern Poverty Law Center, to a total of 892. Among the most worrisome increases: a 164 percent rise in white-supremacy Klan groups, from "only" 72 Klan groups in 2014 to 190 in 2015. At the other end of the spectrum, extremist black-separatist hate groups (not to be confused with Black Lives Matter activists, who advocate peacefully for justice and equality) also increased sharply, from 113 in 2014 to 180 in 2015. In a different category, yet one also marked by extremist ideology and talk of armed violence, antigovernment "patriot" groups and militias—such as the armed group that occupied a federal wildlife refuge earlier this year—increased from 874 in 2014 to 998 in 2015; more disturbingly, such groups have increased more than *sixfold* since 2008.

Not surprisingly, in the fertile soil of extremism— and with liberal applications of the fertilizer of hate speech—murders motivated by extremism flourished in 2015, rising to their highest level in years, with 52 killings by domestic extremists. These were roughly equally divided between jihadists and far-right extremists. At one end of the spectrum was the December 2015 murder of 14 people in San Bernardino, California, by two homegrown jihadists, a married couple. At the other end was the murder of nine African Americans at a Bible study group in Charleston, South Carolina, by a 21-year-old white supremacist and neo-Confederate. Tragically, 2015's total was nearly equaled during a single mass shooting in June 2016, when a lone gunman pledging allegiance to ISIS killed 49 people at a gay nightclub in Orlando: an act that combined terrorism and hate crime on a horrific scale.

The picture is not *entirely* bleak. The FBI reports that hate crimes (including nonlethal assaults and incidents such as vandalism, harassment, and bullying) declined in 2014, the most recent year for which FBI statistics are available—for *most* target groups, including blacks, LGBT victims, and Jews. Still, Jews remain the largest group of hate-crime victims, accounting for 647 of the 1140 hate-crime victims the FBI tallied in 2014—an appalling 57 percent.

But while Jews remained the most prevalent victims, hate crimes against Muslims rose by 14 percent in 2014, according to the FBI, occurring at roughly five times the rate they did before Al Qaeda's September 11, 2001, World Trade Center attacks. And in the wake of the deadly jihadist shootings in Paris and San Bernardino in November and December 2015, a further spike in anti-Muslim violence, harassment, bullying, and vandalism ensued, resulting in a tripling of anti-Muslim hate crimes for the year, according to a non-FBI study.

Another deadly act of domestc terrorism in late 2015 was the murder of three people at a Planned Parenthood clinic in Colorado, gunned down by a self-described evangelical Christian who said he was doing "God's work."

To paraphrase, very slightly, a comment by one of this book's characters: People have been hating and killing in the name of God—one God or another—ever since the dawn of religion.

It's enough to give God a black eye, a bad rap, and some serious second thoughts about whether we humans were such a good idea after all.

ACKNOWLEDGMENTS

THE BODY FARM SERIES began in 2006, and—in the blink of an eye, seemingly—here we are, ten novels later. Fitting, then, we begin by thanking our publishing family at William Morrow: publishers Liate Stehlik and Lynn Grady, executive editor Lyssa Keusch, assistant editor Rebecca Lucash, production editor Stephanie Vallejo, cover designer Richard Aquan, publicist Danielle Bartlett, and marketing guru Katherine Turro. These terrific folks, together with some who helped earlier and then moved on, have made it possible for us to tell more stories, and better stories, than we ever expected. We couldn't have done it without them, and we're deeply grateful.

We also couldn't have done it without our literary agent, Giles Anderson, who took us on when all we had was an idea for a single book, and has been representing us and encouraging us ever since.

We are further grateful to many, many people in law enforcement, anthropology, social justice, the media, and other arenas of crime and punishment, of life and love, who helped us with this story.

Gordon Webster planted the seed of this story, in different form, years ago, while ferrying Jon Jefferson up the Tennessee Valley in the cockpit of a single-engine airplane a few thousand feet up. Many thanks to Gordon—and a word of warning to all: Be careful what you tell a writer!

FBI Executive Assistant Director (EAD) Michael Steinbach, head of the National Security Branch, provided tremendously helpful perspectives on counterterrorism. FBI media liaisons Ann Todd and Betsy Glick were gracious, helpful, and efficient in arranging the interview with EAD Steinbach.

Retired FBI Special Supervisory Agent James McNamara, a veteran profiler who helped us understand serial-killer psychology in our prior novel, *Cut to the Bone*, circled back to help us deal once more with serial killer Nick Satterfield. And former Special Agent Mike Brennan—who worked undercover to infiltrate domestic terrorist groups, and is now a fellow at the Brennan Center for Justice at New York University—explained the far right's little known but systematic creation of "lone wolf" terrorists in recent decades.

ATF Special Agent Michael Knight—public information officer *and* certified explosives specialist—was extraordinarily generous with his time and expertise, going many extra miles to arrange a research visit to the ATF laboratory—the National Center for Explosives Training and Research—in Huntsville, Alabama.

Lieutenant Keith Debow, commander of the

Knoxville Police Department's remarkably equipped and highly trained SWAT team, shared his time, expertise, and encouragement with astonishing generosity.

The Southern Poverty Law Center—Laurie Wood, especially, along with Heidi Beirich, Keegan Hankes, and Richard Cohen—provided cooperation, information, and inspiration beyond all deserving. Laurie's courage in researching hate groups is matched only by her gameness in agreeing to be (loosely) fictionalized in this book.

Forensic ace Amy George, as usual, gave invaluable insights into crime-scene evidence. Emergency physician Charlie Hartness, MD, was generous with both medical information and musical inspiration. Robin Catmur guided us cheerfully through the labyrinth of international education, student visas, and privacy regulations.

Beth Haynes and WBIR-TV were game and gracious, as ever, in allowing Beth to be the bearer of the bloody news of Satterfield's escape. Beth is a good sport, an admirable television journalist, and a messenger we would never, ever shoot! Another good sport—as well as a terrific facial-reconstruction artist—is Joanna Hughes, who cheerfully agreed to a clay-intensive cameo.

Our spirited wives, Carol Bass and Jane McPherson, have supported us—some might say "borne with us"—through far more books, and far more book tours and signings, than any spouses should have to, and for that, as well as an infinitude of other mercies, we are most grateful.

A passel of other anthropologists—forensic, molecular, and biological—provided crucial technical insights, as well as collegiality and friendship. Heartfelt thanks to Drs. Graciela Cabana, Richard Jantz, Angi Christensen, Tony Falsetti, Kate Spradley, Amy Mundorff, and Bridget F.B. Algee-Hewitt.

Last but most important of all: Our readers and fans never cease to amaze us. If only we could complete books as quickly as you can! Your enthusiasm and encouragement—your calls for more and more and more!—have sustained us lo these many years, inspiring us to do more than we ever imagined. It's been an astonishing privilege.

We've ended this book by giving Dr. Bill Brockton a well-earned sabbatical. And now, in the blurring of fact and fiction that have always been a hallmark of the Body Farm novels, we're granting Jefferson Bass a sabbatical, too. It's been our aim to instruct and delight; to make you laugh and cry; to make you root for justice and rage against cruelty, abuse, and narrowness of mind and heart. If we've succeeded in those aims, we've done a good decade's work. And we've had a fine time doing it.

Thank you, and bless you.

Jefferson Bass

Jon Jefferson   *Dr. Bill Bass*

THE SKULL

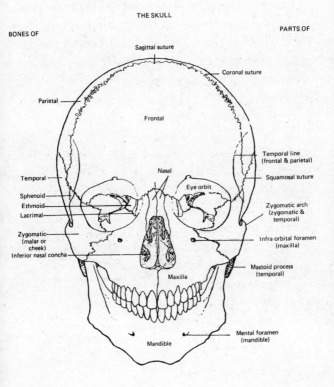

BONES OF

PARTS OF

Sagittal suture

Coronal suture

Parietal

Frontal

Temporal line
(frontal & parietal)

Squamosal suture

Nasal

Eye orbit

Temporal

Sphenoid

Ethmoid

Lacrimal

Zygomatic arch
(zygomatic &
temporal)

Zygomatic
(malar or
cheek)

Inferior nasal concha

Infra-orbital foramen
(maxilla)

Mastoid process
(temporal)

Maxilla

Mental foramen
(mandible)

Mandible

THE SKULL

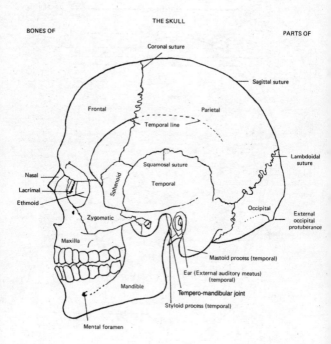

BONES OF

PARTS OF

Coronal suture

Sagittal suture

Frontal

Parietal

Temporal line

Lambdoidal suture

Nasal

Squamosal suture

Sphenoid

Lacrimal

Temporal

Ethmoid

Zygomatic

Occipital

External occipital protuberance

Maxilla

Mastoid process (temporal)

Ear (External auditory meatus) (temporal)

Tempero-mandibular joint

Mandible

Styloid process (temporal)

Mental foramen

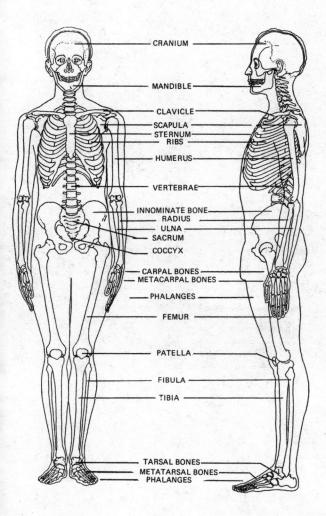

CRANIUM

MANDIBLE

CLAVICLE
SCAPULA
STERNUM
RIBS
HUMERUS

VERTEBRAE

INNOMINATE BONE
RADIUS
ULNA
SACRUM
COCCYX

CARPAL BONES
METACARPAL BONES

PHALANGES

FEMUR

PATELLA

FIBULA

TIBIA

TARSAL BONES
METATARSAL BONES
PHALANGES

THE FINEST IN FORENSIC SUSPENSE
JEFFERSON BASS's
THE BODY FARM NOVELS

THE BONE YARD
978-0-06-227741-1

Dr. Bill Brockton has spent his career surrounded by death at the Body Farm—the scientific compound where human remains lie exposed to be studied for their secrets. On a trip through Florida's panhandle Brockton's team makes a grisly discovery: a cluster of shallow graves containing the bones of teenage boys, all of whom suffered violent deaths.

THE BONE THIEF
978-0-06-227740-4

A routine case for Dr. Bill Brockton, the exhumation of a body to obtain a bone sample for a DNA paternity test, leads to a shocking discovery when the coffin is opened: the corpse inside has been horribly violated. The grisly find embroils Brockton in a dangerous investigation into a flourishing black market in body parts.

BONES OF BETRAYAL
978-0-06-227739-8

Bill Brockton is shocked when an autopsy reveals the cause of Dr. Leonard Novak's death: a radioactive pellet inside the elderly scientist's body. Is the horrific crime related to Novak's role in the Manhattan Project, the secret World War II program that helped create America's deadliest weapon?

BAS1 0217